THE HORUS HERESY®

*Many of these titles are also available as abridged and unabridged audiobooks.
Order the full range of Horus Heresy novels and audiobooks from*
blacklibrary.com

Also available

Audio Dramas

THE HORUS HERESY®

James Swallow

GARRO

Weapon of fate

BLACK LIBRARY

For Toby and Neil, who make me sound good and look good.

A BLACK LIBRARY PUBLICATION

Hardback edition first published in 2017.
This edition published in 2018 by
Black Library,
Games Workshop Ltd.,
Willow Road,
Nottingham, NG7 2WS, UK.

10 9 8 7 6 5 4 3 2 1

Produced by Games Workshop in Nottingham.
Cover illustration by Neil Roberts.

A CIP record for this book is available from the British Library.

ISBN 13: 978 1 78496 758 1

See Black Library on the internet at

blacklibrary.com

Find out more about Games Workshop
and the world of Warhammer 40,000 at

games-workshop.com

Printed and bound by CPI Group (UK) Ltd, Croydon, CR0 4YY

THE HORUS HERESY®

It is a time of legend.

The galaxy is in flames. The Emperor's glorious vision for humanity is in ruins. His favoured son, Horus, has turned from his father's light and embraced Chaos.

His armies, the mighty and redoubtable Space Marines, are locked in a brutal civil war. Once, these ultimate warriors fought side by side as brothers, protecting the galaxy and bringing mankind back into the Emperor's light.
Now they are divided.

Some remain loyal to the Emperor, whilst others have sided with the Warmaster. Pre-eminent amongst them, the leaders of their thousands-strong Legions are the primarchs. Magnificent, superhuman beings, they are the crowning achievement of the Emperor's genetic science. Thrust into battle against one another, victory is uncertain for either side.

Worlds are burning. At Isstvan V, Horus dealt a vicious blow and three loyal Legions were all but destroyed. War was begun, a conflict that will engulf all mankind in fire. Treachery and betrayal have usurped honour and nobility. Assassins lurk in every shadow. Armies are gathering. All must choose a side or die.

Horus musters his armada, Terra itself the object of his wrath. Seated upon the Golden Throne, the Emperor waits for his wayward son to return. But his true enemy is Chaos, a primordial force that seeks to enslave mankind to its capricious whims.

The screams of the innocent, the pleas of the righteous resound to the cruel laughter of Dark Gods. Suffering and damnation await all should the Emperor fail and the war be lost.

The age of knowledge and enlightenment has ended. The Age of Darkness has begun.

~ DRAMATIS PERSONAE ~

The Knights Errant

NATHANIEL GARRO	Agentia Primus, former battle-captain of the Death Guard
TYLOS RUBIO	Former Librarius Codicier of the Ultramarines
MACER VARREN	Former captain of the World Eaters
VARDAS ISON	Former Librarian

The Legiones Astartes

ERIKON GAIUS	Captain of the Ultramarines 21st Company
RAKISHIO	Known as 'the Shadowed', legionary of the Emperor's Children
HAKEEM	Legionary of the White Scars
HAROUK	Techmarine of the White Scars
ROGAL DORN	Primarch of the Imperial Fists
SIGISMUND	The Templar, First Captain of the Imperial Fists
YORED MASSAK	Legionary, former Librarius Codicier of the Imperial Fists
MERIC VOYEN	Apothecary, formerly of the Death Guard

Those who serve the Imperium

MALCADOR	Sigillite and Regent of Terra
KHORARINN	Shield-captain of the Legio Custodes
MIQELL OLEN	Lieutenant, 34th Espandor Rangers, Imperial Auxilia

The faithful, and the lost

TAFF ARCUDI	Deck-captain, *Arc Bellus*, Collegia Titanica
KATANOH TALLERY	Scribe-adepta of the Administratum, second classificate
VOLO KELKINOD	Scribe-adept of the Administratum, second classificate
HALN	Covert operative of the Warmaster
ERISTEDE KELL	Fallen Assassin
EUPHRATI KEELER	The Living Saint
KYRIL SINDERMANN	Former Primary Iterator
NDOLE ESTO	Driver
ZEUN THURUQ	Believer
'CERBERUS'	Lost soul

'Those who cannot hear the aria are fated to believe the performers are insane.'

– Lady El Mar Horobin-La,
The Rapture of Suns [date unknown]

'Torn by shadows, comes the cry. "Bleed more," scream the masses, "bleed more." So they do, and they do; but the masses only howl for blood in other shades.'

– attributed to the remembrancer
Ignace Karkasy [early M31]

I will say this about him – when we first met, he was like a rock. Unbreakable and stoic, possessed of obdurate resolve and unwilling to compromise.

He was not a giant among his brothers as his gene-father would have been, but still he carried himself in a patrician manner. Respect seemed to come to him as rain to the ground. He earned it with every step he took, every word he uttered. Every deed he undertook.

I would not have said that to him. He would have thought it hubris, and he never hewed towards such things. It was not in him.

It is strange, is it not? That after so many years have passed, after so many terrible events and moments of import between then and now, I recall this thing so clearly. One would think that our meeting might have sunk beneath the weight of the horrors and glories that were to come, but it never has.

Why?

Call it simplicity. Yes. That will suffice.

When I looked him in the eyes that first time, I per-ceived clarity. And I must ask you to pause to reflect and consider where my mind was in that instant, and what we had experienced before that point.

What we had seen. What we were running from.

Above all, what we were afraid of.

Then you will understand how exceptional that was. So you see, something as simple as clarity was a prize that I seized upon with all my might.

In our desperation, we who fled had flung our-selves into the Stygian night, had given ourselves fully to faith. Understand that we had no guar-antee of survival, and know that with certainty. Death awaited us. We were given only the chance to choose how it would happen, not to forestall it.

But then we happened upon them, upon him. Guided by voices, by braver souls.

His welcome was to show us that all the gal-axy had not gone mad. Only some of it. Yes, only some of it.

No, he showed that there were still some things we could grasp that had not changed. Despite what we had experienced, all loyalty was not gone from the universe. Good and right and true, these ideals did not die that day. Thank the Throne. Wounded they were, oh yes. Cut to the quick and bloody, indeed. But still alive. Still fighting.

He showed us that. Affirmed it. And with his actions, he gave us hope.

We had expected death. Felt its inexorable approach. We prayed and asked our God-Emperor to take us to His side when the end came.

But that was not His gift to us. He had other plans.

Instead He placed this guardian in our path, a warrior who himself was on a journey, seeking an understanding of this new reality. A shepherd who would carry us away from the madness and beyond the reach of evil.

For a time, at least.

I knew it when that scarred face looked down upon me and I saw humanity written there. I saw a noble soul looking back at me through his searching, distant gaze.

Let me tell you about him. Close your eyes and listen. Hear his voice through my words. See his deeds in your thoughts.

Let me tell you about Nathaniel Garro.

PART ONE
THE SWORD

ONE

Mark of the Sigillite
Calth ablaze
Brothers in arms

ALL ABOUT HIM, the grey terrain of the Sea of Crises glowed monochrome, draining the colour from everything. Through towering windows of once bright glassaic pitted and misted by centuries of micrometeorite strikes, the stark beauty of Luna's landscape reflected back a hard, uniform light that seemed to cast no shadows.

The illumination gave nowhere to hide; something in that truth stirred a sense of *rightness* in Nathaniel Garro. That was how it should be. But in that truth, there was also an edge of sorrow, a longing that he had – so far – been prevented from addressing.

Since his arrival in the Solar System aboard the starship *Eisenstein*, since the conclusion of his calamitous mission to bring a warning to his Emperor, Terra's moon had become Garro's prison in all but name. Hanging there in the black sky, his birthworld seemed fated to be forever in sight, but beyond his reach.

How long had he been here? The days blurred into

one another, and without purpose they were torture.
He frowned, ignoring a twist of pain from his augmetic
leg, and glared out into the dark. The bionic limb was
a recent addition to his flesh, and in quieter moments
Garro would admit to himself that he still felt ill at ease
with the replacement. It was no lie for him to say that
he had truly left a part of himself back in the Isstvan System, in both flesh and in spirit.

Garro's gaze slipped from Terra's occluded ochre
sphere, and he let it be drawn towards the darkness
beyond. Somewhere out there in the black and fathomless void, a newborn war was raging, but for Garro and
the men who had joined him in his mission, there was
only the hush of the Somnus Citadel.

Here in the domain of the Sisters of Silence, under his
house arrest by any other name, the absolute absence of
sound had no end to it. With each turning of the world
in that black sky, he felt as if the silence dissolved a
fresh measure of his soul. To a legionary, this enforced
inaction was poison.

How long? The question pressed at his thoughts. *How
long will I remain here? Until the sky is cut by fire and the
enemy is at the very gate?*

'Battle-Captain Garro.' The words came at a low register, barely a whisper, but in the tranquility of the citadel
they carried like a crack of thunder.

He turned to the sound of the voice. A hooded figure
was silently crossing the chamber, and Garro was certain
he had been alone here only a moment before. He knew
the voice, however, and that explained it all.

'Great Malcador.' Garro bowed slightly towards the
Regent of Terra as the new arrival passed over a floor
of abstract black-and-white tiles. The iron staff in his

hand cast a soft glow from the flames that muttered in the basket atop it, flickering with each footfall; and yet, Garro noted, the Regent did not seem to cast any shadow where he walked. 'I came at your summons, Lord Sigillite,' continued the legionary. 'How may I serve you?'

Malcador gave a thin smile that cut through Garro's rote greeting. There had never been any question, of course, that his summons *would not* be obeyed. He gestured at the glassy walls. 'I recall that the last time we met here, you were angry with me. I saw the colours of your fury like an aurora. Strong and bright.'

Garro's memory kindled a brief echo of that rage and he stiffened. 'Can you blame me? I crossed the light years in a stolen warship, faced the guns of my own battle-brothers, and for what? To bring you warning of a treachery you had already foreseen. To face distrust and suspicion. Forgive me if I remain in ill humour.'

The words balanced on the edge of insubordination and the Sigillite's smile widened. Garro felt the gossamer trace of a psychic touch passing over him. After the Emperor Himself, Malcador was the most powerful human psyker alive, and to be stood before him was to be as glass. Just as the sunlight scoured the lunar surface leaving nothing hidden, so Garro faced the telepathic probe and did not flinch. He had nothing to hide.

Malcador saw the truth of him. Once a company captain of the XIV Legiones Astartes – the unstoppable Death Guard under the primarch Mortarion – Garro had become a man lost. His oaths remained unbroken, while those around him had been shattered. When his master and his kinsmen declared their loyalty to the renegade Warmaster Horus, it was Garro who had dared to refuse.

Garro, who made a desperate voyage across space to carry word of this terrible sedition back to the Emperor.

'You have paid a high price for your fealty, Nathaniel. Your Legion. Your brotherhood. The lives of your men. Yet you still remain.'

'I am the Emperor's hand.' The answer came without hesitation. Did Malcador think he wished for some kind of reward for doing his duty? Garro wanted nothing so trivial. He sought only to return to what he was best at, what he was made for. 'I could not turn from that,' he added.

The Sigillite nodded. 'But without a purpose, a legionary is nothing. A warrior without a war... is no warrior at all.'

Despite himself, Garro felt his annoyance returning. 'I have a purpose,' he insisted. 'Whatever force drives us, be it human will, fate or some higher power, I know that. There is reason for me to live. Just as there was for me to bring the warning, to stand alone as my kindred took rebellion to their hearts.' He gestured around, no longer able to stand rigid at attention, advancing towards the Regent. 'But as long as you keep me corralled here, you deny me the chance to find it!'

The moment the words left his mouth, some part of him wanted to call them back. Few could speak in such a way to the Sigillite and not fear chastisement because of it. But it was done, and he meant everything he had said.

When Malcador met his gaze, Garro felt a chill pass through him, like a shadow cast across his soul. In that moment it came to him why the Sigillite had suddenly demanded his presence here.

'We shall see what purpose you will serve,' intoned the great psyker. 'You are a legionary, indeed, and that will never alter. But you are of the Death Guard no longer. You are a *ghost*.' Malcador put hard emphasis on the word, cutting him with it. 'You are a figure that stands between light and dark, trapped amid the grey...'

Garro found himself nodding. It was true. He had fallen into the cracks of this insurrection, and feared the abyss might swallow him whole.

But Malcador's next words offered a lifeline. 'I have need of such a man.'

His head snapped up. 'Then task me, Sigillite. I ask only for that, and nothing more. Let me fulfil my purpose.'

A slow smile crossed that ancient, thoughtful face. 'For your sins, Nathaniel Garro, I will give you exactly what you have asked for.' He beckoned him with his other hand. 'Come. Follow me.'

Garro did as he was ordered, trailing warily after the psyker, into the gloom of depthless shadows cast by the curve of a half-furled solar shield. Malcador briefly vanished into the shade like a scrap of cloth sinking into an ocean of ink, and Garro heard clanking mechanical footfalls cross the floor, hissing pistons grinding to a halt.

An eyeless humanoid form, far more machine than flesh, presented itself. A blinded tech-adept of the Mechanicum, the Mars-born had a face made of metal plates and nothing that Garro could see in the form of sensors. Yet it approached him as if it saw clearly, opening up tool arms and bunches of serpentine mechadendrites in his direction.

The Sigillite turned back towards him and the stark white light reflected from the lunar landscape made Malcador's face seem spectral and serene. He gestured. 'Kneel, Nathaniel. Let the adept do his duty.'

'As you wish.' Garro reluctantly obeyed, frowning as he

bent down on one knee, the joints of his bionic limb clicking. He placed his sheathed sword upon the tiled floor and held his war helmet to his chest, looking the Sigillite in the eye as the Mechanicum adept leaned in.

The legionary smelled the tang of bitter bio-lubricants and machine oil. Heat flared over the bare skin on his neck as fat yellow sparks leapt and sizzled. He heard the grinding hiss of a meson lance as it cut into the plates of his armour, the particle stream layering levels of infinitely complex nano-scale circuitry into the ceramite.

'With this mark, you swear fealty to me,' said Malcador. 'You will obey my orders without question, to the bitter end.'

The warrior's eyes narrowed. 'I will obey,' he countered, 'as long as it serves the Emperor.'

'It will.' Garro felt the psyker's mind press into his, and he steeled himself, even as he knew he would not be able to resist the Sigillite's harrowing inner gaze.

'I see the fury again, Nathaniel.' Malcador cocked his head, studying the play of psychic streams that only he could perceive. 'But now it is directed outwards. It burns in you, the need to deliver reprisal to your traitorous brothers. You seek to give censure to your former comrade Calas Typhon. Perhaps even to challenge your primarch Mortarion, for daring to believe he might turn you.'

'Aye.' He bit out the word, holding cold anger in his heart. 'I will not deny it.'

Malcador gave a grim nod. 'The time for vengeance will come. But this day hear my orders. Hold your enmity in check. Your mission comes first.'

The legionary accepted this without comment. Just as before, on the deck of the starship *Eisenstein*, when he sacrificed everything he knew to carry the warning of Horus' treachery to Terra, the mission was his first, his *only* concern. If history was to recur, if it was his lot to play that same role, he would do it willingly, in the Emperor's name.

The lance fell silent, and the scent of superheated ceramite was sharp in the air. Garro listened to the crackle of the cooling brand as the adept backed away, head bobbing respectfully. The mark was made, the deed done. Whatever came next, he was committed to it.

Metal rang on metal, as with care Malcador worked to draw the blade *Libertas* from its sheath. Garro saw him strain to hold it steady. The great sword was not meant for human hands. The Sigillite pointed the tip of the mighty weapon at the floor, turning it to present the flat of the blade to the warrior.

'The oath, then.'

Garro removed a single gauntlet and placed his bare hand on the naked blade. With this act, he crossed the point of no return.

The Sigillite went on. 'Nathaniel Garro. Do you accept your role in this? Will you dedicate yourself to my orders, and put aside all other claims upon your honour? Do you pledge yourself in this oath of moment?'

Garro nodded once. 'By this matter and this weapon, I so swear. In His name.'

The Sigillite raised an eyebrow at his choice of words, but made no remark upon them. Rising to his full height once more, Garro took back his sword and bowed low, catching sight of himself in the towering windows. As good as it felt to be back in his armour and eagle cuirass after so long, it was still strange to see the new colours that Malcador had bade him wear.

Gone was the old Death Guard livery, the icon of the skull upon a six-pointed black star. There instead was a featureless ghost-grey that could have been slate or silver, or a shade in between. It stirred an odd emotion in Garro's chest, one that he could not quantify.

'What would you have me do?'

The Regent's steady gaze did not waver. 'Plans are being drawn. Another of my agents has drafted a list of names. You will leave the Somnus Citadel and travel the galaxy to seek the first of these individuals out.'

'Another agent?' Garro echoed, musing upon the rumours he had heard. 'The Luna Wolf, Severian, perhaps?'

Malcador's eyes narrowed at the legionary's insight, but he neither confirmed nor denied his suspicions. 'Twenty warriors from across all the Legions, both loyalist and traitor,' he continued. 'You will find them and bring them to me. You will do this, and leave no mark where you pass.'

Garro's fingers tightened around the hilt of his sword. 'For what cause?'

Malcador turned his back on him and looked out at the clouded orb of Terra, raised high in the lunar night. 'For the future, Nathaniel.'

CALTH WAS A world ablaze.

Deep in the Veridian System, beneath the hard light of a wounded sun, war like no other had come to the planet. A war that sounded its echoes across the galaxy. A war that would change the face of humankind forever.

Grim thunder roared over the distant howl of gunfire. Across the dying fields of blackened grasses, in the rubble of silent cities, through canyons of dark rock and ice-rimed sands, brother fought brother.

The Ultramarines, the sons of the great tactician primarch Roboute Guilliman, had come to the Veridian System to marshal their forces for battle. Their commander, ever the loyal warrior of the Imperium, massed the best of the XIII Legion, and their soldiers from the Ultramar regiments of the Imperial Auxilia. This he did under the orders of his brother, the Warmaster Horus Lupercal. This, Guilliman did without doubt or question.

His fealty was repaid with treason of the most odious stripe. The battle to come – the battle Horus had bade him prepare for – instead arrived shrieking from the skies on trails of blood and murder. The warriors of Lorgar's XVII Legion, the zealot Word Bearers, had come to kill. And with their oaths to the Emperor of Mankind broken, their new turncoat loyalty to Horus still painted fresh upon their blood-dark armour, the Word Bearers stabbed their brothers in the back, and scattered the Ultramarines to the points of the compass.

Now, fire cradled Calth in molten talons of churning gas, great streams of glowing colour that reached around the latitudes and raked the heavens. The aftershock of massed salvoes of thermoplasma weapons and fusion bombs had torn into the planet's atmosphere. The thin layer of fragile sky was broken, and the damage irreversible. No untainted breath of Calth's air would remain, as each new dawn brought it closer to death.

Amid the flames, Lieutenant Olen wondered if he would live to meet the next sunrise. Like his men, Olen was born on Espandor, which along with Calth was one of many worlds in the Ultramar Coalition. And like many souls upon them, he had shared the desire to stand in defence of his Imperium and his Emperor.

Olen wore the sigils of the aquila and of Ultramar with

pride. While he had not had the fortitude to become a legionary of the Ultramarines, he did his part nonetheless. And somehow, even in the darkest of days during the battles of the Great Crusade, Olen had never been in fear for his life. He did not consider this arrogance. It was only that he had never confronted an enemy so powerful that it could not be defeated by Ultramar courage. At least, not until this day. Olen had not faced a legionary in battle before, and there had never been cause to consider that such a thing might even occur. The mere thought of it was... *foolish*. That a single Space Marine might rebel against his liege lord was nigh-impossible to comprehend. And to suggest that an *entire* Legion, or even a primarch, could turn upon the Emperor for their own glory... If any of his troopers had said such a thing, Olen's laughter would have drowned them out.

The only laughter now came from their killers.

When the Word Bearers arrived, they carried destruction with them. Olen saw hundreds of men die in that first barrage. He saw Ultramarines, weapons slung as they moved to greet the surprise arrival of their kinsmen, slaughtered where they stood in a flash of treachery. Ultramar's finest warriors, human and legionary alike, reeled beneath a blow struck from nowhere.

They scattered across Calth in disarray even as Lorgar's sons tore into the planet, and put it to the torch. It was as if the whole world and every living thing on it were to be some vast burned offering.

The last contact Olen's unit made with an allied squad came from an armoured patrol moving north towards Numinus, the capital. The tank crews told the troopers of forces regrouping in the cavern cities, places where they might survive the souring of Calth's atmosphere beneath miles of rock and steel. And so Olen and his troops broke out, intent on a fast march across the Plains of Dera to the caves.

It was a good plan. It had failed when the *monsters* came. They boiled out of the icy gloom, rising from their concealment among the ruins of a burning starport.

Olen had fought aliens, and these were no strain of xenos that he could recall. They were rippling, changing things that hooted and brayed, dragging clawed tentacles and bearing lamprey mouths. They drooled venoms that melted men, glared with orchards of eyes that froze your heart with a look. And some of them – the worst of them – seemed in part to resemble human beings, but seen through a hellish lens of madness and horror.

As they came again, he thought of a word that few would ever speak in these secular days of human empire. A word he had once heard his late grandfather utter in a moment of senility – or, perhaps, of clarity.

Daemon.

In his prime, the old man had been a starship officer, and in the madness of warp space he had glimpsed secrets that had followed him to his grave. He had died a little before young Olen's eyes just to say that word.

Surveying the dwindling charge on his laspistol with grim understanding, Olen knew that he would very soon be joining his elder. The creatures advanced, and he gathered the last of his strength, casting around to his troops.

'Every shot counts!' He roared his final orders, determined not to go quietly. 'Make them pay for all they take!'

The attack began anew. The nightmare spawn ripped into the troopers like a hurricane, cutting them down, eating them raw. Olen's gun ran red-hot in his hand, but they did not drop. The largest of them rasped and screamed as they feasted on the fallen, and little by little the soldiers were forced into a collapsing ring as their number diminished. Death was moments away now.

Then, from above, deliverance arrived on wings of grey steel. A Stormbird drop-ship, falling from the fiery clouds as though it were some great eagle, casting a shadow over the fight, turning in place as spears of white flame held it aloft.

Olen's attention was seized for a brief moment. The ship was clearly Legion-issue, and yet, try as he might, he could not recognise the livery. It was neither the deep arterial-red of the traitor Word Bearers nor the striking blue of the Ultramarines. It was the colour of *ghosts*.

He watched as a brass-leaf hatch snapped open, and from it fell a giant figure in armour the same shade as the ship. As the craft powered away, the hulking warrior landed with a thunderous impact, killing a handful of the fanged monsters with the force of his arrival. Olen saw a shimmer of light on a vast sword as tall as a man, as the grey figure drew it from the scabbard on his back. Then, with a black-enamelled boltgun in his other hand, the warrior threw himself into the melee.

The sword rose and fell, rose and fell. The bolter crashed, each hammering discharge blasting the freakish creatures into gobbets of ragged, bleeding matter. As one, the bestial things turned on the warrior, sensing where the greatest threat to them lay. But this was no soldier, no common man. The figure in grey ceramite was a legionary, and he strode through the ranks of his enemies as an angel of death.

In his wake there were no screams. He left nothing but clean kills, thinning the lines of the monsters as they hurled themselves at him. Olen called out orders to his troops, and bade them support the warrior's fight, but the legionary did not need it. Alone, he did what more than a dozen soldiers had perished attempting. He *won*.

When it was over, the warrior advanced on them, and Olen could not help but draw back. He had seen legionaries on the field of battle many times, but never this close. Never like this, looming over him, the emerald lenses of a scowling battle helmet measuring him with cold intent.

The warrior gave his sword a cursory flick to shake off the tainted blood marring the blade, and returned it to the scabbard. Olen saw a word in High Gothic burned into the metal before it disappeared out of sight. *Libertas*.

'You are in command here.' It was not a question. Olen gave a stiff nod, kneading the grip of his laspistol. He was afraid to attempt to holster the weapon, for fear the legionary might think any sudden motion was an attack, and react in kind. 'I need information, lieutenant,' continued the masked figure.

'Of course.' He nodded. 'You have our gratitude. Are you here as part of a reinforcement detail or—'

The warrior held up a hand to silence him. 'The Twenty-First Company of the Ultramarines, under the command of Brother-Captain Erikon Gaius. You will tell me where to find them.'

The legionary did not raise his voice, and yet Olen's hand was already beckoning to the squad's vox-tech before he realised he was obeying the order. He halted, hesitating. 'Can you tell us what is happening? The Word Bearers... They attacked us. The signals we have intercepted... People are saying that Lorgar and his warriors have turned against the Emperor.' As he said it out loud, the full horror of the situation finally struck Olen and he shivered.

The reply cemented that cold dread in place. 'It is worse than you know. Now tell me. Where is Captain Gaius?'

The lieutenant gave up the data. The 21st Company had last been sighted on the western outskirts of Numinus, and after a moment to glance over Olen's fragmentary data-map, the legionary favoured him with a terse nod of thanks and walked away.

Abruptly, Olen realised he was leaving them behind. 'Sir? Wait…'

Something about the legionary and his armour had sounded a wrong note in the lieutenant's mind, and as he looked on him again, he saw why. The warrior's wargear bore an ornate cuirass dressed in brass and gold. Across his chest was the head of a fierce eagle, and rising up behind his helm was a heavy plate of armour that was cut into another raptor-shape. But what seemed strange was the absence of all other detail. The Legiones Astartes bore their colours proudly, and carried the symbol of their brotherhood on the pauldron of their armour. This warrior had none. Aside from a few flashes of dark-coloured trim, his armour was a uniform stone-grey from helm to boot, bereft of iconography.

'Who are you?' The question was snatched away by the winds, but the legionary heard it and he halted. 'Can you tell me that?' Olen pressed on. 'Before you go, at least let me know the name and the Legion of the warrior who saved our lives.'

For a moment, the armoured figure paused. Then he reached up and removed his helmet. A pale, patrician face, shorn and scarred, looked back at Olen with ancient, troubled eyes. 'My name is Nathaniel Garro,' he said, the words heavy with regret. 'And I am a Legion of one.'

THE ULTRAMARINES OF the 21st had been dug in for days, and if truth were told, they were now a company in name only. They had been at the forefront of the first Word Bearers' assault, and it had been their sufferance to witness the deaths of too many battle-brothers. The captain – hero of the Haddir Uprising, Gaius the Strong, Gaius the Unflinching – had rallied them in the face of the brutal losses. With words and deeds he led them into the fray, and they claimed back in blood a price from the traitors. But not enough. *Not yet enough.*

Now they were here, cut off from contact with their kinsmen, holding one of the railroad approaches to Numinus City. Waiting for this new war to reach out to them once again.

Brother Rubio took a moment to shift his stance. On the captain's orders, he had allowed his catalepsean node neural implant to dismiss the need for sleep, standing watchful and immobile among the lines of makeshift barricades. Before him, highways of plasteel rail reached away, some threading out across the landscape, others vanishing into underground passages. The rails were part of the infrastructure of Calth's society, connecting their network of cities both above the earth and below. Behind him, a wide, yawning tunnel mouth bored into a shield wall of sheer black rock, and far past it lay the capital. The remnants of the 21st Company stood astride a path that any foe would have to take, if they were intent on the capture of Numinus.

And the foe had *tried.* They began with massed forces of human soldiers, cultists gathered by the Word Bearers from distant worlds, whipped into a kill-frenzy and set loose against the legionaries. These slaves called themselves the Brotherhood of the Knife, and for all their ill discipline, they were many. The killing ground beyond the line of the barricades was carpeted with their bodies. Corpses clad in hooded robes that recalled monastic figures of old idolatry, their burned skin bearing ritualistic tattoos of lines and stars.

The Ultramarines had culled them, cutting them down as they ran heedless into their guns, trampling their fallen into the bloody mud. The attack had been broken, but not without its cost. Rubio glimpsed movement and inclined his head. His commander emerged from the shadows of an overturned cargo hauler.

'Brother.' Captain Gaius beckoned him from his post. 'It is time.'

Suddenly, Rubio felt a tightness in his chest. A regret. 'Someone must stand watch, captain.'

Gaius' face reflected a shared moment of sorrow, his breath curling from his lips in a thin wisp of vapour. 'Someone will. But first we must pay our brother his due.'

Rubio gave a solemn nod and shouldered his bolter, falling in to follow the captain deeper into the tunnel, where the glow of lumoglobes cast pools of weak yellow light.

There, surrounded by a circle of his kinsmen, Brother Mieles lay at rest. The Apothecary's white armour, stark in contrast to the deep blue wargear of the warriors standing about him, was marred by streaks of dried blood. The wound that had killed him was an angry rip across his torso, the gift of a cultist who had broken the line and destroyed himself using a vest packed with impact charges. Mieles was the most recent of them to perish, and his death had come without warning. The Apothecary had been a man of great character and good humour, a friend to all. His loss cut the warriors of the 21st as keenly as every one that had come before.

'For Ultramar and for duty,' said Gaius, speaking the words he had repeated many times before in this grim obligation. 'For past and for future. For Terra and the Emperor. No brother falls forgotten.' Then, with care, the captain applied the reductor to Mieles' corpse, reverently extracting the progenoid gene-seed glands that would be carried back to the fortress on Macragge. There they would be added to the Legion's store of genetic material, the bequest of the next generation of Ultramarines.

In this way, Mieles would live on; but at this moment all Rubio could see was death and darkness. Silently he made his farewell to his comrade, and cursed the sons of Lorgar once again for their perfidy. When he looked up, Rubio found Captain Gaius watching him intently. The captain spoke to them all.

'Kinsmen. We are being tested. We cannot know what madness has overcome Lorgar and the Warmaster. We do not know the fate of our brothers and our primarch. But what we do know is duty.' He gestured around. 'Our duty is to hold this approach to the city, to deny it to the enemy. These were Guilliman's last words to us. Mieles gave his life in service of that command, and if called, then so shall we.'

Inwardly, Rubio seethed with cold anger. His fury was directionless, railing at the mindless insanity of the suicidal cultists, the traitorous Word Bearers, the oathbreaker Horus – even at himself, for his failure to protect his battle-brother.

But he was an Ultramarine, and to speak openly of

such things was beneath him. Instead he kept his silence and only nodded.

GARRO MOVED SWIFTLY across the scarred wilderness, his gene-enhanced lungs drawing in the cold, corrupted air of Calth's dying day. The faraway shouts of heavy weapons and the cries of the injured and the dying were a constant refrain, carried to him on the harsh winds.

In the distance, he saw the glitter of habitat towers and hive stacks rising over cliffs of dark stone. Numinus City reached as high into the sky as it did into the caverns below the planet's surface, yet even as the warrior approached it, he saw the once-proud minarets wreathed in plasma fires, and the bright pinpricks of long-range laser bombardment.

As he walked, Garro wondered how long the battle would rage across Calth. The extremist Word Bearers had picked a fight here that would test them to the limit. The Ultramarines were no easy target. They were among the most finely drilled and highly competent warriors of the Legiones Astartes, a firm match for the ruthless, fanatical zeal of the primarch Lorgar's warriors on any battleground. On Calth, Horus Lupercal's civil war was raging in microcosm, but, like the larger conflict written across the stars, there could be no certainty as to how it might play out.

But the fate of Calth was not why Nathaniel Garro had come to this world. His mission here served another purpose.

His gaze dropped from the towers and searched the landscape, until he found the trail he was seeking.

DEEP INSIDE THE tunnel, in the cold and echoing space, Rubio's gaze turned inwards. In his mind's eye he saw the moment of his battle-brother's death. In the rush of Calth's howling winds, he heard the echo of Mieles as the Apothecary called out a warning, a heartbeat before the crashing detonation that tore him open and ended his life.

Rubio had seen the cultist coming, caught sight of the madman just as his bolter ran dry. In those precious seconds, as he raced to slam a fresh magazine home into the breech and bring it to bear, he had been too slow to save his friend. The moment burned like a livid brand, acid guilt searing him. The tragedy of it was, he could have stopped the cultist, boltgun or not. Rubio could have done it with a thought. But such a thing was now forbidden.

Once – in what seemed like another life – Rubio had been more than this. Now he wore the sigils of a Tactical line legionary, but before...

Before he had proudly carried upon his shoulder plate the skull-and-scroll device of a ranked Codicier, the badge of a psyker-warrior in service to the Ultramarines. Once, the company of Rubio and his kind had been feared across every battlefield, and even his fellow legionaries had taken pause at his presence. Once, the power of the warp had coursed from his fingertips, the actinic glow of telekinetic lightning laying waste to the enemies of mankind. Countless foes blasted apart by the sheer power of his mind.

But not now. Not since the gathering at Nikaea, and the passing of the Emperor's Decree Absolute. Many said that those with Rubio's gift – or as some would have it, his curse – were only one step removed from sorcerers, their minds open doors to ruinous powers ready to reach from the darkness and consume them. At Nikaea, out of fear or of jealousy, those voices had finally held sway.

At a conclave of his primarch sons, the Emperor of Mankind had ordered that all psykers among the Legions, every Epistolary, Codicier and Lexicanium, were to abstain from the use of their abilities and return to line duty with their battle-brothers. Rubio was faithful and obedient, and he did as he was commanded, giving up his psychic hood and his force sword. His former status nulled, he accepted redeployment and did not question.

At least, not at first. But now the death of Mieles had set him at odds with his orders. Rubio knew with every fibre of his being that the Apothecary would still be alive, if only he had been given free rein to use his preternatural powers. *And how many others?* he wondered. *What deaths might have been avoided, what adversaries felled, had they been able to call upon the might of a psyker?*

He heard the approach of armoured footsteps and Rubio looked up from his introspection to find Captain Gaius standing over him. 'Are you troubled, brother?'

'It is nothing of import, captain.' It was a poor lie, and his captain saw through it.

'I know where your thoughts are, my friend. I also know that you are one of the finest Ultramarines it has been my privilege to command. No matter where your talents are applied.' Gaius placed a hand on his shoulder. 'Courage and honour, brother. We follow the words of the Emperor and Guilliman, unto death.'

'Courage and honour, brother-captain,' repeated the Codicier, but the axiom rang hollow in his ears. He took a breath. 'It is only that I–'

The words he was about to speak faded in his throat as a sentry called out a warning from the far end of the tunnel. The sudden cry of alarm out at the barricades echoed down to them.

'Report!' Gaius barked the order into the vox-bead at his throat.

'*Intruder sighted*,' came the reply. '*A single legionary approaching our lines. He comes with a weapon drawn.*'

'One of our kinsmen?'

'*It would appear not.*'

The captain did not wait to learn more, breaking into a run. Rubio went after him, bringing his bolter to the ready. 'To arms,' shouted Gaius, as they sprinted towards the tunnel mouth. 'Prepare for enemy contact!'

TWO

A ghost
The choice
Oath of moment

A FIGURE EMERGED from the low wreaths of curdled mist before the blockade about the tunnel mouth. In the dimness, Rubio saw the unmistakable bulk of a figure in Legion-grade power armour, moving towards them with steady purpose. Every weapon on the line of the barricade went up to firing position and drew ready.

The Ultramarines had suffered badly at the betrayal of the Word Bearers, and they would not be so trusting a second time. But as the figure fell into range of the light from the barricade's glowing lumoglobes, Rubio saw not the dark, brazen livery of the traitors, but armour the shade of a storm cloud.

'He bears no Legion's colours,' said the Ultramarine. 'What trickery is this?'

With a whip-crack gesture, Gaius had his men take aim, and he called out: 'You there. Halt and be recognised! In the Emperor's name, stand to and state your intentions!'

Slowly, the figure in grey shouldered his bolter and

surveyed the line of Ultramarines, each of them a heartbeat from gunning him down. He lingered on Rubio's
commander, measuring him with a glance.

'Captain Gaius. You're a difficult man to find.' Heedless of the weapons ranged against him, the legionary
walked boldly through the barricades until he was face
to face with the officer.

It was all Rubio could do not to let a breath of his psychic senses reach out and take the measure of this new
arrival. Perhaps the warrior sensed that, as his helmet
turned, the fathomless eye-lenses scanning the Codicier intently.

'I will have your name and rank,' demanded Gaius.

'As you wish,' replied the new arrival. 'Although I'll warrant you will learn nothing from them. I am Nathaniel
Garro. And as for rank... Once I was a battle-captain, but
now I have none, as you would know it.'

Rubio could not stop himself from speaking. 'Then
what are you?' He studied Garro for a long moment. 'You
stand before us in denuded armour, bereft of insignia,
and this on a battleground where the enemy were once
men we called kindred.' Something in the way this warrior carried himself chimed with a distant memory from
deep in Rubio's past, a glimpse of an image once seen in
a millennia-old reliquary. 'You court death, Garro, like
some ancient knight errant.'

When he spoke again there was a dry smile in Garro's
voice. 'That's as good a title as any, brother.'

Gaius saw little that brooked amusement, however. 'If
you are not a son of Ultramar or one of Lorgar's traitor
whelps, then why are you here on Calth?' The captain
eyed the intruder coldly. 'I am in command here, and
you will answer me.'

Garro's manner hardened. 'I do not dispute your command, but the higher authority here is mine. *See.*' He bowed slightly, and by the glow of the lumens, a hidden rune across the shoulders of his plate suddenly became visible.

Rubio saw a stylised eye, scribe-encoded into the atomic lattice of the ceramite sheath by meson beam. 'The Sigil of Malcador...'

He knew the symbol; they all did. It was the personal mark of the Regent of Terra, and those who bore it were proxy to the Emperor's closest confidante. The rune would allow this Garro to go where he wished, and as the instrument of Malcador's will, to countermand any order – even that of a ranked officer. The sharp intake of breath from Captain Gaius told Rubio that his commander shared his thoughts.

'My mission on Calth is at the behest of the Sigillite and the Emperor, captain,' Garro went on. 'That is all you need know, for now.'

Gaius' steady gaze did not waver, but Rubio saw the slight stiffening of the captain's jaw and knew it for the signifier it was. 'So be it,' allowed his commander. 'But I warn you not to interfere with my mission. That mark of yours will be no shield to you when the turncoats attempt to breach our lines.'

The captain stalked away, and Rubio found the new arrival's gaze on him once more. 'You are Brother-Codicier Tylos Rubio,' said Garro.

He shook his head. 'I am only *Brother* Rubio. Nothing more.'

After a moment, Garro gave a nod. 'As you wish.'

THE MATTER OF the intruder dealt with for the moment, the legionaries manning the rail tunnel barricade returned to their duty, and slowly the poisoned night faded. Now dawn was coming, but it would be a sunrise like no other over Calth's frigid, frost-rimed landscape. Through the night, oxygen levels had continued to drop until now, only a toxic breath of atmosphere remained to shroud the planet. Soon it would be a wasteland, all native flora and fauna suffocated and dead. Only the war would live on.

Silent inside the seals of his wargear, Brother Rubio watched the warrior Garro prepare his bolter for combat with swift and careful motions. It was clear he knew the weapon intimately, and from the numerous honour lines acid-etched into the frame and grip, it had seen many battles at his side. The warrior made a pretence of keeping to himself, but Rubio saw through that. Garro was observing everything around him, his attention returning time and again to Captain Gaius, as the officer moved among his men.

Is Garro here for the captain? Rubio examined the question in his thoughts. *Has Gaius transgressed in some way, and now this stranger arrives from out of the darkness to claim him?*

He had no answer to that, but he was certain of one thing. Nathaniel Garro had come to Calth to judge them. A dark impulse in the depths of his mind stirred at the thought of being found unworthy by an agent of the Sigillite. And yet, another inner voice dared to ask by what right this man could put the Ultramarines of the 21st to the question. What conviction there was in Rubio had been severely tested in the last few days, and it was close to breaking point.

It would be simple to gaze into him, he thought. It would only require the most infinitesimal use of his prohibited witch-sight. Just to see, to know if Garro was what he appeared to be.

In that moment, for one fraction of a second, Rubio's iron concentration wavered, and something slipped into his psyche. He stiffened, and suddenly–

A vision came to him.

The real world hazed and turned to fluid, slipping away, becoming dreamlike echoes all around. He heard the thudding of his own heartbeat. Skeins of absolute and infinite frayed in Rubio's mind, unravelling and reordering themselves. He tried to reel back and shutter the sensation away, but it was too late. The vision was upon him, his silent Codicier's power engulfing him for one brief instant. And in that crystalline moment he saw–

A battle in full flow, bolter fire and the screams of crazed attackers. Battle, red in blade and black in shell. And there, fallen upon the icy ground…

Gaius.

Armour cracks and snaps under a terrible weight. Gaius cries out in agony, dying. Rubio sees himself reach out, his blood roaring in his ears, desperate to reach his commander, to save him before his life is crushed from his flesh–

'Rubio!'

Garro's voice shattered his hallucination and the Ultramarine gasped and shook off the moment, the taint of psychic energy dissipating faster than it had arrived. He cursed his brief lapse of control and rose, waving Garro away, but the other legionary strode closer. Did the grey-armoured warrior know? Would Rubio's moment of distraction cost him dearly? He struggled to process what he had witnessed in the flash of future-seen. The captain, struck down. Dying. Dead?

'No,' he whispered. 'It has not come to pass…'

Rubio shrugged off the fragments of the vision, denying it. He had shown weakness, that was all. A moment of lost focus, and it had been enough for the warp to poison him. The Emperor's decree was not to be questioned.

'Brother!' Garro was at his side, reaching for his arm. 'Do you not see them coming? Quickly, to your gun!'

'See what?' Belatedly, he understood that his reverie had been deeper than he'd realised. The words had barely left his lips before the first report of mortar fire shrieked through the air and blasted a rockcrete piling into shrapnel. The stone walls trembled, dust raining down on them, and in the echo of the blast a new sound reached Rubio's ears. The oncoming roar of massed attackers.

'The enemy returns,' said Garro, 'and in great number. We must make ready for battle.'

'The captain...' Rubio cast around, searching for his commander, fearing the worst. His brief stab of dread faded when he found him. Gaius stood atop a barrier across the tunnel mouth, his battle cloak flaring open behind him, his bolt pistol aimed and ready. The captain raised the giant mailed glove of his power fist and punched the sky.

'Hold the line, my kinsmen!' he shouted, earning a roar from his men. 'For courage and honour!'

Rubio bared his teeth and set forward as bolt-fire and las-beams cut into the rails and the stony ground, the ruined dawn finally breaking beyond the barricade. He raced into the fray to meet the hordes of the enemy, and found Garro at his side. The scarred warrior drew his shining silver sword and set it cutting arcs through the air, to cleave chests and take heads. The masses of the Brotherhood of the Knife, clad in makeshift breather masks and pitiful remnants of armour, died in their droves.

Gaius led the way, at the very tip of the arrowhead that was the legionary blockade. The cultists, screaming and shivering in the frigid cold, were pushed to greater and greater heights of bloodthirst through madness and fear. Their masters among the Word Bearers had driven them into this mad tumult, and their only respite would be to die choking the guns of the loyalist Space Marines.

The captain fought deep, as an army of insane zealots rode over him in a wave. There were so many of them that by sheer weight of numbers they toppled Rubio's commander from his feet, slamming him into the steel rails criss-crossing the ground. For long seconds, the heap of screaming, murderous cultists heaved and shivered – and finally exploded outwards as Gaius burst free of their suffocating grip. Every hammer-blow strike from his power fist took a life, shattering their brittle bodies.

Rubio stepped to his post and followed his captain's example, ignoring the torrent of pain that lanced through his skull in echo of his vision. He tried to force it away, ignore it. He did not succeed.

Close at hand, Garro fought hard, the lone warrior's grey armour now smeared with blood and smoke-dirt. He was possessed of keen, intense focus, and every stroke of his sword, every bolt shell expended, was placed where it would do the maximum amount of damage. Rubio saw light glitter off the brass eagle-head on Garro's ornate chestplate, and once again wondered who this man might be. He fought with the poise and cold lethality of a seasoned veteran.

Then Garro spun in place as something caught his sight. He stabbed out with his sword, towards a ridge in the middle distance. 'There! This is only the precursor! Enemy incoming! Close the line!'

The Ultramarine heard a sound like the grinding of gigantic break-tooth gears, and from behind the ridge-line emerged a great construct of plasteel and cables, armour and brass. With a grating noise, with pistons spitting foul steam, it clattered across the stone on six jointed piston-hissing legs, crab-walking as it crushed the unwary in its path. An angular turret thrust up from the centre of the machine-thing's mass, overloaded with gun cupolas and missile tubes in organ-pipe profusion. It had a main cannon made of black iron, the yawning muzzle dripping with penitent chains.

The mechanism moved like it was alive, its flanks daubed in arterial-red and dressed in the ebon detailing of the Word Bearers. It defiled the ground underfoot with every heavy step.

As one, the Ultramarines turned their fire upon it, but if anything the attack seemed to enrage the monstrosity. Rubio watched as it rocked forwards and broke into a skittering run, far faster than something of such bulk should ever have moved. Mass-reactive bolt shells, plasma rounds and short-range missile impacts all found their mark on the war machine, ripping into it. But on it came, catching afire, bearing down on the central barricade. And upon it, the captain of the 21st Company.

Rubio's blood turned to ice. 'Gaius!' His shouted warning split the air, but too late, things fell into place. Too late, he saw the moment unfolding once again. The battle, red in blade and black in shell. Rubio broke off and threw himself into a heedless, headlong charge, swatting aside any enemy that dared to block his path. He had to stop it. He knew what was coming and *he had to stop it*.

Gaius' helmet turned, as the captain registered Rubio's cry and saw him come running; but then the battle engine's cannon spoke and Rubio was ripped from the ground by the catastrophic shock of impact. He tumbled and spun, landing hard with a bone-shaking crash that brought the taste of copper to his lips. He tried to rise, and there before him, he saw a metallic leg collide with his captain's chest and ram him down.

GARRO TURNED AS he heard Rubio's cry of anguish. The shout was immediately lost in the brutal noise of armour cracking and snapping under a terrible, inexorable weight. Captain Gaius' ornate chestplate splintered with a sound like the snapping of bones, and his dark blood spattered across the rail lines in wet splashes of colour, freezing instantly where it fell. Garro's teeth ground behind the forbidding mask of his helmet, and he silently cursed the defiler-machine as it ended the life of another loyal scion of Terra.

It howled and grumbled as it half stumbled on legs damaged by sustained fire. One metal limb was hanging lifeless from oil-spitting hinges, but the construct still fought on, returning chugs of cannonade towards the defenders around the tunnel mouth. It reared up like an angry arachnid, and the legionary caught sight of Brother Rubio as he fought to drag the captain's battered body into cover. The construct hooted and went for him, intent on ending the Ultramarine's life as brutally as his captain's.

'No,' snarled Garro, and he bounded from a tumble-down marble column, boots crunching on broken stones as he marshalled his strength to leap high. The warrior in storm-dark armour led with his sword and landed with a resonant clang atop the traitor engine's turret. It rocked and twisted like a bear attacked by a wolf, trying to dislodge him.

Garro spun the length of *Libertas* around his gauntlets and plunged the point of the power sword into the apex of the turret, where a screaming skull-mask glared out with eyes of burning black. Oily fluids jetted from the savage cut and the machine shook, almost as if it were in agony. Ultramarines from the company's Devastator squads were closing, heavy lascannons, plasma weapons and multi-meltas in their mailed fists. His close-quarter attack was enough to distract the machine, giving Rubio time to get clear and the Devastators the moment they needed.

He shouted into his vox, struggling to hold on. 'Kill this thing! Do it now!'

An inferno of white heat, las-beams and rocket strikes engulfed the traitor engine, and it recoiled. The legionary heard an echoing rattle that was almost a screech, before the spider-legged tank finally threw him off in its shuddering death throes.

Garro landed hard, still clutching his sword, and rolled behind a slab of rockcrete as the machine met its end. The tank-thing exploded in a blast of flame, sending a storm of cursed metal fragments clattering to the frozen ground. The detonation broke the lines of the few cultists still standing, and those not executed by bolt-fire from Rubio's kinsmen died from the force of the explosive shock wave.

As Garro pulled himself to his feet, silence fell, the dead air leaden and threatening. He took a moment to climb atop the remains of the shattered barricade where Captain Gaius had briefly stood. From the vantage point, Garro could see out across the ridgeline to where the next wave of the enemy were massing. The optics in his helmet picked out targets at a distance, matching silhouettes to known threat vectors.

Word Bearers. The army of the primarch Lorgar, his most dedicated warrior-fanatics, and until recently, men considered kindred battle-brothers under the aegis of the Emperor of Mankind. Cold, repellent rage rose in Garro's chest as he beheld them. Was there no end to the spread of traitors' rot through the Legions? The Sons of Horus, the World Eaters, the Emperor's Children, even his own Death Guard, all had taken the turncoat path against the will of the Emperor. *Against His divine will.*

And now the Word Bearers would be counted among the renegades, damned forever for their rebellion, their betrayal marked in the blood of the Ultramarines. His aspect grim, Garro stepped down and turned away. They were coming, and in a force far greater than the remnants of the 21st Company could muster. Gaius' men would die defending the tunnel to Numinus, and the route to the city would be lost. It was inevitable.

But that was not his concern.

Garro's objective lay elsewhere.

BROTHER RUBIO'S HEAD was bent over the body of Captain Gaius as he approached. The Ultramarine crossed the dead warrior's heavy ceramite gauntlets over his chest in the sign of the Imperial aquila, and then saluted again, this time in the old pre-Unification manner, a balled fist to his chest. Rubio glanced up at him, and Garro imagined he felt the warrior's angry eyes glaring out through the ruby lenses of his helmet.

'My captain is dead,' he said, at length. 'He gave his life with nobility.'

'Aye.' Garro nodded, and framed his next words with care. It was time to make his mission plain. 'That he did. But you could have prevented this.'

Rubio reacted as if he had been struck, stiffening in shock. 'You dare–?'

'I know what you are, brother, what you are capable of.' Garro spoke quietly, so their conversation did not carry beyond them. 'I know what you once were, before Nikaea, before you gave up your hood and your blade. A *psyker*.' He gestured at the captain's corpse. 'You could have mind-spoken to him. You might even have been able to shield Gaius with a wall of psychic force. Yet you did not.'

Rubio's manner shifted and he advanced on the other legionary, his armoured hands balling into fists. 'I have my orders!' He spat the reply back at him. 'I will not challenge the decree!'

And yet, even as he spoke, Garro heard the conflict churning beneath the surface of Rubio's words. The Ultramarine was caught between bonds of loyalty to brethren and company, and his oath to primarch and Emperor. *What torment must it be for him to know that one had been sacrificed to the demand of the other?* It was a pain that Garro knew only too well.

'My captain is dead,' Rubio went on, his bitterness strong and dark. 'Whatever you wanted with him, knight errant, you came too late.'

Garro gave a slow shake of his head. 'I didn't come to Calth for Gaius. I came for *you*, Tylos Rubio, under orders from Malcador the Sigillite.' He let that statement register with the Ultramarine before pushing on. 'Malcador has commanded me to gather a host of warriors from across the Legions and bring them to the Imperial Palace. You are the first of that number, and if my mission is to be fulfilled, we must leave now.'

Rubio's anger ebbed and he shook his head, disbelieving. 'What you ask is impossible.'

'Not so. Time is against us and we must move quickly. If the Word Bearers launch their attack, we will be trapped here.' He looked up into the tormented sky. 'I need only transmit a machine-call signal to summon my Storm-bird. We will recover to my ship, and then–'

'No!' Rubio spoke over him. 'You would have me leave the side of my sworn battle-brothers in their dark-est hour? I *refuse!*'

'It is the Sigillite's command,' Garro repeated. 'His word is the Emperor's word.'

The other legionary stood silent for a long moment. Then he drew himself up. 'The Sigillite's command be damned. You give me no recourse, Garro. And so, on my honour as a son of Macragge, I choose to defy it. Even if it means I will perish here, even if you colour me a rebel like Lorgar's turncoats, I defy it.'

It was not the answer he had expected. Garro looked down at the sword in his hand. The impassive reflection of his battle helmet was reflected in the sheen of the ada-mantine blade. The fire in the Ultramarine's heart burned strong, and the other warrior felt the echo of it in himself.

If our roles had been reversed, Rubio's words would be my own. He felt the flash of cold certainty at that, and he could find no fault with them. 'Very well,' said Garro. 'If that is so, then I choose to stand with you... We will embrace defiance together.'

Rubio eyed him. 'If you have leave to escape this place, you should take it. Remain and there will be only death. An honourable death, perhaps, but an end nonetheless.'

Behind his helmet, Garro smiled. 'We shall see.'

SHOULDER TO SHOULDER, they met the advance of the traitors at the entrance to the vast stone tunnel with a clamour like unleashed thunder. The horde of armoured warriors stormed the barrier in unfettered wild array, their boltguns blazing and vile battle-cries in their throats. The absolute ferocity of the assault was a shocking, brutal thing, breaking in a wave of fire and blood across the barricades and the dug-in lines of the defenders. The Word Bearers threw themselves into the attack with a mad fervour that outstripped even the crazed offensive of the cultist hordes.

Every Ultramarine's gun was discharged, but for each of them there were five times that number of Lorgar's fanatic warriors, and the punishing momentum of their onslaught tore through the barriers, shattering the lines and riding forwards in a surge of blackened armour. The Word Bearers had always been known for their extremist, militant behaviours. During the years of the Great Crusade to reunite the lost colonies of humankind, many worlds that had fallen under the shadow of the XVII Legion had felt their wrath. Those who did not pay proper obeisance to the Emperor were punished mercilessly, so much so that the Master of Mankind had personally rebuked their primarch Lorgar, chastising him for fostering idolatry of his father, and violence beyond the pale. Some believed Lorgar and his Legion had heeded these lessons, but now it seemed clear that if anything, they had rejected their lord and found a new path. A path of cruelty and carnage, fuelled by raw hate and new gods.

Garro's blade sang and his bolter roared as the battle lines crossed and recrossed. He silenced the inner voice that rebelled at the notion of fighting fellow legionaries and bore down, reminding himself that these turncoats were no longer worthy of that name. These were traitors of the basest nature.

The armour of the Word Bearers, usually a uniform ebon shade, was deliberately smeared with what could only be human blood. The Legion symbol of a burning book upon their pauldrons had been daubed over with an eight-pointed star and a crude rendition of a screaming face. This self-desecration only stoked Garro's anger higher, and he fought with righteous fury, striking down traitors with sweeps of his sword and blasts of bolt shells. Close by, Rubio released bursts of bolter fire that blasted attacking warriors back in spiralling, bloody heaps. With each man they put down, more took his place.

Garro's gorge rose as he saw a group of Word Bearers kill an Ultramarine with a hurricane of storm bolter fire. To his disgust, even when the legionary fell dead to the ground, they continued to desecrate his body, unloading round after round into the twitching mess of the corpse; and as they did so, he heard them laughing. The wicked malice was like nothing Garro had ever seen from another legionary. The Word Bearers took delight in what they were doing, savouring it. He felt sickened inside.

'They keep coming.' Rubio ground out the words. 'Eyes of Terra, have they brought the whole Legion to fight us?'

Garro refused to flinch in the face of such odds. 'This will not end well, but in His name we will make them pay for every step of their advance.' He raised his blade and bellowed. '*Ave Imperator!*' His battle-cry echoed and he killed another traitor-kin, but his words rang a hollow note.

All around, the defenders were running low on ammunition, pacing each shot, making every bolt and beam count. Meanwhile, the Word Bearers were crazed in their abandon, strafing the barricades and filling the air with the stench of promethium and spent cordite. The press

of death was close at hand, and finally, as a fresh surge
of attackers pushed forwards, the cry went up among the
lines of the Ultramarines.

'Fall back!' shouted Rubio. 'To the tunnel, close up
and fall back!'

Garro followed, silently cursing circumstance as he
sprinted out of the icy air and into the gloomy, frost-
rimed stone of the rail tunnel. Behind him, the Word
Bearers screamed their hate and came running.

Rubio beckoned, and Garro's blood ran cold as he
dared to glance over his shoulder. He spied a gathering of hulking, angular shapes emerging from amid the
howling lines of the traitors. The giant forms pushed
forwards, shouldering their own men aside, bringing up
heavy, multi-barrelled weapons bristling with firepower.

'TERMINATORS!' THE ULTRAMARINE spat a curse at the
enemy cadre, as they advanced in steady, iron-limbed
lockstep.

The towering, thickset figures were twice the mass
of any line legionary, and the suits of heavy powered
armour lumbered forwards, effortlessly dismissing the
rain of las-bolts and mass-reactive shells sleeting from
their wargear.

Rubio ranged around, but it quickly became clear that
there were not enough heavy weapons to put down the
line of steel-ceramite leviathans. Krak grenades pushed
them back, but only for a moment. The line advanced on,
breaching barricade after barricade, while the rest of the
Word Bearers fell in behind them, delivering a cascade
of support fire. The Terminators tore open every target
they chose. Lines of tracer from massed combi-bolters
and the spinning muzzles of autocannons shredded the

bodies of the defenders. Ultramarines fell dead, red ruins marring the flawless blue of their power armour. Rubio felt a hand on his vambrace and turned to find Garro pointing with his sword.

'We cannot hold this line,' said the warrior in ghost-grey. 'We have only a few moments before the Terminators enter the tunnel. We must pull back.'

'To where?' snarled Rubio. 'Do we keep retreating down this tunnel until we reach the gates of Numinus? We have no cover in here! If we show them our backs, we will be cut down.' He shook his head. 'The colours of Ultramar do not run.'

'Then we will die here.' Garro's matter-of-fact reply only served to stoke Rubio's annoyance further. 'You will have defied one order to perish for another, and your battle-brothers along with you.'

The Ultramarine's face twisted in frustration. 'Damn you, Garro! You leave me no choice.'

Garro shook his head. 'No, brother. You have already made this choice. It is only now that you understand that.' He loaded his last clip into his bolter, and opened fire. Rubio watched the survivors of the 21st Company as they were forced back, deeper into the throat of the tunnel by the endless deluge of rounds.

What little daylight could enter the wide passageway was lost behind the lumbering shapes of the Terminators, as they crossed the railhead and entered the tunnel proper. The black shadows were illuminated by the cruciform muzzle flashes of their guns, stark light showing scowling, feral-faced helmets crested with horns and tusks. Rubio heard his comrades screaming as they fell. This was no longer an attack; it had become an execution.

Not again. No more. The flash of pain Rubio had felt

at the death of Captain Gaius lashed through him once again. *I will suffer this no more.*

The Ultramarine let his spent bolter fall from his grip to the floor and sucked in a shuddering breath, raising his hands before him, curling them into claws. He let it happen, allowing himself to reach deep inside and draw out what was needed.

Immediately he felt the old, familiar crackle of eldritch power dwelling at the base of his skull, twisting and turning like a spear of lightning confined in a bottle. All the cantrips and the memes, the key-phrases and thought-forms he had banned from his mind after the passing of the decree, all these things he allowed to return to him. The tainted air around Rubio took on a greasy, electric texture, the sense of a force beyond human understanding dancing at the edge of awareness. Rubio saw Garro giving him the distance he needed, saw his battle-brothers shaking their heads, but it was too late to stop it now.

The power was there. It had never left him, instead following Rubio through his actions like a shadow in the warp. It came easily. It was potent, heady, and like his fury, it strained for liberation.

Tiny flickers of electric discharge danced between the tips of his fingers as he aimed his hands towards the advancing line of enemy Terminators. Without the shroud of a psychic hood to collimate it, his power would be fierce and hard to control, but Rubio was ready. If he did not do this, they would all die.

He knelt, and gave his rage its release.

A blinding blue daybreak took brief life as a massive blast of shimmering energy cascaded down in a wave, striking the Terminators. The brief storm of psionic discharge swept across the passageway and engulfed the Word Bearers, for the first time forcing them to scream in torment rather than zeal. Then, as the power found its level, the mouth of the tunnel above cracked and fractured, breaking under the strain of warp-kissed energy.

With a thunderous rumble, the roof caved inwards. Like the closing of a set of vast jaws, black stone slammed down, sealing off the passage and burying the Terminators under tons and tons of shattered rock.

TIME BLURRED, THERE in the aftermath. Garro stalked through the lines of the other Ultramarines, all of them hesitant and unsure at what they had just witnessed. He knew by the motions of their helmets that they were speaking to one another on a coded vox-channel that he could not access, but it mattered little. He did not care to hear what they believed.

Garro found Rubio crouching in a circle of seared, fused stone. He offered his hand and the young Ultramarine took it, pulling himself up from the ground with a grunt of effort. The psyker removed his helmet and for the first time looked upon him with his own eyes. Garro mirrored the gesture, and the two warriors measured each other. He saw a great sadness and felt a sting of guilt at the knowledge he was its author.

'It is done,' Rubio said, his tone bleak. 'The enemy is beaten and this path to Numinus is denied to them. And all it cost me was to defy my primarch and my Emperor.'

'Your brothers survived,' said Garro. 'Take that as a reward.'

Rubio did not answer him. Instead, he moved around the figure in grey and took a step towards the other

Ultramarines, who now gathered in a loose group, tending to their wounded.

They halted in their ministrations as Rubio came closer, and he stopped, seemingly unsure of what would happen next even as he had to know that it would.

As one, each of the battle-brothers of the 21st Company averted their eyes and turned their backs on Rubio. No matter that he had saved them, no matter that he had protected the path to the city from enemy invasion; he had disobeyed a decree absolute, and for that, the sons of Guilliman had no forgiveness.

Garro drew *Libertas* and Rubio spun at the ring of the blade upon its sheath, fixing him with a furious glare. 'Are you satisfied?' The other warrior spat the words. 'Do you have what you came here for?'

'Not yet.' Garro held the sword out, the point down towards the ground. 'Place your hand upon the blade.'

Rubio advanced, his anger towering. 'You forced me into this! You cost me my brothers, and now you demand an oath?'

Garro shook his head slowly, and he gave voice to the truth of it. 'These men are no longer your brothers. You are a ghost. Now place your hand on the blade.'

A torrent of conflicting emotions raged across Rubio's face as the reality of his circumstances became clear, undeniable and resolute. At length, he removed a gauntlet and let it drop to the ground. Then he reached out and touched the sword. Garro gave a grave nod.

'Tylos Rubio. Do you accept your role in this? Will you dedicate yourself to the orders of the Regent of Terra, and put aside all other claims upon your honour? Do you pledge yourself in this oath of moment?'

Something dark like sorrow flickered in the warrior's

eyes. 'By this matter and this weapon, I so swear.' He said the words as if they were a sentence of death. 'I can do nothing else.'

THREE

Remade
A summons
In Bellus, Veritas

WHEN THE SHIP left the warp, Tylos Rubio finally understood where he was being taken, and gained the first true inkling of what that might mean for his future. He sensed the vessel transition from the madness of the warp and return to real space, the impression of the change pressing in on his mind even though he did not wish it.

There were no guards posted outside his quarters, but he had no doubt he was under surveillance as he made his way down the corridor, to an observation cupola that grew out of the starship's outer hull. There, he stood and watched as the smoky disc of distant Jupiter passed by them, and knew that he had come to Sol. To the seat of the Imperium itself.

Rubio had never seen Terra with his own eyes. A son of the Five Hundred Worlds, born and bred on mighty Ultramar, he felt a connection to the Throneworld in the loyalty to Emperor and Imperium that was central to his nature as a Space Marine. But that connection was an ephemeral thing, an ideal rather than an emotion. In a way, Terra had always seemed *distant* to Rubio, far removed from the battles and duties he fought in its name.

But now it was real. He stood watch for hours, until the planet grew through the cupola from an indistinct dot against the void to a dark orb lit by a halo of gargantuan works about it. Shipyards. Gun shoals. Command stations. The decorations of war-to-come surrounded the planet, and the sight brought an odd chill to Rubio's blood.

Then the ship turned away and the dead landscape of Luna filled the view.

He became aware of a crew servitor waiting in the corridor nearby. 'Speak,' he told it.

The machine-slave did not. Instead, it offered him a folded slip of plaspaper bearing an embossed seal – and within he found what would be the first order of his new existence.

THE SUMMONS BROUGHT Rubio to the highest tier of the Somnus Citadel, and in the harsh monochrome light he saw Garro on the far side of the glass-walled chamber. The other warrior stood like a sentinel, a statue of ceramite and steel, bone and flesh. In his plain armour, the former Death Guard seemed somehow unfinished. His hairless, scarred scalp was lined with the furrow of his brow, and his eyes were eternally watchful. If Rubio looked closer, he knew he would see the edges of regret that ran deep in the warrior's heart. But it was not seemly to speak of such a thing. It was not his place.

His place. Was there such a thing for Rubio now? He pulled his nondescript robe tighter around his shoulders.

Beneath it, he wore fatigues of simple cut, the sort of thing in which a Legion-serf or indentured helot might be garbed.

They had taken away all that had showed his Legion and his fealty, and Rubio had not given it easily. The Ultramarine had finally allowed his armour to be removed, and only then on the express order of the Regent himself. Still, he greatly begrudged it.

There was a truth that he had never voiced, but standing here in this great hall, it made itself plain to him. Little by little, the Great Crusade had chipped away at Tylos Rubio.

At the start, he had been a Codicier, a ranked brother of the Librarius. A war-psychic at the head of his Legion's 21st Company, fighting for the triumph of Ultramar with courage and honour. Alongside his primarch, he marched for Macragge beneath banners of blue and gold. Memories of those days were bittersweet. There had been such glory, with many enemies dispatched and many worlds saved from the abyss. Through it all, Rubio had used his unique, preternatural talents as a superlative weapon. He was a psyker, a warrior of the mind, capable of calling lightning from his hands and spinning dread through the hearts of his foes. He had been so very, very good at it.

Magnus the Red took that from him.

The lord of the Thousand Sons Legion, a mighty psyker in his own right, had earned the Emperor's displeasure by dabbling with the darker powers of the psychic realm. Magnus' reckless games with the warp earned harsh censure, and in the aftermath, the Emperor forbade the use of any psychic power across all Legions, to preclude any future chance of misuse. With a single edict, Rubio's ultimate ability was forbidden to him.

But he was still a warrior of the Legiones Astartes. Even without his mind-amplifying psychic hood and with his greatest weapon silenced, he could still fight for the Imperium with blade and boltgun. And in the moments when his hobbled status troubled him, Rubio would remain stoic and show nothing. After all, he had still been an Ultramarine.

But now that too had been taken.

On battle-scarred Calth, as the sky blackened, Rubio lost something that could never be measured. To save the lives of his kinsmen, he had made a terrible choice, and the echo of it had clouded his mind all the way back to Sol. Rubio had broken the Emperor's edict and called upon his shackled powers to beat back the enemy. In doing so, he had betrayed a sworn oath. His battle-brothers lived, but as one they turned their backs upon him.

Does that make me... a traitor? Rubio pushed the disturbing thought away, but it lingered, like a thunderhead on the far horizon. 'I am here, Garro,' he said. 'What do you want of me?'

The battle-captain turned to study him, his eyes searching Rubio's face for some measure of his mood. 'The voyage back from the Veridian System was arduous. Are you rested?'

'I am ready to return to the battle, if that is what you mean.'

Garro shook his head. 'We have not been called to fight a war, Rubio. Other men will challenge Horus' rebellion in open conflict. We... We are on a different path.'

'And where does it lead?' Irritation flared in him. 'You dragged me away from my brethren. You took me from my rightful place. Tell me it was for good reason!' Rubio cast a look down at his characterless robes. 'What duty can I undertake like this? Where is my armour? Where are my weapons?'

The other legionary's reply was solemn. 'Your wargear was your last connection to your Legion, brother. You no longer need it.' Garro turned towards the windows and gestured towards the black and grey beyond. 'Look out there.'

Rubio frowned, but did as he was asked. Out past the thick glassaic panes, there was only the airless wilderness of the lunar surface, and rising up above the rocks and craters, the curtain of great night. Stars, hard and bright like diamond, cast out the lines of the galaxy beyond.

'Millions of worlds and billions of souls upon them,' said Garro. 'Each one with a gun to their head, for assurance of fealty. Each with a blade at their neck, ready to take blood for sacrifice. But you know as well as I, brother. I imagine you hear the cries of the dead and the betrayed louder than I ever could.'

Unbidden, the spectre of distant gunfire, of screaming and the sounds of battle, rose and fell in Rubio's thoughts, as if from a faint memory. He stiffened.

Garro went on. 'A war like no other has come to the Imperium of Mankind, and I was cursed to be there at the birth of it.' He opened his arms to the other legionary. 'I was once a battle-captain of the XIV Legiones Astartes, the Death Guard. Like you, one of the Emperor's chosen Angels of Death. We shared the same mission as the sons of Ultramar... The *bringing of illumination*. The greatest undertaking in human history, to forge a transgalactic empire that would be glorious and eternal.' He looked away, sorrow flashing in his eyes. 'Such a grand dream. A magnificent endeavour. But broken now. Shattered and crumbling to ashes. The Emperor's plan has been ruined by the most petty and human of things. Treachery.'

'Horus Lupercal.' The name fell from Rubio's lips in synchrony with Garro's statement. The Warmaster and his foul deeds were so inexorably linked in the legionary's thoughts that it could be no other way. The primarch of the XVI Legion had rebelled against his father, and even after days of reading the reports and missives explaining the horror of it, Rubio still found it hard to grasp.

'Some said it was from a kind of madness, others that he had been poisoned by xenos influence,' said Garro. 'But I have come to believe it was something base and simple that took Horus to betrayal's path. Jealousy, resentment, distrust... These most human emotions are still extant in a warlord like Horus, even though the great primarchs were meant to be above such matters. It is troubling to admit, brother. If those so mighty can fall, what hope is there for us?' His gaze turned back towards the legionary. 'Can we transcend what we are? Will true illumination forever be beyond our reach?'

Rubio could find no answer. Against all reason, Horus' call to revolt had not died unborn. Others – the Emperor's Children, the World Eaters, Iron Warriors and Word Bearers among them – were joining the bloody rebellion. And now, across a galaxy split by terrible warp storms, they burned planets once held in the Imperium's name. If what he had been told was true, then world by world and star by star, the madness he had witnessed first-hand on Calth was inching ever closer to Terra and the Emperor's throne.

Garro's gaze dropped, and his voice became a whisper. 'To my eternal disgrace, I saw my own Legion follow Horus into disloyalty, led by my gene-father Mortarion. I watched powerlessly as my battle-brothers spat on their vows and took the Death Guard to the traitor's banner.'

'And yet you live still. Spared by both your turncoat kinsmen and those still loyal.' Rubio's bitterness coloured the words. 'How so?'

If Garro noted Rubio's mordant tone, he did not comment on it. 'In defiance of my master, for daring to choose Emperor over Legion, I was marked for death. And in the end, I fled the devastation at Isstvan where the war began, racing for Terra to carry the warning of Horus' intentions.' He took a long breath. 'I am Death Guard no longer. My armour has no mark upon it but for the brand of the Sigillite. As Horus – may his name be cursed – and his followers threw off their loyalty, so I have shed my old identity and been made anew. I stand before you now, a warrior without brothers, a legionary with no Legion.' A bleak smile pulled briefly at his mouth. 'What was the name you gave me on Calth? *Yes.* I recall. I am a *Knight Errant,* cast against a dark background. I have a new oath, to be the Sigillite's hand amid the murk and the fire of this hateful schism.'

Despite his circumstances, Rubio could not hold back his curiosity. 'To what end, Garro?'

'For the future...' He gestured towards the darkness, and Rubio followed his direction, finding Terra low in the sky, half in shadow. 'Somewhere upon that sphere, the Emperor is at work on designs so complex that none can comprehend them. In the meantime, we must protect Him from whatever threats come to pass. And there are such great threats at hand, Rubio. You saw a sliver of that on Calth, and I must tell you there is far, far worse ahead of us.'

The hard certainty behind Garro's words gave Rubio

pause. There was no deceit in him. The other warrior's expression spoke of what sickening truths he had been exposed to, and of the anger it kindled.

At length, Garro beckoned Rubio to follow him. 'Come with me. We will make you ready.'

'For what?'

'For the new conflict.'

THE SOMNUS CITADEL'S armoury was a forge of war, with dozens of machine-slaves and techno-serfs busy at the repair and maintenance of battle gear. The golden armour and shining great-swords of the Sisters of Silence, the Citadel's keepers, dominated the chamber. Their blades hung from every wall, alongside powerful flame cannons and assault guns. But as impressive as they were, none of these instruments of conflict could ever match the weapons of the Legiones Astartes.

Garro led Rubio towards an alcove where a group of patient servitors stood at attention. 'There, brother. Do you see?' He pointed towards an arming rack six metres in height, upon which lay a suit of power armour almost identical to his own wargear.

It was a highly advanced build, fresh from the manufactorum, and like Garro's armour, it was denuded of sigil and symbol, save for the discreet rendition of a stylised eye, almost indistinct upon one of the pauldrons – the mark of the Sigillite. A simple Librarius tabard hung from the waist. At Rubio's approach, the arming rack hissed open and servitors gathered, ready to assist him in donning the ceramite plate.

He hesitated. In his service to the Imperium, Rubio had never worn anything but the cobalt-blue of the Ultramarines, never borne any sigil but the Legion's revered

Ultima. To consider doing so now would seem like a kind of betrayal. Garro understood the sentiment only too well.

'If I accept this…' began Rubio, 'what becomes of me? I will lose what I was. I will no longer be a son of Ultramar.'

'This is not about Legion or birthplace,' Garro told him. 'This is a matter of greater import than the world you called home or the primarch you saluted. You and I, and the others to come – we give our loyalty to a new truth. A new ideal. We remember what we were, but rise to something beyond. We serve the Emperor of Mankind. That will never change. You swore an oath of moment on Calth, Rubio. Now make it whole. Take the armour. *Join me.*'

For a long moment, Garro thought the Codicier might refuse him and strike out in fury, but then that urge faded from his eyes and he nodded. 'Very well.'

Rubio mounted the rack, and spread his arms wide to accept the martial embrace of open brassarts, vam-braces and breastplate. Servitors secured the torso sections and greaves, the thick-set boots and gaunt-lets. He tipped back his head as the gorget locked into place, and with a low, bone-deep purr of coiled power, the micro-fusion generator in the armour's backpack became active. Next, the pauldrons settled into place. Piece by piece, Rubio became a war machine in the figure of a man.

Garro recalled the moment where he had stood in the same place, remembering how it had troubled him deeply. Rubio was passing through the same turning point now, uneasy with the oath he had cemented by this act. His former identity was lost to him now, and in its place he had gained a new status, one he had yet to be certain of. *I know, brother,* Garro wanted to say. *I know how this feels.*

The arming process halted and silence fell. 'It is done,' said Rubio, with the air of a man facing the gallows.

But Garro shook his head once more. 'Not yet, brother. There is still your greatest weapon.' He gestured to the servitors and bade them set the final piece of armour into place.

A black iron capsule suspended above the arming rack cracked open and from it descended a construct of arcane power, humming with latent energy. The psychic hood was a complex array of crystalline matrices and energy conduits, attuned to the unique resonance patterns of the immaterium. The servitors set it in place around Rubio's head and the device came to life, immediately bonding itself to his telepathic engrams.

The Codicier tensed as familiar power reawakened in him, a force of will that had been silenced for too long. Garro watched the potency return to him as abilities that had lain dormant since the Decree of Nikaea danced at Rubio's fingertips. '*Now* it is done,' he said.

THE ARMING FRAME hissed open and Rubio stepped down, fully armoured and ready for battle. The armour was a second skin. Plasteel and ceramite matched to meat and bone through the conductive surface of the black carapace bio-implant interface beneath his flesh. He tested the gauntlets, flexing the fingers. It felt right, but the conflict within him did not entirely fade.

'You accept your duty,' said Garro, with formality. 'Take these weapons and use them in the Emperor's name.' The other warrior handed him the heavy frame of a bolter and a sword in its scabbard.

Rubio smiled slightly as he held the blade in his hand. It was a gladius, the traditional sword-form of the Ultramarines, and upon it in a most subtle manner was the shape of the revered Ultima. He realised that Garro was allowing him to retain one small token of the Legion he was giving up.

'Gratitude, brother–'

The words turned to ice and ashes in his mouth. A sudden flash of psychic energy bloomed, the tremor of mind-sense came from nowhere, pressing in on Rubio's thoughts. He hesitated, fixing Garro with a hard gaze.

'What is wrong?'

Rubio did not answer. His telepathic skills were slow with disuse and unfocused, but still he felt a strange sense of something buried deep in Garro's mind. Another kind of truth, hidden under layers of the stoic Death Guard's thoughts. A secret belief that could not be read.

A fleeting image passed across his mind's eye. *An icon. A golden aquila.*

Every part of Rubio wanted to question what he had sensed, but now he felt another presence looming closer. Burning brighter than the chemically neutered thinking of the servitors, fierce and harsh, with the razor edges of a mind used to the act of killing. 'Someone approaches...'

'Who?' Garro turned as a hatch ground open to admit a broad figure clad in shining and ornate golden armour.

The figure scanned the room with the gaze of a killer, finding the two legionaries and taking their gauge in an instant. He towered in the hatchway, tall enough that Rubio was forced to look *up* at him, a rarity in itself. Yet the warrior in gold seemed uninterested in the former Ultramarine.

'You are Garro.' It was a statement, not a question.

'I am.' The legionary bristled at the open challenge in
the words.

'You will bring your cohort and follow me. *Now.*' The
new arrival did not wait to see if they would obey; he
simply turned on his heel and returned the way he had
come, marching down the citadel's vaulted corridors
towards the primary airlocks.

Garro's lips thinned at this blatant show of arrogance,
but he followed nonetheless, with Rubio a step behind.
On the face of it, they both had little choice. One did
not simply refuse a member of the Emperor's Custodian
Guard without good cause.

HE IDENTIFIED HIMSELF as Khorarinn – at least, that was
all he was willing to give them for the moment. The
warriors of the Legio Custodes possessed honour-names
of varying length, each supplementary appellation presented to them in recognition of services to the Emperor
and the Throne of Terra. Garro had heard of Custodians
with more than a thousand names, every one inscribed
across the inside of their armour. He could not help but
wonder how many names came after 'Khorarinn'.

It was said that as the legionaries were to their primarchs, so the Custodians were to the Emperor. The
personal guard of the Imperium's ruler, they were His
ultimate defenders. Indeed, it was a rare thing to encoun-
ter a Custodian *off* Terra. They only left the Imperial
Palace for matters of the greatest import, and then alone
or in small numbers.

The warrior cut an imposing, threatening figure, taller
than Garro even in his war-plate. The Custodian's ornate
golden armour was emblazoned with intricate designs of
lightning bolts, Imperial aquilae and complex scrollwork.

A blood-red cloak fell back over his broad shoulders, and under one arm the Custodian held a tall, conical helmet with a sculpted eagle across the brow, and a plume of crimson horsehair at the tip. He had an olive-toned complexion and dark eyes, and instead of the guardian spear more typical of his kind, Khorarinn was armed with a heavy, broad-bladed sword that mounted twin boltguns in its hilt.

He marched swiftly and with purpose, never once deigning to cast a glance towards the two legionaries. The aggrandised superiority of the Legio Custodes was well documented, and their manner was often the source of friction with outsiders. Garro had no reason to suspect that Khorarinn would disprove that assumption.

Rubio was the one to break the silence. 'Where are we going?'

Khorarinn answered without acknowledging the other legionary. 'A shuttlecraft has been prepared. You will both accompany me to the Imperial fleet battleship *Nolandia*. The vessel is in lunar orbit, awaiting my return.'

A scowl darkened Garro's face 'To what end?'

'That will be made clear when deemed necessary, *Death Guard*.'

The barely veiled insult could not have been clearer if Khorarinn had simply said 'turncoat' and been done with it. 'Perhaps I consider it necessary now. And to be clear, I no longer serve the Fourteenth Legion.'

'Of course,' the Custodian allowed. 'If you did still march for the traitor Mortarion, you would have been executed by now.' Garro's temper flared at the slight, but Khorarinn did not allow him the chance to respond. 'The command I bear comes from Lord Malcador, Regent of Terra. You are sworn to obey him, are you not? He wishes it, and so you will join me in my mission, despite my insistence that your presence is not required. For the moment, that is all that it is necessary for me to reveal.'

'As you wish.' It took effort not to rise to the bait, and Garro exchanged a grim look with Rubio.

The Codicier said nothing, but his expression was enough to make his thoughts clear. Warriors of the Legiones Astartes were not used to being ordered around like the common mortal soldiery of the Imperial Auxilia, and such a lack of respect would have earned other men a sword-point at their throat. But to speak out of turn to a Custodian was seen almost as insolence towards the Emperor Himself.

Garro was conflicted. He had respect for any warrior judged worthy enough to stand at the Emperor's side and bask in that divine glory. But he chafed at Khorarinn's ill-concealed and misplaced distrust. The Custodian was not reticent to show that he considered Garro unworthy of his regard, doubtless casting the battle-captain in the same light as the rest of his former Legion.

As they reached the airlock, Rubio could hold his silence no longer. 'If you will say nothing else, can you at least tell us what kind of enemy we will face on this endeavour?'

Khorarinn came to an abrupt halt and turned a hard glare on the Codicier. 'The worst of them all,' he growled. '*Traitors.*'

KHORARINN'S SHUTTLE WAS a sleek Aquila-class courier, a heavily modified surface-to-orbit variant painted in the gold-and-crimson livery of the Custodian Guard. Unlike the workhorse Stormbirds and Thunderhawks that the legionaries were used to, the shuttlecraft was almost extravagant in its design. It seemed out of place compared to the slab-sided monolith that was the *Nolandia*, a bright jewel resting against an ingot of crude iron.

The capital ship was kilometres long, heavy with countless weapons batteries. Great sheets of ablative armour gave the vessel the look of a massive, elongated castle, as if an ancient stronghold from Terra's prehistory had fallen through time and space, to be mated to powerful warp engines and cannons mighty enough to crack open moons.

As soon as the smaller craft had been pulled aboard, the *Nolandia* accelerated away, its drives echoing through its hull like the rumble of captured thunder. Her Navigator charting a course out of Terra's orbital path towards the perimeter of the Solar System, the vessel passed the great shoals of construction satellites busy with urgent builds to bolster the fleets, and the autonomous gunnery platforms bristling with macro-cannons and defence lasers. Other cruisers of smaller tonnage and system monitor ships without warp engines crowded out of the *Nolandia*'s way, obeying the pennants of high rank flying from its signalling masts.

The battleship left Terra behind in its thrust wake, the last sight of the Throneworld passing into eclipse behind a gargantuan, shining fortress – the *Phalanx*, star fort and monastery of the VII Legion, Rogal Dorn's Imperial Fists. Out across the orbits of Mars and the Jovian Colonial Axis, the *Nolandia* burned hard and fast towards the haze of the Kuiper Belt, the region of scattered ice asteroids that marked the edge of Solar space.

Out there at the Mandeville point, where warp ships could revert to normal space at the end of their transits, the sun was cold and distant, the stars alien and unwelcoming. Out there nothing moved but perimeter patrols of frigates and destroyers, and the swarms of machine-mind warning drones. All of them watching and waiting for the first sign of the invasion that would inevitably come.

A week or a month, a year or a decade; however long it took, eventually the Warmaster's fleets would reach this empty expanse of the void. It was only a matter of time.

A FEW DAYS into the voyage, after it became clear that the Custodian was in no hurry to brief the legionaries on their mission at hand, Garro sought out Khorarinn. He was drawn to the sounds of power swords tearing plasteel and the crash of weapons striking, the low animal grunts of constant exertion from a fight that showed no sign of coming to an end.

No one among the vessel's crew had dared challenge the Custodian when he demanded exclusive use of the *Nolandia's* combat training ring. Khorarinn's orders to the shipmaster had been succinct. Nothing, short of the arrival of the arch-traitor Horus himself, was to interrupt his sparring.

Garro learned that he had steadily worked his way through the ship's entire complement of training servitors, leaving them in smoking heaps as he dispatched them, one at a time or in groups. Each servitor learned from the mistakes of the one that preceded it, but still, after hours of duelling, not one of them had been able to lay a single blow upon the Custodian.

The legionary watched the flash and fire of Khorarinn's sentinel blade as it obliterated a mechanoid wielding dual chainaxes, in short order. It was an impressive sight.

'Slave!' Khorarinn sensed the presence in the chamber with him and called out, expecting to be obeyed. 'Clear away that wreckage. Bring me another.'

Garro stepped into view. 'There are no others,' he explained. 'You have destroyed them all.'

'Pity.' The Custodian was filmed with sweat, panting with exertion, but he seemed by no means fatigued. 'I was hoping to find something that might test me. For a moment at least.' He pointed with the sword-bolter in his hand, towards Garro's scabbard. 'The blade you carry is a fine tool. You call it *Libertas*, yes?'

Garro's hand slipped automatically to the sword's pommel. 'You are well informed.'

Khorarinn showed his teeth. 'I would see how it fares in combat.'

'That has all the colour of a challenge.' The legionary said the words carefully, without weight.

'Does it?' The Custodian gave a derisive snort. 'I don't expect you to be imprudent enough to accept. The Death Guard have never tolerated the reckless or the foolish in their ranks, after all.'

Libertas rang as it left its scabbard. 'You'd be surprised,' said Garro, crossing the perimeter of the fighting ring.

Khorarinn's grin widened. 'Very well. To the first mark, then?'

'Aye.' Garro turned the weapon in his grip, pushing aside the doubts in his thoughts. 'First mark.'

They saluted with their blades, and then the storm began. Swords clashed violently, sparks flying, mirror-bright metal dancing back and forth.

Khorarinn was unlike any opponent Garro had faced. It was said that even a primarch would hesitate at meeting one of the Emperor's Custodians in the arena, and as he fought to hold his ground through the whirlwind of Khorarinn's blade strikes, Garro could believe it.

It was almost impossible to do anything other than defend, and he was quickly at the limit of his skills, fighting to place his power sword at the points where the Custodian stabbed and slashed with his own weapon. He parried every hit, but the blows were like thunder, shaking his bones inside his battle armour.

There was a moment when an opening showed itself, and Garro almost took the chance, turning the hilt of *Libertas* by reflex. But he stopped himself and let the moment pass.

Too easy. Too inviting. A flicker of annoyance in Khorarinn's eyes confirmed it. It had been a feint to catch him off guard. The Custodian's attack pattern changed abruptly, intensifying, pushing Garro back across the training ring towards the piles of wrecked servitors. He suddenly realised that Khorarinn had been toying with him. This was his real intent, blade ringing upon blade as he beat him down with precise, brutal force.

He had one chance to escape with his honour intact, but he would need to be fast, faster than ever before. For an instant, their swords locked, edge against edge, and Garro took the split-second opportunity.

With a supreme effort, he found his chance and forced the blades apart. If the Custodian had a weakness, it was his arrogance. In his rush to mark Garro, he already thought him defeated. The legionary turned that upon him, disarming him with a shout, even though it was a huge effort to unseat the sentinel blade from his hand.

Khorarinn froze, his face reddening with sudden fury, before he drew back a step. Garro held his sword steady, aiming the tip at his opponent's chest. 'You disengage?'

he asked, breathing hard. 'The bout is not ended. I owe you a mark.'

'If that blade ever touches my armour,' growled Khorarinn, meaning every word, 'I will tear you limb from limb.'

Libertas dropped away and Garro stepped back. 'You're a poor loser.'

'And you were lucky.' The Custodian turned, gathering up his fallen sword-gun. 'I underestimated you. It won't happen again.' He made a sharp gesture with the blade of his hand. 'You are dismissed, Garro.'

The legionary's choler shifted towards annoyance. 'You overstep your bounds, Custodian. You do not command me. And you have no reason to hide the scope of this mission from my sight.' He returned his sword to its scabbard, daring the other warrior to disagree with him.

Khorarinn only paused, musing. Then he glanced over his shoulder. 'Very well. I suppose you've earned that right as your victory's reward. Come with me, and be illuminated.'

HE STRODE TO the battleship's strategium, and Garro trailed warily after him. The compartment was an oval chamber where walls lined with gas-lens viewers and scrying scopes provided real-time data streams from the zone surrounding the *Nolandia*. In the centre of the room was a tall hololithic display tank, cast with a globe made of motes of coloured light. The tactical plot showed the Solar System and the orbits of the planets, overlaid with the *Nolandia*'s course.

Khorarinn barked a single command, and within moments he and Garro were alone in the chamber, with only mindless servitors as witnesses. The human crewmen dithered out in the corridor as the strategium's hatch irised shut.

'What requires such a need for secrecy?' said Garro.

'You will see.' The Custodian removed a memory capsule from a pouch on his belt and inserted it into a socket at the base of the hololith. The display shifted and transformed into a grainy loop of pict-images. Garro saw ships, a dozen of them, a ragged flotilla drifting in space. 'This recording is from a perimeter drone stationed beyond the far orbit of Pluto,' continued Khorarinn. 'It detected multiple warp space events and moved to intercept. This is what it found. This is what we go to confront.'

The vessels were of classes known to Garro. Imperial transport craft, bulk carriers and the like. 'Those are all civilian ships.'

The Custodian gave a nod of agreement. 'But they fly no pennants of authority and marque. Their origins are uncertain. And they did not come alone.'

The image tracked to reveal the vessel at the head of the small fleet. It could only be a warship. The bladed prow and the layered turrets of cannons formed the distinctive shape of a fast-attack frigate, a class of ship most commonly found among the expeditionary fleets of the Legiones Astartes.

Khorarinn shot Garro a look. 'You recognise the frigate's livery, of course.'

'White, trimmed with blue. That ship belongs to the Twelfth Legion.'

'The World Eaters.' Khorarinn's words were bitter. 'The warriors who followed their traitorous gladiator-king Angron to Horus' banner.'

The bow of the frigate became clear and Garro's eyes narrowed. The name he saw there triggered a flash of memory. 'The *Daggerline*... I know this ship. I've seen it before. At Isstvan Three, in the hours before the attack. It was part of the Warmaster's assembly.'

When Khorarinn spoke again, he gestured dismissively at the hololith and made no attempt to conceal the sneer in his tone. 'You should feel a kinship with these... *refugees*, Garro. The crews of these ships claim to have fled the Warmaster's betrayal of the Throne. There are civilians, soldiers from the Imperial Auxilia, merchant envoys from across the Eriden Sector and others, allegedly gathered along the path of their escape route. They say they have come through the warp storms to Terra, searching for a safe haven. Just as you did.'

Garro remained silent for a long moment. When the Death Guard had turned from the Emperor, he and seventy other legionaries had commandeered the cruiser *Eisenstein* and escaped the horrors that followed. Months had passed since that day, but it seemed like an eternity. Garro had carried word of the insurrection, holding tightly to his oath to Emperor and Throne, but he had been judged by many for the deeds of his wayward primarch, and tainted with suspicion. The same suspicion that burned in Khorarinn's eyes.

'And this is why Malcador sent me here. To pass judgement upon them?'

The Custodian frowned. 'Given your experience, he considers your insight to carry some weight. You are to assist me in the evaluation of these refugees, but their ultimate fate will be decided by the Council of Terra.'

There was no doubt in Garro's mind that whatever the full scope of his orders were, the Custodian had already categorised the new arrivals as a threat. 'You don't trust them.'

'I trust nothing but the Emperor's word. This schism created by Horus means we no longer have the prospect of any other conviction. Insurrection corrodes such bonds.' The Custodian fixed him with a gaze that shone with icy fire. 'A battle line has been drawn across the galaxy. Anyone who comes from the Warmaster's side is an enemy until proven otherwise.'

'Do I fall within that description?' demanded Garro. 'Do you consider me unreliable because my former Legion betrayed the Emperor?'

'You begin to understand.' Khorarinn eyed him coldly.

Garro met his gaze. 'I am no traitor.'

'History will judge that, just as these exiles will be judged. The Warmaster is a cunning enemy. It would be like him to send ships under cover of such a ruse, so he might infiltrate spies into the heart of the Imperium. His invasion is coming, Garro. It is unstoppable, like my hatred for his treachery.' Khorarinn recovered the capsule and the hololith stuttered. He turned to leave, then hesitated. 'While we speak, one other matter must be aired. The witch-mind, Rubio.'

Garro scowled at the insulting descriptor. 'Brother Rubio is a legionary. A Codicier–'

'Such a rank no longer exists within the Legiones Astartes,' Khorarinn broke in. 'Malcador may have given you permission to flout the Emperor's edict, but I will not tolerate it.' He raised a mailed hand and pointed at the legionary. 'Know this. If Rubio uses his damned powers in my presence, I will put him down.'

Khorarinn strode away, leaving the open threat hanging in the air.

FOUR

Faithless
Gathering the lost
The *Mistral*

'THOSE WERE HIS exact words?'

Garro nodded. 'The esteemed Custodian is not one to leave ambiguity in his statements.'

Rubio grimaced, turning to glare out of the window of the cabin. 'Khorarinn has no right to give me orders. He's an arrogant martinet.'

'The same has been said of the warriors of the Thirteenth Legion, in the past,' offered Garro.

Rubio rounded on him. 'But I am not an Ultramarine, am I? I'm like you now. Knight Errant, a ghost in armour.'

'True,' said Garro. 'But for now, stay out of his way. We are called to work with him, so we will. Khorarinn's personal prejudices will cloud his judgement, so it is important we keep our own focus clear.' Returning to the spartan quarters he and the Codicier had been granted aboard the *Nolandia*, Garro had relayed the scope of his conversation with the Custodian to Rubio. Like the former Death Guard, Rubio was troubled by what the revelation of the *Daggerline* and its ragtag fleet represented.

The younger warrior paged through the contents of a data-slate, examining sensor reports from the first contact with the refugees. 'This matter is more complex than it first appears. Look here. If this data is correct, the refugee ships have far more civilians on board than military personnel. Non-combatants, Garro. Men and women, families fleeing the collapse of Imperial rule before the Warmaster's advance. These are the people we are oath-sworn to protect.'

'I do not disagree. But Khorarinn does not see such delineations. In his eyes, all aboard those ships, whether they be Space Marines or base humans, are equally dangerous.'

When Rubio spoke again, he was grim-faced. 'Earlier, as I walked the corridors, I... overheard members of the *Nolandia*'s bridge crew discussing the mission. At the time I had no context for their words, but now I do. They spoke of Khorarinn, of how he has set actions in motion. He has already decided how this mission will play out.'

Garro folded his arms across his chest. 'Explain.'

Rubio sighed. 'The Custodian has placed standing orders with the shipmaster and the gunnery commander. A "zero option" to be employed if circumstances demand it.'

'Again, he exceeds his remit.' Garro's jaw hardened.

'If the *Daggerline* or any other of the refugee ships poses a threat, the *Nolandia* has been granted authority to destroy it, and every other vessel in the fleet.'

'That would be a massacre,' snapped the legionary. 'The *Nolandia* is a Retribution-class battleship, a burner of worlds. A single frigate and a handful of freight barges would stand no chance against it.' Garro's blood ran cold as he remembered his own flight from rebellion aboard the *Eisenstein* and the moment his ship fell beneath the shadow of the great *Phalanx*. With someone like Khorarinn in command, he might never have lived to deliver his warning to the Imperium.

Could it be that the Council of Terra were so afraid that they would be willing to let the Custodian kill a hundred thousand innocents, rather than risk the infiltration of a single spy? The question was chilling. It went against everything in the spirit of the Emperor's bright, shining Imperium.

'We cannot allow that to happen,' said Garro firmly.

'And yet...' Rubio seemed unwilling to say the words. 'There is a chance Khorarinn is right.'

'A chance, Rubio. Not a certainty. This is the Imperium of Mankind, this is the domain of Sol and the Throneworld. We do not take life without cause. We draw the sword in necessity, in truth. We do not kill out of blind fear and prejudice!'

The Codicier was silent for a long moment before he spoke again. 'The rebellion is changing many things.'

IN THE SILENCE of the void, the *Nolandia* drew to a halt, station-keeping thrusters firing in great jets to place it abeam of the *Daggerline* and the exile flotilla. The battleship's cannons swung into ready position with careful menace, dozens of domed turrets drawing clear firing solutions on the leading vessels.

As a show of force, it was a theatrical gesture, but nevertheless a serious and uncompromising threat. The refugee ships had been corralled in this same zone of far-orbit space for some time, hemmed in by a cluster of gunship drones that tracked their every move. The arrival of the *Nolandia* and the aiming of its weapons only served to underline what the fleet captains already knew. For all intents and purposes, they were prisoners.

The *Daggerline* drifted off the arrow-sharp bow of the battleship, directly in line of sight to the larger ship's spinal-mount nova cannon. If fired, at this range even a near-miss from the *Nolandia*'s main gun would open up the frigate and boil its atmosphere into the dark in a matter of seconds. In return, the *Daggerline*'s full complement of weapons would need a warlord's luck just to penetrate the bigger vessel's void shields and strike a palpable hit.

In another time, these ships would have welcomed each other as honoured comrades, the flotilla afforded escort to home dock. But there was rebellion now, civil war in full effect, and few could draw deep enough to find a fresh wellspring of trust.

From the strategium's vantage point, Khorarinn studied the loose, poorly ordered clustering of the refugee ships and worked at a small hololith with one gauntleted hand. He considered spreads of fire and torpedo barrage patterns, plotting the most efficient attack models for reducing the other craft to whirling wreckage. With the element of surprise and no unforeseen events, he estimated it could be done in no more than five minutes.

Khorarinn did not look up as the grey-armoured warriors entered the chamber. He had not summoned them, but neither could he bar them from the command centre. The presence of Garro and his witch-kin cohort were an impediment the Custodian would simply have to endure.

'My lord?' One of the *Nolandia*'s duty officers dared to raise his voice. 'We are receiving a signal via ship-to-ship vox. A message from the *Daggerline*. They are hailing us and requesting direct communication.'

'No reply,' ordered Khorarinn. 'Not yet. Let them wait.'

'What purpose will that serve? They've been waiting out here for days,' said Rubio. 'Is that not long enough?'

Khorarinn answered without meeting the psyker's gaze. 'It is important to enforce the lesson of who is in command here.'

'That is very true,' said Garro. Then in the next moment, the grey-armoured legionary was barking an order at the man who had spoken. 'You, officer of the vox! Open a channel to the *Daggerline*, now!'

Khorarinn turned sharply, glaring at Garro as he casually countermanded his orders, but it was too late to stop him.

A gruff voice, all hard edges and broken stone, issued out of a brass speaker horn on the console. '*Daggerline hears you*, Nolandia. *I would say "well met", but your gun crews seem to have mistaken us for target drones.*' The timbre and set of his words betrayed him. The frigate's commander was undoubtedly a legionary, as few humans would have dared to be so defiant in the face of such superiority. And yet, there was an edge of weariness in him that could not be hidden.

'These are dangerous times,' said Garro. 'You will forgive us if we are cautious.'

'*Cautious, you say? As you wish. Who am I to judge if you feel threatened by a handful of tankers and cargo sloops.*' Garro smiled at the jibe, although he saw that Khorarinn found no such amusement in the cynical retort. '*At any rate, we are ready to follow to Terra in your wake, at your convenience.*'

'I am Nathaniel Garro. Whom do I address?' He leaned forwards, peering out at the starship.

'*Garro?*' He heard surprise. '*They said that Typhon killed you...*'

'I do not meet my end easily.'

That earned him a rough chuckle. '*You speak to the poor fool who has become commander of this wayward fleet of the desperate and the weary. I am Macer Varren, former son of Angron.*'

'Former?' echoed Garro.

The reply was rancorous. '*He tried to murder me. I would think that to be full indication that the bonds between my gene-father and I are severed.*'

Garro gave a quick nod to the vox-officer to mute the signal, and glanced at the others.

'You know him?' demanded Khorarinn.

'By reputation,' said Garro. 'A company captain with a fearsome battle record. A frequent victor in the gladiatorial pits. A hard fighter, but said to be honourable with it.'

Rubio raised an eyebrow. 'A rare accolade for one of Angron's berserkers.'

The Custodian remained unimpressed. 'I am not interested in his kill-count or his laurels.' He glared at the vox-officer and ordered him to resume communications, addressing his next words to the fleet. 'Captain Varren! I am Khorarinn of the Legio Custodes, leader of this mission. The *Daggerline* and all attached fleet elements are to maintain their position and remain with engines powered down. Disobedience will be met with immediate reprisal. Do you understand? You will not proceed to Terra.'

Varren's irritation was plain. '*What idiocy is this? You hold us here as if we were enemies, threaten us?*'

Garro stepped forwards, but Khorarinn was already speaking. 'Your status as friend or foe is unclear. The

World Eaters have broken with Imperial rule and conspired against their Emperor. Your Legion is in league
with the arch-traitor!'

'Do you think I am ignorant of that fact?' Varren's voice
cracked like a whip. *'Why else would we be here? I defied
my primarch to escape the shadow of his treachery! Do you
have any understanding of what that means?'*

'It is clear that Varren and his cohorts have endured
much to reach Terra,' Garro broke in. 'Something I know
only too well. Perhaps if we were to speak face-to-face,
matters will become clearer for all of us.'

'We can take a shuttlecraft across to the *Daggerline*,'
suggested Rubio.

The offer seemed to mollify the World Eater, at least
for the moment. *'Agreed. Come look me in the eye, if you
dare to call me traitor.'*

'Vox-channel has been cut,' reported the officer.

Khorarinn fixed Garro with a hard gaze. 'You had no
right to make that offer.'

'And you had no right to provoke him!' Garro's patience
with the Custodian's intractable manner was thinning by
the moment. He took a breath. 'But if you fear a trap may
await us, you are free to remain on board the *Nolandia*.'

Predictably, Khorarinn did not react well to the suggestion of weakness on his part. 'Very well. Lead the way.'

THE AQUILA SHUTTLE hove through the void barrier
across the open maw of the *Daggerline*'s landing bay,
the crackling energetic membrane holding out the cold
kiss of space, keeping the ship's atmosphere in check.
Khorarinn's pilot put the craft down on a vacant platform
with swift, practised ease. Discreetly concealed lascannons twitched beneath the eagle-like wings, tracking the

figures gathered on deck below. The drop-ramp fell open and Garro was first to step down, with Rubio and the Custodian a step behind.

Heavy shadows grew from all sides. The chilly air of the landing bay was thick with a sense of foreboding. Garro saw it in the eyes of the crew-serfs who clustered on the upper maintenance galleries to watch the arrival, all of them silent and morose. They were afraid of what word was to be brought to them. There could be no one in the refugee fleet who did not fear the choices that distant Terra might make.

'Captain Garro. You don't look like a dead man.' A figure in war-plate detached from the cluster of armoured figures and strode towards them.

'In many ways, kinsman, I am indeed a ghost.' Garro kept his arms by his sides, doing his best to project a neutral aspect.

Varren looked him up and down as he came closer. 'I've never seen armour like yours before. Is that what a ghost wears into battle?'

'You could say that.'

'Huh.' The World Eater seemed amused by his reply. He offered his hand in the old manner of greeting. Garro accepted it, and they clasped palm-to-wrist, each meeting the gaze of the other.

Varren was every inch a warrior of the XII Legion. His white-and-blue power armour was weather-beaten and battle-worn, adorned with oath papers and honour-marks alongside savage gouges and impact points that were themselves tributes, of a kind. A heavy power sword with a spiked guard lay at his hip, within easy reach. It was a mute warning that he was not to be considered powerless here.

The captain's face was like a clenched fist, eyes deep-set and searing. Service studs and victory tattoos warred with lines of old scarring to tell the brutal story of his life. Garro felt Varren take the measure of him in return, in the long moment before the World Eater released his grip. 'How is the leg? I heard you lost it against the war-singers. Damned augmetics never feel the same as meat and bone, do they?'

'That is so,' Garro agreed. 'But it means I can walk, and if I can walk, I can fight.'

'And if you can fight, you can win.' Varren nodded towards the others at Garro's side. 'So who is this?'

'Brother Rubio is my comrade. You've already spoken to Lord Khorarinn…'

Varren deliberately ignored the Custodian, turning his gaze on the psyker instead. 'A second spirit in ghost-grey? But I think you are no Death Guard. The mystery deepens.'

'We both serve Lord Malcador,' Rubio said tightly.

'And is he the one who has kept us here?'

Khorarinn broke his silence. 'There is a civil war in progress, World Eater. And you wear the colours of the wrong side. Be thankful you were not blown out of space the moment you arrived.'

The warrior's dark eyes glittered with anger. 'Such gratitude shown towards true sons of the Imperium! Men who refused to follow the path of rebellion, when their battle-brothers turned away as one. We kept to our oaths, Custodian. That should count for something.'

'You would have done the same, had the circumstances been reversed,' insisted Khorarinn.

Varren gave a harsh laugh. 'No, I would have just killed you and been done with it.' He turned to Garro once more, those dark eyes searching for someone he could trust. 'Our flight home was hard-fought, cousin. I lost many of my best men to Angron's Devourers. But we followed your example and made the break.'

Garro took in the other legionaries standing in the shadows nearby. 'There were others who joined you?'

'Aye. More perished than survived.' Varren's face creased in a frown. 'A handful of World Eaters – *loyalist* World Eaters – remain with me aboard this ship.'

But Garro's genhanced sight picked out more liveries than just that of the XII, and Khorarinn saw it too.

'Who else stands with you?' snapped the Custodian. 'I demand you reveal them to us!'

Varren glared at Khorarinn, his lip curling at the command. Then he beckoned them to follow him. 'Come meet them, then,' he muttered. 'Or remain here and cower by your shuttle if you suspect this is an ambush.'

RUBIO HAD SENSED the other legionaries in the chamber from the moment he stepped off the shuttle, their minds guarded like flickering candles shrouded from the wind. He had deliberately kept his psionic abilities dormant, even though part of him longed to return to their full use once again. It was difficult for him to advance slowly back to the power and the might of a Codicier's way, but Garro had warned him about the Custodian's inflexible manner, and to openly display his talents would only add to the tension of the moment.

Among the gathering of the refugee Space Marines, Rubio saw other World Eaters of similar character to their captain, and with them warriors representing two more of the Legiones Astartes.

Varren gestured to the closest of them. The legionaries

in finely wrought plate of purple-hued ceramite, detailed with fine gold filigree and handsome artistic flourishes. 'This is Rakishio, late of the Third Legion.'

The Emperor's Children had been declared enemies of the Imperium, but it still seemed strange for Rubio to think of them in that fashion. He had fought alongside Fulgrim's sons in the past, and while they might have been peacocks in manner, they were strong in martial spirit. Rakishio and his battle-brothers bowed low, and Rubio saw the places where their purple armour had been badly damaged by bolter fire.

'We remain so,' said the other warrior. His voice was at once arch and sorrowful. 'To our shame, our primarch no longer sees the Legion as bearing fealty to Great Terra and his father. We are marked by this betrayal, to our hearts.'

'Did any other warriors from the Third escape Isstvan?' said Garro. 'Captain Saul Tarvitz was an honoured friend of mine. Does he live still?'

Rakishio shook his head. 'I'm afraid I can't say.' The warrior shared a brief look with the World Eater. 'Brother-Captain Varren offered me and my men a way to avoid the high disgrace of our brethren. We took it. The only other alternative would have been to end our own lives.'

'That might have been the better choice.' The Custodian's hand rested on the hilt of his sentinel blade, in a clear suggestion of forewarning. 'The World Eaters and the Emperor's Children both declared for Horus. But here we find you claiming otherwise.'

Rakishio was about to reply, but others came forward from the shadows to answer for him. What Rubio had first thought to be more of Varren's legionaries instead bore armour of white trimmed with red. Upon their pauldrons, as stark as blood, was the lightning-bolt sigil of the V Legion.

'You are so quick to judge, Custodian.' Rubio immediately recognised the coarse tones of a Chogorian accent. 'Tell us, what judgement do you have for the White Scars?'

For the first time, Rubio saw something like surprise on Khorarinn's face. The riders of the White Scars had always been one of the Emperor's most devoted and loyal Legions, and His son Jaghatai Khan had never once shown anything but unswerving allegiance, in his own unpredictable fashion.

'We are all equally loyal,' insisted Varren. 'We would not be here if that was a lie.'

Garro accepted this with a nod. 'How did you come to gather, captain?'

Varren gestured at the walls of the frigate around them. 'Rakishio helped us secure an escape passage for the *Daggerline* and a few of the civilian ships. We picked up more refugee craft at the perimeter of the Isstvan System.'

'The lucky ones…' Rakishio said, grim-faced.

'Then we set course for the Segmentum Solar. Short transits, at first. The warp was so turbulent, we could barely cover a dozen light years before the storms forced us back into normal space. But then we crossed paths with Hakeem and the rest of his warriors.' Varren went on, explaining how Hakeem's force had become becalmed and separated from their fleet in the warp. It was only blind chance that had brought them into the path of the *Daggerline* flotilla. Together, they had charted a new course and made for Terra.

'I have never believed in fates or luck,' noted Rakishio. 'But if I were to do so, then perhaps such a force put the

White Scars before us. Once Hakeem granted us the skills of his Techmarine, Harouk, we were able to repair critical damage to our navigational systems.' The warrior gestured to one of Hakeem's men, who wore the cog-and-skull sigil of the Legion's technical savants.

'We would not have made it this far without them,' concluded Varren.

Rubio saw the Custodian's attitude shift as he stepped towards Hakeem and held out his arms, inclining his head in the manner of a traditional Chogorian greeting. '*Sayan banu, hata Hakeem.*'

Hakeem seemed surprised, but responded in kind. '*Sayan.*' A smile split his face. 'You know our ways, Lord Khorarinn.'

The Custodian nodded. 'I once ran a Blood Game with the warriors of the Great Khan. I was impressed by the prowess of the White Scars.'

Rubio said nothing. It was the first time he had seen the Custodian show anything approaching respect for a legionary, but he clearly had good reason. The Blood Games were an incredible test of a warrior's skill and those who could participate in them deserved their accolades. Each game took place on Terra, a live exercise designed to test the defences of the Imperial Palace against assassins. The Custodian Guard used them to constantly assess their skills and seek out weak points in the Emperor's aegis.

Rubio saw Garro give a solemn nod, seizing on the moment as a way to find common ground for them all. 'Cousins... Brothers. Whatever circumstances brought us together, we are all in agreement on one point. We stand on the right side of this accursed schism, and no matter what Legion insignia we wear, our oath to Terra and the Emperor remains supreme. So believe me when I say this, the matter of your homecoming will be dealt with in quick order, and with surety. Our enemy is out there. Our enemy is the Warmaster, and in unity we will face him.'

'That is all we ask,' said Rakishio, and Rubio did not need to exercise his psionic ability to know that he spoke for all assembled there.

The meeting concluded, the Codicier turned back towards the shuttle. He took only a step before, for only the briefest moment, he felt something at the edge of his thoughts. *The faintest shimmer of psychic shade, a tone of emotion that could have been… untruth?*

But then it was gone, and they were marching back towards the shuttle.

GARRO PACED THE length of his chambers, deep in thought. No one had spoken on the return trip from the *Daggerline*, Khorarinn's stern visage remaining intractable, his thoughts unknown.

There were more than enough variables in the situation with the civilian ships and the contingent of World Eaters, but with the addition of two more groups of warriors – one from a Legion known to be loyal, another from one known to have turned traitor – the matter had grown to new complexity.

A heavy fist knocked twice on his hatch. 'Who seeks me?' asked Garro.

'It is I.' Rubio's manner was troubled. Garro bade him enter, and the Codicier came close, speaking in low tones. 'I need to talk to you. I made certain I went unseen. Khorarinn would doubtless wish to know if we were thought to be conspiring in secret.'

'He sees sedition everywhere,' Garro noted. 'But then,

that is his remit.' He dismissed the thought. 'On the shuttle, you seemed troubled. What is it, Rubio?'

The Codicier frowned. 'I believe we are being lied to. Aboard the *Daggerline*, just as we were leaving, I sensed deceit.'

'From whom?'

The frown deepened. 'I'm not certain. It's been a long time since I was called upon to use my abilities in a subtle manner, Garro. I'm out of practice. But someone in that room was desperate to hide a vital truth from us.'

'Do what you can–'

A strident chime sounded before Garro could say more. He stiffened, touching the vox-link in his gorget. An encrypted message was being transmitted to the machine-call module built into his wargear.

'What is it?' said Rubio.

'Uncertain,' said Garro. 'Someone is attempting to reach me by breaking into my Legion vox-net...' He gestured to Rubio to remain silent and spoke into the link. 'Who contacts me?'

Heavy with static, the growl of the White Scars warrior filtered through. '*Captain Garro, it is I, Hakeem. Forgive this clandestine method of communication, but I must converse with you directly. Are you alone?*'

He gave Rubio a look. 'We may speak in confidence.'

'*I must warn you,*' insisted Hakeem. '*Things are not what they seem in the fleet. I contacted you in secret because I believe there are allies of the Warmaster at large among us.*'

Garro felt a chill run through him. 'Why have you come to me with this, instead of speaking to Khorarinn?'

He heard the scowl in the other warrior's reply. '*He may respect my brethren, but he is not of the Legions. The Custodian will not understand. But you were at Isstvan, Garro. You saw what happened there. You know full well what Horus is capable of. And you know this war is not a matter of black or white.'*

The White Scar's words were, if anything, an understatement. 'Indeed. Go on, kinsman.'

'I believe that Macer Varren is an honest soul,' said Hakeem. 'He's too blunt and forthright to hide any stripe of duplicity. But the World Eater is being duped by Rakishio and the Emperor's Children. They are still following Fulgrim's commands, I am certain of it.'

Garro's eyes widened. 'You have proof of this?'

'Not enough to take action. They call Rakishio "the shadowed", and he's far too adept at deceit to allow anything to incriminate him. But my brothers and I have been watching the Emperor's Children over the course of our voyage. They're planning something. They meet in secret aboard one of the tanker-transports in the fleet, the Mistral, and allow no one else aboard it. They call these meetings "lodges".'

'I have heard of such things,' Garro said gravely. The lodges were at the root of Horus' rebellion, secret gatherings spread from Legion to Legion, where new oaths could be sworn and the unspoken given voice. Garro had seen his own warriors drawn into these assemblies, and he knew full well that the Warmaster had used them to prepare his traitors for their insurrection against the Emperor.

Hakeem went on. *'Rakishio and his legionaries have been acting suspiciously since we arrived in the system. I fear that they may act soon, unless we move to prevent them.'* There was a moment of silence, and then Hakeem spoke again. *'I must end this conversation. Be on your guard, Garro.'*

'Can it be so?' muttered Rubio.

The White Scar's words were deeply disturbing. If such

a thing was happening among the refugees, if Khorarinn were to learn of it… Garro had no doubt that the Custodian would use this revelation as a pretext for the most ruthless actions, and fate take whomever was caught in the crossfire. 'This is a matter for caution,' he said, thinking aloud.

Rubio's gaze turned inwards, considering. 'We have to take control of this, and soon. Every moment we delay the refugee ships out here, lives are under threat. I reviewed the data-captures from the flotilla. The civilians and crew-serfs aboard are malnourished and sickly, their supplies depleted in their escape. If we do nothing, innocents will perish.'

Garro eyed him. 'And if we go forth with gun drawn and blade high? Khorarinn may show some esteem to the White Scars, but his finger lays heavily upon the trigger. He will be quick to kill, innocents or not. In his eyes, a perceived threat to the Emperor will excuse even the most extreme of deeds.'

But then, as if mere mention of his name were enough to summon him like a creature of mythology, the *Nolandia*'s intercom crackled and the Custodian's harsh snarl sounded through the ship. '*Garro! Rubio! Report immediately to the strategium.*'

'What now?' Rubio muttered. 'Did he intercept Hakeem's transmission?'

'Whatever the cause,' Garro told him, 'it will not bode well.'

THEY ENTERED THE compartment to find Khorarinn barking orders to the *Nolandia*'s weapons crew, jabbing his gold-armoured finger towards the flotilla rendered in the hololithic tank. 'All gunnery crews are to remain at action stations until the order to stand down is given,' he growled. 'They will stay at their posts around the clock. We cannot allow our attention to slip. The danger remains.'

Garro approached him, eyes hard. 'Explain yourself, Custodian. Why does the *Nolandia* remain on combat alert?'

'Officer of the vox, stand by to transmit by machine-call and hololith. I want every last vessel in that flotilla to hear my words. No exceptions.' Khorarinn gave the order and then turned to Garro. 'Pay attention, Death Guard. These words are for you as well as those refugees.'

'And Hakeem?' asked Rubio.

'The White Scars will see the necessity of my orders,' said the Custodian. The vox-officer nodded to him, and Khorarinn took a breath. 'Attention, vessels of the *Daggerline* flotilla.'

Garro glanced at the strategium's great window ports, and beyond it the loose grouping of the refugee starships. The tension of the last few hours was suddenly pulled tight, close to breaking point.

'All fleet ships will stand by to accept search operations,' said Khorarinn. 'Boarding parties will be dispatched from the *Nolandia* to each vessel in turn, to conduct deck-by-deck surveys. Only after these searches have been completed will your ships be permitted to cross the outer marker into the system.'

Rubio shook his head. 'It will take *weeks* to search every ship from bow to stern. Those people don't have that much time!'

Khorarinn's commands continued. 'This order is mandatory and cannot be refused. Any resistance will be met by lethal force. Operations will commence in three hours, Terran standard. *Nolandia* out.'

Garro turned on the Custodian, his jaw set. 'Is this your plan, then? To keep these people out here until they starve to death, and thus let the problem remove itself?'

'If they wish to request aid supplies, they may do so. And if your heart bleeds so much, Garro, you and your psyker are welcome to go and fetch those supplies for them.' Khorarinn turned away.

'Those are the lives of the Emperor's subjects you dismiss so easily!'

The Custodian gave him a sideways glance. 'Their lives are not my concern. *Security* is my concern. The protection of my Emperor and His throne. All else is of secondary importance.'

The vox-officer looked up from his console. 'Lords, there is an incoming hail from the *Daggerline*.'

Rubio looked at the Custodian. 'I imagine Captain Varren will not be silent on this.'

Khorarinn directed his reply to the crewman. 'I have no desire to speak with him. Hail denied.'

Garro leaned closer, his voice low and cold, meeting Khorarinn's stony gaze. 'What you have done will sow panic and fear amongst the civilians. These are not soldiers who will salute and say nothing. They are common people, terrified and at their wits' end. If you give them no choice, they will react poorly.'

His words fell on stony ground. 'You are here because I decided to keep you informed, not because I want your counsel. Don't presume to tell me how to prosecute this mission.'

Anger blazed in Garro's eyes at the Custodian's intransigence, but any retort died before he could give it voice, as an alert siren cut through the air.

'What now?' shouted Khorarinn. 'Report!'

Rubio stood over the hololithic scope. 'Scry-sensors detect a power surge aboard one of the ships in the flotilla. Engines are going active. A single vessel is moving out of the formation, velocity increasing.' His expression hardened and he turned to Garro. 'It's the tanker, the *Mistral*.'

'Show me,' snapped Garro.

The hololith shifted to a view of the vessel. Burning sun-bright, the drive nozzles of the tanker-transport flared as it powered away from the flotilla. The *Mistral* was an ugly ship, heavy in girth and rounded. It resembled a giant artillery shell, pockmarked by docking ports and vent hatches. It was easily the mass of an Imperial frigate, but it wallowed into its turns, lacking the nimble motions of a warship.

'The vessel's command deck does not answer,' said the vox-officer.

Garro strode to the great windows at the fore of the strategium in time to see the *Mistral* surge forwards into the first sheets of beam fire from the drone gunnery platforms. The tanker took blows that ripped into her feeble void shields, but it showed no signs of reducing speed. If anything, the attack seemed to goad the crew into pouring more power to the engines, in the wild hope of punching through the defence barrage.

Below, lined up along the *Nolandia*'s dorsal hull, the warship's multiple cannon turrets turned with lethal ease, shifting to place the fleeing vessel in their kill-zone.

Garro spun, calling out, 'Khorarinn, *no!*'

THE CUSTODIAN PUSHED past Rubio and strode across the strategium to the gunnery master's station. Surveying the weapons display, he stabbed a finger at the icon representing the *Mistral*. 'I want a firing solution on that craft. Prepare a full las-barrage. Engage at point-blank range!'

'Custodian! Wait!' Garro came across the chamber at a pace, his hand raised.

Khorarinn's expression was carved from stone. 'The orders were quite clear, Garro. That ship is in open defiance of lawful commands. Its intentions are unknown. It is moving onto a course directly towards the core planets, and Terra.'

'Damn you,' spat Garro, and the legionary stepped away, activating his vox-link, opening a channel to the fleeing vessel. '*Mistral*, this is Battle-Captain Nathaniel Garro. Halt or you will be destroyed. You must cut your engines now!'

Instinctively Rubio reached out with an invisible tendril of psionic presence, grasping through the void towards the fleeing craft, in the hope of sensing some shade of emotion from those on board.

Something *was* there, but it was sickly, ink-dark and repellent.

Rubio's breath caught in his throat. 'On the ship…' His voice dropped to a whisper, so only Garro could hear him. 'There's a presence over there. Dark and lethal… Hiding itself. *Hiding from me.*'

Across the compartment, Khorarinn called out his final commands. 'Target is locked. Charge the guns.'

'*Mistral*, if you can hear me, turn back!' Garro tried one last time to reach someone on the tanker.

But it was already too late. The Custodian gave the order to open fire, and the backwash of livid laser light flooded the strategium with the colour of blood.

FIVE

Splintered
I name you traitor
A piece of silver

IT WAS NOTHING short of overkill.

One single pulse-barrage would have been enough to crack the tanker's compartment bulkheads and destroy its reactor core. Instead the salvo of beam fire from the *Nolandia* obliterated the transport vessel completely. The *Mistral*'s heedless, headlong flight was over before it could begin, and the brief supernova of its death throes cast a shimmering light over the bows of the other craft crowding behind the *Daggerline*. Fragments of white-hot hull metal and clouds of vaporised plasteel billowed in the darkness, backlit by flashes of radiation and plasma-fire.

Their lesson delivered, the *Nolandia*'s turret guns returned to their previous stations.

For a moment, a stunned silence held sway across the warship's command deck; then Garro was advancing on the Custodian, his hand on the hilt of *Libertas*.

'You callous–'

Rubio stepped into his path, grabbing his hand before

he could fully draw his sword from its scabbard. 'Captain, don't.'

Khorarinn stepped forwards, opening his hands, inviting attack. 'No, "captain", please *do*. Please defy me as well, so that I may confine you to the brig and complete my mission without further interference.'

'You forced that to happen,' snarled Garro. 'Just as you goaded Varren. There was no need to destroy that ship. There was time. Rubio and I could have teleported aboard, taken control of it...'

'Perhaps.' The Custodian gave a broad shrug. 'But I do not deal in vagaries, Garro. There is either obedience or anarchy. *Order or chaos.* I gave those fools fair warning. They ignored me at their own peril.' He advanced, pushing Rubio aside until he and Garro were a hand's span apart. 'There is no room for confusion here. And now every ship in that fleet understands, as you too should understand. Those who do not obey will suffer the same fate.'

It took all of Nathaniel Garro's will to let *Libertas* slide back into its scabbard. 'To hell with you.' He ground out the words and marched away.

'I do not believe in such delusions,' Khorarinn said to his back, as Rubio followed after him.

THE DAGGERLINE WAS an ancient vessel, old at the start of the Great Crusade, and a veteran of many, many wars. The ship had been tested to its limits hundreds of times over its lifespan, and this was to be its last voyage.

A final, heroic race across the void leading those who still held to their oaths. A pilgrimage, if one would dare to speak so pious a word in the heart of Terra's secular empire. But all for nought now, so it seemed. The ship would never fall under Earth-light again. It would rust and corrode out here among the ice asteroids, forever in sight of Sol but forbidden to approach it.

Macer Varren did not think in such ways. His cunning, martial mind was not open to sorrowful ideals. He lived in the moment, fought his way through life second by second. And he was ill at ease, angry. This was not why he had come back to Terra. Not to see his ships destroyed, his liberty sundered.

Such was his preoccupation that he almost missed the figure waiting for him in the corridor's gloomy shadows. He halted, and turned his cold eye to the darkness. In the wake of the *Mistral*'s obliteration, nothing could be trusted.

'I know you are there,' he snarled. 'Show yourself, or face a bolt-round!'

'Brother-Captain Varren.' A ghost emerged from the shadows.

'Garro…' Varren's bolt pistol was instantly in his hand, the muzzle only inches from the legionary's face. 'You *dare* to call me brother? I should kill you where you stand. You have no right to show your face here! How did you even get aboard this ship?'

Garro inclined his head. 'The *Daggerline*'s tertiary shuttle bay is poorly guarded. And I made sure we were not tracked by the *Nolandia*.'

'*We?*' Varren's grip on the gun tightened.

'Rubio waits below. He guards our transport. He clouds the thoughts of any who might look too closely.'

'So Khorarinn did not send you.' Slowly, Varren's finger curled away from the pistol's trigger. After a moment he let the gun drop.

'I have already ignored his orders by leaving the

battleship,' Garro insisted. 'I had to come back, Varren. To speak with you. So we might gain the full measure of one another, and speak plainly.'

'Plainly?' He gave a harsh laugh. 'That gold-plated whoreson destroyed an unarmed transport ship, and you did not stop him! Is that plain enough? If the *Daggerline* were not such a wreck, I would pilot it into the battle-ship's bridge to spite that braggart.'

Regret clouded Garro's scarred face. 'Believe me, I tried to prevent it. But Khorarinn is inflexible. He considers you traitors in all but name.'

'But not the White Scars, eh?' Varren's pistol went back into its holster. 'The rest of us he would hang, but not Hakeem's cadre. How is that fair and just? How is that the Imperial Truth?'

Garro paused a moment before he replied, framing his words. 'It is true the sons of the Khan have proven their loyalty in this schism.'

'But the rest of us are thought corrupted by the actions of the greater number.' Varren wanted to fling the accusa-tion back at him like a blade, but Garro knew it already. His Legion, like Varren's, were vow-breakers. 'You know the sting of that, I'll warrant,' he went on.

'Aye,' admitted the other warrior, regret weighing heavy in that admission.

'I was not cut out to lead like this, Garro. I am a killer, a meat-cutter!' Varren shook his head angrily. 'Not a brood mare struggling to protect a clutch of weak and feeble runts. I lead warriors, not common folk.' His gauntlet closed into a heavy fist and cold fury burned within him. '*Damn Horus Lupercal for this.* Damn him for his treachery and false prom-ises. If he had not sundered the Legions, we would not be here. No one would need to die without purpose!'

'I feel as you do, brother,' said the former Death Guard. 'The Warmaster has turned warrior against warrior. Oaths made in blood and fire have been broken. His betrayal casts the blackest shadow across the Imperium. It threatens everything we have worked for, fought for... *died for*. Everything has changed, Varren. Trust turns to sand. Men like the Custodian Guard are ascendant now. Ruthless men with too much to lose, and a gaze too narrow to see the complexities of the moment.' He took a step closer, opening his hands in a gesture of comradeship. 'We must work together if we are to end this spiral of suspicion. Find the truth before Khorarinn's distrust leads him to even greater bloodshed.'

'What truth?' Varren asked warily.

RUBIO WAITED AT the foot of the Arvus lighter Garro had co-opted from the *Nolandia*, casting a glance back at the blank-eyed pilot-servitor enclosed behind the cockpit bubble. The machine-slave was a savant, highly trained to fly the little shuttle but utterly incapable of any other interactions or thought processes. It had been relatively simple to appropriate its punch-card control memes and order it to take them across to the frigate. In the aftermath of the tanker's destruction, the zone of space around the battleship was heavy with particulate debris that fouled the scry-sensors. On low power, it had been possible to make the transit from one ship to another unseen. Getting back would be a different matter, though. They would not be fortunate enough to slip the net twice.

He retreated back into the shadows under the wings of the Arvus, where the only light came from the eldritch glow of his psychic hood. The illumination bathed his face in cool whispers of energy, his power helping to hide him and the lighter from passing gazes.

His abilities were returning to full potential, to the strengths they had reached before the Decree of Nikaea. For Rubio, it was like staring at an indistinct image as layers of haze faded away. In time his gifts would be at their peak once again.

He reached into his memory and felt for the ghostly shimmer of psychic noise that he had felt last time they were aboard the frigate, grasping telepathically for the brief but distinct form–

–*and he found it.*

'It comes again...' A shock passed through him. The impression of the hidden and the dangerous, the same ephemeral trace he had sensed aboard the *Mistral*, but here, *now*.

Rubio took a step forwards, and hesitated. Garro had charged him with guarding the Arvus while he set off to find Varren, but the inaction chafed upon him. He knew they were risking much to come here, but to stand by and do nothing... That seemed like weakness.

He could not wait for Garro's return, and the sense of the untoward was already starting to fade from his thoughts. He could not ignore it. With grim determination, Rubio threw a last look at the lighter, and set off into the depths of the *Daggerline*.

Garro studied Varren carefully. He knew that with a single wrong word, at the slightest trace of duplicity, the World Eater would turn on him. The sons of Angron went to violence as their first tool in all things, and he could see that Varren's temper was worn paper-thin by the events of the day. 'Whom do you trust?'

Varren answered without hesitation. 'My kinsmen.'

'The ones who came with you,' Garro corrected. 'But not the ones who stayed to follow Angron.'

'Don't play games with me,' spat the World Eater. 'You know what I mean. It is not easy to see an oath you lived for ripped apart by those you once called brother.'

Garro nodded gravely. 'I do. What Horus has done… It will change the Legions in ways we have not yet begun to comprehend. He has broken something that can never be remade.' A thought that Garro had never before voiced, one he had carried since Isstvan, now left his lips. 'From now until the last of us perishes, there will always be a doubt in the minds of every legionary, as he looks upon his brother. He will wonder, even if only for a moment, *Will my kinsman ever turn from the Emperor?*' Varren nodded, knowing it was true. 'We know that potential is in us,' Garro continued. 'It has been revealed and proven. A splinter of suspicion that will forever lie in our hearts. Tell me, what do you know of the "lodges"?'

The other warrior's expression became a brooding scowl. 'That idiocy that came from the Davinites? A pointless thing. I forbade my men to participate in them. Secretive meetings in shadowed alcoves are for the fops of the Imperial court, not Space Marines.'

Garro nodded again. He had avoided the lodges for similar reasons, and like Varren he had paid the price for standing alone. 'What about Rakishio? Does he share that sentiment?'

'Do I trust him, you mean?' Varren's hand strayed to his face, rubbing at the scars on his chin. 'Like all of the Emperor's Children, he's a peacock, but put a sword in his hand and he becomes a hurricane of blades. I would be dead a dozen times over if not for Rakishio. He found us a way out from Isstvan. Lost plenty of his men doing it, too.' At length, he nodded. '*Yes.* He shed blood for me. I trust him.'

'In these turbulent times,' said a voice from above, 'that is good to know.' A legionary in full armour descended from a walkway crossing the corridor and Garro turned to face the other warrior, his hand falling to the hilt of his sword. Neither he nor Varren had been aware of his approach, and that was of grave concern.

'What did you hear?' he demanded.

'Enough.' Rakishio approached them, his hands open but his aspect cold. 'First you and the Custodian challenge us, then you massacre innocents? Now you return to cast doubt upon our honour and call us to heel like lapdogs? I might expect such behaviour from a mortal, but not one of us, Garro.' He struck the golden palatine aquila across his chestplate with the heel of his fist, and the ceramite rang with the impact. 'Did you forget what this means?' His anger began a slow rise. 'Or did you lose that along with the colours of your Legion?'

'I forget nothing,' Garro retorted. 'And I need not prove myself, to you, or any other. I had no hand in the destruction of the *Mistral*. But perhaps you can explain why it fled the line?'

The question seemed to take the warrior by surprise. 'Do you seek to accuse me of something? Look to Khorarinn. His words sparked a panic. And now he shouts out orders to us, as if we were neophyte recruits, or fresh from our mother's breast!'

'What orders?' said Garro.

'The reason I came down here.' Rakishio turned to Varren. 'Brother-captain, the Custodian has demanded that representatives of the Legions assemble on the landing deck to await his arrival.'

'How far is he going to push us?' Varren spat on the deck. 'Does he want us to draw our weapons?'

'I assure you, I have no knowledge of this,' insisted Garro.

Varren seethed. 'Then if we wish to know more, it seems we have little choice but to come to heel.'

'And where will you stand, Garro?' said Rakishio. 'With him, or with us?'

Garro opened his mouth to reply, but the answer was lost to him.

GARRO'S PRESENCE IN the *Daggerline*'s landing bay drew a collection of stares from the assembled legionaries, some of them authored by surprise, others cold disdain or outright disgust. He showed nothing, but behind the blank mask of his face, he was conflicted. They placed the blame equally upon him as they did upon the Custodian, and the sting of guilt was strong. No matter how hard he tried, Garro could not accept that the brutal execution of the *Mistral* was justified.

He was not one to shrink from hard choices. He had made many in his time as a legionary and a commander, but Garro had never been ruthless. That cold, dark well of intent that some men drew from did not exist in his heart. He hoped it never would.

Garro glanced up at the landing bay hatch, waiting for it to grind open on its massive brass cog-wheels, but he soon realised that Khorarinn had opted for a different entrance, one with a much greater display of shock and awe.

In the centre of the deck, a flickering seed of emerald energy faded out of nothing. It cast out flails of lightning, sketching an expanding sphere of shimmering colour.

Rakishio saw it first and called out to the others, forcing them away. 'Back! Back, I say!' He shouted across the bay. 'Clear the umbra!'

Each of them knew the signs of a teleportation precursor. Anyone caught too close to the displacement aura would risk being sucked in, to merge with the new arrivals in a malformed mess. Garro shielded his eyes as a viridian orb crashed into existence upon the deck, the phantoms of dozens of figures within gaining solidity and dimension.

At their head, Khorarinn surveyed the chamber with that same imperious manner he had on first meeting Garro. 'Stand to,' he ordered.

Varren did not obey. 'What is the meaning of this?'

Khorarinn advanced, stepping away from over a dozen armed Naval troopers in full carapace armour, his sword-bolter already drawn. 'Any one of you who touches a weapon will be considered an enemy of the Emperor and treated as such.' His eyes found Garro, and he sneered. '*Of course.* I should have known you would be here with the rest of them. Did you bring the witch-mind too?' He shook his head, dismissing him. 'No matter. I'll deal with you later.'

Garro could stay silent no longer. 'I came here to correct your mistake, Khorarinn.'

'It is you that is mistaken,' he said, without even a look. Instead, the Custodian addressed the other legionaries before him. '*Heed me!* I am hereby taking direct command of the refugee flotilla. You will submit to my authority, in the Emperor's name.'

'I won't allow it,' said Varren.

'You won't stop me,' he replied.

'You think so?' Varren stood before the Custodian. 'Call

back to your battleship for a few more platoons of those troopers, and I might just start to take you seriously.'

For a moment, Garro thought Khorarinn was about to strike the former World Eater, but instead the warrior in gold and crimson beckoned to a Mechanicum emissary hiding amongst the soldiers, and the adept ambled forwards on iron feet. 'It seems you are the short-sighted barbarian I took you for,' he began. 'This isn't about posturing or your honour, Varren. This is about facts. *Truth.*'

At a word from Khorarinn, the adept operated a portable hololith capsule, beaming a hazy image into the air over their heads. Garro recognised what appeared to be the bridge of a civilian starship, and saw a halo of data indicators flickering across the display.

'After the *Mistral* was interdicted, I dispatched a team of Mechanicum scouts to survey the wreckage of the tanker-transport.' Khorarinn's voice took on a lecturing tone. 'Their drones recovered the ship's central archive record. It preserved the last few moments of the vessel's life.'

'Why show us this?' said Hakeem, eyeing the image.

'Watch, and be illuminated,' Khorarinn told him.

All of them turned to do so. There on the hololith, clear as day, came a figure in the full power armour of a legionary. A heavy bolt pistol filled his fist. The log recorder showed him as he strode across the *Mistral*'s bridge, carefully executing the tanker's crew, one after another. It was as if the atmosphere was suddenly excised from the landing bay.

Dread marred Rakishio's perfect face. 'This is impossible!'

Garro stiffened at the sight of the sudden, brutal burst of carnage, as a ripple of grim disbelief echoed from the legionaries around him. He felt a terrible, familiar sensation wash over him; a sickening horror at such open butchery from the hands of a battle-brother. He had witnessed such things before, at Isstvan, and again at Calth, all at the command of Horus.

With the bridge crew dead, the murderous warrior moved to the helm console and turned the ship's yoke, putting power to its engines. Almost as an afterthought, the legionary looked up and found the sensor head that was recording the images. He raised his gun. A shot rang out and the hologram dissolved into a fall of static.

Khorarinn pointed with his sword, his face like thunder. 'For the record, let the colours of the killer be known. He wears the purple and gold of the Third Legion, the Emperor's Children! And so I name Rakishio and his warriors *traitor!*'

RUBIO ALLOWED HIMSELF to become free of distractions, and he moved down through the mid-decks of the frigate, with a degree of stealth that one might have thought unattainable for a legionary in battleplate. He was adept at becoming invisible when he needed to, and Rubio knew these ships well, having spent many a year aboard such craft in the Ultramarines expeditionary fleets, at the height of the Great Crusade.

On the eighth level of the *Daggerline* were the Legion barracks. Usually home to dozens of squads of warriors, here they lay mostly empty. The renegade World Eaters, the lost Emperor's Children and the White Scars were sharing the compartments, but no one walked there at this moment, save for mindless servitors intent on their tasks.

It troubled Rubio that his psychic inkling had drawn him here. The closer he came, the sense of what his thoughts had touched grew clearer – and with them, his misgivings.

He wanted so much to be wrong, even as he knew he was not. For a moment, he allowed himself to feel a measure of sorrow, then smothered the jolt of emotion. This was not the time or the place.

Moving through the compartment, he reached for a particular cabinet at the back of an arming alcove.

Here, he told himself. *Here is the place where the darkness has collected. I must know what is within.*

What he was about to do was a gross violation of a battle-brother's personal effects, a grave insult that no legionary would overlook. But he had no choice. He had come this far. Rubio sensed the residue of intent around the locking mechanism and dialled it open with great delicacy, taking care not to disturb the cleaning cloths, tins of lapping powder and other items used to maintain a legionary's wargear.

The cabinet slid open, and the Codicier felt the temperature in the compartment fall by degrees.

THE GUNS OF the troopers in Khorarinn's escort were raised and ready, but they wavered, some aiming towards Rakishio and his men, others drifting back and forth between the other legionaries assembled before them. In another time or place, such an act would have been met with immediate violence, but for the moment the attention of the warriors was turned elsewhere.

'Rakishio…' Varren's words were low and menacing. 'You will explain what we witnessed. Tell me now!'

'I… I can't say!' Garro watched as the warrior in purple and gold shook his head, his eyes wide. 'I don't know. All my warriors are here, accounted for. I don't know who that was!'

'Some kind of illusion,' offered Hakeem. 'An impostor, perhaps.'

'No,' insisted Khorarinn, brooking no challenge to his words. 'The adepts assure me the images are genuine. It would take incredible skill to falsify such a recording. I deem it true!'

'How closely did you look?' Garro glared at him. 'Did you want it to be disproved? You seem very ready to accept it at face value.' He advanced on the Custodian, eyes flashing.

Khorarinn showed his teeth. 'When we return to Terra, I will see Malcador strip you of that armour and bury you under the craters of Luna. Do not think you have the right to question my intent, Garro.'

'If what we saw is fact…' Varren was struggling to grasp what he had seen. 'Answer me, Rakishio. Do you still serve Fulgrim? Have you rejected the Emperor?'

'No, brother. *No!* I fought and killed my own battle-brothers to come with you. You know that.' The warrior was almost pleading with his comrade. 'Fulgrim betrayed us all!'

'Indeed,' said Hakeem, 'and in turn the Emperor's Children took the Warmaster's side.' There was no pity in the White Scar's voice. 'Perhaps *all* of them did so.'

'You will surrender now, or you will die.' Khorarinn said the words and the armed troopers took aim. 'I call to all those loyal to Terra to take aim and fire upon these turncoats if they do not comply.'

As one, the White Scars followed suit, turning their bolters towards Rakishio and his brothers. Hakeem's nod had been subtle, but enough for Garro to see it for what it was, just as his men did. They trained their weapons on the Emperor's Children, each prepared to make a

head-shot kill. In turn, Rakishio's followers had their
guns at the ready to fire back.

'I am sorry, Rakishio,' intoned Hakeem. 'But this must
be done. Do not resist.'

'No!' Varren strode forwards, into the line of fire. 'We
will not carry the horrors of Isstvan with us. The legacy
of that act must not reach here. Lower your guns!' The
World Eater's power sword flashed into the air and Varren raised it across his chest, daring anyone to oppose
him. 'I said lower them! I did not claw my way through
the madness of the Ruinstorm for this.'

Garro sensed the moment tipping towards open violence and he followed Varren across the deck. 'Stay your
hand,' he called. 'No more blood must be shed.'

Khorarinn walked forwards, bringing his sentinel blade
to a guard position. He glared at the World Eater. 'If you
wish to die here, captain, I will see it done. You will
not oppose my commands, nor will your men.' His gaze
momentarily took in Garro, and the warrior knew the
threat was meant equally for him.

When Varren spoke again, his words were an angry
hiss. 'You expect me to let you execute Rakishio like you
did those poor fools on the *Mistral*?'

'The Emperor's Children are culpable,' said Khorarinn.
'You saw the recording. If you defend them, you share
their guilt.'

Garro stepped between the two warriors, his hands
open and raised. 'Whatever you suspect to be true,
Khorarinn, Rakishio is still a legionary, and he answers
to authorities higher than yours.'

The Custodian snorted. 'Unless he surrenders peacefully, that point is moot.'

A heartbeat more and there would be open conflict,

brother fighting against brother, Legion against Legion. In this place, the great misery of the insurrection was being played out in microcosm. Garro turned to Varren, imploring him to step back from the abyss. 'Brother-captain, he will listen to you. Don't let this go any further.'

For a moment, Garro feared the World Eater would spit out a war-cry and attack; but then the fire in his eyes ebbed, and with sullen mood, he returned his sword to its sheath. 'Rakishio,' he said, in a dead voice, *'Stand down. Cousin, I promise you that this matter will be resolved and your honour restored.'*

'Very well.' After a moment, Rakishio bowed his head. 'You have brought us this far, Varren. I will trust your judgement now.' Grudgingly, the warriors of the III gave up their guns and blades, the grave symbolism of the act taking place without a word spoken.

Varren's gaze had never left Khorarinn's. 'Are you satisfied, Custodian?'

Khorarinn did not answer, instead turning to the White Scars. 'Hakeem. You and your men will accompany me below. We will escort these prisoners to the *Daggerline's* brig for detainment and questioning.'

'Very well.' Hakeem made a terse motion with his hand in battle-sign, and his warriors took up positions around the disarmed Emperor's Children. Garro and Varren watched the warriors march away across the landing bay under the guns of the White Scars, with grim, solemn expressions.

At last the World Eater turned to him. 'Is this how our world must be from now on?'

Before Garro could answer him, another voice spoke, crackling from the vox-bead in his armour. *'Garro. Do you hear me?'*

'Rubio? Where are you?'

'Below decks,' said the Codicier, a warning in his tone. *'I've found something you need to see.'*

ON THE PSYKER'S insistence, they gathered in a maintenance corridor beneath the *Daggerline's* secondary heat-exchanger array, amid a rain of moisture dripping onto catch-trays below.

Rubio stepped out of the shadows as Garro approached, casting a cautious look up and down the empty corridor. 'You were not followed?'

'No one saw us,' said Garro.

'Us?'

Varren moved into view, his aspect set and cold. 'If you have something to say, psyker, you may voice it to me also. This situation is growing worse by the moment, and I will not be left behind by any development.'

Garro gave him a nod. 'The situation has changed, Rubio. We owe him the right to know the truth.' With quick, blunt words, Garro relayed what had taken place in the landing bay. Rubio listened with mounting concern, feeling the colour drain from his face.

When Garro was done, Rubio released a low breath. 'I fear what I am about to say will only create more disorder.' He held up a metal disc, slightly larger than a Throne gelt coin or a five aquila piece, stamped out of silver with an intricate design on both faces. 'Do you know what this is?' Turning it in the low light of the corridor, the etchings conspired to make the shape of a crescent moon.

Garro reached out and took it, and from the expression on his face and Varren's, both captains were aware of what the object represented.

'It is a lodge medallion,' said Varren. 'Only those who

are sworn initiates to the secret host may carry such a thing. He who holds this, holds loyalty to Horus, I'll wager.'

Rubio's lips thinned. He had suspected as much, but now confirmation made his gut twist. 'I found it on the barracks deck,' he explained. 'It was hidden in an arming cabinet. I sensed it, like the sound of a distant scream on bloody winds. There is a psychic trace on the object. The last time I encountered such a warp taint was on Calth, when the Word Bearers attacked us with their hell-beasts and cult-slaves. I think it may be somehow bonded to its owner.'

The medallion flickered as Garro examined it, the lines and forms upon the surface moving almost as if they were threads of mercury. 'It is cold to the touch, this eldritch thing. Aye, this is the mark of treachery.'

Rubio thought he saw a circle upon it, a wavering line, a star with eight points, one changing into the other, an inconstant and shifting illusion.

'If there is no mistake, then this makes the claim of Rakishio's disloyalty certain, and his men doomed along with him.' Varren spat angrily on the deck. 'Curse this war. I believed in him!'

'By the Throne,' said Garro. 'Khorarinn was right.'

But Rubio was raising his hands, shaking his head. *They do not understand.* 'No, you mistake my words. The lodge medallion does not belong to Captain Rakishio, or any of the Emperor's Children.'

Varren grabbed him by the wrist. 'Then where *did* you find it?'

'Among Hakeem's personal effects.' Garro stared at the disc in stunned silence, and for an instant, Rubio fancied that he glimpsed the shimmering patterns upon it become a mimicry of the V Legion's lightning-bolt sigil.

'How can this be?' Garro was shaking his head. 'The Khan's sons are loyal to Terra. They have proven it.'

'All of them?' said Rubio. 'Just as every son of Mortarion and Angron is blindly loyal to the Warmaster?' The counter cut hard, and he saw Garro accepted it with a grave nod.

'But if Rakishio is truly innocent–' Varren blurted out the words.

'Then Hakeem cannot allow him to live,' concluded Garro. He tapped the vox-link on his gorget, tossing the medallion away, into the depths of the sluice tanks. 'Garro to Khorarinn. Do you hear me? *Answer, you fool!*'

The quiet murmur of a dead communications channel was the only reply.

SIX

Daggers
Sword of truth
Destroy them

KHORARINN'S ARMOURED BOOTS sounded an echo with each footfall across the broad expanse of the cargo bay. At his side, the trooper party from the *Nolandia* and the White Scars moved carefully about the pack of Emperor's Children they surrounded. Rakishio and his men did not speak, seemingly resigned to their fate. The Custodian scanned their faces, seeing nothing to disabuse him of the belief that they were deserving of their chains.

Curious, he thought, *how easy it is to think them like the rest of us. The loyal. But the face shown to the light is never the true one...*

He did not finish the notion. Something was amiss, and it took him a second to realise what it was. 'This route does not lead to the brig.' He had memorised the frigate's deck plan as a matter of course before boarding it.

'That corridor is sealed off,' Hakeem said airily. The White Scar's topknot caught the light as he moved. 'The

Daggerline was damaged in the escape from Isstvan. This path will take you to your destination.'

Khorarinn hesitated, glancing back at the warriors. The wide, low compartment around the group was a cargo storage bay, but empty now, the supplies that had once filled it gone to feed the civilian refugees.

There was no cover here, he noted. No method of quick egress. His martial mind saw it instantly for what it was – a perfect kill box. The first real sense of something truly awry settled in his mind, and the Custodian grabbed the handle of his sentinel blade, as a static-smothered voice crackled over his vox-link.

'*Heed me!*' It was the Death Guard, but his words were barely intelligible. '*You are in great danger!*'

Rakishio's head snapped up. 'What did he say?'

The White Scars halted abruptly and Hakeem turned to cast a withering gaze over them all. He spoke before Khorarinn had the chance to respond. 'Kill them all.'

Their guns spoke in thunder, and across the rusted space of the cargo bay the flash of muzzle flares blazed like lightning strikes. The Naval troopers were cut down like chaff, dying together as swords flashed and blood jetted in arcs of wet crimson. They were dispatched in seconds, their murders merely the opening act of the deception. Rakishio's veteran sergeant and his equerry were the next to die, each legionary perishing instantly as bolt-rounds blew their skulls into red mist.

The captain reacted quicksilver-fast, throwing himself at the nearest warrior, desperate to try to wrestle a gun from him and fight back, but Hakeem had him in his sights and he stitched a three-round burst up his thigh and chest to blast him down to the iron deck. Rakishio collapsed, blood streaming through the cracks in his ceramite armour. He struggled, his leg refusing to obey him, clawing at the deck as he tried to right himself.

Then Hakeem was upon him, combat knife in his hand. The White Scar cut the other warrior's throat as though he were butchering a herd animal. The warriors of the Emperor's Children died around him in short order, brought low by bolt shell, sword's edge and callous treason.

Khorarinn was not so easy to kill. The traitor White Scars slaughtered their fellow legionaries and *then* turned their attention to the Custodian. It was a tactical error, allowing him to terminate the first of Hakeem's outriders by planting his sword through the warrior's chest.

He moved swiftly, but it was impossible to avoid every shot. Khorarinn let his heavy armour absorb glancing strikes, trying to pick off the traitors one at a time. But the odds were not in his favour. Khorarinn ended the life of another collaborator with a swingeing snap of a neck, but they were closing in on him, tightening the noose.

The Custodian had killed prey enough times to see the hunter's pattern as it formed around him. They had his measure, and his life was now counted in moments. In a brutal flurry of gunfire, he took a dozen close-range hits in the span of a heartbeat. The Chogorian warriors were careful and deadly with their guns, like the patient battle-riders of the steppe-world they had risen from. He fell, and they took aim.

'I always wondered how many of us it might take to put one of them down,' offered Harouk, the machine arm curving over his shoulder brandishing a combat blade. 'Now we know what is needed. Their arrogance. Our surprise.'

Blinking away blood and pain, Khorarinn groped

for understanding. *The White Scars are loyal.* That fact crumbled to dust before his eyes, and he knew the kill would come next. 'This is treason, Hakeem!' He spat the accusation at the legionary. 'You have renounced your birthright. You have shamed your Legion!'

'No, Custodian. We will *save it.*' Hakeem stepped closer, preparing to take the final shot himself. 'Horus Lupercal will win this war – it is written. And all those who side against him will be ashes and bones. You will not be the last.'

Their bolters howled, and ran until every one of them had emptied their magazines.

'KHORARINN?' GARRO CALLED into the silence. 'Custodian, do you hear me?' After a moment, Garro silenced the vox-channel and gave Rubio and Varren a grim look. 'It seems that our communications are being disrupted.'

'The Custodian is dead,' said Rubio quietly.

Varren eyed him. 'How can you be sure?'

Rubio ran a hand over the glowing crystalline matrix of his psychic hood. 'I'm sure,' he said.

The World Eater shook his head, trying to make right the sudden reversal of what he had held to be true. 'How could I have been so blind? Curse me, I am a fool.' He looked to Garro, almost imploringly. 'Hakeem and the others, they were White Scars like any other but... They had a different way about them. I paid it no mind. The warriors of Chogoris stem from so many different tribes, I thought it only a variant in company traditions. But it was the lodge. They hid it from me!'

'It must be so,' agreed Garro. 'Rakishio and his men were never in league with Horus. All this, the *Mistral*, everything, it was to isolate them and distract us. To allow Hakeem to make his move.'

'He has been following the Warmaster's banner from the start,' said Varren. 'It is the only explanation. But we can fight back. I still have many warriors on board this ship.'

Rubio frowned. 'More than Hakeem?'

'No,' admitted Varren. 'But if I can alert them...'

'How? If they're jamming our vox, we are silenced.' The psyker cast around, as if he could find an answer at their feet.

The World Eater straightened, the call to action upon him. 'Then we have to move, right now!'

Garro held up a hand to halt him. 'Wait! Listen...'

The *Daggerline*'s intercom system crackled to life, broadcasting throughout the vessel, and the voice they heard was being sent further still, back to the *Nolandia* and out to all the refugee starships in the fleet. *'This is Hakeem of the White Scars Legion. I have hard news.'*

'What is that whoreson doing?' growled Varren.

'Moments ago, the traitor Rakishio, now revealed as a spy for the Warmaster, escaped captivity with his followers and assaulted my men...'

'And now it begins,' muttered Garro. 'The gallows of lies.'

'It is with deep regret I must report the death of the esteemed Custodian Khorarinn, who fell in glorious battle with Rakishio and his turncoats. Rest assured that my warriors and I have avenged Khorarinn's murder. The Emperor's Children have been executed, one and all. But the danger has not yet passed. Before he died, Rakishio revealed that other spies lurk amongst you. These collaborators must be found and expunged. Therefore, I am declaring martial law throughout the flotilla. The White Scars will hunt down all traitors. There will be no mercy!'

The transmission ceased and left the three of them to take in what they had heard. Rubio spoke for them all: 'The only truth in those words is that Khorarinn and Rakishio are dead.'

'We must attempt to make contact with the *Nolandia*. This will spiral out of control unless we act with alacrity and focus. They'll be looking for us. We are all that stands between Hakeem and his greater treachery.' Garro placed a hand on Varren's shoulder, meeting his gaze. 'I know your blood sings out for battle, kinsman. I know your soul at this moment better than any man alive, believe me. But there are more lives at stake than just ours. I need to know you will follow me if I ask it of you.'

'The traitors will pay for their duplicity,' hissed the World Eater.

'That has never been in question.'

Varren's hard, scowling face did not alter, but at length he gave a single, sharp nod. 'I will follow you, brother. For the moment.'

OUT IN THE darkness, Hakeem's words rang out from ship to ship, his voice the only sound that could be heard.

'I am declaring martial law throughout the flotilla.'

The crews of the refugee ships had been pushed to the ragged edge of panic by the destruction of the *Mistral* and the menacing threat of the *Nolandia*. Aboard each craft, different microcosms of the same drama unfolding on the *Daggerline* were playing out.

On the cruiser *Sylvinus*, the refugees had rioted and the Naval crew all lay dead. Now they were fighting amongst themselves, pushed beyond reason into mindless mob rule. Aboard the *Tessen*, a colonist barge, a

vicious mutiny had been put down, but the ship had
lost all life support and the crew were suffocating. On
other ships, the fearful and the desperate were looking
past the gunnery drones and the battleship, wondering
if the risk of flight was one worth taking.

'*The White Scars will hunt down all traitors. There will
be no mercy!*'

Anarchy, fuelled by terror, took hold, and the fleet collapsed into disarray. A formation kept in line by fear
suddenly broke apart, engines flaring as a dozen ships
tried to escape at once.

The *Sylvinus* burned too hard and too fast, colliding
with the *Tessen* before either craft could veer off. The
cruiser's needle-nose bow sliced down the side of the
barge, a lance opening up the flank of a wallowing beast.
Together they bled fire and atmosphere into the vacuum,
great plumes of breathing gases flash-freezing into clouds
of oxygen ice.

Eight thousand souls across two ships were immolated
in a sphere of fusion fire. Their terror had killed them as
readily as any boltgun. And still the tide of panic rose.

Nearby, the *Nolandia*'s gunners readied their weapons
and took aim, Khorarinn's last order ringing in their ears.

THE DAGGERLINE'S VOX-ARRAY should have been a hive
of activity, with dozens of servitors and tech-adepts operating the frigate's internal and external communication
systems, but the compartment was a charnel house
scattered with their corpses. The three legionaries took
in the bloody display in silence. Crimson vitae pooled
on the deck or dripped from ornate brass consoles, where
it had been cast by the opening of throats.

'Hakeem's men were thorough,' noted Varren.

'It is how they are trained,' said Garro. 'The White Scars will not take prisoners.'

Rubio shook his head ruefully. 'Hakeem doesn't deserve to hold that name any more. The Khan would never accept what he has done.'

'The lord of his Legion is not here,' said Varren. 'In this moment, I fear we are beyond the sight of *all* reason.'

Garro picked his way through the bodies, searching in vain for any sign that someone might have survived, but Varren's estimate was correct. He moved to the primary communications console, with its multitude of controls and viewer-lenses. The system was an order of magnitude more complex than the vox-module built into his battleplate, and without an adept to operate it, he could not hope to amend its functions. But still, Garro knew enough to fathom what had been done here. 'All contact channels are being jammed. Squad-level vox-communication, internal, ship-to-ship. Hakeem has made certain that only his words will be heard.'

'What of the astropaths?' said Varren.

Rubio shook his head again. 'He won't have let them live.'

'Hakeem can broadcast whatever fiction he wants and no one will be able to challenge it.' Garro frowned, piecing together the whole of the treachery from the pieces before him.

'Harouk, the Techmarine in Hakeem's command. He would be capable of such subterfuge,' added Rubio.

'And more, no doubt.' Varren nodded at a gas-lens viewer. 'The hololith from the *Mistral*.'

'It could be done,' agreed Garro. 'Perhaps Hakeem sacrificed one of his own to take the tanker, and Harouk worked a lie to alter the visuals of the log record.' He considered the bleak implications of the deduction. Tarring Rakishio's contingent of Emperor's Children was only the first element in the traitor's plan. If unchecked, Hakeem would be able to engineer events so that only he and his brothers would survive the unfolding turmoil.

Garro imagined the treacherous White Scars returning to Terra, without anyone to speak against them. Unchallenged, they would be free to tell any tale they wished, to set themselves up as the heroes of the day. And once on Terra, they would be perfectly placed to do the secret bidding of the Warmaster.

'This is a fool's errand.' Garro gestured towards the hatchway with his weapon. 'Hakeem is intelligent. He may guess that we will come to this place.'

'*I did.*' The gas-lens flickered and came to life, framing the White Scar's craggy aspect. He leered at them through the display. '*Ah, Garro. That is the greatest weakness of the Fourteenth Legion. You are as predictable as the turn of the seasons.*'

'To arms!' Rubio shouted out the alarm and Garro spun around to see a group of warriors in white-and-red armour crowd into the chamber, their faces hidden behind plumed battle helms. He froze, as did Rubio and Varren. The White Scars halted with their weapons trained.

Varren's lip curled in disdain. 'Have you not the courage to face us yourself, traitor swine?'

'*There are more important tasks,*' grinned Hakeem. '*It matters not who kills you, World Eater, as long as you die along with the Sigillite's lackeys. I've already executed all the men you brought with you. It's fitting you lived long enough to learn that. To know you led them to their deaths.*'

'You lie!' thundered Varren.

'*You wish that were so.*' Hakeem waved a gauntleted hand towards the other White Scars. '*End them and be done with it.*' The lens viewer went dark.

IT WAS THE most grave of errors to force a World Eater into his rage. These were not warriors who would experience emotion in the same fashion as other legionaries. To them, agony and fury were constant companions, the air in their lungs and the blood pumping through their veins. Unleashed, a son of Angron was rage made real. He was butchery and brutality. He was hate and vengeance.

Varren gave a wild shout of anger and attacked the White Scars in a frenzy of gunfire and sword blows. Hakeem's provocation set him loose and he became a berserker, smashing his way across the vox-chamber and into the midst of the White Scars. He took on the squad alone, and belatedly Rubio and Garro followed to assist him, though they could not come too close for fear of Varren's wild state.

Rubio saw Varren spear the throat of one legionary through his neck-seal, then rip the helm from another and beat him to death with it. The World Eater took hit after hit but dismissed every one of them. His aura was a searing blood-red, wreathing him in invisible flames.

The stories of the XII Legion, of their pain-blocking brain implants and their blood-soaked way of war, were well known. But he had never seen it so close at hand. It shocked him to wonder how such martial power would fare in the hands of those who plotted death for the Imperium.

Varren killed the last of the squad with a slash of his sword, and halted. His white armour was patterned red with splashes of fresh gore. 'Not enough,' he hissed, through clenched teeth. 'My brothers are dead and *it is not enough.*'

IN THE VOID, the flotilla fragmented. Drive plumes flashed like burning torches in the darkness, and a dozen different vessels made their panicked bids for freedom. Some called out for lenience across deadened vox-channels, hoping that their entreaties might stay the hands of the *Nolandia*'s gunnery crews. Others went to their own ineffectual point-defence batteries, as if the las-weapons built to fight off local pirates and asteroid storms could even scratch the armour of an Imperial battleship. All of them hoped to flee the madness, but they had done no more than offer up their own death warrants. To disobey the Custodian's final order was suicide, the very act that Hakeem had driven them to take.

A storm of coherent light and particle beam fire left the muzzles of the *Nolandia*'s turrets, joined micro-seconds later by slaved shots from the drifting drone platforms. Force walls designed to deflect space debris were instantly punctured, void shields collapsing in flickers of false-colour radiation. The torrent of burning brilliance melted fissures through hull plating and into the delicate internal spaces of the civilian ships. Iron evaporated, plasteel became slag, and those who did not perish in the immediate heat-surge died when they were vented into the pitiless void.

Bursting like rotting fruits, the freighters and tugs, tankers and transports became expanding globes of glittering, metallic ash and sparking wreckage.

DISTANT ALERT SIRENS sounded as they made their way aft from the vox-array, encountering more of Hakeem's warriors, and with them new reinforcements.

Rubio did not hesitate and unleashed a blast of psionic lightning, immolating the common soldiers who had made new fealty to the White Scars. 'Naval troopers,' he scowled. 'They've turned the crew against us.' Rubio cast white fire from his fingertips, but he took nothing from the act. He had little stomach for the culling of the unwary. 'Damned fools! Why do they resist?'

'Because they are more afraid of Hakeem than they are of us,' said Garro. He cast a look over his shoulder, watching Varren as the World Eater brought up the rear. The bleak cast across the other warrior's face held firm, and his eyes were unreadable. A dozen wounds bled fiercely, but Varren paid them no heed. He seemed numb.

Garro pointed with *Libertas*. 'This way. We'll make for the landing tiers. We can take a Stormbird, get off this craft, and return to the *Nolandia*.'

'That is a coward's plan.' Varren grated.

Garro shot him a look. 'It is a *survivor's* plan, Captain Varren. I know your pain, I know you want vengeance... But we must pass on the truth of what is happening here.'

'Then you go. Take the psyker, and flee. I will stalk the halls of this ship until I have found and murdered every last one of these bastards.'

Rubio snorted. 'You won't last long on your own. They outnumber us three to one. And if Hakeem has rallied the *Daggerline*'s crew to their side, told them we are the traitors, he'll have even more arrows to his quiver.'

'I care nothing for those odds.' Varren drew himself up to his full height. 'I am an Eater of Worlds! Gladiator Son! I will stand, and fight, and avenge!'

'And die?' Garro met his gaze.

'Without hesitation. And so will you. Hakeem has your measure, Garro. Even now, he has warriors covering each approach to the landing bays. You won't get within a hundred metres of a Stormbird before a lascannon blasts you apart.' He made a snarling noise in his throat. 'I said I'd follow you. But to war, Garro. *To a glorious death.*'

'I have another option.' Rubio halted before them, the crystal matrix of his psychic hood glowing with ethereal light. 'There is another way off this vessel. If we take it, we can reach the *Nolandia* and end this madness. Hakeem will have to face his crimes.'

'He will do that at the tip of my sword,' said the World Eater.

'And will it be enough, Varren? Your life for his? We can give you a chance to carry your vengeance forward. To Horus. To Angron. But you must *live* for it.' Garro's words seemed to reach him, and behind those sullen eyes, something changed. Varren gave a slow nod.

'I will hear you out, psyker.'

'If we are to live beyond this day, I must find a spectre of the newly dead.' Rubio closed his eyes, extending feelers of telepathic power away down the corridors of the frigate. 'We don't have much time. *The spirit fades.* Follow me.'

IF THE SIGHT of the massacre in the vox-chamber had not been enough, what awaited them in the cargo compartment sickened Nathaniel Garro to his core.

'Blood's oath...' He had witnessed butchery before, but to find it here, so close to Terra's halls, was grotesque.

Cold air thick with the odour of coppery blood and the stinging burn of cordite clouded the space. The chamber was littered with the fallen, the full number of the warriors from the III Legion lying discarded where they had dropped. The Emperor's Children had suffered honourless deaths, executions instead of fair combat. For want of a better word, a cull had taken place here.

'This is a galaxy gone mad,' rumbled Varren, his rage momentarily stilled.

Rubio knelt by one of the corpses and grimaced as he examined the massive blast-crater in the dead man's armour. 'Shot in the back, at close range. This one perished without the grace of knowing who killed him.'

Garro had seen much that he struggled to accept since the beginning of the Warmaster's rebellion, but nothing appalled him so much as this, the central and fundamental horror upon which the whole insurrection was based. Brother killing brother, setting aside oaths of comradeship and honour, murdering without pause or regret. He simply could not comprehend where such an impulse could stem from. It made him feel hollow inside.

Rubio moved from one body to another, grimly cataloguing the names of the dead. He came across the commander and paused. 'Rakishio… His throat was slit.'

The World Eater pointed towards the shadows, to bodies lying in a lake of spilled blood. 'I see gold, there. Though it seems that Khorarinn took many of the traitors with him before he perished.'

'What kind of honourless war breeds this slaughter?' said Garro. 'Is this how Horus wishes to fight for the Throne? This is not our way. There is no principle in it.'

'I do not–' The psyker froze as he moved towards the Custodian's body, stiffening. His head jerked suddenly, and he glared into the deep shadows. 'We are not alone!'

From out of the blackness in the far reaches of the chamber, came figures in white battleplate with fire-red trim. At a count, it was the full number of Hakeem's warriors on board the *Daggerline,* all gathered here for this last confrontation.

'What is wrong, witch-mind?' Hakeem smiled. 'Did you not sense us waiting for you? Were your preternatural powers fogged?' He nodded languidly towards one of his warriors, who turned another of the silver lodge medallions over between the armoured fingers of his gauntlet.

Varren took steps forwards, his sword flashing to life, but Garro held him back, his own blade in hand. 'You did this, Hakeem,' he said, trying to understand. 'To your kinsmen. How can you justify it? How can you live with this deed on your conscience?'

The White Scar seemed amused by the questions. 'I do so with ease. How many legionaries have *you* killed, Garro? Warriors you might have shared battle with, in years past?'

'Too many,' he admitted. 'But I never wished for it. A part of my spirit was lost with each one I fought.'

'What sentiment.' Hakeem's smile became a mocking grin. 'I did not think a Death Guard capable of such a thing.'

'And I could not believe a White Scar capable of this atrocity!' Garro gestured angrily at the carnage all around them. 'Why, Hakeem? *Tell me why!*'

The Chogorian nodded to his men, and they spread out into a skirmish line, blocking all routes of escape, surrounding the three warriors. His manner shifted, becoming one of ruthless zeal. 'You know the answer already, Garro. You were at Isstvan Three. You saw the absolute determination shown by the Warmaster. The *vision.*'

'Is that what you call it?' said Varren.

'Horus Lupercal is the first among equals!' cried Hakeem. 'He is Warmaster! And if he wants the galaxy, he will have it. His victory is inevitable. It is unquestioned. The old order has grown stale. The Emperor's time is over.'

Garro glared at him. 'How can you believe that?'

'I know it, as I know Horus. We served alongside the Sixteenth Legion. There was much to admire about them. We share similar hearts, the same free souls resistant to those who would corral us, like your master the Sigillite and the so-called Council of Terra. Administrators and bookkeepers dictating the paths of warrior-kings?' He cleared his throat and spat. 'That shall not stand. The Legiones Astartes are masters of their own destiny. Horus will carry us to victory!'

'So the White Scars have rejected the rule of the Emperor?' Rubio asked the question Garro could not countenance. 'Has Jaghatai Khan denied his father?'

A flicker of annoyance crossed Hakeem's face. 'No. Sadly, my primarch is still blinded by the Emperor's lies. And many of my battle-brothers have yet to see the same truth I have. But they will, eventually.' He held up his blade. 'And if they do not...' Hakeem let the statement hang.

'The Khan will never go to Horus' banner,' said Garro. 'You are deluded to believe that it could be so. Give up this insanity before it ends you, Hakeem. The lodges have tainted you, but you can still atone for what you have done.'

'Repent, you mean? Like some religious heretic?' Hakeem released a bellowing, cruel laugh. 'I will not recant my words. I have set them in blood. My warriors follow the same path. The *Daggerline*'s crew follow me. Only you stand in our way.' Hakeem lowered his sword, the tip touching the deck, and held out his hand.

It slowly closed into a fist. 'I would offer you the chance to join us, but I know that you would never do so. I see you, Garro. I see how you bask in the Emperor's light as if it were some holy radiance. You will never reject Him. And if, when the moment comes, my battle-brothers amongst the Fifth Legion speak the same words, then they too will be put to the sword as Khorarinn and Rakishio were. Even the Great Khan himself, if he fails to kneel to the Warmaster, will not be spared.'

'You are mad,' muttered Rubio.

'Am I?' Hakeem's grin returned. 'We will see.' The warrior's words hung in the still air of the chamber, the moment stretching to breaking point.

Fittingly, it was Varren who gave voice in reply. 'We finish this.'

THE BATTLE WAS blood and it was fire.

It was sword and boltgun, fist and helm. White clashed with grey. Blood jetted and bones shattered. The Imperium's gene-forged warrior sons were turned against one another in a fight that only death could end.

And that end seemed certain, a span of seconds, minutes at the most, before the overmatched legionaries were beaten down and terminated by the superior numbers of Hakeem's traitors. Nonetheless, Garro, Rubio and Varren fought with the full measure of their martial skills, never once flinching from the fight, putting aside the nature of their foes. This was the war in microcosm, the battle for ideology and fidelity become action. Each side believed that they carried the sword of truth, and with that weapon they were justified in the acts they committed.

Brother against brother, loyalist against traitor, rebellion against conformity. Ultimate victory would grow from a thousand small battles like this one, or else it would breed an eternity of waste and devastation.

Rubio was drawing into a small war of his own, fighting down a pair of White Scars renegades as they attempted to flank him. He released a surge of telekinetic force to blast them back against the bulkhead, but no sooner had he turned than another of Hakeem's men was upon him.

It was Harouk, the Techmarine. A single augmetic eye glared at Rubio from the warrior's sallow face, and arching up over his back, like the tail of an iron scorpion, a third machine-limb swooped down to bludgeon him. It ended in a heavy, sawtoothed claw that snapped open and clamped about his shoulder, contracting on hissing pistons. Rubio's armour cracked and deformed under the bone-crushing pressure. In moments, the inexorable force would splinter ceramite and plasteel, grinding his bones and flesh into pulp. Gritting his teeth, he raised his hand and channelled a burst of psionic lightning from his fingertips.

The Techmarine took the full force of the mind-power and died screaming as the energy savaged him from within. Rubio shrugged off the juddering claw and cast around, ready for the next attack. As a new adversary came in to challenge him, he saw Garro and Varren nearby, side by side in the full flow of combat.

'YOU CAN'T WIN,' spat Hakeem. 'Surrender, and I'll grant you the mercy of a swift death!' He engaged them both, crossing a paired set of curved power tulwars to meet their blades.

Varren advanced on the White Scars warrior. 'You may have my life, traitor. I give it freely. You need only meet the price.'

'Name it.'

'You die first!' The World Eater's blade creased the traitor's face and slashed across Hakeem's eye, splitting it. But for all his fury, Varren was slowing. His wounds were many, and not even a berserker could go on taking such punishment without consequence.

'Varren, raise your guard!' Garro called out a warning, but even half blinded, Hakeem saw the opening and took it, crossing both his swords to slash at the World Eater's throat.

Varren fell, and the killing strike came down after him. 'You will not kill him!' shouted Garro, and *Libertas* flashed in the air, blocking the blow before it could land.

'Then you die in his stead, Death Guard!' Hakeem roared, his eyes alight. 'I'll take your head as a gift for Mortarion!'

'And I will end the shame of your betrayal, in the Khan's name!' His power sword blazing, Garro forced the White Scars renegade to retreat, fighting with the same unchained wrath that Varren had shown his enemies. He broke one of Hakeem's blades in two with the violence of his blows, and the other he unseated, sending it spinning away. The fury of it felt worthy, it felt *true*.

Hakeem fell back, into the line of his warriors, his face streaked with crimson. 'I grow weary of this blade-play,' he grunted. 'Bolters high! Take aim!'

The rest of the turncoat White Scars fell back, bringing their guns to bear.

'Garro, Varren!' Rubio roared their names. 'To me!' Garro turned to find the Codicier crouched over Khorarinn's corpse, his hand upon the dead Custodian's chest.

'He can't aid us, psyker,' said Varren wearily. 'We die now.'

Rubio shook his head. 'You are wrong. Look here.' Garro saw something in Rubio's fist, pulled from Khorarinn's belt. A rod-like device, webbed with a matrix of flickering indicator lights. 'I told you there was another way.'

The warriors drew up, boldly facing the guns of the White Scars, and Garro fixed Hakeem with a thin smile.

'I will wipe that grin from your face,' snarled the traitor. 'We will cut you down like the animals you are.'

'Not today.' Garro heard the high tones of energy crackling from out of the air around him. 'You will shed no more loyal blood.'

Khorarinn's teleport homer went active in Rubio's grip with a flash. Sheets of emerald fire enveloped the three warriors, and in the blinking of an eye, they were gone.

NO ONE ABOARD the battleship *Nolandia* had expected to see the legionaries again. Garbled transmissions from the *Daggerline* and Hakeem's pronouncement had been enough for the shipmaster to reassume direct command. He was a loyal, if unimaginative officer of the Imperial armed forces, and he had no intent of fulfilling any orders other than the ones Khorarinn had left.

And so the *Nolandia* remained at station, her gun crews calmly and systematically exterminating every refugee ship that tried to flee, or fight back. Thus, the return of Garro and his cohorts was akin to death itself striding into the strategium. The battle-captain's blood-smeared, smoke-darkened face was fierce and wrathful.

'You will cease fire!' Shock robbed the crew of immediate action, and Varren loomed over the commander, reeking of murder.

'Silence those guns!' The World Eater knocked the shipmaster to the deck and finally, the lasers went dark.

Garro strode to the centre of the chamber. 'Pass this to all decks, all crew. The Custodian Khorarinn was killed by agents of the Warmaster Horus. We have isolated the traitors aboard the frigate *Daggerline*. Gun crews are to rearm and make ready to fire, on my command.' He threw the psyker a look. 'Rubio. See that the astropaths are prepared for communion. I want all details of what has transpired here to be sent directly to the Imperial Palace. Malcador must know the truth of this before rumours can spawn.'

'Aye, captain.' Rubio hesitated. 'What about Hakeem and his turncoats? They'll try to run now, escape back to Horus and his rebels.' He nodded towards the frigate, hanging in space beyond the *Nolandia*'s bow.

Garro did not answer him. Instead he gestured to the battleship's master of gunnery. 'Target the *Daggerline*. All weapons.' The warrior hesitated, then beckoned Varren to him. 'This choice is not mine to make, kinsman. Capture or execution. I will leave the method of Hakeem's punishment to–'

'Destroy them.' Varren bit out the words and marched to the great oval portal at the bow, there to bathe in crimson death-light.

GARRO WAS STARTING to think of the moon's silent tower as the closest thing he had to a home. Given that the Somnus Citadel had been, for a time, as much a prison as it was his place of solace, that was a sorrowful reckoning indeed.

He had hoped that in his new mission for the Sigillite, he would find purpose. And he had, to a degree. But not the full measure of it, not yet. The light of events in the distant Kuiper Belt had thrown this into stark relief for the warrior. Garro was looking for a truth that he had yet to discover, an elusive certainty that seemed to recede each time his mind tried to frame it.

Where is this path leading me? He had no way of knowing.

'And what happened then?' said Malcador. He hesitated, glancing up at the Regent of Terra. His master studied him from beneath his hood, the details of his face lost in the shadow. But the eyes... The Sigillite's eyes were always clear, always watching. Garro was as glass to him. He could hide nothing.

'Hakeem was executed, along with the rest of the traitors. There were no survivors.'

Malcador nodded slowly. He had said little during Garro's report on what had transpired aboard the *Daggerline*, only clarifying small points here and there as the legionary relayed the grim story. Just once had he shown something like a true reaction, at the description of Khorarinn's death. Garro knew that it would fall to the Sigillite to tell the Emperor the details of how one of His trusted Custodians had perished.

'Grave events indeed,' said the Sigillite. 'The loss of life is regrettable, but the safety of the Imperium was upheld. You served the Emperor well, Garro. My instinct to send you was affirmed. Had your... "Knights Errant" not been at hand, circumstances would have favoured the arch-traitor Horus.'

'*Regrettable?*' The word seemed almost an insult to the dead. 'My Lord Regent, no ship in that flotilla survived the day intact. They came to us with hope and we met them with suspicion and death.'

'These are the times we live in, Nathaniel.' Malcador looked away. 'The luxury of trust no longer exists. Each confrontation is a stone in the water, spreading out ripples that create new battles to be fought. In the confusion following Khorarinn's death, when the refugee fleet splintered, a single ship was lost in the melee. It escaped detection and passed deeper into the solar system. I suspect that whomever was aboard it is an agent of the Warmaster. But I have already set other operatives to work on that matter.'

Garro silently assimilated this new information as Rubio approached, pausing to bow to the Regent. At the Codicier's side was Varren, the World Eater's expression morose and distant. His blood-spattered wargear had been taken from him, and now he too wore the same featureless slate-grey armour as Garro and the psyker. Varren's power sword lay inert in its back-scabbard, the heavy brass grip the only flash of metallic colour upon him.

Malcador raised an eyebrow. 'Your next recruit?'

'It seemed fitting, Lord Sigillite,' said Rubio.

Varren lifted his head. 'Garro told me that your mission serves the Emperor's will and punishes the traitors.'

'In a way,' Malcador allowed.

'Good enough,' said Varren. 'My sword arm is yours, until the day dawns that I die or I run out of enemies to kill.'

The Sigillite inclined his head. 'Then you are welcome within our ranks, Macer Varren. But I warn you... I warn *all* of you. What happened out there, what Hakeem did... You may well see the like of it again. The lines between loyalist and traitor are blurring, as the opposing forces in this war take shape for the battles ahead. Hakeem's renegades are not the only turncoats you will face.' He walked away, his staff tapping against the floor. 'Even now there are conspirators walking the corridors of power, on Terra and the core worlds. Men and women, fools, dupes and zealots. They are paving the way for the invasion that must come. For Horus' attack upon the Imperium's beating heart.'

'Show them to me,' said Varren. 'They'll die.'

'In time.' Malcador nodded to himself. 'All things will come in time.'

Garro studied the Sigillite's unreadable expression, searching for some understanding of Malcador's intent. He did not find it. 'What do you wish of us now, Lord Regent?'

'I have many missions for you to undertake, Captain Garro,' came the reply. 'And when they are done, I promise that you will pass full circle to the black roots of this bloody insurrection. But before that day, you will be my eyes and ears, my knife in the darkness. You will find these collaborators, and terminate them.'

Garro bowed his head and placed his hand on the hilt of *Libertas*, pushing away the shadow of something dark at the edges of his thoughts. 'As you command,' he said, 'so shall it be.'

PART TWO
THE SHIELD

SEVEN

The *Phalanx*
Stone man
Burden of duty

IN THE SKIES above Terra, the forces of the Imperium of Mankind were preparing for war. The birthworld of the human species turned beneath a haze of ash, the surface pockmarked by colossal city-sprawls and hive-plexes. It was a clenched fist of iron and stone, and from it rose spindly orbital elevator towers and the thruster trails of heavy transports.

The planet was ringed by platforms and way-stations of varying size and complexity, littering the low orbit and the gravity-null clusters of the Lagrangian points. Ships crossed between them like motes of mercury over black velvet, engine exhausts glowing. A shroud of ever-moving armour turned about Terra, constructs as large as continents drifting as if they were gargantuan metal clouds. Some were gunnery complexes, little more than free-floating weapons aimed outwards into the void, like cannons atop ancient castle battlements. Others were command-and-control facilities, staging posts. Shipyards and star-docks bristled with battle vessels of every make and tonnage, old hulls being refitted with new weapons.

Some orbitals were the private habitats of Imperial nobles and dignitaries, but even their exalted status did not protect them from the Order of Fortification. No one was exempt from the diktat that the Emperor had handed down. Terra was on a war footing, donning her chainmail and sharpening her blades. Watching. *Waiting*.

Out past the orbit of Luna, secondary and tertiary lines of defence were already in place. Fields of autonomous cannon-drones and sensor webs floated in the darkness. Asteroids dragged in by tenders from the belt beyond Mars formed the bastions of the Ardent Reef, the Hecate Shoal and other portcullis groups.

They prepared for the day they knew would come, the day when the sky would brim with the battlefleets of Horus Lupercal's rebellion. The turncoat Warmaster had never let his gaze fall from Terra.

The planet was more than just the spiritual heart of the Imperium, more than the capital world and origin-point of mankind. Pragmatic tacticians could say that a successful war against the Emperor might never even need to reach the light of Sol, but no one truly believed that it would not.

Horus *would* come here. This was his father's house. If he did not burn it or take it for himself, then he could never claim that ultimate victory. This, the Emperor knew full well. And so He made ready.

The architect of the fortification was one seemingly born to such a task. Rogal Dorn, most steadfast and unswerving of the Emperor's sons, primarch of the VII Legiones Astartes, the Imperial Fists. It was said that Dorn was the greatest master of defensive strategy in the galaxy, and that a stronghold designed by the Fists could never be breached. Horus would put that claim to the test.

Dorn oversaw the great reinforcement effort from his flagship and star fortress, the mighty *Phalanx*. The size of a small moon, it was forced to remain clear of Terra's shipping lanes for fear that its great mass would exert a tidal pull on the lesser orbitals. Standing sentinel over the ongoing work of the defences, the star fortress was a grand artifice of gold. Ramparts and towers, cathedral-like halls and acres of domes covered its flanks. The *Phalanx* was not only the flagship of the VII Legion, but also their home, with room for hundreds of thousands of warriors and support serviles in its habitat tiers. Lines of military traffic and freighters dotted the approaches to the fortress, a complex dance of starships moving back and forth under Dorn's supreme command.

Among them, lost in the mess of auspex returns and radiation back-scatter, a small shuttle-pod crept closer on stealth-cowled engines.

THE SHIP WAS barely worthy of the name. No bigger than a Land Speeder, the shuttle-pod carried only a single occupant, a rudimentary drive system and auto-navigator. What other space remained inside the seamless, scan-resistant hull was packed with sensor baffles and reflex shield devices. Craft such as this were typically deployed by Imperial agents or the killers of the Officio Assassinorum. But in this instance, the passenger was of a markedly different intent.

The pod spiralled in towards the hull of the *Phalanx*, autonomic systems waiting until the last possible second to fire braking thrusters to slow its approach. Magna-grapples extended and drew the pod the last short span towards a service hatch, and locked on. Stealth protocols ran from the craft's cogitators, misdirecting the docking sensors and masking the unscheduled arrival. The window of opportunity was only a few moments, but it was enough.

Unnoticed by the Imperial Fists, an intruder had boarded their vessel. *A ghost by any other name.* Its sole function completed, the shuttle-pod disengaged and drifted away, blending back into the clutter of the space lanes.

The lone passenger risked a single communication, a burst-transmission message encrypted on a deep-level vox-channel. There would be no reply. One signal alone was enough to chance detection.

'I have boarded,' he whispered into his vox-bead. 'Proceeding with mission as planned.'

THE WARRIOR LET the long shadows conceal him, the bulk of his ghost-grey power armour half hidden in the gloom. He wore a large, thin robe of shimmering material over the battleplate, giving him the look of a monastic figure out of old legend. Pulling it close, he activated a device sewn into the sleeve and the surface of the robe shimmered. He became a glassy sketch, a shape disrupted as if seen through a rain-slick windowpane. The technology was rare and fragile, but the Falsehood could shroud even an armoured giant from a passing observer.

Beneath the hood, Nathaniel Garro grimaced. He did not approve of such clandestine acts, but he had no other choice. He was here on the direct command of Malcador the Sigillite, as one of the Regent of Terra's covert agents amidst the turmoil of the galactic civil war.

Months had passed since Garro had made his new

oath to Malcador's service and taken on the mantle of a
so-called 'Knight Errant'. Months since that first mission
to Calth and gathering of the first name on the Regent's
list of recruits. Since then he had found more, swelling
the secret ranks of the Sigillite's secret militia.

It was easy to lose himself in the work. He had been so
desperate for purpose after his escape from Isstvan that
the simplicity of tracking, isolating and recovering the
legionaries Malcador required was enough to sate him.

Until recently. Garro frowned and silenced the traitorous doubt before it could fully form in his mind. He
could not afford to be distracted, not here of all places.

He moved in the gloom cast by huge ornamental columns, shifting from point to point when the eyes of
crew-serfs or Imperial Fists legionaries turned away. Garro
crossed the Great Hall of Victories, following the lines
of the Statue Garden and the Gallery of Heroes. He had
been aboard the *Phalanx* once before, but under very
different circumstances. Then, Garro had been a guest
of the VII Legion, plucked from certain death by Rogal
Dorn himself. It sat poorly with him that his return came
under a shroud of secrecy.

The corridors and chambers of the flagship were magnificent works of functional, martial architecture. Heavy
with banners from a hundred thousand victories, lined
with works of art that celebrated Dorn's Legion and the
high ideals of the Imperium, they were a glorious sight.
Garro had no time to admire them. For the duration of
this mission, he considered himself in enemy territory
and would act accordingly.

The only exception he had made to his usual preparation was to come bearing only his sword, *Libertas*.
Garro had left his boltgun behind. That act signified

that he would not, could not, shed blood in the prosecution of this duty. But if he were discovered now, he doubted that the Imperial Fists would extend him the same consideration.

He froze in place at the sound of footsteps. A dozen armoured Space Marines passed close to his place of concealment, oblivious to his presence. Careful to remain unseen by his fellow legionaries, Garro let the Falsehood and his training carry him slowly and carefully into the inner halls of the vast star fort.

The warrior's objective lay deep inside the *Phalanx*, on the lower decks towards the flagship's gargantuan engine cores. The chamber was known only as the Seclusium.

WITHIN A FEW hours, he had made his way to his target. A huge oval gate, titanium-blue and ringed with locking devices, rose up before Garro, and his eyes caught the symbol etched into the metal above the latch. A mailed fist against a white disc, the emblem of the VII Legion. Rogal Dorn himself had struck that sign when this door had been closed, and if Garro opened it, it would be Dorn that he defied.

Inside the sealed chamber, behind humming forcefields, walls of deadening black phase-iron and psychic countermeasures from the Dark Age of Technology, the primarch of the Imperial Fists had wilfully imprisoned a cadre of his own sons. They had committed no crime, done nothing to dishonour their brethren. These were steadfast warriors taken from front-line battle duties, men ordered to disarm and stand down by the father of their Legion. They were Imperial Fists, sombre and steadfast in character, and to every last degree Dorn's true sons. Yet they had accepted their primarch's command without question.

The only offence that these legionaries had committed was to be cursed with the gifts of the warp – Lexicanium, Codicier or Epistolary, they were the battle-brothers of the Librarius, trained to use the power of their minds as a weapon. The Emperor's passing of the edict after the conclave on Nikaea had ended that service in a single moment. In the wake of the sorcerer-primarch Magnus the Red's dalliances with the mercurial powers of the warp, their weapons had been denied to them and now Dorn's Librarians spent their long days in quiet meditation, isolated from their kinsmen and their future uncertain.

Garro paused, considering the great seal, the edict and the men he had recruited. He thought of Rubio, the Ultramarines Codicier who had been the first. The act of bringing Rubio to Malcador had been in direct violation of the Emperor's Decree Absolute, and so it would be violated again if he were to proceed now. Yet it was necessary for the safety and security of the Imperium. Garro believed that wholeheartedly.

The troubling duality of the situation weighed heavily upon him, and not for the first time. In the end, he did what he always did, and silenced his misgivings with action.

Garro reached into a pouch on his belt, removing a device that Malcador himself had pressed into his hands. The origin of the small crystalline object, its radiant glow soft and ethereal, was unknown to him. Still, Garro could not entirely banish the feeling that it was somehow *alien*. When he had questioned the Regent of Terra on that suspicion, Malcador had said nothing, merely holding him in that steady, stony gaze.

He held it up to face the sigil on the gate, and tendrils

of faint energy reached out to caress the locks. The glow brightened and the arcane device began its work, the seals holding the gate shut opening in swift order under its influence. But the act did not go unnoticed.

Hidden alcoves spun open to reveal a pair of armoured gun-servitors in the yellow livery of the Fists. They marched towards him, weapons spinning up to firing speed, targeting lasers flashing in the cold air. A vox-coder grille in the chest of the nearest cyber-hybrid produced a pre-programmed demand. 'In the Legion's name, halt and identify.'

The Falsehood's image-collapsing effect seemed to confuse them, and the machine-slaves dithered, struggling to track the cloaked warrior. Garro did not give them time to target him.

Libertas came to life in his hand. He allowed the servitors no opportunity to raise the alarm before he attacked, the power sword making swift, deadly arcs. The servitors barely managed a screech before they were cleaved apart. Oil and blood spurted, electricity crackled, and with their neural cords severed, the mind-wiped helots stumbled and crashed to the deck.

Leaving them where they fell, Garro turned back to the gate as the last of the seals disengaged. Slowly, the Seclusium began to open.

BROTHER MASSAK WAS dreaming.

He did not truly sleep, for the bio-implants of the Legiones Astartes ended the need for such a thing. But he did dream, in the strange mind-space of his meditations as his thoughts turned in upon themselves, and there he contemplated his fate.

In the darkness, he sometimes saw glimpses of things that appeared unreal.

Skies, black with warships. Creatures beyond the alien, warped and monstrous. Fire and thunder. War, burning the galaxy from spiral arm to core.

Time had become meaningless to Massak and the other psykers. Isolated from the universe at large, the passage of weeks into months, and months into years had fallen away until there was only the now. Massak was ready to wait as long as his primarch wished him to, contained within this chamber. That was his duty.

'When the time is right, he will come.' His voice echoed into infinity. 'When the Imperium needs us, *Dorn will return.*'

The words came from nowhere, but the conviction beneath them seemed transient. None among the isolated Librarians had given voice to any doubts about their confinement, but a bitter thought buried deep in Massak's mind threatened to rise to the surface.

What if Dorn did not *return?*

Then the moment faded. At some great distance, he heard the faint sound of complex locks opening, of gunfire and sudden death.

The Seclusium gate? Brother Massak's mind snapped back to wakefulness and he rose swiftly from his pallet. Something was wrong.

He sensed the flicker and fade of the gun-servitors as the dim candles of their minds were snuffed out, and then the hazy shape of another psyche. One hidden behind hard walls of counter-telepathic training and rigid thought. It could only be a legionary, but the identity of the warrior was impossible to grasp, and to call upon his powers to push deeper would be to violate the decree.

'Brothers!' Massak sprinted towards the opening gate, rousing a handful of the other Librarians around him, calling them to arms. 'The gate should not open so readily. This must be some sort of attack!'

The great hatch yawned, light flooding in from beyond, and Massak's kinsmen stood ready as a vague shape moved like heat-haze in the air. Then the phantom was revealed, a grey-armoured figure appearing as a Falsehood about it opened and fell to the deck. The figure was haloed by the glow from the corridor beyond, a power sword crackling in its grip.

By contrast, the Librarian's weapon of choice was a force axe, two curved blades of psychically resonant metal forming the killing edges. It was in his hand in a heartbeat, and at his side his brothers drew their swords and force rods from arming racks about the chamber. 'You wear no colours or sigil, intruder! Give me your name and Legion. Surrender your sword.'

'And if I do not?' said the stranger. 'Those weapons in your hands are nought but dead metal without your psionic powers to charge them.'

Massak's knuckles whitened around the shaft of his axe. The invader was quite correct, but months of isolation with little else to do but train had sharpened the Librarian's already excellent skills of blade-play, enhanced or not. 'They will be enough,' he countered.

The warrior in grey smiled at that. 'Come with me, and we need not cross blades at all.'

'You do not command us,' Massak retorted. 'Now surrender your sword.'

The smile faded. 'I do not wish to fight you. But I will not give up my weapon.'

'Then you will pay for your trespass!' Massak and his battle-brothers advanced upon the intruder, launching a string of connected attacks that were each met and parried. The Librarian tried to find the measure of the warrior. He moved with a fractional hesitance, betraying the presence of an augmetic replacement limb, but he was not slow. His great power sword deflected Massak's own weapon and forced the Librarian back a step. The nameless one had the scarred face of a hardened battle veteran, and the prowess to match it.

The Imperial Fists outnumbered him, but he held them at bay with unparalleled focus and skill. Massak grimaced, advancing. He let his brothers move in a swift feint and then he struck, swinging the axe hard. Their blades met and locked, sparks flying. Massak glared at the trespasser, searching his expression for some understanding of why he was here.

'Who are you?' he hissed, and for a moment he allowed his emotions to take the upper hand.

A flicker of psionic power sparked across his thoughts. Despite his iron self-control, in the melee some tiny fraction of Massak's preternatural power brushed across the mind of his opponent. A flash of insight came to him, the briefest glimpse of why the legionary had come to the Seclusium. The shape of his true intention was almost within reach…

… but then the moment broke like brittle glass as a new force entered the chamber. The burning, stony mind of a warlord.

'*Cease!*' shouted Rogal Dorn, in a voice that had ended battles and split mountains. Hard as granite, radiating dark fire, his psyche eclipsed everything else in a silent inferno of pure will. 'By my command, put up your weapons.'

None dared defy the order. Dorn filled the chamber with the great weight of his presence, his aura the very echo of the mailed fist upon his ornate armour. Flanked by his huscarls, the primarch of the Imperial Fists threw his stormy gaze across the psykers and watched them each sink to one knee, bowing their heads. Massak followed suit, as did the grey-armoured intruder.

Dorn was a son of the Emperor, a walking fortress of a man more invincible and unyielding than any construct of stone and steel. Few could have had the courage to meet his gaze without flinching, but to Massak's surprise the veteran warrior did so.

'Well met, Lord Dorn,' he said.

Something like surprise flickered briefly on the face of Massak's master, before quickly vanishing again. 'Nathaniel Garro. I wondered if our paths might cross again. Did *he* send you?'

The warrior named Garro looked away. 'With all due respect, my lord… I believe you already know the answer to that question.'

Dorn's eyes narrowed, and he gestured to one of his men. 'Take him to my chambers. I will have words with this one.'

Massak watched Garro sheathe his blade without resistance and walk away in custody. As he crossed the Seclusium, he threw Massak a nod. *A gesture of respect, perhaps?*

'Your isolation should not have been disturbed,' Dorn said tersely. 'Those responsible will be punished. Return to your meditation.' He turned away towards the threshold of the hatchway. 'The gate will be secured once more.'

'Master?' The Librarian spoke before he could stop himself. Dorn halted but did not turn back to face him. 'My lord, before you leave us, if I might ask of you…' He mustered his will to put forward the words. 'How goes the Great Crusade?'

The primarch was silent for a long moment. The question – not what he had uttered but the true question – hung unspoken in the air between them. *When may we return to our Legion?*

Dorn's tone became grim. 'Matters have become complicated. It is a crusade no longer. It is a war now. A war of brutal dimension and great sorrow.'

Massak drew himself up to attention. 'We stand ready to serve.'

When his gene-father replied, the psyker heard sadness in the words. 'I know you do, my son. I know.'

GARRO LOOKED AROUND, taking in the scope of the primarch's sanctorum. Little had changed since his last visit to this chamber, other than a new profusion of documents, pict-slates and data charts ordered in neat piles across one great chart table. The matters of the Order of Fortification presented for Dorn's guidance were many and complex. The ornate chambers, atop the tallest of the *Phalanx*'s towers, commanded an impressive view of the star fortress. The wide, oval space seemed now like an arena, and Garro felt like a sacrifice sent to perish upon its azure floor.

He tensed as he sensed a presence behind him.

'Do you recall what happened the last time we stood together in this room?' Dorn's voice was deep and resonant, like a faraway storm.

'I watched the noble *Eisenstein* meet its end.' Garro felt an unexpected pang of guilt at the memory of the steadfast ship and its destruction.

'After that.'

The warrior stiffened. It had been here that he had first revealed to Rogal Dorn the facts of Horus Lupercal's betrayal. Dorn's reaction had been that of any loving brother: first denial and then great anger, severe enough that Garro had feared for his life. Considering his next words carefully, he turned to face the primarch. 'I brought you a hard truth. The burden of my duty.'

'As I recall, you asked me if I was blind. And perhaps I was. But no longer. I see clearly now – I must so that my duty can be completed. The Emperor has charged me with the defence of Terra and command of all His armies. That is *my* burden. I am now Warmaster in all but name.'

'Much has changed for both of us, my lord.'

Dorn loomed over him, his eyes glittering like shards of flint. 'I know what you are, Garro. I know of Malcador's plans and his secret endeavours. I know that you and that old wolf Iacton Qruze are among his agents. The Sigillite uses you to gather materiel and to recruit men, many of them psykers, for reasons as yet unrevealed. And all of it in apparent defiance of the Emperor's commands.' The primarch's heavy gauntlets closed into fists. 'That ghost-armour you wear, with Malcador's brand upon your shoulder, it may give you leave to go where you wish elsewhere in the Imperium, but not here! The *Phalanx* belongs to my Legion. You do not come to my domain in stealth and expect no censure. You will explain yourself to me.' He raised his hand to point at Garro. 'Or this time, I will not hold back when I strike you.'

There was only truth in the threat, and all too clearly Garro recalled the grievous pain that had shocked through him when Dorn had lashed out at him once before. He still had the scars from the day. But still, the primarch's order was one he could not readily obey. 'I mean no disrespect, my lord. But my mission cannot be revealed. Even to you.'

'You owe your life to me, Garro.' Dorn's fury seethed beneath the words. 'It was the Imperial Fists that rescued you and your men from deep space. You were adrift and facing certain death. Have you forgotten that so readily?'

'I forget nothing, my lord. True enough, I know the full weight of the debt I owe you, but my duty to the Sigillite is greater still.'

Dorn's eyes narrowed menacingly. 'What duty can require you to steal aboard my ship like a thief, break my commands and disturb those whom I hold in isolation? We have already recovered your shuttle-pod, Garro. How were you going to escape? What did you want with the Librarians? *You will answer me!*'

Garro breathed deeply, steeling his courage to openly defy the primarch. 'I regret that I cannot, my lord.'

For a long moment, Garro feared that Dorn would make good on his threat and knock him to the deck. But then the primarch stepped back, his aloof rage simmering. 'I do not accept your refusal. You will remain a prisoner aboard the *Phalanx* until such time as you decide to provide me with the answers I have requested. Here you will stay, if need be until the stars themselves burn cold.'

Before the Master of the Fists could summon his guards to escort him away, the sanctorum's doors opened of their own accord and Garro saw the psyker he had spoken with standing there, held back by the praetorians. 'Lord Dorn, forgive my intrusion, but I must speak with you!'

'Brother Massak.' Dorn dismissed him with a glance. 'I did not grant you permission to leave the Seclusium. Return there at once.'

'I shall,' said Massak, 'but first I must beg this audience with you.' He shot a look at Garro. 'I know why *he* is here.'

Dorn waved a hand, and his praetorians stood aside to let Massak enter. The primarch's narrow gaze turned its full, withering power on his son. 'Explain yourself.'

'I can sense the truth he is hiding,' insisted the Librarian. 'It lurks beneath the surface of his thoughts. With your permission, I can reveal it.'

The warrior-lord's huge arms folded across his golden chestplate. 'Do you dare suggest the use of psychic power? You know better than any Imperial Fist that my father forbids it!'

But even as he said the words, Garro saw the conflict in Dorn's eyes, the same questions he himself had wrestled with. Even as Dorn knew he was honour-bound to follow the Emperor's edict, he could never ignore the great value of a psyker as a weapon of war in the arsenal of the Legions.

Massak shook his head. 'He can hide nothing from me, master. If only you will allow me to put Garro to the question. I swear to you I will not defy the Decree of Nikaea.'

'But you will. Even the smallest exercise of warp-born power is defiance. It opens the door to misuse, just as my brother Magnus misused it.' Dorn scowled. 'No. The Imperial Fists are loyal to the Emperor in all things. My father's decision is the final word.'

In that moment, Garro saw an opportunity and took it. 'If I may speak... I would offer a compromise, Lord Dorn.'

The primarch eyed Garro. 'I will hear you out.'

'Your Librarian's instincts are strong,' Garro went on, 'and they are correct. I came here for *him*.' He pointed at the psyker. 'I will reveal Malcador's orders, but to Brother Massak and no other. He will know if I am truthful.'

Dorn studied him, his expression impassive. 'And if I refuse?'

Garro managed a rueful smile. 'Then, my lord, as you say, you will have my company until the stars burn cold.'

THE INTERROGATION CHAMBER on the *Phalanx*'s dungeon decks was no larger than the interior of an armoured transport. Dull, featureless metal walls rose up to a ceiling studded with lumen orbs, and a sluice-grate in the centre of the floor betrayed the spilling of blood that had often occurred there.

A heavy hatch slid closed on oiled pistons, the thud of magnetic locks sounding as it sealed them off from the rest of the vessel. Garro and Massak stood opposite one another across the empty room. The former captain was as still as a statue. The Imperial Fist studied him, watching his face for the first sign of some telltale micro-expression that might reveal Garro's true intentions.

'Are we being monitored?' he asked.

'No,' said Massak. 'Even the primarch cannot hear us in this place. Whatever you have to say to me, it shall be between us alone.' He took a breath, preparing himself for what would come next, reaching for a point of calm neutrality in his thoughts.

Garro nodded. 'Tell me about the dreams, Massak.'

Of all the words he had thought to hear, the Librarian had not expected those. Massak had told no one of the disquieting images that had visited his meditating mind in recent weeks, their appearance growing more frequent with each passing day. 'I do not dream.' The lie came too easily to him, and Garro saw it immediately.

'We *all* do, kinsman. Perhaps not in the way that common men think of it, but we dream. And you, with your abilities… You dream very differently indeed. You haven't spoken of it, have you?'

For a moment, Massak considered prolonging his denials, then thought better of it. They were truly alone here, and in that there was a kind of liberation. 'I have not,' he admitted.

'Yet the Sigillite knows.' It troubled Massak greatly to see that his thoughts were open to others, but then Malcador *was* the greatest living psyker in the galaxy, after the Emperor of Mankind, and it was said that any mind was as an open book to him.

'I said nothing because I feared my brothers would not understand.' He took a breath. 'I have dreamed of the skies above Terra filled with black warships, a baleful eye emblazoned upon them. I dream of hordes of malformed horrors in league with traitors, laying waste to the planet. Atrocities. Creatures the like of which have never been seen before in mortal realms.'

'Daemons?' Garro offered the word without weight, but Massak instinctively knew that it carried grave meaning for the warrior.

'That name is good enough,' he said.

Garro nodded. 'They are no mere fancy, no trick of the mind. They are *real*.'

With blunt, steady words, he told the Librarian of the insurrection spreading under Horus' hand. He revealed the whole bloody truth of it to him, as at first shock, then revulsion and finally fury warred across Massak's face as he struggled to take it all in.

'I have fought these creatures,' Garro concluded. 'I have seen them born from the flesh of the dead. Your visions are—'

'The future, then?'

'A possibility,' he corrected. 'What you have seen is why I am here.' Garro took a step closer, his manner sobering.

'The Sigillite sent me to retrieve you. Malcador seeks men of strength and honour for an endeavour that will defend the Imperium against such threats for millennia to come. He chose you, Massak. He chose you for a duty that goes beyond your loyalty to Rogal Dorn and the Imperial Fists.' The grey warrior offered his gauntleted hand. 'Come with me, kinsman. Your seclusion will be at an end. Your power will be returned to you.'

Brother Massak looked down at Garro's outstretched hand. He knew what the offer meant. A chance to end his isolation, to be useful again. To fight for the Imperium.

But he shook his head, turning away. 'No. *I refuse.* Tell the Regent of Terra that I must decline his offer. I am an Imperial Fist, a son of Dorn, and subject to my primarch's command over all else. I will not leave my Legion.'

Garro's hand did not drop. 'You realise what you are rejecting, Massak? If you do not come with me, Lord Dorn will return you to the isolation of the Seclusium. You will be a prisoner there, an outcast among your own Legion. You may never have another chance to be freed from the Decree of Nikaea.'

'That may be so,' Massak told Garro, a resolute cast rising in him. 'We are iron and stone, captain. We do as our primarch commands us. I do not seek to be free of the Emperor's mandate. *I embrace it.* I am of the Seventh Legion, and we obey.'

'Even if the order brings you to doubt?' For a moment, it seemed as if Garro's question were directed towards himself and not Massak.

The Librarian drew up to attention, his gaze unwavering. 'If Dorn speaks the words, then there is no doubt. My visions...' He hesitated, framing his words. 'If what you say is true, Garro, if the Warmaster has betrayed us, if he makes pacts with monsters, then I must stand side by side with my primarch and my battle-brothers, and meet this treachery head-on.'

'When the time comes, that may not be enough to stop him.'

'I have faith that it will.' Massak's reply seemed to strike a chord with the warrior, and at length, Garro nodded in reluctant acceptance.

'I understand. I too know the burden of duty all too well. I will see your words carried back to Malcador. He will not be pleased, but I will make him appreciate your choice.' Garro saluted Massak with the sign of the aquila and strode towards the hatch, but he held firm, musing upon his words. 'Farewell, Massak,' Garro added, as the heavy door hissed open once more. 'I hope one day I will have the honour of fighting the enemy at your side.'

Unbidden, a dark mood settled on the Librarian, and the memory of stark, dreamlike images clouded his thoughts. 'That day will come sooner than we expect,' he said, the words coming from nowhere.

ROGAL DORN STOOD waiting for Garro in his sanctorum, staring out of the great gallery windows towards the distant sphere of Terra. The primarch's praetorians escorted him into the chamber, before executing a flawless about-turn and retreating to the corridor beyond.

'An unscheduled transport vessel flying the colours of the Regent's Court is approaching the *Phalanx*, requesting permission to land,' said Dorn, when they were alone. 'Your passage home, I imagine. It seems that the Sigillite is always watching.'

'That has been my experience, lord.'

The primarch spared him a glance. 'I am within my

rights to kill you, Garro. This is a time of war, and deeds done in shadows are dealt with in most harsh a manner. Is it not enough that we must guard against assassins and spies from the traitors? Must I protect myself from my own side as well?'

'I would not presume to say.'

Dorn's expression shifted. 'Of course not. You are a loyal son of the Imperium. My issue is with he who gives your orders. Your only error is that your loyalty may be misplaced. *Or misused.*' At last Dorn turned to look directly at him, starlight throwing the hard lines of his face into stark relief. 'My sons make me proud. Tell me, are you proud of *your* duties, Nathaniel? Does it elevate your spirit to be a soldier in a silent war, out in the darkness chasing deeds of questionable provenance?'

'I do... what must be done.' Garro faltered on the words, as Dorn's pitiless gaze bored into him.

'Malcador and I...' Dorn paused, his gaze turning inwards. 'We want the same things. In a way, we fight the same battles and we prepare the same ground. But *his methods!* I cannot countenance them. And it saddens me to see a warrior of your calibre at his side. He will put you on a certain path, captain, if you allow it. And it will lead you to ruin, to the fulfilment of his need and no other.'

'The Sigillite serves the Imperium,' said Garro, echoing words that Malcador himself had once uttered.

'But does he serve the Emperor?' said Dorn.

Garro's throat felt arid. 'I am clear-eyed in this. I know the dimensions of the bargain I have struck.'

'Do you?' Dorn's simple question thundered through the canyons of Garro's soul.

Did he really understand? The uncertainties that had

been building since Calth and the incident in the Kuiper Belt could not be ignored. It was as if the primarch's words had removed a veil from Garro's gaze and forced him to see them, straight on and without obfuscation.

'Question yourself, Nathaniel,' Dorn went on. 'Question *him*. Ask why he keeps so much from you.'

A chill crept through Garro's bones. 'What do you mean, lord?'

'I will show you.' Dorn walked to the chart table and picked out a particular data tablet. 'Do you know where your brothers are, Nathaniel? Not the traitors. I speak of the ones who risked all to come with you.'

'The Seventy?' He was describing Garro's own command cadre, the warriors who had joined him in his desperate race to warn Terra of Horus' betrayal at Isstvan V. 'They remain at the Emperor's pleasure in the Somnus Citadel on Luna, in the care of the Silent Sisterhood.'

Dorn shook his head. 'Not all of them.'

He handed the tablet over, and Garro scanned the words there, his eyes widening as he read on. 'What is this?'

'Intelligence comes to the Imperial Fists as we fortify and prepare. I had considered directing my sons to investigate the report you have in your hand. But now you are here, and perhaps it is better that you look into the matter personally.' Dorn studied him for a moment. 'And when you do, ask yourself why Malcador did not speak to you of it.' The primarch walked away, towards the towering windows looking out onto the blackness of space. When he spoke again, it was with stern, unbending conviction, his brief flash of liberality extinguished. 'Do not test the tolerance of the Imperial Fists again. That warning is to you and to Malcador. Make it clear to him.' He waved him away. 'You are dismissed, Captain Garro. Take what I have given you and leave.'

Garro bowed, his thoughts churning, but still he hesitated a moment longer. He could not leave without one more thing said. 'Lord Dorn… Your warrior, Massak. He has great insight that goes unheeded in his confinement. There will come a time when you will have use for him and his fellow Librarians once again.'

'I value Massak's insight more than you can know.' Dorn spoke over him. 'The Sigillite believes I act out of ignorance and fear. He does not understand. The Librarians are *precisely* where they need to be.'

Garro's brow creased. 'Locked in a vault, in the bowels of your fortress? They mark time like condemned men waiting for the scaffold.'

'No,' Dorn corrected. 'They stand *ready*. Close at hand, in the heart of my Legion. I will choose the right moment, Death Guard. Not you. Not Malcador.'

'You ask much of them, my lord.'

The father of the Imperial Fists nodded grimly. 'These times ask much of us all.'

EIGHT

Errant
Ashes of fealty
Consequences

THE LONG IRON hall was filled with shadows.

In the echoing space, nothing human moved. No one had the courage to enter, for fear of what lay beyond. No one dared to set foot inside, to take a breath of the air within and challenge fortune.

At least, no *man* dared.

Concealed in the gloom, a heavy hatchway opened with a hissing chorus of pressure-locks and two hulking figures entered the chamber. These were not men. They towered over common humans, these scions of battle. Once, both of them had been proud to stand amongst the Emperor's Legiones Astartes. Brothers in conflict, comrades against adversity. Now fate had set them upon separate paths.

One was clad in wargear the colour of storms, adorned with a golden eagle cuirass, his helm mag-locked at his waist and his sword at his back. Nathaniel Garro, Knight Errant and Agentia Primus of the Regent of Terra. The other, a former warrior stripped of his armour, weapons and the desire for war. Meric Voyen in his robes, once an Apothecary of the Death Guard Legion and now a soul in search of peace.

'Captain! Please, no! *Wait!*' cried Voyen, trying in vain to halt Garro's furious strides.

'I will not,' came the reply.

'Stop! I beg of you, let me explain!'

Garro shook his head angrily. 'Nothing you say will sway me.'

'*Nathaniel!*' The shout echoed through the chamber, with such force behind it that both of them halted.

Garro looked down at the hand that Voyen had placed on his vambrace, a warning flashing in his eyes. 'Step back, brother. *Now.*'

'Hear me out,' said the former legionary. 'That is all I ask.'

'There is no explanation you can voice, Meric.' Garro's ire ebbed, replaced by a sadness. 'I am disappointed in you.'

'I have not done this for your approval, my captain,' Voyen said stiffly. 'I did it for a greater good. For our battle-brothers and our Legion.'

Garro's scowl returned. 'The Death Guard are no longer our Legion. They broke that faith when Mortarion turned against the Emperor.'

'We can bring them back.' Voyen's words gave him pause, as did the light of certainty in his old friend's eyes. '*I* can bring them back.'

'With that?' Garro turned and gestured tersely towards the only object in the hall, a heavy cylindrical cryo-casket made of plasteel and armoured glass. 'A harvest of poisoned dregs and foul detritus?'

Voyen raised his hands. 'How does one cure a disease, Nathaniel? First you must capture the virus. Analyse it and conquer it. Only then can a vaccine be feasible.'

The warrior sneered. 'A vaccine? We do not speak of some malady to be treated by balms and potions! You cannot… *recover* from this corruption. I have seen it, at close quarters and with my murder in its fangs! I have looked this foulness in the eye and glimpsed the true shade of its hatred.'

'You are not alone in that,' insisted Voyen. 'I was on the *Eisenstein* too, remember? I know what happened to Grulgor and Decius! I saw the pestilence that overtook their bodies.'

Silence stretched between them. It seemed like an aeon had passed since they had fled to Terra. Garro and Voyen, and Solun Decius, Andus Hakur, Iacton Qruze and the rest of the Seventy, who dared to oppose their primarchs when all loyalty to Terra had been burned to ashes.

In the aftermath, amidst the airless wastes of Luna, they had awaited an uncertain fate. Warriors orphaned by their traitor kinsmen, trusted by few, feared by many. In that silence, their brother Decius had been taken by the same insidious taint that even now was undoubtedly corrupting the rest of their Legion.

Garro had been forced to kill Decius out there in the Sea of Crises, destroying the aberrant creature he had become. And perhaps, in the act, the battle-captain had known that he had been spared for something greater.

Voyen saw something different that day. A sickness that he could not turn away from. The Apothecary surrendered his birthright as a Space Marine and dedicated his existence to finding what Garro now thought impossible.

'A cure,' said Voyen. 'I believe it exists. It *must.*'

Garro shook his head. 'No matter how hard you wish for it, Meric, no matter how much either of us would wish it to be true... Believe me when I tell you that it does not.' His harsh retort robbed Voyen of any immediate reply. 'Now get out of my way, or I will put you aside by force.' He pushed past his comrade and strode towards the dais and support frame upon which the casket rested.

'You cannot know that,' Voyen called after him.

'What I know...' Garro tried to find the words that would convince the Apothecary. 'What I know is that corruption is absolute. It is subtle and constant.'

'Do you see that in me, my lord?'

He released a slow, sad breath. 'You kept something from me once before, brother. Your membership in the lodges.' At Garro's mention of the covert gatherings instigated by Horus' Legion, Voyen hesitated. Guilt soured his expression.

'I have atoned for my mistake!' He looked at the deck, chastened. 'I foreswore that clandestine pact when I learned they were the tool of the Warmaster's perfidy.'

'Indeed,' allowed Garro. 'But still you kept all of *this* from me as well.' He opened his arms, gesturing at the walls. 'You began your work in secret and hid it from the world. Why? Is it because you knew what I would do when I learned of it?'

'I did not think you would understand,' Voyen said hesitantly. 'I am a man of science, and I think in such terms. But you are...'

'I am *what*?' snapped the legionary. 'Do you think me a credulous fool?' He snorted. 'You know me better than that.'

Voyen eyed his former commander, choosing his words with care. 'You have always put great stock in the

numinous. I believe only in what I can see and touch
and know.'

Garro hesitated before the steel-blue cylinder. 'Aye, I
have faith, brother. But that does not mean I have abandoned reason. It is you who cannot see clearly. You cling
to the truth you were born with, that this is a rational
universe of immutable laws. You tell yourself you could
understand all of existence, if only the structure of it were
visible to you. But that is not so.'

'Then what do you say is true?' There was open challenge in the words.

'The truth is that we live on the surface of a great
maelstrom, populated by powers we can only begin to
comprehend.' Garro had rarely been called upon to frame
such thoughts to voice to others, but now he did so,
they came to him clearly. 'That we must oppose those
threats unto death, on that point you and I fully agree.
But if your only compass is the lucid and the possible,
then you have already lost! The Archenemy lies beyond
human constructs like reason and logic. To fight them,
to beat them, we must see past the veil.'

Voyen waved at the air, as if he were dismissing a nagging insect. 'If I can save the lives of the Death Guard–'

'You cannot save their *souls*,' Garro broke in. 'It is
already too late for that.' The warrior studied the container. Through misted, glassy panels, a dark grey mass
of particulate matter was visible. It resembled volcanic
ash, clumps of it accreting around objects that might
have been fragments of mutant bone or distorted chitin.

It was all that remained of the ground where Solun
Decius, transformed into a monstrous Lord of Flies, had
perished. Where he fell, Decius' ashen remains polluted
the lunar surface like a toxic spill. In any other place

but the moon's magnificent desolation, the residue of death would have spread like a canker. And now that material had been scooped up and gathered here for transit off-world.

Garro glanced at his former battle-brother, unable to mask his dismay. 'Where did you hope to take this?'

Voyen took a moment to reply. 'The moon Io, the Jovian installation. There is a facility there that rides atop the sulphur oceans. It belongs to a loyal faction of the magos biologis who rejected the rebellion of Mars. We could examine the remains there, in safety.'

He considered the Apothecary's use of that last word carefully. 'How many men died to gather it all?'

'Seven men perished in the recovery process. Each from a different chimeric disease vector.' The answer was a reluctant one. 'They were dead before we could get them to an infirmary.'

Garro frowned. 'And still you wonder why I came to stop you.'

When Voyen spoke again, his manner was different. Something had changed in him now, and there was almost a beseeching tone to his words.

'You left us behind, Nathaniel, those who remained of the Seventy. You went away and you were given purpose. But not the rest of us. *Not I.*'

Somehow, the Apothecary seemed to have been lessened by his experiences. He went on.

'So I forged my own. We legionaries are functionally immortal, are we not? Away from battle and threat of violent demise we might live for millennia. So I chose to rededicate my existence to finding a cure for that hideous living death that took our former kinsmen.' He met Garro's piercing gaze. 'I need this purpose. Without it,

I am only the cast-off son of a Traitor Legion. Lost and forgotten, distrusted and maligned. I have no Knight Errant's armour, no sanction from Malcador the Sigillite to elevate me. I have only my hope. You understand that, don't you?'

Garro did, only too well. 'More than you can know, my old friend.' He shook his head. 'And that is why, for the final time, I refuse you. This must end here.'

'If you do this,' cried Voyen, 'then there will be no chance of redemption. You will doom the name of the Death Guard to live in infamy for thousands of years!'

'It is our gene-father, Lord Mortarion, who made that choice, Meric,' Garro said sadly. 'Not I.'

The shadows were at their heaviest here, thick curtains of night-dark that made the wide space of the hall seem enclosed and oppressive. As Garro reached for the casket, he felt the flesh on the back of his neck prickle. That innate war-sense, bred into him through the gene-works of the Legions, came alive. An intuition he could not name, an animal impulse warning him of a danger as yet unrevealed.

His armoured fingers touched the curved lid and he knew that something was amiss. There, along the seam that held the casket closed, the thick brass mag-locks that should have each been sealed tight were hanging wide, the latches like slack jaws.

'It is *open...*'

Garro heard the shock in his old friend's voice. 'What? That's impossible!' But then the low moan of a deathly, unearthly wind blotted out his words.

Suddenly the air tasted of foetor and rancid meat. A wave of slaughterhouse stench and decay arose, potent enough to curdle the air in Garro's lungs and repulse even a legionary's constitution. He took an involuntary step backwards, though some instinct made him reach out towards the black, shadow-wreathed stanchions supporting the casket. Light moved strangely upon the iron pillars, almost as if it were being absorbed by the dark, and Garro had the sudden sense that the unnatural shadows he saw were not falling from the play of illumination and shade.

Darkness coated everything in a fathomless slick. His fingers scraped at the metal and encountered thousands of tiny, chitinous forms, clustered so densely together that they were a thick, black mantle.

The shadows were flies.

Hidden in the gloom, the silent, unmoving insects now exploded into horrible, freakish life. Their tiny mutant wings were sharper than razors, their warp-tainted mandibles wet with acidic venom, and they craved warm flesh and spilled blood. The droning swarm rose up and attacked them both in a shimmering black tempest.

'*Back!*' shouted Garro. 'Get back!'

Voyen stumbled as the cloud of insects writhed and turned in the air. 'Where did these things come from? There was no living organic matter in the ashes. They could not have come from the casket. This chamber was hermetically sealed. Nothing can get in or out. *Nothing!*'

'They came from the immaterium,' Garro shot back. 'They are born out of madness and corruption. Do you see now, Meric? This is the nature of the enemy.'

'The warp?' The Apothecary struggled to grasp the reality of it.

'Aye,' he said grimly, and he shoved Voyen towards the heavy airlock hatch behind them. 'Go! You are unprotected! These things will feast on the meat of you, make your body a nest for their maggot hatchlings. We cannot let the swarm move beyond this chamber. Go now, and seal the door behind you!'

Garro's former comrade nodded, but he could not take his eyes off the casket. Of its own accord, the metallic cylinder was deforming, cracking open, and a torrent of newborn insects flooded out, filling the air with a hurricane of glistening wings.

Although he carried no weapons other than *Libertas*, Garro knew he had to find a way to destroy these things. As if seeing his thoughts on his face, Voyen cried out to him. 'You can't fight them with a sword!'

He waved him away. 'Let me worry about that!' Voyen stepped over the threshold and Garro slammed his mailed fist into the hatch controls.

The metre-thick barrier of solid plasteel slid into place and locked shut. Garro reached down and donned his sharp-snouted battle helm, securing it against the dithering cloud of carnivorous flies. Through a portal of armoured glass, Garro saw Voyen's face looking back at him from the safety of the corridor beyond. The Apothecary's aspect was that of a man shaken by a truth he did not wish to face.

'I warned you,' he said, his words distorted by the helmet's vox. 'This is what the enemy is capable of. And when we try to fight them on a battleground of reason, they shift the sands beneath us. We are at war with the impossible.'

He marched into the storm of flies, but did not draw his power sword. Voyen was right; even with the weapon's energy-charged edge, Garro would only destroy a handful of the swarming horde. He had a different manner of attack in mind.

With each step closer to the casket, the density of the flies increased. He heard the scratch and snap of thousands of microscopic fangs biting into the ceramite sheath of his armour. The flies chewed at the flex-joints, trying to pierce to the plasteel beneath. They clogged the breather slits of his faceplate with a wet paste of their own crushed bodies. His helmet's glowing eye slits drew them in like moths to a flame, blinding him. Step by step, Garro felt his way back to the casket on the dais. A colossal mass of flies crawled and writhed across the plasteel surface, acid venom sizzling from their maws. For a moment, the warrior thought he heard the echo of Solun Decius' warped laughter in the buzzing of their wings.

He knew what needed to be done. In a way, he had known from the moment Rogal Dorn had handed him that data tablet on board the *Phalanx*. He blink-clicked an image-icon inside his helmet lenses and opened a vox-channel to a preset frequency. 'This is Captain Garro. Execute emergency protocol. Open the doors.' As the words left his lips, he activated the magnetic pads on the soles of his boots, and tensed against what was to come.

The blank bulkhead at the far end of the hall shuddered and then, in the manner of a magician's trick, it became a series of great panels that shifted on hidden rails, retreating back into the walls. Behind it, a blinding, yellow-orange inferno was suddenly revealed, blazing beyond the retracting doors, filling his vision.

The turbulent surface of Sol, Terra's great sun, seared him with its incredible radiance.

The tainted atmosphere inside the compartment was immediately blown out into the vacuum beyond, and with it went the creatures of the swarm. The mutant insects were simultaneously flash-frozen and burned to a crisp, and even their warp-tainted origins were not enough to save them from the titanic power of the star.

The screaming air howled around him until it trailed away into the silence of space, and then the only sounds Garro could hear were the internal mechanisms of his power armour and the steady pace of his own breathing. After a moment, soft alarms began to chime, and he felt the withering solar heat even through the dense layers of his wargear.

Crimson warning runes lit up across every read-out visible to the legionary, as the temperature and radiation inside the compartment rose towards lethal ranges. The heat burned off the dead flies and scorched the front of Garro's grey armour a dull, sooty black. He felt it beat at him, slowly boiling him alive. He had little time to finish what he started. With effort, he reached for the casket and took hold of it.

The intelligence intercepts that Dorn had given him were thorough, as one might have expected of the Imperial Fists. The primarch's Legion watched all that took place in the boundaries of the Solar System, and it was their agents who had logged and tracked the works of Meric Voyen and the cadre of men from the magos biologis on Io. Dorn's sentinels looked for anything that carried the slightest suggestion of sedition, and it did not surprise Garro that they made special effort to watch the warriors of the Seventy, the Death Guard battle-brothers who had become lost in the no man's land between their traitorous kinsmen's misdeeds and the new oaths sworn by Garro as a Knight Errant.

Even after everything they had done, after all that had been sacrificed, they would never be trusted. The Fists watched them and waited for treason to bloom, even as

Garro knew that it never would. It would forever be a weight they would carry, to realise that they would never be able to do enough to erase Mortarion's betrayal.

So then, what must Dorn have thought of poor Meric's foolhardy venture? The primarch of the Fists had given Garro permission to intervene personally in this instance, but he had to have known how that would play out. He imagined that the primarch gauged this as some kind of test. The legionary had no doubt that Dorn would not have given him this opportunity without planning in an alternative.

There were warships out there in the void, shadowing them. He had not seen them, but Garro knew Dorn's ways, and so he knew they were there. Ships with orders to obliterate this vessel and everything aboard it, if Garro did not end this today.

The Fists would have seen Voyen's scheme as dangerous, as a thing to be stamped out and destroyed utterly. Dorn's sons never chose subtlety where the application of naked force would better serve. Giving Garro the gift of dealing with this on his terms was an act of kindness, in a strange way, but it was also an act with an agenda behind it.

If Dorn knew of Voyen's desperate, doomed plan to disinter Solun Decius' warped remains and take them to Io, then so did Malcador the Sigillite. Yet the Regent of Terra had said nothing of it to Garro.

What did that mean? How, in all the complex strata of the Sigillite's scheming, did this circumstance benefit *him*? Had Malcador wanted the Fists to terminate Voyen's experiment? Had he wanted it to succeed? Or had the Regent of Terra known all along that his Agentia Primus would end up in this place, on this ship, standing before a casket filled with death and corruption?

When Garro had intercepted Voyen's ship out past lunar orbit and forced his way on board, his first act had been to convince the vessel's commander to divert course and accept no countermand of that order, save from Malcador himself. And as the ship turned away from Io and Jupiter, directly towards the sun, Garro had gone below to find his brother.

He pushed all other questions aside and concentrated on the moment, until nothing lay before him but the blinding oblivion of the great solar furnace, putting his full strength into the action and tearing the casket from its support with a snarl of exertion. He lifted it high, marshalling all the potency of his genhanced musculature and the power armour that encased him, and then he hurled it through the open hatchway and into the void, into the eternally hungry grasp of the star's gravitational pull.

He watched the blackened, twisted mass of the container tumble end over end, spilling streams of decayed and desiccated matter from within. Dead clouds of chitin glistened in the orange light, and the casket began to break up. Passing into the corona, it would be stripped down to plasmatic gas and absorbed into fuel for the raging fires of the chromosphere, every last molecule of its uncleanness burned and purged from space.

He turned away, chemical sweat streaming down his brow and blinding him. 'Garro to bridge,' he told the vox. *'Close it.'*

The shutters silently slid closed once more and locked back into place. The sounds of the world outside Garro's armour returned by degrees as air rushed in to refill the chamber, and at length he removed his helmet.

He took a wary breath. He tasted the oily tang of

burned metal and the ozone of machine-cycled air, momentarily grateful that the foetid stench of decay that had so sickened him before had been completely expunged. 'It is done,' Garro said aloud.

Is it done? The question in his thoughts countered, nagging at him.

FROM THE CORRIDOR beyond, Voyen saw Garro standing amongst the trace ashes of the burned swarm, and the horror of full understanding at last came to him.

All his hopes to search out a cure for the malaise he had seen in the diseased forms of Ignatius Grulgor and Solun Decius were gone. His fears for the future of the Death Guard, his wish to save his brethren. This need that defined him... *It was in vain.*

His own eyes had shown him the truth. Garro was right. This new war was a thing of daemonic powers and foul magicks as much as guns and blades, and if that were so...

'How can a rational soul face *that?*' He faltered over the words as a wave of weakness came over him. Voyen felt his throat tighten and a sudden burning in his blood. A stinging sensation made the flesh of his forearm twitch and he pulled back the cuff of his robes, part of him knowing, fearing what he would see.

There, on his skin, was the reddening mark of an insect bite and, already forming, a trio of tiny sores. He thought he heard the tinny, high-pitched buzzing of a fly, and his hand came up to swat at the air around him.

Voyen struggled for breath and turned in place as an alien, unfamiliar sensation filled him. Horror welled up inside like bitter bile. He shot a look back towards the sealed hatch and through the armoured glass panel, the

Apothecary saw Garro standing on the far side of the door. His former commander was watching him with a sorrowful expression. Voyen tried to speak, but no words formed.

Garro's eyes were bleak. 'Show me,' he ordered, his words muffled through the thick glass.

Voyen shook his head, raising up his hand, almost as a gesture of warding. He felt the skin on his palm tighten, and he turned it to his face. There were more lesions and puckered flesh there, red and damp and newly formed.

Garro looked away, saying something into his vox-bead. A moment later, Voyen heard the grinding of gears at the far end of the corridor as a thick pressure door emerged out of the deck and rose to seal off the length of the passage where he stood. He looked back towards Garro in time to see his old friend don his battle helmet once more. Then the door between the two of them began to slide open.

The Apothecary reached for his courage and stood his ground.

RUBIO FOUND HIM in the Citadel's landing bay, surrounded by a quartet of patient gun-servitors, all with their cannons at rest but all in active pre-combat mode.

Garro sat in the middle of the machine-slaves upon an overturned cargo crate, the hard lunar light glistening off his armour. Another work serf was slump-shouldered and inert by his side, dirty with the remains of whatever it had cleaned off the other legionary's wargear. The stringent odour of powerful chemical purgative agents lingered in the air. For his part, Garro was working at the blade of *Libertas*, the weapon lying across his lap. With metered, careful motions, he cleaned the sword, dabbing away spots of what could only be dried blood.

Where have you been? Rubio wanted to ask the question, but he hesitated. It was unlike Garro to simply disappear without a word for days on end, and yet that was exactly what he had done, commandeering a Stormbird with no flight plan and no mission at hand.

Instead he asked the question that preceded. 'What happened to you on the *Phalanx?*'

Garro looked up at him, then back to the sword's blade. 'You know. The mission was a failure. The Imperial Fists Librarian, Massak. I could not convince him to join us.'

'There's more to it than that,' Rubio countered. He sensed the shape of Garro's surface thoughts, even without having to actively probe his mind. '*Dorn.* Dorn spoke to you.'

'Stay out,' Garro said quietly, the warning gentle but no less firm for it.

The psyker tried a different tack. 'Since you came for me on Calth, over these past months we have grown to respect one another, yes? To share the trust of brothers in battle.'

'Of course.'

'But you cannot speak to me of where you have been?'

'It was a duty,' he replied, cleaning the blade with infinite care. The naked crystalline-metal edge shone, all traces of spilled blood gone from its surface. 'One that is complete now. You need not concern yourself over it.'

Rubio hesitated. He knew of no such mission that had come from the Sigillite, but the changing shade of Garro's aura became marbled with a deep sorrow and suddenly the Codicier felt a stab of guilt, as if he were trespassing upon some private moment.

'What do you want of me, kinsman?' The other

legionary looked up at him, before returning the sword to its scabbard.

'Orders,' said Rubio, nodding to himself. 'There is news from Malcador's prognosticators. They predict a brief path will be opening through the Ruinstorm, a treacherous one to be sure, but enough to serve our purposes. It is time. Time to venture out and find the last of them.'

Garro rose to his feet and the gun-servitors flinched in unison, but then after a moment, the machine-slaves seemed to think better of it and they retreated away across the landing bay, their smaller servile cohort trailing behind.

There was an uncountable distance in the other warrior's gaze, a melancholy that Rubio had sometimes glimpsed but never seen fully revealed until this moment. 'The last,' he echoed, and in those words the psyker knew he was counting a cost that would never be repaid. 'If only that were truly so.'

Rubio found he had no reply to that, so he gestured across the bay to where a fuelled and ready drop-ship sat waiting for them. 'Command is yours, battle-captain,' he said, deliberately using the old Death Guard honorific. 'Give the word.'

But Garro said nothing, only marching away towards the Stormbird.

With each step he took, his grim demeanour shifted until only his resolute and familiar aspect remained.

NINE

Blighted
The hound at the gates of hell
Lair of the beast

MOVING ACROSS THE stars like a line of flame, the rebellion of the turncoat Warmaster, Horus Lupercal, raged on. Inching ever closer to Terra and the throne of his father, the Emperor of Man. Step by step, consuming worlds, shattering the great Imperial design. Horus, first among equals of the primarchs, the Emperor's gene-forged sons, had embraced treason. And in his wake, nothing remained but ashen, silent battlefields choked with the bodies of the dead, mute witness to the murder of loyalty and honour.

This planet was such a place. Here, the traitors had sealed their revolt with an act of the greatest betrayal, and left behind the corpse of a world to mark the moment. It was a charnel house. A cooling ember thrown from the passing inferno.

Nothing but death lingered.

From the poisoned, churning skies came an iron raptor, moving fast and low across a ruined landscape that had formerly been a magnificent city of great spires and ornate minarets. The Stormbird was the colour of ghosts, and no icons or insignia marked the hull to give trace to its origins. Alone in the wilderness, it settled to the ground in a cloud of dust, a hatch in its flank dropping open.

Three warriors disembarked. Each wore a suit of Mark VI Corvus-pattern power armour, the most advanced build of wargear yet created for the Legiones Astartes. They carried boltguns and power swords, but went without helmets, faces bare to the biting winds. And like their ship, they bore no markings. Sigils of echelon and honour, of Legion and fealty were absent – all save a stylised eye etched into the metal and ceramite. The mark of Malcador the Sigillite, the Regent of Terra and adjutant to the Emperor.

'Ready your weapons, brothers,' said Garro. 'Be watchful.' He took in the ruined vista, his gaze looking to the far horizon of the battleground. *Just one burned world among many,* he thought, remembering his first sight of such destruction wrought by the Warmaster's hand. It seemed like a long time ago. Much had taken place since then. *Prospero. Calth. Signus Prime.* A litany of worlds engulfed in the fires.

At Garro's side, Rubio knelt and gathered up a handful of earth, sifting it through the fingers of his gauntlet. About the Codicier's head, a subtle halo of delicate, crystalline circuitry gave off a faint blue glow. It had been more than a year since his recruitment to Malcador's duty, and he had yet to make his peace with his changed status.

Rubio closed his eyes and a shudder ran through him, as he allowed his psionic senses to extend and take the measure of the ruins all around them. The invisible traces of human souls littered the landscape, shades of them left in the ethereal like burn shadows after a nuclear detonation. 'This place,' he began. 'There is torment... And so much sorrow.'

'We know full well what happened here.' The third warrior bore the aspect of a veteran, the scars of countless conflicts upon a chiselled, granite-hard face. 'You have no need to rake the ashes and stir the memories of the dead.' Garro had offered Macer Varren a role as one of Malcador's operatives after his refusal to follow his kinsmen to Horus' banner, but in truth, the duty sat poorly with him. Quick to anger like all the World Eaters, he longed to be out in the thick of the war, facing his former battle-brothers. He lacked the cool detachment of the Death Guard or the stoicism of the Ultramarine. 'Why have you brought us here, Garro? What reason could there possibly be for us to visit these blighted wastes?'

'Because the Sigillite commands it.'

'Does he?' Varren scowled. 'And with ease, I do not doubt. The halls of the Imperial Palace are a long way from where we stand, brother. A long way from the memory of the atrocities committed in this place.'

The psyker gave a slow nod of agreement. 'All I sense here is death. Would Lord Malcador have us bring him skulls and bones?'

Garro took a deep breath and gestured around. 'The scent... Do you smell it? An odour in the air, dry and acrid? *Human ash.* The remains of countless corpses, reduced to powder, cast to the winds. It is fitting that we set foot on this world. Where this war began, there will be an ending, of sorts.'

Varren eyed him suspiciously. 'What do you mean?

These tasks we completed for the Sigillite, the conscripts
we have gathered...'

Garro silenced him with a raised hand. 'I will tell you
what Lord Malcador told me, in the Somnus Citadel on
Luna. *This will be the last.*'

Neither Varren nor Rubio raised their voices to question him, both legionaries reflecting on his words. This
ruined world would mark the end of their quest in the
Sigillite's name, and yet all three warriors knew in their
marrow that their greater purpose was still yet to be
fulfilled.

FAR ACROSS THE shattered city, buildings flattened by
orbital strikes lay like great fallen trees. Those few that
remained partly intact reached up, broken, skeletal fingers
clawing at an overcast sky. Down in the rubble-choked
streets, the voice of the wind was the moan of a dying
animal, but upon the crumbling ramparts, it was a cease-
less torrent of dust and grit.

From the haze came a twitching, feral figure clad in
blackened, war-damaged armour, moving across the rooftops to stand at the very edge of a broken parapet. He
opened his arms wide to embrace the windstorm, the ragged, torn cloak at his back snapping like unfurling wings.

'Shall I die, again?' His voice was a broken, cracked
thing, directed at the sky. 'Shall I step forwards, into the
embrace of gravity? Fall and be dashed upon the broken
stones far below? Shall I try... to die again?' He gave a
cold, brittle chuckle. 'If only it were so simple. If only
I could...' He paused, leaning out, almost as if he were
daring fate to claim him. 'You cannot take me!' He bellowed the words, a slow burn of mad anger rising within.
'You do not know me. You do not know my name. I...

I am become *Cerberus*, the wolfhound at the gateway to hell. I am untouched. Do you hear me?' He filled his augmented lungs and roared. '*Do you hear?*'

The chainsword at his side was as ruined as the rest of his wargear, as broken as his mind, and yet, like those tools, it too could still function. Could still kill. At the push of a power-stud, the ravaged blade stuttered into life.

The one who named himself Cerberus kept speaking, his torrent of words like a hushed litany, like a madman's confession. 'This destruction will never end. I have seen into the darkest heart of it. I tasted blood on the blade at the birth. I will see it rage on, and on, and on… For the future will only be *war*. I see the city as it was and as it is. A nest of traitors spun into treachery by the songs they sang in the night. I see the light of madness in my own eyes. I do not know the face beneath my helm. I see the dead and the dead and the dead. Palaces of corrupted stone. Steel rusted by hate. The killers and the killed. Crying out. Spreading their filth and their poison. I see the Mark of the Three. I know what it means. If nothing else, I know that!' His eyes searched the gloom below, desperate for prey. 'I am Cerberus, *yes*. I have been rejected by death itself. The peace of the grave will only be mine when the scales are balanced. I am the last loyal man under a galaxy of traitor stars… The undying among the dead.'

Then the warrior saw his foe, and he leapt into the air.

'And I come for you.'

THOSE WHO CALLED this world home had not been spared the fate of their planet. Tides of lance fire, kinetic kill rods and the vicious lash of bio-weapon bombardments took their toll. Life was ripped from their flesh, savagely torn away, and yet, even among the ashes of their dead kindred, some pitiful remnants remained. They could not be called human, not any more. The force that animated them was life, but of a kind born of horror and pestilence.

Bodies saved from instant death by happenstance or blind luck, these were the ones who had died slowly in the aftermath. Vomiting up black, tainted blood, choking on their own fouled fluids. These were the unlucky ones, denied the mercy of the quicker kills, their flesh intact enough to become host to colonies of virulent disease. Whatever remained of who they once were had gone. Now they were only vectors for the plague to spread itself, mindless meat-things stumbling in the ruins.

Cerberus hated them. He loathed them with a furious, insane passion that had no end. He hated them as he hated himself; for like the risen dead, he had perished and yet lived, but untouched by their infection.

The unliving fought him, their groaning howls sounding through the mist, but the warrior ripped through their lines like a hurricane, annihilating everything that moved. Death had rejected him, thrown him back. And so he would kill, until it embraced him once more.

'I am the storm's blade!' he screamed at them. 'I am justice! I am defiance and the oath-keeper!'

And in only moments, all of the creatures were torn apart, and silence fell.

'I am alone,' he panted, even as a part of him was longing for the next fight.

HERE, AT THE edge of the dead city, a great plain of blasted land lay churned and broken. Defence bunkers were cracked open like looted tombs, trenches filled with floods of dried, blood-laced mud. Garro, Varren and Rubio marched past the corruption and destruction, into the teeth of the constant, mournful gale.

'Those winds,' muttered Rubio. 'The sound chills the marrow.'

They navigated around deep impact craters, where lakes of toxic water gathered. The rusted, burned-out shells of Land Speeders and assault tanks lay across the silent battlefield. Here and there, the grimy skeletons of soldiers spared the mercy of death by vaporisation.

Garro's gaze crossed the myriad bodies of the dead. 'No sane man could look upon this place and not think it a vision of hell.'

'Hell?' Varren snorted. 'There is no such thing. It's a figment of old idolatry, nothing more. We have no need for a place of horrors beyond death. Horus makes it for us, here in the real.'

The battle-captain did not respond. A glitter of something golden caught his eye, in the lee of an overturned Rhino-class armoured transport. It reflected the weak, watery daylight. Garro approached and found the remains of a man, scraps of a grey-green uniform clinging to blackened bones. He bent down to take a closer look.

Rubio approached him. 'What is it?'

Garro leaned in, and with a delicacy that belied the bulk of his armoured hand, he plucked a smoke-dirtied icon from the cracked fingers of the corpse. It was a simple chain made of low-purity metal, and hanging from it, a two-headed aquila of the Imperium rendered in gold. It seemed tiny, lying there in the palm of his ceramite gauntlet.

'The uniform… This one was a soldier in the Imperial Auxilia. A rifleman,' noted the Codicier.

Garro knew full well what the icon represented.

Outwardly, an ordinary trinket, the aquila symbol was a touchstone for those who followed a secret faction within the secular Imperium.

Those who carried such a thing were followers of the *Lectitio Divinitatus*, they who believed that the Emperor of Mankind was worthy of godhood. These beliefs hid in shadow. They had no churches, no agency but those who believed. The Emperor was the most powerful human being who had ever lived, an immortal psychic of matchless power, and He had dismantled every religion in human history in favour of His great Empire. It was said that the Emperor Himself did not wish to be worshipped as a living deity, but His deeds had taken that choice away from Him. His true divinity was bestowed by those who had faith in His majesty.

Before the civil war, before the treachery, Garro had held to the secular dominions of Imperial Truth. But since then, the things he had seen, the horrors and the miracles... He had been challenged, and along his path, the warrior had found a new, secret faith. 'The Emperor protects,' he whispered.

A faint hum of power murmured through Rubio's psychic hood as he examined the dead man. 'Those words you speak... As the rifleman perished, they were his last thoughts. How could you know that?'

Garro frowned and let the icon fall from his fingers, and moved away. 'It does not matter.'

'Kinsmen! Over here. You should see this.' Varren was calling them from where he stood at the edge of a wide, low blast crater, and as Garro and the psyker drew close, both legionaries saw that the earth about the hollow had been fused into dull, glassy sheets by some tremendous discharge of heat.

Rubio glanced at Garro. 'A fusion blast, perhaps?'

The other warrior gave a curt nod.

Varren held a twisted curve of blackened metal in his grip, the fragment trailing broken cables and bunches of fibres that resembled muscle. His face was set in an expression that was equally sorrowful and angered. 'Another relic of the dead to lay at the bastard Warmaster's feet.'

Garro's breath caught in his throat. The fragment was a piece of power armour, a pauldron warped by thermal shock. The original colours of the cracked ceramite sheath were barely discernible, marbled white with dark emerald detail. But it was the scarred, pitted symbol upon the armour piece that, for a moment, robbed Garro of his voice. There, staring back at him, was the device of a white skull on a black sun.

The old sigil of the Death Guard Legion.

He looked away, and with mounting dread, saw what at first he had thought to be more drifts of blasted rubble were actually the scattered remains of legionary wargear, left to rust and decay. Garro's fingers tightened into fists, and he felt the mirror of Varren's cold fury rise in him.

'I know where we stand, World Eater. This place, this graveyard… This is where my battle-brothers perished at Horus Lupercal's command. Here they died when Mortarion – my own primarch! – gave them up.' He swallowed a surge of powerful sorrow. 'You said we should not stir the ashes of the dead, Varren. You are mistaken. *We need to hear them.* We must listen to the tales of their deaths. And then, on the day the turncoat Warmaster is given his due, we will be their voices.'

The Codicier gave a curt nod, the soft glow of his psychic hood framing his face. 'I hear them, even now. At the edge of my senses, like the rush of the wind–'

Rubio did not complete his thought. Instead, he suddenly turned in place, bringing up his bolter to the ready, aiming into the gloom. Garro and Varren did the same, ready to face whatever danger the psyker had intuited.

They came out of the smoke-haze slowly and carefully, making every effort to show no fear, and failing with it. What weapons they had were meagre and barely enough to scratch the armour of the legionaries. There were fewer than twenty of them, a haggard and dispirited flock. Young and old, male and female, their bodies malnourished and their faces hollowed with hunger and fatigue.

Varren was incredulous. 'Survivors? *Here?* And common men at that! It's not possible...'

'It would seem otherwise,' said Rubio. 'If they had made it to a refuge, waited until the bio-agents dissipated...' He trailed off, examining their faces.

'Do not underestimate the will to live,' added Garro. 'You need not be a legionary to possess that trait.' He turned to address the survivors. 'Lower your weapons in the presence of the Emperor's Space Marines, or answer for it.'

A mutter of surprise passed through the group. An older man in a torn military jumpsuit stepped forwards and gestured for the others to do as Garro had commanded. Doffing his forage cap, he took a few paces closer. 'Space Marines, you say? Of what Legion are you, lord? Your colours are unfamiliar.' His accent had the distinctive tones of a Cambric-born, a people of hardy stock from a system in the Segmentum Solar.

'You dare to question us?' Varren hissed. 'We carry the Mark of the Sigillite!'

'All you need know is that we serve the Emperor of Mankind,' Garro told him.

'Not Horus Lupercal?' The Cambrican asked the question with raw fear in his eyes.

Garro gave him a pitiless glare. 'The oath-breaker Horus, and all those who side with him, have been declared Excommunicate Traitoris by the Council of Terra. Now you will answer *my* questions. Who are you, and how did you survive the virus bombs?'

The man told them his name was Arcudi. He had been a deck-captain in the motive crew aboard a Titan, *Arc Bellus*, but the war machine had been crippled and beheaded early in the battle with the traitors. Arcudi explained how he and some of his men escaped into the city even as the bombardment began. They took shelter in a series of underground transit tunnels, moving to the deepest levels as the bombs fell. By sheer, blind luck they had become sealed in down there, buried under tons of rockcrete and stone. Many had perished as they worked to dig themselves out, and in the months that passed, the battle above their heads burned itself out. The turncoats had moved on.

'We have been crossing the great span of the city on foot, but the passage has taken a long time,' he went on. 'We move only at the speed of our slowest. We are searching for a way to flee this dead world. A ship, if such a thing can be found intact. But our morale and our strength runs thin, my lord. We endured such hardships... Such horrors...'

Varren's lip curled. 'We cannot help you. We have a mission here. Your circumstances are not part of it.'

'You would leave them to die?' snapped Rubio, dismayed by the World Eater's callous words.

Arcudi held out his hands in entreaty. 'Please, help us! If you truly are loyal to Terra... I have always believed, the Emperor protects...' Tears filled his rheumy eyes. 'The Emperor protects!'

'What did you say?' Garro strode over to the old soldier, and he stiffened in fear. Arcudi did not resist as the warrior took his arm and pulled back the ragged, torn sleeve of his tunic. There, about the soldier's wrist, was a gold chain with an icon of an aquila. Garro gently released his grip. 'The Emperor protects. He does indeed. And here and now, we three are the instruments of His will. You will come with us.'

Varren's craggy face creased in a frown. 'This is a mistake. We are not here to rescue a litter of wounded strays!'

Garro gave the other warrior a hard look. 'You do not know the letter of Malcador's orders for this mission. Or do you believe you would be more suited to direct this duty than I?'

Varren said nothing, and at length shook his head. Still, his soured expression spoke volumes. On some level, Garro knew the other legionary was correct, but it was clear that Arcudi and many of his group were also followers of the *Lectitio Divinitatus*. And whatever duty the battle-captain had to the Sigillite, his faith in the Emperor transcended it.

Arcudi saw something in his eyes and spoke to him in careful, conspiratorial tones. '*He* sent you. I prayed and *He sent you*. The moment we saw daylight again, I knew we would be delivered... If only we could escape the beast...'

'Beast?' Varren caught the scent of terror around the word and eyed the old man.

'Explain yourself, deck-captain,' Garro prompted.

A new fear, strong and potent, shimmered in the soldier's eyes, and he threw a worried glance over his shoulder. 'There is a revenant that prowls the ruins of the city, lords. A terrible, monstrous thing. It has been stalking us. I have seen it. A hulking form, wreathed in a tattered cloak, stinking of blood and death. It has already killed many of us, returning again and again to prey upon our numbers. I fear it will end us all before we can find safety.'

Arcudi's terror lingered in the air like the dust in the wind, and something in his description sounded a cold, steady clarion in Garro's mind. When he spoke again, he spoke to all. 'This revenant. If it is beyond you to defeat it, then we will do so in your stead. We will not wait for an attack to come.' He glanced towards Varren and Rubio. 'Brothers, ready yourselves. We will take the fight to this beast. We will battle it on our terms.'

'Every man who has tried has perished,' Arcudi warned.

Garro nodded. 'We are not men. We are legionaries.' He pointed back towards the ruins. 'Show us where to find this thing.'

IN THE CENTRE of the city, a building that had once defied the beauty of the heavens now lay collapsed in upon itself. A basilica of stately and imposing character, now reduced to a hill of dust-caked rubble and broken glassaic.

Inside the fallen structure, there were still cavernous spaces, slope-shouldered voids where support columns of marble had fractured but not fallen. Successive damage wrought by fires and the sluice of acidic rains made the bombed-out building a dangerous place.

Any mistake of footing could bring down a precariously supported wall or swallow a gap in a heartbeat. And yet the warrior returned to the basilica time and

again, drawn back here by a compulsion he could neither understand nor deny.

Cerberus picked his way across the rubble, in the
gloom and the damp air, returning to the place of his
rebirth. A silent, ruined figure in scarred armour waited
there, slumped against the remains of a broken lectern.

'I am here once more, brother. Cerberus is here. Will
you speak to me this day?'

There was no reply. There was no sound but the drip
of water on stone.

It was here that he had died. Here, that he had reawakened, buried beneath the debris and the stone. It was
here in this memorial to wanton destruction that he had
dug himself out, driven by a single-mindedness that bordered on lunacy.

'If you will not speak to me, brother, I will talk to
you. I will tell the tale again, and take the pain. Do you
remember it? I know you do. How many times must I
ask you to share the moment with me? I search my own
thoughts and there are voids. Dark places. Broken shards
of memory. Jagged, and harsh.'

He gave a low moan of pain. All attempt at recollection brought agony unlike any other. Razors, clawing
across the surface of his mind. Fire enveloping his soul.

And yet, he still tried to grasp it.

As Cerberus struggled to pull the memories out of
his tortured thoughts, the phantom traces of gunfire,
of screams, rose with them. He experienced anew the
clash of sword on sword, the shriek of falling bombs.
'I will see! You and I in these halls… The traitors at the
lectern… The hate in them! The Ruinous Powers! The
sword… This sword in my hand. Stop! *Stop!* You must
not! Stay your hand!' He collapsed to his knees, feeling

the misery of those moments anew in a flash of brutal, terrible empathy. *'Do not do this!'*

And yet, for all the agony he endured, his fractured mind could not bring him the understanding he so desperately wanted. No measure of truth made itself clear to him. The precious, ephemeral knowledge of himself remained forever out of reach. This *death-that-was-no-death* had done that to him. The betrayal and the fire, the blades and the bombs, the wounds they gave him bled out his spirit into the stones. Lost and forgotten. He lived through that moment once more.

'Betrayal… Madness and betrayal…' Each word was agony for him. 'The red god… And darkness… Darkness…'

He collapsed, fighting to breathe like a drowning man pulled from a lake. In that death, the warrior had been broken inside. Some vital part of the man he was had been torn open, the fragments of him spilling into the dust.

Ruined and burned, time held him in its cradle as the war passed about him. The line of flame moved on, and he was left behind. Discarded by the turncoats in the ashen wastes.

'Brother… Kinsman! Each time the death cuts closer, but still I am rejected. *You know why.* Will you not tell me?' Hand over hand, he dragged himself across the rubble. 'Death took you! Why not me? *Why not me?!*' With a sudden burst of furious energy, he launched himself across the broken stones, to where the other figure lay slumped upon the lectern. *'Speak to me!'*

But no answer would ever come. The warrior's brother lay dead and mouldering, as he had every day since the ignition of the rebellion. His kinsman's neck ended in a bloody stump, his severed head lying in his lap.

Blackened crusts of dried fluid surrounded the pale, bloodless lips. Sightless eyes, set in a ruined face tended by flies and slow rot, stared out at nothing.

'I am sorry,' he whispered. 'I wish I could remember your name, brother. Please forgive me.' The warrior looked down at his hands. His body seemed disconnected from his thoughts, as if they belonged to some other being. And in that instant, he felt the briefest touch of lucidity. 'What has been done to me? Who–'

A rattle of stones sounded across the broken chamber as rocks were dislodged by the shifting of weight. The warrior fell silent, sensing movement somewhere above, and the moment was gone.

'Who dares?' he growled, rising to his feet, drawing his battered chainsword and finding the answer to his own question. 'Intruders.'

NIGHT HAD FALLEN across the shattered cityscape, and the broken spires and toppled towers became a nest of shadows and darkened spaces. Acres of windowless voids glared out like black, predatory eyes, and the wind never ceased.

Garro led the others on their approach, but at distance the old soldier skidded to a halt and refused to go any closer. 'This is the place. The beast is in there.'

'Are you certain?' asked Varren.

Arcudi nodded nervously as Rubio studied the fallen structure. 'It appears to be the remains of an official building.'

'I saw ten men enter with intent to kill the beast,' said the old man. 'I heard them dying only seconds later. This is where the killer hides. On some nights, the screams of torment it makes are carried to us on the wind.'

Garro's hand went to the hilt of *Libertas*. 'Return to the rest of your group,' he ordered. 'Varren, go with him.'

'What?' The World Eater glared at him, affronted. 'You put me aside?'

The two legionaries locked gazes, and Garro lowered his voice. 'I give you a command, brother. Remain here. Watch Arcudi and his people. Be on the alert.'

Varren's reply, when it came, was cold and sullen. 'As you wish.'

Garro watched him go, then turned to Rubio. 'What do you see?'

The psyker studied the tumbledown remnants of the building, peering into the stone, measuring the telepathic resonance of the air around them. His face was lit by the glow of his hood's crystalline mechanism. 'I am uncertain,' he admitted. 'Emotion clouds this place like smoke. It is difficult to filter out the noise. So many died here. So many voices.'

'I only need you to find one.'

Rubio nodded and closed his eyes, the blue aura of the psy-matrix casting strange, jumping shadows. Garro felt the air tingle with a metallic tang, the trace of psionic spoor, a tiny measure of the immaterium crossing into the real world.

Garro watched Rubio work his art, the psyker's hands moving as if feeling in the dark for something unseen. The talents of espers, psychics and warp-seers had always seemed strange and alien to him, even in the days when he had fought as a battle-captain in the Great Crusade. The Sigillite had given Garro leave to employ Rubio's prohibited skills as he saw fit, with no word of censure. What that meant for the future, Garro could only guess at.

'Something... *Someone* is here with us,' said Rubio,

breaking the silence. 'But the shadow of the mind is unusual. In the past, I have read those recently dead and seen the echoes of who they were, like the rifleman. This is the same, but it is a mind that yet lives. Almost as if his thoughts are caught between life and death.'

'We shall find him, then, and learn to which extreme he lies. Come with me.'

But Rubio held out a hand and halted Garro before he could enter the ruins. 'And what will you tell this tortured soul when we find him? *The Emperor protects?*'

'If you have something to say to me, brother, I would hear it,' Garro said sharply.

The psyker's hand dropped away, but he held the former Death Guard's steady gaze. 'Varren was correct. Arcudi and the survivors are not our concern. Our duty is our sole focus. I learned that hard lesson when you recruited me on Calth.'

'I give the orders. Lord Malcador chose me as his Agentia Primus.'

'Aye, he did,' agreed Rubio. 'But this is not the first time I have heard you say those words, Garro. *The Emperor protects.* They have more meaning than you will admit to. And those aquila icons, too. They are more than mere trinkets.'

Garro said nothing, watching the younger legionary carefully. Was Rubio probing his surface thoughts even as he spoke? How would he react to learn that Nathaniel Garro, hero of the *Eisenstein*, chosen of the Sigillite, dallied with belief in a deity?

The psyker answered the question. 'It matters little to me what you may hide, Garro. We each have our daemons and our secrets. But be sure that you do not allow your agenda to come into conflict with our sworn oath.'

'That will never come to pass,' he insisted.

Rubio drew his weapons and pointed with his battle sword. 'Lead the way, then.'

TEN

Legion of one
Maelstrom
True name

GARRO LED THE way into the fallen basilica with *Libertas* held out before him, and Rubio followed close behind. His eyes narrowed as they picked out shadows among the broken stonework. Here and there, bottomless black pits fell away into the spaces below the massive building, where sublevels had collapsed into one another.

Taking care with his footing, Garro cast a look down at an electromatic device hanging from his belt, and frowned. 'Readings from the auspex are confused. The metals within the wreckage fog the sensors. Do you have anything, Rubio?'

The Codicier heard his own voice, as if it were coming to him from a great distance away. 'There are ghosts in this place. Be content you do not hear them.' The echoes of the dead were everywhere, thick as mist.

'What do they say?'

'What all ghosts say. They want *revenge*.'

Garro studied the other warrior for a moment, and

Rubio could tell he was uncertain if the psyker was telling the truth or mocking him. Ultimately, he decided not to press the matter and turned away, spying something in the shadows.

Rubio saw it too, a distinctly human silhouette amid the broken beams and cracked supports. He recognised the familiar shape of Maximus-pattern battle armour. Garro approached the figure, sword raised. 'You. Stand and face us.'

'It would be a horror if he did so,' Rubio told him, reaching out with his mind and finding nothing. 'No spirit remains in that one. He is long dead.'

'You are regrettably correct,' Garro allowed, moving closer. What at first appeared to be a bowed head was in fact the ragged stub of a neck. He looked away, disgust colouring his expression. 'This is no way for a legionary to be remembered,' he added.

As Rubio's gaze cast around, searching in the damp corners of the chamber, Garro examined the damaged armour. 'Blast marks here. The gouges are from the edge of a power blade.' He paused, then brushed at the surface of the cracked ceramite. 'The livery... Beneath the dust, the colours and insignia are still visible. This warrior was a captain of the Sixteenth Legion.'

The psyker stiffened, his preternatural abilities grasping something beyond Garro's ability to sense. 'The Legion of Horus Lupercal.'

Rubio's words were suddenly drowned out as a caped abomination burst from beneath the rubble at his feet. Buried there, waiting for them, it now exploded into violence. The Codicier barely had a moment to react before a snarling chainblade came roaring down on him. Blocking with his vambrace, ceramite armour meeting tungsten teeth with a flash of brilliant yellow sparks.

He caught the briefest glimpse of a scowling, furious face before a renewed, savage attack was unleashed upon him. The pommel of the chainsword slammed into his head, fracturing bone and shattering psionic crystal. He stumbled, fighting to regain his balance, but the assault was psychotic in its intensity. Dimly, he was aware of Garro coming to his aid, but his foe howled with laughter and tore an object from the depths of his tattered cloak.

'My tomb will be yours, traitor bastards!'

'*Krak grenade!*' Garro's shout of warning sounded as the fist-sized device went bouncing and skittering away across the uneven floor.

The cloaked warrior knocked Rubio down and left them behind, sprinting towards the tumbledown entrance. In a single, lightning-fast motion, Garro captured the grenade where it had fallen and threw it with all his might into the black depths of the nearest sinkhole. Rubio heard it clatter its way into the collapsed underlevels.

'Run, damn you!' bellowed the Death Guard, but in the next second Rubio was deafened by a shuddering crash of detonation. All around, the fractured walls and drooping ceiling surrendered to gravity and came down upon them.

AFTER MONTHS OF slow decrepitude, the basilica was finally destroyed. It collapsed in a last outburst of black dust and displaced air, falling into the abyss that cracked open beneath it. The earth swallowed the ruins, dragging them into the dark.

Varren staggered backwards as a massive shock-front of powdered rock and earth reached for him. He heard the panicked cries of Arcudi and the rest of the survivors, and ignored them, calling into his vox-bead, 'Throne and Blood! Garro! Rubio! Do you hear me?'

There was no response, and he watched, his boltgun in his hand, as the great flood of dust rolled in and engulfed the survivor camp where he stood guard.

'All of you, get down!' He snarled the order at the cowering refugees. 'Cover your faces and do not move.'

'I warned them...' said Arcudi. 'The beast comes.'

'Be silent, old man.' Varren bit down on a flash of annoyance at the old soldier's morose pronouncement, and checked his bolter's magazine. 'Stay down.'

He heard the flutter of a torn cape, and so did Arcudi. 'What was that? In the dust cloud–'

'I said be silent!' Grim-faced, Varren drew up his bolter to his shoulder and aimed into the haze, searching for the one errant motion that would give him a target. All else was forgotten. The fate of his battle-brothers was not his concern. All he sought now was the enemy he knew was coming.

A voice muttered, out in the dust. 'Traitors are paid only in steel, and you will pay for defying the Emperor!' Before he could react, something moved, a form like a leaping wolf or a raptor given wing. Varren glimpsed the dull glitter of a chainsword looming and he opened fire. The legionary saw his enemy come running.

'The beast!' howled Arcudi, as the armoured figure came charging in with a roar.

The two warriors collided with a clash of weapons. 'You are dead!' the attacker screamed wildly. 'You are all dead!'

Even as every instinct in him called out for him to meet this foe in rage and battle, Varren tried to halt the tirade before it went too far. 'Stop!' he bellowed. 'You cannot fight–'

'In the Emperor's name, I will destroy you!'

The words were ignored and pain lanced through him.

In the training pits of the World Eaters Legion, Varren had battled warriors of every stripe, from those pure of body and mind, to those driven to the edge of madness with lobotomaic taps and neural implants. But still, he was staggered by the sheer venom with which this new enemy attacked. Every legionary, no matter what his parent Legion might be, no matter what primarch he called his sire, fought to live and to win. This beast did no such thing. He fought like a madman, with no thought to survival. Everything about him was pure fury.

He fought as if he craved the embrace of death itself, but in his eyes, there was something *lost*.

'Damn you!' Varren bit down on another shudder of agony.

'Too late for that!' came the reply. He was pulled off his feet and slammed against a broken stone pillar. His bolter left his grip and Varren slumped, half dazed from the force of the blow. He turned, bringing up his guard to defend against any killing strike, but his foe had left him behind.

'This will do...' He blinked through the pain and saw the ragged warrior gather up his boltgun and work the slide. Then, he marched slowly towards Arcudi and the survivors, who quaked in fear at the sight of the cloaked figure, the bolter's wide muzzle turning in their direction.

Varren dragged himself back to his feet. 'What are you doing? They are civilians!'

No glimmer of remorse crossed the warrior's scarred face as he opened fire on the unarmed people. 'I am Cerberus!' he declared. 'The gatekeeper of hell! *I am justice!*'

'Not in this world!' came a shout. Varren lurched around and saw Garro and Rubio emerge from the haze. Wounded, but still very much alive, the other Knights

Errant had dug themselves out of the rubble and returned to the fray.

Rubio threw out his hands in a gesture of power. The psyker tapped into the quickening at the heart of his warp-touched soul and turned it to lightning. With a sweep of his arm, an arc of crackling blue-white power blasted across the debris-strewn ground and tore it open. The ragged warrior – this so-called 'Cerberus' – cried out in pain and tumbled over the edge of a new abyss, into black oblivion. All around, the earth shook and caved in, howling and grinding before finally settling once more.

By degrees, the dust fell, coating everything in a thick layer of grit and ashes. His injuries sending brutal jags of pain through him with every step, Varren limped to the edge of the cave-in. In passing, he saw the survivors tending to their wounded; there were precious few of them. Almost all of Cerberus' shots had blasted their targets into smears of blood and meat.

Varren spat blood into the new crater and glared down into it. He saw only shadows.

'Is he dead?' Garro approached, his armour caked in the same dark ashes.

'No. There would be a body.' Varren turned away, looking the other legionaries up and down. 'I might have said the same about you. The ruins fell, and I thought that was an end to you.'

'We were trapped for a moment,' said Rubio, 'but my gifts made escape possible.'

'It will take more than the collapse of a building to kill a legionary,' said Garro. 'What happened here?'

'Rubio's smiting blast struck true, but the stone beneath the foe's feet gave way. This entire city is nothing but layers of rubble and ruins, one atop the other.' Varren cast a look towards Arcudi and the remains of his party. He knew full well that Cerberus would have ended them all, had Rubio not intervened. He glanced at Garro, and fixed him with a steady gaze. 'That was no beast, battle-captain.' Varren had expected to face some kind of warp-spawned monster, but not what could only be a gene-forged warrior-born. 'That was one of *us.*'

'Aye. It must be so.' The psyker's expression soured. 'He called us *traitors.* I saw only a glimpse down there…' His gaze swept up to meet Garro's. 'Tell us the truth. Is this enemy what I think it is?'

Garro's expression hardened. The burden of the question appeared to age him. 'Yes. I see now that he is too far gone. He has been consumed by madness. What happened here has broken his mind.' He looked away. 'He must be killed.'

'What?' Varren felt a strange jolt of emotion. Was that… *empathy?* Despite the killer's crazed assault, the World Eater could not help feeling some strange kind of kinship with Cerberus. *We are alike,* he thought. *I could be him, had circumstances played out another way.*

Rubio nodded sadly. 'We all saw what he did. He ignored us in favour of attacking defenceless civilians. Old men. Women and children.'

'You did not look in his eyes, psyker,' spat Varren. 'You did not see what I did. Torment and blackness. Can your witch-sight divine that?' He struggled to articulate himself. 'My words before… I was *wrong.* He is a beast. A man become an animal. But he is still one of us. He is not a traitor.'

'I could not touch his mind,' admitted the psyker. 'The turmoil there is too strong, like a great maelstrom.'

Varren reached out and grabbed the battle-captain's

arm, his craggy face lit with purpose. 'Garro, heed me. We
have lost so many brothers to this schism, this damned
bloody war. A traitor I will kill without hesitation. But we
do not speak of a traitor. Our kinsman is lost. You must–'

'What I must do.' Garro snarled the words back at him,
for a moment furious at the legionary's demands. Then
the heat faded and the weight of the words seemed to
settle on him. 'What I must do is make the choice. It is
my duty, and mine alone, Varren. If I give an order, then
so shall it be. Do you understand?'

It took the World Eater a long time to reply. 'I understand,' he lied.

THE DAWN CAME slowly, the weak glow of a distant sun
casting only the most ghostly light upon the destroyed
city. The dust and the clouds robbed everything of shade,
rendering all things in grey. The only patches of colour
came from the spills of blood around the bodies of the
dead and the wounded.

While Garro and Varren stood watch, Rubio walked
among the survivors, the coppery scent of their blood
strong in his nostrils.

He found Arcudi dressing an injury on his arm with
a length of dirty cloth, surrounded by the weary remnants of his band. 'I can spare you a medicae pack,
deck-captain. There are bandages and–'

'No,' Arcudi replied, almost too quickly. 'No need,
legionary. It is nothing, a scratch at best. Of no concern.'

'As you wish. Perhaps one of the others, then? I see
there are some in your group with greater wants.'

The soldier shook his head. 'Your offer is well taken.
But I must refuse. Please understand. It is our way.'

'To bleed?' The psyker gave the old man a hard look; he

sensed what could be the gossamer touch of a lie in Arcudi's thoughts, but he could not be certain of it. When the soldier did not reply, Rubio relented and walked away. *Perhaps I should not be surprised,* he thought. *It was legionaries who brought this destruction down on them, a legionary who stalked and murdered their number. Why should they wish to trust us?*

Still, he could not shake a steady sense of disquiet. He came across a line of corpses arranged in a row, all of them wrapped in makeshift death shrouds. Compelled by an impulse he could not express, a half-formed suspicion that welled up in his chest, Rubio knelt by the closest of them. With care, the psyker took the arm of a dead woman and opened her sleeve, letting his preternatural senses guide him. His gaze traced the length of the pallid limb and found something strange.

There were contusions and scarring, as he expected, but the corpse-flesh showed something more. Lesions, of a kind Rubio had never seen. He was no Apothecary, but he had seen radiation burns and cancerous growths before. The flesh-marks resembled those kind of injuries, but it was the pattern that struck him as odd. Whatever afflicted the dead woman manifested in triangular threefold clusters, almost like a deliberate mark. Rubio examined another body, and then a third. Each showed the same strange infection, each time hidden away from plain sight.

'What are you doing?' He looked up as Garro approached, a searching look on the battle-captain's face. 'Why do you disturb their dead?'

The psyker showed him the marks. 'Have you ever seen the like, Garro?'

Even as he asked the question, Rubio saw the answer

to it in the other warrior's expression. Disgust, anger, hatred – all these emotions swept across Garro's face in an instant. Behind him, Arcudi and the other survivors had stopped and turned to watch the legionaries.

'I have seen such a mark before,' said Garro, with cold ferocity. 'And it is the herald of horror and ruination.'

In the depths of the warp, aboard the frigate *Eisenstein*, Nathaniel Garro and his battle-brothers had fought beings touched by the same threefold sign. They were the dead, traitors from the Death Guard Legion, bodies reanimated to new and pestilent life by some dark power from the immaterium. Those undying creatures were animated by disease and raw hate, driven by corruption – and now that same power swarmed here in the ruins, hiding in plain sight.

'You were not meant to lay your eyes upon the mark.' Arcudi's voice was solemn and full of regret. 'Now you too must meet the blessing of the Grandfather.' The old soldier looked Garro in the eyes and smiled. 'He has been waiting for you, Nathaniel.'

Then as one, the survivors threw back their heads and screamed. It was the same mournful howl as the blighted winds that scoured the surface of the planet.

Arcudi's skin sloughed from his face, a papery mask of decaying flesh crumbling into fragments in the blink of an eye. All around, his cohorts transformed too, any pretence at humanity falling from them in shed rags of flesh. Pallor burst across their faces, torrents of triad scabs bursting into livid, pus-wet blushes. They shed their disguise, revealing themselves to truth.

Whatever dark potential had kept them balanced on the edge of life now withdrew, and in turn accelerated them into decay. What a moment ago had seemed human became stumbling, moaning carcasses. At their sides, the cold-skinned corpses twitched and rose to their feet, torn and bloodied flesh hanging off them, limbs ruined by bolt-fire.

Varren came running, his weapon at his side. He was aghast at the sight before him. 'That sound!'

'A call to their kindred,' said Garro, drawing his weapons. 'We are betrayed, brothers... Curse me for a fool.'

'Combat wheel formation!' Rubio sprang back, closing the gap with his comrades. 'They surround us.'

Swords drawn, boltguns raised, the three legionaries drew together as the undead shambled forwards, gathering around them.

Garro raised *Libertas*. 'Destroy these abominations, in the Emperor's name!'

The creatures rushed forwards, into the flash of gunfire and the shriek of swords as the legionaries dispatched them.

They fell like wheat before a scythe, and Rubio let out a harsh bark of laughter. 'These few, they are no match for us!'

In answer to him, a new chorus of wraithlike howling sounded out of the ruined cityscape, and the rasping of decayed limbs on cracked stone grew louder and louder. Hundreds of the horrors stumbled brokenly out of blackened doorways and caved-in passages.

'You spoke too soon, psyker,' Varren grated. 'There's a lot more than *a few*.'

'We are the countless dead.' The thing that had been Arcudi wavered before them, pressed forwards by the mass of its corpse-fellows. '*Join us.*' From every shadowed corner they came, digging themselves from the rubble, rushing from the ruins, emerging from every shallow

grave. A horde of the undying fell on them in a howling
tide, overwhelming the legionaries by their sheer force
of numbers.

'*Never!*' Garro shouted his denial back at the creature and
Libertas sang in the air once more. The sword rose and fell
as he took the heads from the necks of the corpse-things,
but for each plague-ridden victim he dispatched, three
more arose to take its place. The press of dead flesh was
forcing them back, cutting off all lines of escape.

Rubio called upon his powers to cast bolts of snarling energy into the mass of them, but he could not hold
back the flood. 'They just keep coming!'

'Must we face every victim taken by the virus bombs?'
snarled Varren, his own weapons a blur of steel and fire.
'How can they die and yet live?'

'Cerberus,' said Garro. 'He must have known what they
were all along.' A thunder of shots blasted apart more
of the pestilent monstrosities. 'Stay close, brothers! If we
perish here, then we will perish together.'

But then a new voice joined the chorus of madness.
Like the summons of some mythic creature, the mention
of his name had brought Cerberus to the fray.

'I see you!' came the distant cry. '*I come for you!*'

The ragged warrior was suddenly there, a whirlwind
of blades, taking heads and ripping open torsos. The
undying monstrosities were torn apart, limbs rended,
skin carved by the spinning razor-sharp teeth of the
chainsword. The legionary in his ruined armour was a
black phantom, and he fought like the spirit of vengeance itself, never tiring, never faltering, ignoring every
clawed slash and clubbing blow upon his wargear, his
blood flowing freely from countless wounds. And still
he battled on, killing the dead, returning the pox-riddled

flesh-puppets to the bombed-out tombs they had crawled from. In his eyes there was only the pathological, perfect focus of the true madman.

In this deadly melee, Garro would take whatever reinforcements would offer themselves. 'The numbers thin, do not falter,' he called out to the others. 'We must survive. Our duty must be done!'

'Finish them!' Rubio barely got the words out before a mob of undead dragged him off his feet and to the ground. The psyker stumbled under a surge of corrupted bodies and they slammed him to the ground. He vanished under a mass of snarling undead, their taloned fingers raking at his armour.

But only for a moment. A wash of telekinetic energy turned the creatures into new drifts of ashy powder, and Varren strode in to bring his comrade to his feet, slashing with his power sword to behead any foes that still moved. 'In Terra's name, tell me there are no more of these rotting freaks.'

Rising, Rubio shook his head. 'The fight's not done yet.'

Varren turned to see Garro stride towards Cerberus, as the maddened legionary fought his way through the last mass of the undying.

THE CHAINSWORD FELL, trailing a rope of old, spoiled blood through the air, and the ruins fell silent again, save for the endless winds. All about him lay a mass grave of decapitated corpses, bodies in varying states of pestilent decay heaped atop one another.

Panting, the warrior who called himself Cerberus looked up, his kill-fury high and ready, and found a legionary in grey, unadorned battle armour advancing to him.

'Enough,' said Garro. 'The deed is done. The enemy dispatched.'

The words were enough to stoke the ragged warrior's rage still higher. 'You dare command me? Traitor swine! I'll salt the earth with your blood!'

Garro let the tip of his blade drop and returned his spent bolter to the mag-plate holster on his back. 'Lower your sword,' he said carefully. 'Don't force me to make the choice... Do not make me fight you.'

'Never!' Cerberus screamed his denial to the sky. 'I will never stop! I am the last loyal son! I will end all Horus sends to test me!'

'This is your last chance.' Varren's earlier words echoed in Garro's thoughts, the World Eater's demands that they try to end Cerberus' rampage without further bloodshed. *Too many brothers lost. Too many.* 'Refuse and you will die!'

'Do your worst!' He attacked, and if anything, the fury Cerberus had displayed moments before was now revealed as only the spark of the flame burning inside him.

As their swords met, clashed and met again, Garro saw this lost soul for what he truly was. Through a hurricane of blows, sparks leaping as metal ground on metal, he glimpsed fragments of the man behind the madness. Garro was tested with every attack and riposte. He knew in an instant that this was one of the most lethal foes he had ever faced in the arena of blades. Every strike, parried. Every lunge met in kind.

Warrior to warrior, they fought and fought. Time stretched until there was only the moment, and the fight caught within it. They struggled back and forth, seeking tiny nicks and cuts but never finding the defining blow. Each was the equal of the other; they battled on in search of the single fractional instant of inattention that would mean a death-strike.

Sword hilts locked, and suddenly they were struggling against their coiled, enhanced muscles. 'I know what you are!' hissed Cerberus. 'Traitor! Liar!'

'I know what *you* are,' Garro shot back. 'Like me. A legionary! The man the Sigillite sent me to find!'

'Deceiver! I am Cerberus! The wolfhound at the gates of hell! I am death denied!' Spittle flew from his mouth with every murderous shout, and his eyes were black pits of despair.

'Your mind is clouded, brother.' Garro put every iota of his strength into holding the swords in lock. 'Help me. Break through the veil of madness!' He met those dark eyes with an unflinching gaze. 'Remember who you are!'

'*I am Cerberus!*' Striking out with all his might, the warrior batted Garro away with a brutal blow and staggered backwards, opening up the distance between them. He pointed his sword to where Varren and Rubio stood poised to join the fray. 'Bring your bastard brothers in, if you dare. I'll finish you all!'

Garro shook off the flashes of pain in his head and held up his hand before the other legionaries could make their approach. 'This matter will be put to rest between us.'

'You die first, then,' snarled his opponent. 'They will follow you in short order.'

Desperation tore at him. 'Listen to me!' Garro drew himself up. '*Cerberus is a myth!* It is the name of a legend, a story, nothing more. It is not your name. It is not who you are.' Finally, in the instant between heartbeats, he saw doubt flicker in those depthless, crazed eyes. There was a moment of hesitation, and Garro seized upon it.

If he failed now, then death would be the only conclusion. 'I am Nathanial Garro, Knight Errant of Malcador the Sigillite.' He drew his sword to him, as if he were at a ceremony of arms. 'I am a loyal servant of the Emperor of Man. And you–'

The ragged warrior froze where he stood, and he seemed to falter beneath an invisible force. The gravity of his existence was crumbling as Garro watched. Whatever shell of madness that had hardened around him was cracking open. The trauma that smothered this brother in battle was finally loosening its grip on his war-damaged sanity.

'Who am I?' he whispered, sorrow and fear beneath the words. He looked down at his hands, as if seeing them for the first time, then cast around at the sight of the ruins surrounding them. 'What is this place?'

Garro gave voice to the name, to the last of the secrets he had been carrying since the moment Malcador had given him his list of recruits to recover. He spoke the words that would make this final one, the last of the Knights Errant. '*Your name is Garviel Loken.* This world is Isstvan Three, where your primarch Horus Lupercal and your battle-brothers betrayed you, and left you to perish.'

'No…' He shook his head, denying it.

Garro nodded sadly. 'Yes, brother. You know this truth. You have not forgotten.'

The scream that left his lips was a howl of pure pain, the sound of a man's soul being sundered, the thunder of betrayal's knife cutting deep into his hearts. He flew at Garro in a mad rage, his cloak snapping around him. 'I have no brothers! Only traitors remain! I am a Legion of one, and I will kill you all, until death comes to claim me!'

Garro opened his hand and released the hilt of *Libertas*, letting the power sword fall free from his fingers and clatter to the dead earth. 'Then do so,' he said, tipping back his head and showing his bare throat. The scarred warrior raised his chainsword, the roaring blade hesitating at the apex of the motion. 'I cannot best you,' Garro admitted. 'So I offer no defence. Only a choice. The same that faced me when I came to this world. If you kill me, you murder a kinsman, an ally. That single act will make *you* the traitor. You know this.' He held the other warrior's gaze. 'Brother. Join us, and prove that you are still loyal to the Emperor.'

'The Emperor…' He grasped at the words, anxious to understand them.

'The Emperor protects,' said Garro, fully knowing that his death or life now rested in the hands of a broken, damaged spirit. *But I have faith*, he told himself.

The chainsword's spinning teeth clattered to a halt and the weapon fell.

'Yes,' said Loken. 'He does.'

WHERE BLADES HAD failed, words and deeds brought victory. Garro reflected on this truth and felt a new certainty course through him. Even the deepest pits of madness could not blight the allegiance and fidelity of a true legionary, and if that were so, then there was still hope in the darkest reaches of the insurrection. Now the last of the lost sons had been found and Malcador's mission was complete, Garro allowed himself to wonder what would come next.

Before, with the names of those yet to be found at the fore of his thoughts and deeds, it had been a simple matter for Garro to put aside the questions that dogged him through his duty. The questions that Rogal Dorn's words had thrown into harsh relief, the questions he had silenced in himself aboard the *Daggerline* and later in the aftermath of Voyen's revelations.

He could not silence them any longer.

Varren's heavy footfalls crunched over the rubble, and Garro looked to him. He jerked a thumb at the drop-ship across the way, waiting in the ruins of a tumbledown plaza. 'The Stormbird is ready to depart.' The vessel's thrusters were already idling, and Rubio was climbing aboard. The psyker did not look back, and Garro could not blame him. He could not imagine what horrors one gifted with warp-sight would see in this place of desolation and misery.

He nodded. 'Aye. I'll bring him.' Garro turned to seek out his new charge, but Varren held out a hand to stop him.

'He could have cut you down where you stood,' said the World Eater. 'You took a great risk to save him from himself.'

'I had no choice. You were right. We have lost enough of our brethren to this war.'

As Garro walked away, Varren called out to him. 'It isn't over yet, Nathaniel.'

'LOKEN. TIME TO GO.'

He found the Luna Wolf standing at the lip of another sinkhole, staring down into the fathomless abyss, and for a moment Garro was afraid the younger warrior might be considering an end by his own hand. 'Where?' he asked, at length.

'To Terra,' he told him. 'And the future.'

Loken looked away, finding Garro. 'Why did you come for me? I was dead. Forgotten. Why bring me back?'

'You duty is not ended, my friend,' he said. 'In truth, it has been renewed and transformed, for all of us. I know only the edges of what the scheme will be, but I trust in it.' Garro hesitated. The words seemed hollow. Was he trying to convince his kinsman or himself? He pressed on. 'You are the last, Loken. The final recruit the Sigillite bade me seek out.'

'For what purpose?'

I do not know. He almost said the words aloud, and it took a near-physical effort to hold them back. Finally, he went to the truth, as he always did, to guide him. 'The answer to that, we will learn together, brother.' He offered his hand, in the old gesture of friendship and fealty. 'The true trial begins for us this day.'

'No, Garro,' said Loken. 'The truth is, it has never ended.'

ELEVEN

Hunted
Tell me your truth
Othrys

SHE KNEW THEY would find her.

It was only a matter of time. The pursuit squad she fled on the administration level was the first of many. Blind luck saved her from their clutches, that and the adrenaline coursing through her system. But others followed them, blocking her at every turn. Each avenue of escape was being meticulously closed off, one after another. The public shuttle terminal, the cargo bays, even the mass conveyors, all were barricaded by hunter patrols.

In the old days, back when this place had been policed by humans and not machines, she would have taken her chances and risked an attempt to slip past the officers of the Adeptus Arbites. But not now. She dared not pass before the unblinking synthetic eyes that tirelessly scanned the streets of the city.

Dropping into cover behind a towering service gantry, she took pause and made an attempt to compose herself. 'Panic is an unproductive emotional state.' Her words came out in panting gasps. 'Can't just keep on reacting. Have to *think*.' She looked up, following the lines of the massive cranes moving overhead, seeing the flashing motions of beam-welders.

Warships were taking shape in the titanic dock-spaces all around her. Bulky things with chisel-shaped prows that bristled with crenellated missile turrets. Brass-clad system boats built around spine-mounted mega-lasers. Autonomous platforms packed with kinetic kill rods. Forever adrift on anti-gravs miles above the surface of Terra, the untethered city of the Riga orbital plate had always served as a lathe for the Imperium. But the fall of Mars, and the struggle to control what remained of the Ring of Iron about the Red Planet, had changed much. The city's work was now the building of smaller craft for the Solar System's defence fleet, in vital preparation for the coming conflict.

Since word had arrived of the Warmaster's insurrection, the aerial platform had not known a moment's peace. The rebellion of Horus Lupercal against the Emperor had put the galaxy on a war footing. Riga looped forever on a slow course back and forth between the rad-lands of Merica to the region in Old Ursh after which it had been named. And all the while, the planet beneath, like every other Imperial world, prepared for invasion.

She had been born down there on the ground, thirty years ago, at the edges of the Atalantic Scarp; but Riga had become her home ever since her assignment here as a scribe-novitiate of the Estate Imperialis. She had come to love it, in an abstract way, to know the great floating metropolis as though it were an old friend. But that conceit seemed foolish now. The sky-city had turned against her. There was no place on the floating plate for her. She would be found. The tireless hunters would come.

As if the thought itself had summoned it, an armoured Thallax machine-soldier crossed a catwalk high above, its bronze head turning this way and that as it moved. A fan of sapphire laser light washed across its path as scry-sensors peered into the gloom. *Looking for her.*

Shrinking into the folds of her hood, she did not dare to move, to breathe, to exist until it was gone. One mistake, one slip, and they would take her. It terrified her to think of what would happen if she were captured. She might have been able to reason with a human. But a combat cyborg would only see her as a target, as an objective to be captured or killed, and the accursed artificials never needed to rest.

Carefully, shifting from cover to cover, always staying in the shadows, she moved on down the length of the dockyard. To one side, the edge of Riga fell away into a sheer drop towards open, polluted skies, and she kept a wary distance.

Metal shapes moved out there, endlessly circling. The hawk-like gunship drones governed by synthetic bio-mechanical brains cultured in vats, and they too were looking for her. She imagined that every machine in the city knew her face and ident code.

I won't make it easy for them. She rolled up her sleeve and exposed the pale skin of her forearm. Gritting her teeth, she felt for the tiny bulge in her flesh. Her subdermal data-implant was not designed to be removed by something as crude as a writing stylus, but she had nothing else to hand. Silently, she cut into herself. Slick with her blood, she levered the microscopic device out from beneath her skin until she had the glistening sliver of silicon between her fingers. Then with a grunt of effort, she threw the implant over the edge and watched the wind take it. That might keep them off her back a little longer. Long enough, she hoped, to come up with something approaching a plan.

The new pain from the self-inflicted wound helped her to focus. She feared that if she dwelled upon her circumstances, it would be enough to sap her will. A few days ago, she had been nothing more than a minor functionary, a scribe in the employ of the monolithic records division of the Departmento Munitorum. Now she was a criminal, declared Excommunicate Traitoris and marked for high crimes against Terra. The words had been spoken across the enforcer watch-wire for all to hear, but such accusations sickened her. They were lies, fabrications created by those who wanted her silence, and as the Emperor was her witness, she was afraid they would soon have it. There were no more places to hide.

For it was not just the machines that were hunting her. There was something else. At first, she thought it to be a trick of the mind, some element of the fatigue creeping over her. She was human and so she was subject to human frailties. She could not run forever. She would have to rest eventually.

The hunter that shadowed her did not seem to suffer the same limitations. She glimpsed it on rooftops when she had pushed through the crowds on the mainway, heard its weighty footfalls in back alleys. She caught a shimmer of twisted light, like rays of the sun through a rain-slick window. It was tracking her, cloaked beneath the mantle of a Falsehood. The camouflage mimetic adapted moment by moment, rendering her seeker near-invisible.

And now it was close at hand, closer than it had ever been before. Her blood turned to ice in her veins as she rolled back her hood. She peered through the dimness, towards a nearby landing gantry.

And froze.

There, a brutal, hulking figure twice the size of a man stood watching her, the rippling mirror-effect of the metallic cloak gathering at its back. An armoured giant, heavy with menace and the promise of terrible destruction, it resembled an ancient war god from the histories beyond the Age of Strife. It was not a machine, she knew that instinctively. Nothing mechanical could move like this warrior did, fluid and martial, as if born to the business of a death-dealer. In lattices of shadow cast by the moving cranes on the upper docks, the eye-slits of the figure's helm glowed green above a sharp, angular snout.

Every fear she had ever experienced, every night terror and irrational dread, paled before this sight. *They had sent a legionary to end her.* One of the Emperor's Angels of Death. Like some mythic revenant, it slowly raised one hand and pointed towards her. The meaning of the gesture was clear.

There is no escape.

And because she was only human, in that second her will broke. Reason shattered like glass. In its stead, panic rose in a tidal wave and she was suddenly running, heedless of where her path might take her. She fled towards a low-hanging gantry and scrambled beneath it, tearing her robes as she threaded through a gap too small for the legionary to follow. Bursting out the other side, she emerged into a canyon formed by lines of cargo modules.

The warrior's pursuit did not slow. He came crashing over the gantry at speed, seemingly too swift for something so heavy. She felt the deck plates beneath her feet resonate with each step as he bounded after her.

At the last second, she jack-knifed into a narrow alley between two bulk tankers, choking as she pushed through a vapour of spent promethium fuel. Beyond, there was darkness, the safety of deep shadows, and for one giddy moment she thought she might actually get away. But too late the price of her headlong flight was revealed. The shadows did not conceal an escape route, as she had hoped. Instead, they ended in a sheer wall of iron rising high towards the docking towers.

'Oh, Throne. No...'

With a crash of metal on metal, the legionary forced his way between the tanks and strode after her. The heavy footfalls slowed and the warrior drew a massive sword from a scabbard across its back. Power humming through the shimmering edges of the blade, the weapon almost as long as she was tall.

She saw him clearly now, the full threat of the armoured Space Marine revealed under the sodium-bright lights of the shipyard. He spoke for the first time, the words flattened by the hiss of a vox. 'You are Scribe-Adepta Second Classificate Katanoh Tallery.' The fact that he knew her name was strangely the most terrifying notion of all. 'You are accused of treason,' he concluded.

Her every instinct was to *kneel*, and she fought to remain standing, her legs trembling. She had never been in the presence of a warrior of the Legiones Astartes before, only glimpsed them at a distance or in the still images of a pict-slate. But now, close enough to touch this one, she knew that all the stories of their menacing aura were true. This was a gene-engineered killer standing over her, a being created only for war. How could she ever have hoped to escape him? The turncoat Warmaster had thousands of such warriors at his command, so was it any wonder that one of them could come to end her with such ease?

But for all the fear that gripped her, Katanoh Tallery was not ready to die in silence. 'I am not a traitor,' she whispered. 'I am loyal!' Shaking, she managed to draw herself up. It took all the effort she could muster to look the legionary in the eye. 'You will not cloak this act in lies. I have done nothing against my Imperium, no matter what has been said against me!' Tallery turned away, her hands trembling. She pulled at a golden chain about her wrist, hidden inside the cuff of her robe. From it dangled a tiny charm resembling the great symbol of the Imperial aquila, the two-headed eagle that looked both to the future and to the past. She took it between her fingers, as if to draw strength from its noble form. *'The Emperor protects…'* The words became a prayer for deliverance. *'The Emperor protects…'*

The stagnant air lay still for the passage of long, chilling moments. Then, with a hiss of pressure-seals, the legionary removed his helmet. 'Look at me.'

She did as she was told. The face behind the legionary's dread helm was revealed to her. Flesh that was a map of healed wounds, old scars and the near-touch of death. *And yet, those eyes.* For all his fearsome aspect, the warrior's eyes had a kindness in them.

'The icon you wear about your wrist,' he said. 'The aquila. Where did you get it?'

'What does that matter?' Tallery's answer was bitter and resigned. 'If I am to be executed for a lie, what is any truth worth?'

The tip of his great sword dropped towards the deck, and Tallery felt him take the full account of her. There was doubt on that scarred, ravaged face. He was not what she had expected. The warrior seemed almost *human.*

'I am Nathaniel Garro,' said the legionary. 'Tell me your truth, scribe, and perhaps you will live to see tomorrow.'

A jolt of emotion shocked through her, a sudden ray of hope piercing the darkness. 'What... do you want to hear?'

'Tell me why you are here,' he said. 'Tell me how this began.'

IT WAS, ON reflection, remarkable how circumstances could change so radically after just one unexpected event. That was all that it had taken to begin the unravelling of Katanoh Tallery's well-ordered world – the breaking of a single link in the chain of fate.

The unanticipated ending of a life.

She had been deep in her duties, as was her way. 'Attention, servitor. Addendum number six-three-six-one-two-one. File Gamma. Protocol Omnia Majoris. Scribe Tallery recording – let it be known that the four hundred and ninth supply convoy to the Mertiol System has been diverted via the colony on Rocene due to anomalous stellar navigation hazards. This datum to be recorded and transmitted by astropathic medium to all relevant contact points, see sub-clause eight-alpha.' She stood behind her operations lectern and pawed at the hololithic panels that appeared and disappeared around her, isolated in her cubicle among all the other hundreds of adepts hard at work.

'*Servitor confirms. Scribe Tallery.*'

She barely glanced at the mind-blank machine-slave, her attention turning to new sheets of photic parchment emerging from glass capsules, each deposited at her terminal by the chugging vacuum tubes running overhead. The tubes were a complex network, resembling the root system of a tree as if viewed from below. Capsules bulleted back and forth in endless volleys, carrying all kinds of data from station to station.

'Stocks of class-two engine coolant modules for Javelin-variant attack speeders are to be increased from forty thousand extant to sixty-seven thousand, expedite imme-diate,' she dictated smoothly, as a chattering ticker-tape spooled out a physical record of her words. 'Refer and submit docket.'

So the axiom of the great Terran Administratum held, there was no more serious task than the logistics of empire. In an Imperium that spanned not just planets and star systems, but an entire galaxy, the business of maintaining government, of financing war and peace, of keeping supply lines open, was an endless challenge. If the warriors of the Legiones Astartes were the fist of the Imperium, the Navigator Guild its eyes and the astro-paths its voice, then the monolithic Administratum was the heart pumping vital lifeblood through its veins. Noth-ing moved from world to world, not a starship, not a man, not a morsel of food, without the great machine of the Administratum to manage it. And in a time of con-flict, the vital responsibility of this office became even more important.

Tallery gestured at the servitor to be certain she had its attention. 'Record that battle salvage from engagements on Zhodon and Hellicore is now cleared for repurpos-ing. Wrecks and deadships pending dispersal to primus forge worlds.'

'*Docket confirmed,*' the helot droned, and did as Tall-ery ordered.

This was her life, this kingdom of numbers, and she was proud to be a part of it. One amongst many ranked scribes on Riga now working for the Departmento

Munitorum, it was her task to see that the food, supplies and weapons passing through the orbital plate's docks moved seamlessly across the vast span of the Emperor's domain. It was a task that she was ideally suited for, with her natural eidetic memory.

'Next item. You will request a signal confirmation from the proxy server array on Luna, refer to–'

'Tallery!'

Her concentration was broken as a hooded figure came barrelling towards her at a run. 'Scribe Tallery,' he piped, his manner urgent. 'Your attention!'

Confused by this disturbance, the machine-slave dithered, glancing back and forth between the two of them. *'Please. Restate. Command.'*

'Dictation halt.' Tallery told the servitor. She gave a deep sigh and glared at her colleague. 'Kelkinod, you cannot simply interrupt me in the middle of–'

'This is important,' he snapped, putting the lie to her declaration. 'Stop what you are doing!' The impromptu appearance of Scribe-Adept Volo Kelkinod was never something that Tallery enjoyed. A fussy, self-absorbed man, he always seemed swamped by his official duty robes, in direct contrast to her rake-thin and somewhat angular aspect. Although they technically shared the same rank in the complex operational structure of the Departmento Munitorum, Kelkinod always spoke to her as though she were an inferior. He had an irritating habit of taking an interest in logistic operations that were nothing to do with him, offering so-called 'advice' that was never anything more than thinly veiled criticism. But that day, his usual querulous manner was absent. In its place, there was real panic.

'What has happened?' she asked, genuine concern rising in her thoughts.

'It is my burden to bring grave news.' Kelkinod's voice dropped to a conspiratorial whisper. 'Our honoured Adept Senioris, Curator Lonnd… He was found dead in his dormitorium this morning.

'What?' Tallery's mouth dropped open in shock. 'How?'

Kelkinod's hands found each other and twisted. 'The medicae say it was heart failure.' He shook his head sorrowfully. 'He did work so hard.'

She took in the reality of it, and frowned. 'Only in death does duty end.'

The other scribe shot her a severe look. 'And it does not end with Lonnd! Come with me. We must take steps.' He beckoned her to follow him. 'And do not speak of this. It is imperative that the workflow remains constant.'

CURATOR LONND HAD only become notable by his absence in the Riga Munitorum complex. Given to sequestering himself in his private chambers for days at a time, Tallery's superior was barely visible to those who toiled under his orders. His existence was only confirmed to her by the steady tide of advisory notes and information requests that flowed from his data queue to hers. Or so it had been until today.

The two scribes entered Lonnd's cramped work chamber and peered into its gloomy shadows. Kelkinod made a noise of distress and dashed to the dead man's lectern. 'Look. Do you see? We have a problem. Lonnd's work is piling up and we cannot allow it to bottleneck in this office.' He gave a shudder. 'The last thing any of us want is… *an audit.*'

'Agreed,' said Tallery, with feeling. The stringency of the Administratum's inspectors was legendary in its rigour and ruthlessness, and no one on Riga wanted to invite their presence there. 'We should contact the centrum office, then. Inform them of the situation.' She drew herself up, putting the sad matter of Lonnd's death aside, already thinking of what might be done to expedite matters in its wake.

'I have already done so,' Kelkinod said, with an arch sniff. 'A new curator will be dispatched from Terra to take up Lonnd's post as soon as possible.'

'Oh…' She suddenly felt foolish. 'I thought–'

'You thought I was going to suggest you be promoted to take his place, is that it?' The other scribe gave a sarcastic, snorting chuckle. 'You forget yourself.'

'I have more than enough experience,' she insisted.

'The man's flesh is not even cold, Tallery!' he retorted. 'I hardly think it appropriate to brush him aside so swiftly.'

'They turned you down for the post, didn't they?' The other scribe's face took on colour, and she knew that her guess had been on the mark.

He grimaced and moved to Lonnd's wide desk, gesturing sharply at neat piles of data-slates and sheets of photic parchment. 'Our late curator's work in managing the movement of military hardware, starships and assorted materiel through Riga's docks was… It *is* a vital cog in the battle to oppose the treachery of the Warmaster.'

She chafed at his attempt to lecture her. 'I am well aware of that,' she snapped.

'Then you also know that something as trivial as one man's untimely demise cannot be allowed to slow the processing of our data. The flow of permissions, certifications and other sundry formulae must continue, in order to oil the gears of the Imperial bureaucracy. Without that, there will be–'

'*Chaos.*' Tallery nodded gravely. 'Yes, of course.'

Kelkinod's hands knitted again and he showed a sly smile that made Tallery cringe. 'I have been granted authority by the centrum office to shift all of your current assignments to your servitor adjunct for temporary processing.'

'That half-witted cretin? I don't want a brain-wiped menial blundering through my data queue!' Suddenly, she had an idea of what was really going on here, of the true reason that Kelkinod had brought her to Lonnd's office. He ignored her interruption. 'You are now tasked with completing all of Curator Lonnd's unfinished assignments, until such time as his replacement arrives on Riga.'

She cast around, seeing a hill of paperwork piled atop the lectern. 'For Throne's sake, there must be two hundred incomplete dockets here!'

'At the very least.' He made a pinched face at her use of the near-profane oath. 'So, I suggest you get started *immediately.*' Kelkinod scurried out of the room before she could say more.

Tallery scowled, and by force of habit her free hand went to her wrist, to the golden chain and the icon hidden beneath the cuff. 'Emperor, give me strength,' she whispered, quietly enough so that the vox-monitors in the room did not hear her.

GARRO STUDIED THE woman as she spoke, sifting her every word of her recollection for the slightest hint of mendacity. He found none. 'This Curator Lonnd. Do you believe his death was unnatural?'

'No. Well, at least, I didn't at first,' Tallery said, warily. 'But now I look back over everything that has happened since then and I cannot help but wonder. Did Lonnd make the same mistake that I did? Was he silenced the way they want to silence me?'

'Who are *they*?'

She hesitated before speaking again. 'It is complicated, my lord.'

'In my experience, things usually are.' Garro frowned. He did not add that his own circumstances were complex enough without becoming entwined with those of a wanted fugitive. But the legionary could not deny that he felt a compulsion to know more about the woman and the reasoning behind the death sentence that had been placed upon her head.

Garro had come to the Riga Orbital Plate for his own reasons, troubled by motivations he found it hard to quantify. And now this; by rights, he should have left Tallery to the local peace officers to deal with and never got involved. But old instinct, that ingrained sense of the wrong and the unjust that was at the soul of his character, it came to the fore and demanded he be part of this. He had learned long ago never to argue with it, no matter where it took him. 'Continue, then,' he said.

She gave a rueful smile, and briefly the fear that marbled the scribe's aspect faded. Tallery did not seem like any kind of traitor-kin that Garro had crossed paths with before, but the warrior was not about to lower his guard until he was certain of her character. *The enemy excels at betrayal*, he reminded himself. He would offer trust if he could, but only if he were sure.

'I suppose a warrior of the Legions would think my work to be dull and inconsequential,' she began.

'We all fight the war in our own way.'

'Yes.' Her head bobbed. 'That is what I kept telling myself. But now I wonder if I have unwittingly served the enemy all along, and never known it. Have I become complicit by my own ignorance?'

In the clouded skies above the dockyard, a raptor-like gunship drifted past, suspended high on plumes of jet thrust. Tallery flinched back towards the wall, but the machine dithered, its sensors probing at the air, before moving on to search another area. 'It cannot see us down here,' Garro told her. 'The metal of the cargo modules disrupts any long-range scrying. Go on, scribe.'

She swallowed hard. 'The evidence was all there. In Lonnd's dockets. One only had to know what to look for.'

'Evidence of what?'

Her expression turned bleak. 'High treason.'

'So you submit that the curator was working against the interests of the Imperium?'

His accusation shocked her. 'No! Oh no, not at all. He may never have known what was going on. The poor fool... I wish I could have been as blinkered as he was. Then none of this would have happened.'

Garro looked up, watching the gunship recede. They still had time, before the machines would return to this quadrant. 'I would hear everything,' he said.

THE HOURS THAT Tallery had spent in Lonnd's chambers soon turned into days. For each docket that she pursued, another three were uncovered. The work grew like weeds, every assignment or protocol sprouting into multiple additional tasks that each required her careful scrutiny.

She ate sparingly, ordering menials to bring her rations to the chamber, leaving only to see to her bodily needs. Tallery quickly took to sleeping on the grox-hide couch tucked in the corner of the office, rather than return to her own quarters on the dormitory tiers. She soon lost

track of time, day and night becoming abstract concepts
in the windowless chamber.

Lonnd's data queue had fallen far behind, and it was a
struggle to drag it back onto schedule. But she worked dil-
igently to do so, knowing that a single erroneous docket
could mean the difference between life and death to some
distant colony world. A misplaced decimal point, and a food
shipment would never arrive, a vital reinforcement would
never be sent. Still, there seemed to be no end to it all.

And so it was there, in the dark hours before dawn,
that she found the first anomaly.

To begin with, Tallery thought she was looking at a
correlation error, perhaps an incorrect datum entered by
some other functionary who was not as conscientious as
she. An auxiliary ship, a cargo lighter called the *Shepherd
of Borealis,* was carrying the wrong amount of fuel for the
mission profile to which it was assigned. It was a tiny
mistake. One figure a point higher than it should have
been. Easily corrected.

And yet, something pricked at the scribe's thoughts.
The error nagged Tallery like a paper cut, raw and irritating. On an impulse she could not quite explain, she
put aside her work and looked at the document again.
She drilled down, following the line of permissions that
the paperwork had taken to reach Curator Lonnd's desk.

To her horror, the mistake was not the only one. There
were many more. And as she went deeper, as she looked
more carefully, the number of anomalies Tallery discovered increased. She considered the likelihood that it
could be the result of some programming error, something broken in the great wired network of cogitating
devices that supported the work of the Estate Imperialis
and the Munitorum.

But such a failure would have been rooted out immediately, detected by the cohort of tech-adepts employed
from the Mechanicum for just such duties. Even though
there was still distrust between the nation states of Terra
and their Mechanicum cousins from Mars, the legacy of
disloyalty by the followers of the old Fabricator General,
Tallery could not believe that they would so wilfully corrupt Riga's systems. She dismissed the idea as foolish.
The points of data were too well ordered to be random,
too careful to be destructive in nature.

The anomalies were indicators left behind by changes
that had been made, deep in the complex, ever-shifting
flow of information. *Changes made in secret.*

Her assignments fell by the wayside as she became
consumed by this new problem. What at first glance had
seemed to be nothing more than a handful of small
discrepancies was now forming into a disturbing, regu-
lar pattern. The errors were always in the same places.
Shipping dockets and bills of lading. Navigational route
advisories and scrapyard permissions. Secretly, quietly,
hidden beneath the everyday running of Riga's administration, someone had been using the orbital plate as a
base for a wide-ranging, clandestine operation. The roots
of this deed reached far beyond Riga, Terra and the Solar
System. It touched countless Imperial worlds, and it was
insidious in its ingenuity.

She found that fractional amounts of cargo bound for
the war effort were being diverted, each one painstak-
ingly concealed so as not to raise an alert. There were
shipments of equipment, materiel, weapons. Even personnel and whole vessels that were being sent away from
the lines of battle. *But to where?*

At Tallery's command, a hololithic display shimmered

into being over Curator Lonnd's great desk, and she set
a datum search to work, calling for destination data for
all of the suspect transfers. In return, a torrent of information flowed down the phantom pane hanging in the
air before her. She studied it for some clue as to the end
point for all the diverted shipments.

Each one terminated with the same fragment of information. An alias that was attached to nothing. A single
word.

Othrys.

GARRO SEARCHED HIS recollection and his mnemonic-
imprints for the identity and came back with nothing. 'I
know of no world by that name.'

Tallery nodded. 'That's because there isn't one. I ran a
cross-check with the entire Munitorum astrogeographical
archive, the Navigator Houses' Great Catalogue, everywhere. Nothing. And there is no starship, space station or
orbital with that designation, nor a city or planetside outpost. It was only when I expanded my search to include
historical records that I found a match to the name. It
was just a passing reference, in the piecemeal historical
libraries that survive from the time before Old Night.'

He considered that. 'It is a Terran word?'

'Just so. A place. Othrys was a mountain in what used
to be the islands of ancient Hellenicae. It no longer exists,
now ground to radioactive sand by acts of forgotten war
and time's passing. The references to that name are the
sole constant in the discrepancies I discovered.'

'Then it is a codename for the location where these
materials are being sent.'

She nodded once again. 'That is my guess. But I confess I do not know *why* it is happening.'

Garro had an inkling, however, and it chilled him. 'Weapons. Supplies. Men. Ships. These are the elements one would gather to build an army, Scribe Tallery. If what you say is so, this discovery is of grave import.'

For the first time, he saw something other than fear on the woman's face. She was elated that someone finally believed her. 'Yes! You understand.'

But he did not. 'Why did you not take this information to your colleagues, or to the Mistress of Riga herself? And if this conspiracy holds true, why are you the one named traitor this day, and not the architect of this subterfuge?' There had to be more to this than the scribe was saying.

'I didn't know who to trust,' Tallery retorted, defiant against his allegation. 'What I have revealed to you is part of a grand conspiracy, lying right here in the heart of the Imperium! I knew I had to act, but I was paralysed. Anyone on Riga could be a part of this lie – Lonnd, Kelkinod, even those in the court of the mech-lords…' She trailed off. 'You see my dilemma?'

Garro took a breath, and the scars of cold memory briefly pulled tight upon his thoughts. 'I have lived it,' he said, with plain honesty. 'I know what it is to face treachery in your own halls, among those you hold most trusted. But all the more reason to stand opposed to it. Deceit dies in the light, Tallery. It must be exposed, no matter the cost.'

She looked away, abashed. 'Perhaps if I had your fortitude, I might have found it easy to be so bold. But forgive me for my frailty. I am human, and I am fallible. It is hard to go against all I know.' Tallery sighed, and her next words were a declaration of belief. 'I am convinced that agents of the turncoat Warmaster have infiltrated the Departmento Munitorum. I believe these agents are working to undermine Terra's defences by diverting key materials from where they are most needed. They are weakening us, before the invasion comes.'

He eyed her. 'You speak of Horus coming to Terra as if you think that it is inevitable.'

'Don't you?' she said, tensing at the mention of the Warmaster's name.

It was not a question he wanted to answer at that moment. Instead, he posed another. 'What did you do with the information you recovered?'

'I did what any loyal subject of the Emperor would,' said the scribe.

TWELVE

Puppets
Bound by law
Decision

KELKINOD HAD BEEN waiting for her when she returned to the work tiers. Tallery imagined that he had been searching for her, by the florid cast of his face and the anger in his close-set, beady eyes.

'Where have you been?' he demanded. 'A summons was transmitted over the watch-wire four hours ago! You did not respond.'

She brushed off the hand that grasped at her sleeve. 'Not that it is any concern of yours, but I went down to the deep stacks. I had to check something.'

He jogged to keep up with her long-legged strides. 'This is most irregular. I demand you halt this instant and explain yourself.'

'What I have to say is for the ears of the new curator only,' Tallery retorted. Her dislike and her distrust of the other scribe had hardened into a full and complete loathing.

Kelkinod had gaped like a landed fish. 'He has barely

set foot in the building! You cannot simply barge into his chambers and demand attention.' He gave a snort of derision. 'After your failure, I would expect you to stay out of sight.'

'What did you say to me?' She rounded on him at the accusation.

'You failed to complete the tasks the centrum office assigned to you.' He shot back the words, as if her misdeed was the highest of all crimes. '*You have put us behind schedule!* Curator Lonnd's dockets remain incomplete, and that lies at your door, Tallery. You were told to expedite them.'

'Something more important came up.'

'More important than our documentation?' The other scribe scoffed. 'Are you deluded?'

She pushed past him towards the door of the curator's office. 'I don't have time for this conversation. Get out of my way.'

Kelkinod watched her go, spluttering with impotent ire. 'You'll be lucky if you aren't sent to count spent bolt shells on some backwater forge world before the day is out!'

CURATOR LONND'S REPLACEMENT had set up in his predecessor's workspace, and all trace of the previous occupant had been erased. The great desk, the couch, the sparse human touches about the place, all were gone. Now the chamber was featureless and gloomy, lit only by the faint light of a hololith table, and filled with the staccato chatter of fingers on a bone keyboard.

Tallery approached slowly, her eyes adjusting to the dimness. 'Sir? My name is Katanoh Tallery, I am a Scribe-Adepta Second Classificate. May I address you?' At first, the new curator did not respond to her presence. She saw a thin, drawn face emerging from a heavy hood, eyes fixed upon a ghostly, projected screen floating between them. She pressed on. 'Curator, I must speak with you on a matter of the greatest urgency. I have discovered criminality at work in this office. *Treachery*, sir.'

The motion of fingers over keys halted at her last words, and Tallery heard the faint buzz and whir of clockwork mech-implants.

'I have a set of shipping logs here from the eighth and eleventh dock sectors,' she said hesitantly. 'These are just the most recent examples. Curator, it appears that someone is wilfully diverting important supplies away from the war effort, towards some unknown destination.' The curator seemed to notice her then for the first time, augmetics clicking as he focused on Tallery's words. After so many days of bottling up the evidence she had uncovered, the scribe could barely stop herself from disclosing it all. She had to share it, if only to expunge the sense of toxic paranoia that tainted the information. 'I have imparted this to no other, sir. My colleagues here... They are not above suspicion.'

The curator said nothing, taking in every word, his thin fingers hovering suspended over the keypad before him.

'I could find no terminal ident to trace these alterations to their source. I have no way to locate the person or persons responsible. The only recurrent factor in this phenomena is the reference to a location designated as "Othrys".'

'*Oth-rys.*' The curator sounded out the word in a curious, toneless diction, showing not a flicker of understanding.

'There's no listing for that location in any of our records. Does it mean anything to you, sir?'

'Othrys.' He repeated, his head tilting gently forwards. *'Processing.'* She heard the clicking of oiled machine parts once more. 'No,' he said, at length. 'Nothing. Scribe Tallery. Do not be concerned. Resume your duties.' The long-fingered hands dropped back to the keyboard and the endless rattle of typing resumed.

A sickly sensation rolled through Tallery's stomach and before she could stop herself, she was coming forwards in a rush, disrupting the gossamer hololith as she moved to stand over the figure at the keypad. Reaching out, she pulled away the hood covering the curator's head.

He did not shy away from her touch as a normal human might have. Instead he sat serenely, continuing to work at his tasks as the hood fell back to reveal his true nature.

Once it had been a man. Years or decades before, this curator had been someone with a name, a life, a full identity. But all of that was gone from him now, excised like the portions of his skull and brain missing beneath the hood. In their place, there were fine mechanisms of brass and silver clockwork, tiny cogs spinning endlessly amongst networks of mnemonic crystals and data capsules. This thing that sat before Tallery lived and breathed as she did, but it was no more self-aware than the dumb terminal cogitator she used to input her dockets. Curator Lonnd's replacement was nothing but a mind-wipe, a servitor run by programs on punch-card wafers and remote commands from… *somewhere.*

The first trickle of fear rose in Tallery as her gaze found the thick cables snaking down from sockets on the curator's bird-like neck. They disappeared beneath the folds of his robe to emerge again near the floor. She followed them across the room, peering owlishly into the shadows, until she came to a hollow in the wall where the cables terminated. The curator-servitor was wired permanently into the Administratum data network, a body modification that smacked more of the Cult Mechanicum than the Departmento Munitorum.

Tallery looked into those glassy, dull eyes, seeing no recognition, no understanding. He – *it* – was only a puppet for some distant master elsewhere, and she wondered who it was that was looking back at her from behind them.

'Resume your duties,' repeated the curator.

'Yes, of course,' she told it, recovering her composure as best she could. 'You're quite right, I'm sure it's nothing. Just a rounding error or some such, no reason to be alarmed. I will do as you say.' Tallery crossed the chamber to the heavy wooden door and it was all she could do not to run.

Out in the office quadrant, she was suddenly aware of each and every scribe in their cubicles turning away from their work to look up at her. Some seemed indifferent, some fixed her with cold, measuring gazes that bore her nothing but ill will. She had no allies amongst her colleagues. She had never been one to socialise with the others between shifts, and that had bred suspicion of her. Before, Tallery had been indifferent to such petty behaviour, but now, when she badly needed support, she knew there would be none.

Then she spied Kelkinod across the far side of the room. His words were lost to her, but he was in animated conversation with a maniple of bulky humanoid mechanicals, the four of them towering over him. Each of the machines was detailed with a complex livery, a kind of hexadecimal heraldry that Tallery could not read. She

knew only that the symbols designated them as combat-
ant serviles in thrall to the Mistress of Riga herself, the
ruler of the floating city-state and a scion of the Legio
Cybernetica. The mistress' cyborgs were what passed for
law enforcement on the orbital plate, stripped-down ver-
sions of her cadre's battlefield Thallaxii. They tirelessly
patrolled the city's streets, dealing out harsh, dogmatic
justice to any criminals unlucky enough to attract their
attention.

Tallery's heart sank as she saw Kelkinod say her name
and turn to look in her direction. He pointed, and as
one all four of the cyborgs set their gazes upon her. The
glinting faces of the machines were featureless and utterly
devoid of emotion.

'Katanoh Tallery. Remain still.' The voice of the Thallax was harsh and grating. 'You are bound by law under
the authority of the Imperium of Man.' The other scribes
muttered in fear and confusion, many of them shrinking back into their cubicles so as not to be seen by the
mechanoids.

'There must be some mistake,' she insisted. If the cyborg
heard her words, it gave no sign. Instead, it advanced
across the room with its cohorts in lockstep formation,
iron arms rising to present capture claws and the maws
of electro-guns. She backed away, the action purely reflex-
ive. Her thoughts raced. Was this how Lonnd had met
his end, at the hands of these machines? Had she said
too much, foolishly betraying what she had learned to
the very forces trying to conceal it?

Tallery had the sudden and very certain impression
that if she surrendered to the cyborgs, her life would
be over. She was a good citizen, a loyal subject of her
beloved Emperor... And more besides. But this day she

had looked up to find herself at the centre of a whirlwind of distrust. If she were to vanish, no one would know about Othrys, the missing ships and the stolen munitions. That could not be allowed to happen.

'Katanoh Tallery,' repeated the machine, as it reached for her. 'Remain still.'

'I-I'm sorry,' she stuttered. 'I can't take the risk…' The machine was almost upon her when the scribe burst into motion. She pushed away from a grasping claw, and almost collided with a drooling servitor pushing a wheeled hod filled with heavy ledgers and data-slates. Reacting without conscious thought, Tallery grabbed the shoulders of the servitor and shoved it hard towards the Thallaxii. The thick books and glassy slates tipped from the hod and came down around the machine-soldiers like an avalanche. Their advance was momentarily blocked and she used the confusion to make a break for the corridor.

Pulses of energy lit the air as they opened fire. Tallery heard a choked-off scream as one of the other functionaries was too slow to get out of the line of attack, and she saw him go spinning to the floor, writhing as a discharge meant for her shocked through him.

'Do not resist arrest,' called the machine.

'Tallery, what have you done?' She heard Kelkinod cry out to her a moment before she slammed through a set of doors. Bursting into the corridor, she ran full tilt for the conveyor shaft at the far end.

In her mind's eye, she was plotting out the route she would follow. The conveyor would take her all the way down the length of the Munitorum tower to the sublevels. From there, Tallery could lose herself in the thronging crowds of people, finding safety in numbers. She would need to seek a way off Riga, perhaps by shuttle or freight barge, then find someone she could trust to tell...

Her plan crumbled to dust in an instant as a second maniple of cyborgs rounded the far corner up ahead and took up a position directly in front of the conveyor shaft.

'Throne and blood, no!' She was trapped, her escape route cut off, with the other mechanicals close at her heels.

'Remain still,' droned the cyborg's vocoder. 'Do not resist.'

Tallery cast about desperately. She had committed herself to this course of action, and she could not draw back from it. She knew that the machines would never listen to her explanations. They considered her a flight risk now, and she would be lucky to avoid being gunned down where she stood. The rebellion of Warmaster Horus had put Terra on a war footing, and with that change had come others, more sinister and repellent. The shadow cast by the turncoat was not just from fear of him and what he might do, but from fear of his father the Emperor as well. The Imperium's grip on its citizens was tightening as people imagined treachery in every shadowed corner. And they were right to do so. There were traitors on Riga, and they wanted Katanoh Tallery.

'I won't surrender!' she shouted, shrugging off the near panic and fighting to concentrate. A few metres away, light flooded in through a tall window of colourful glassaic, depicting farmers hard at work in the fields of some agri world. Without hesitating, Tallery grabbed the end of a short bench resting along the wall and upended it, shouldering it through the glass.

'Halt. You are bound by law. *Halt now.*'

Ignoring the commands of the machine, she vaulted

up to the window frame and pushed out onto the ledge through the broken panes, where the bulky cyborg could not immediately follow. Tallery had never really considered how tall the tower was. Not until then, as she looked down towards the thronging streets far below. Cargo transports and smaller tilt-jet flyers charted courses around the building and the habitat blocks nearby.

As a passenger skiff shot past, she called out and tried to flag down the pilot.

'Hey, you! *Help me!*'

But the skiff did not come back around. If Tallery could not get off the ledge, her pursuers would find a way to get out after her. *Surely someone will come to my aid?* A whole city's worth of sky-traffic was racing past just a few metres away; would they all ignore her? Was everyone on Riga afraid to lift up their heads and call out injustice when they saw it? Was everyone too scared to get involved?

Part of the tower's structure fractured with the force of a heavy impact from within, and a wide crack appeared. 'There is no escape,' said a synthetic voice from within.

With flawless logic, the relentless machines had chosen a more direct approach to Tallery's capture. Reconfiguring their talons into mailed fists, the Thallaxii set to work smashing an opening through the wall of the tower, sensing her through the stonework with their thermal imagers. A thick plasteel arm emerged through a rent in the masonry and grabbed at Tallery's robes, snatching at the material.

She cried out and tried to pull free. 'Release me!'

'Do not resist.' Stone crumbled and cloth ripped. She saw it happening, and Tallery knew there was nothing she could do to stop it. The stone ledge beneath her feet cracked and broke away, her robe tearing as gravity pulled her down. For one sickening second, she hung suspended by what remained of her hood.

And then she fell.

GARRO EYED HER coldly and without pity. 'You should be dead.'

'I thought so.' The scribe was shaking, reliving the terror of her ordeal. 'But there was a cargo flyer – it passed beneath me and I struck it as I fell. I grabbed on for dear life…' Tallery paused to wipe tears from her cheeks. '*I survived.* The Emperor protects.'

'He does. Fortunate for you.' Garro shook his head. Had Tallery really been spared by providence? Blind luck was more likely the reason, but he couldn't bring himself to voice that thought. 'You made the worst choice you could have. The window was a foolish decision. Where did you possibly hope to go? What were you thinking?'

'I was terrified!' she cried. 'I reacted on instinct. I told you before, I am merely an imperfect human. Not a fighter like you. This is all new to me.'

'That much is certain,' he allowed. 'Your choices have been flawed, simple to predict. It is why I was able to track you so easily. Count yourself lucky that the Legio Cybernetica's machine-soldiers are lacking in such insight. If they could think instead of just react, you would have been in their clutches days ago.' He frowned. The woman represented a complication of the kind he wished to avoid. But with each passing moment he realised with greater certainty that Tallery's dilemma could not be easily resolved.

'Perhaps this is meant to be. It is fated.'

Her words gave Garro pause, and he considered his

own circumstances, his own experiences. 'I have thought the same, in days past.'

She went on, finding her composure once more. 'I heard the warrant in my name being broadcast over the watch-wire. They have labelled me a traitor. My own colleagues are turning on me, that rodent Kelkinod and all the others. They all believe that I am guilty of treason against my world and my Emperor. But nothing could be further from the truth!' Tallery stared at him, her eyes ablaze. 'Do you believe me?'

The question caught Garro off guard. He stopped short of nodding in agreement, and looked away. 'What I believe… is that there *are* lies here. And traitor or not, you are bound up with them, scribe.'

'If you take me to the authorities, I will be executed.' Tallery's bleak summation of her situation was as honest as it was brutal. 'If the Mistress of Riga is part of this, she will want me silenced. If not, those who have manipulated events up until now will manipulate her as well. No one can be trusted.'

He eyed her. 'And yet you trust me with what you know, to make me stay my hand. How do you know I am not a part of it?'

She gave a quick, brittle smile. 'Because you would never have let me speak. That great sword of yours would have taken my head from my neck.'

Garro brought his weapon up from where its point rested against the steel decking, and to her credit, the scribe did not flinch. 'This blade is called *Libertas*,' he explained. 'The name can mean many things, among them "truth". And I believe that is what you have given to me.' He drew himself up. 'Do you know what I am? What it is that I do?'

She nodded. 'You are one of the Emperor's Angels of Death, a Space Marine. Although I confess, I do not recognise the colours of your armour. Of what Legion are you?'

'A question now often asked of me, it seems,' Garro replied. 'I have no brotherhood, not any more. The Legion I was born to has fallen to infamy, and I have been renewed in a greater duty. I have a new purpose. I serve as Agentia Primus for Malcador the Sigillite, Lord Regent of Terra. I hunt for him, scribe, to find warriors of like spirit, and to track and terminate the Warmaster's spies.'

'Is that why you are here, in the city? You were sent to end my life?'

Garro ignored the question. His reasons for being on the Riga orbital plate were his own, and for now he had no desire to reveal them to anyone else. 'I was drawn to your hunt when I heard the warrant on the watch-wire. My presence here is a secret, even to Malcador.'

Doubt filled Tallery's eyes. 'The Sigillite sees all.'

'So he would like us to think,' he corrected. 'But I have learned that there are some places where his gaze does not fall.' He put away his blade, and Garro considered the slight, unassuming woman. Her story of this missing materiel, of the insidious turning of Imperial might against itself, all of it rang a familiar note.

A few years earlier, as Horus pulled the trigger that began his bloody rebellion, another incident of treachery like the one Tallery described had taken place. The gargantuan warship known as *Furious Abyss* had been stolen by traitor forces from the shipyards of Jupiter. It was a great failure of Imperial security, the culmination of a clandestine plot that revealed exactly how vulnerable the

Solar System was to the Warmaster's network of spies. Despite the purges and pogroms that had followed, it was certain that traitors still lurked close to the Throne-world. As close as Riga, so it seemed.

There was another reason why Garro had let Tallery live. It was not just to hear her tale. His gaze was drawn again to the golden aquila about her wrist. 'I know what you are, Katanoh Tallery. I know what you believe in.'

'What do you mean?' She failed to conceal her shock at his words.

'The charm you wear. It is the secret sign of the cult of the God-Emperor. You believe that the Master of Mankind is more than He claims. You consider Him a living deity, worthy of your worship even as He forbids it. Your church, your faith, is forbidden by the Imperial Truth.' He said the words without weight.

She stared at the ground and nodded slowly. 'It is true. I believe in Him. It is by His grace that I live still. It must be so.' Tallery took a shaky breath. 'You think me a fool for admitting this.'

Garro gave a rueful smile and shook his head. 'Then I too am a fool. I have learned with blood and fire that faith is the only true constant. The Emperor protects, Tallery. If that is a lie, then there is no purpose to this conflict, and I will not accept that.' He shook off the moment of introspection and beckoned her. 'To your feet, scribe. We cannot stay here. The gunships will return.'

WITH A CIVILIAN in tow, Garro no longer had the luxury of using the Falsehood to shroud his movements. The camouflage cape folded back over his wargear and instead he returned to baser tactics, sticking to the depths of the shadows as they made their way through the shipyard.

To her credit, the scribe was a quick study and she mirrored Garro's motions as best she could, stepping where
he stepped, staying well clear of anything that could get
them noticed. She did not question him, and that spoke
to her character. His genhanced senses could smell the
sweat on her skin, hear the urgency of her breathing,
and he knew that terror walked with her. He imagined
that it was only fear of death itself that ranked above
her fear of him.

The common humans of the Imperial citizenry, people
like Katanoh Tallery, had been taught from birth that the
Legiones Astartes were war incarnate, scions of battle to
be revered and dreaded. Sometimes Garro and his kinsmen lost sight of that. He turned and gave her what he
hoped was a nod of approval, but it was difficult to tell
if she took it as such. He wanted to explain to her that
they were not so different, the warrior and the scribe,
both the victims of betrayal in their own ways. Garro
too had been called traitor by short-sighted men, and he
knew how that accusation burned. Even if he understood
nothing else of Tallery, he understood that.

He pointed. 'That way. Move quickly.'

'Where are we going, my lord?'

'To find–'

The words died in Garro's throat as without warning,
bright beams of light stabbed down from the gantries
above their heads, drenching the deck with a stark glow.
He hissed as his augmented eyes adjusted to the glare.
But Tallery had no such genetic enhancement and she
shielded her face with her hands, staggering backwards.

The grating snarl of a Thallax's amplified voice sounded
out around them. 'Remain still. You have been detected.
Do not attempt to flee.'

Garro cursed their luck. He had gambled that doubling back along their path would sneak them through the patrol lines of Thallaxii, but it appeared that the machines were not as dull-witted as he had hoped. 'How many of these things have they sent?' He asked the question aloud. 'All this just for an *accountant*?'

Bulky metallic forms were visible as shadows behind the sharp illumination of the spotlights, and he picked out the shape of electro-stunner weapons and shock mauls. One such cyborg would have been no match for him, cut to shreds by the edge of *Libertas* in short order, but there was a full cohort of the machines descending towards them, and with Tallery to keep safe, the balance of any engagement would slide away from Garro's favour. He chose to wait, keeping his hands close to the hilt of his sword and the bolt pistol holstered at his hip.

'They're going to kill us,' murmured the scribe.

'I will not allow that,' he vowed. 'Stay back.'

A dozen of the mechanoids marched out to surround them, covering every avenue of escape. Sapphire light flashed over Tallery's face and she cowered; then the beams crossed up over Garro's armour and his stoic countenance. 'Your presence in this sector is not sanctioned,' grated one of the machines. 'Identify yourself.'

'I am Battle-Captain Nathaniel Garro, Agentia Primus of the Regent of Terra.' He made certain to stand so that the faint tracery of the Sigillite's Mark on his armour was visible to the cyborg's sensors. 'By my authority, I order you to lower your weapons.'

The Thallax responded without pause. 'Your authority is not recognised. Step aside. Surrender the scribe to our custody.'

'You defy the will of Lord Malcador?' He tapped the

lone sigil on his pauldron, the literal representation of the Sigillite's official sanction. 'You know what this means, machine. Stand down. I command it.'

'Command refused,' said the cyborg. 'Termination of target supersedes all other authority. We answer only to the Mistress of Riga.'

It was not the answer he had been expecting, and Garro sensed Tallery tensing behind him. No human would have dared to speak so to a representative of the Regent, even if Garro *was* operating outside the Sigillite's orders at this moment. But the masters of the Riga orbital plate were not mere humans any more, he reminded himself. Unique amongst the floating cities that drifted over Terra's surface, rulership of Riga had been granted to the mech-lords in exile after their new master, Fabricator General Kane, had escaped the Fall of Mars. In the aftermath of those events, certain loyal houses of the Legio Cybernetica had gained favour in the Imperial Court, and Riga had been a reward for their constancy. Garro was not privy to the politicking behind such power games, nor did he wish to be. All this meant to him was that there were emotionless machine patrolmen standing in his way, instead of flesh-and-blood Arbitrators who he might have cowed more easily.

'Scribe Tallery has been designated Excommunicate Traitoris,' said the cyborg. 'Her life is forfeit. Final warning. Stand aside.'

'I refuse. She is under my protection.' So it would come to battle, then. A part of Garro welcomed the honesty of it.

The Thallax took aim at him. 'Then you will be reclassified as an accessory to her crimes, and treated accord–'

In the blink of an eye, *Libertas* left the scabbard on

Garro's back and he used it to draw a shimmering arc through the air, ending in a seamless cut that beheaded the machine-soldier.

'Scribe, seek cover!' he shouted, and his other hand brought up the bolt pistol and fired a close-range shot into another of the Thallaxii, before it could discharge its electro-gun.

'Attack. Apprehend. *Terminate.*' The cyborgs spat a metallic chorus of commands and came at him in a mob.

Garro waded into the engagement and let the old, familiar battle-sense wash over him. In combat with these machines, he had no need to pull his blows as he might have if he were engaging human opponents. The warrior's lip curled as he began to take the artificial beings apart with swift, forceful and deadly strikes. Blow by devastating blow, shot by pinpoint shot, Garro battled the small army of machines. The lesson he taught them was that transhuman flesh and bone could be every bit as unyielding as plasteel and brass.

SHOCKED AND AWED, Tallery watched the legionary fight. Garro dismembered the Cybernetica's machine-soldiers with brutal precision, weathering blows from their shock mauls with grim determination and beating them back. The decking beneath his feet ran dark with spilled oil and organic fluids. Severed robotic limbs twitched where they had fallen, grasping blindly while power still ran through their systems.

The grey-armoured warrior killed another mechanical with a point-blank shot, blasting fragments of metal shrapnel into the air. He had cut a gap in their line, and as Garro risked a glance towards her, Tallery instinctively knew what she should do.

'Scribe!' he bellowed '*Run!*'

She felt a pang of guilt as she broke into a headlong sprint, a strange reaction towards someone who a short time ago had been on the cusp of executing her. But with this deed, and with his willingness to let her speak, Garro had proven himself a good soul, ready to defend her. *To believe in her.* It had been so long since anyone had believed in Katanoh Tallery that she hardly recognised the feeling.

She half turned as she ran. 'Come on! They'll be calling in reinforcements!' A gasp caught in her throat, as she saw the quick, deadly machines marshal their strength and attack the legionary as one.

'Don't look back!' he shouted. A salvo of shock-blasts bombarded Garro from every angle as the machine-soldiers fired in concert. Serpents of brilliant lightning slithered over his battleplate and into his flesh. Pain that would have killed ten men tore an agonised howl from the warrior's throat and he stumbled, falling to one knee, struggling to stay conscious. *Or so she thought.*

With a monumental roar, Garro took in the agony and endured it. He rose again, shrugging off coruscating webs of blue fire. His sword shone in the hard glare of the spot -lamps, coming around in a blazing arc of murderous steel. Tallery understood. He had let the machines come close, reeling them in so that he might end this engagement with a single, perfect strike. The sword crossed the necks of the remaining Thallaxii, beheading them one after another. *Libertas* flashed, ending the fight in a final, breathless instant.

There was something magnificent in the power of it, and terrible too. 'It is as they say,' she breathed. 'Your kind are the hammer of the Emperor. His will is made manifest through you.'

Garro approached, shaking droplets of dark fluid from his gauntlets. 'That is one way to see it.' He frowned at her. 'I told you to keep running. What if I had been defeated by their superior numbers?'

'That did not seem a likely outcome.'

His lips thinned. 'I am not invincible. No one is. Not even the Emperor, no matter what we may think of Him.'

Tallery did not want to consider that Garro's words might be true, and she nodded towards the heap of wrecked machine limbs. 'It would seem the Mistress of Riga wishes me dead.'

'Perhaps,' said the legionary. 'But a machine can be made to think anything you tell it to. They have only the loyalty they are programmed with. Other influences may be at work.'

'Whoever is behind this, they'll be coming for both of us now.'

'No doubt.' He rubbed his chin in thought. 'So it falls to you and I. We must find the truth.'

'I don't know where to begin,' she said; but whatever reply the warrior was going to make was suddenly lost in a shrieking storm of jet noise from above.

The raptor-like gunship drone hovered over them, wings curving downwards, its thruster wake striking with the force of a tornado. Heavy ballistic cannons, powerful enough to rip through the hull of a battle tank, turned to target them. It came in low and Tallery saw the blank sensor eyes of the machine-mind predator lining up for the kill.

Garro scowled at the bolt pistol in his hand and gestured with his sword. 'My pistol is empty. Scribe, get behind me!'

'Targets located.' The words sounded from a vox-horn on the underside of the autonomous aircraft. '*Terminate.*'

GARRO SNEERED HIS defiance at the drone aircraft, brandishing *Libertas* before him. 'I will not perish in this place, at the hands of some clockwork avian!' he shouted. 'Come then, try to kill me if you dare!'

The machine paused, ready to open fire, but briefly uncertain of its targets. Garro realised why as the scribe suddenly ran out into the open and sprinted directly towards the gunship. 'Tallery, *no!*'

The drone recalculated and shifted its aim to the woman, to its primary programmed target. Garro thought that the woman was making some brave, suicidal gesture, willingly putting herself in harm's way to save him from being fired upon; but then he saw Tallery throw up her hands and address the twitching sensor head of the drone directly. She was *calling* to it.

'Heed me!' screamed the scribe. 'Command input directive, Officio Centrum Omnis Pentalia!' To the legionary's surprise, the gunship's machine-brain actually hesitated.

'What in Terra's name… ?' he murmured.

Garro heard Tallery shout a series of numeral code strings, clusters of ones and zeroes that meant nothing to the legionary. And yet, the effect they had on the drone was stark and immediate. The massive cannons powered down and the machine's targeting lasers winked out. As abruptly as it had descended upon them, the gunship powered away into the sky without firing a single shot.

'It worked,' said Tallery, amazed by her own actions. 'Praise the Emperor, *it actually worked!*'

'What did you do?' Garro came to her side, glaring

into the shadows in search of any other lingering threats. 'Those words you said, that was a Mechanicum code.'

She nodded briskly. 'A base Gothic form of binaric, yes. I used a departmento override command to convince the drone that its weapons were in need of rearming. It's heading back to the hangar right now.' Tallery paled as the adrenaline in her system ebbed away. 'A machine can be made to think anything you tell it to, isn't that what you said? You just have to know how to talk to them, of course.'

Despite the woman's reckless act, Garro could not help but be impressed by her resourcefulness. 'Clever. Could you not have done that with the machine-soldiers as well?'

'Different mechanoids have different command protocols,' she explained. 'I remembered those of the gunships from an addendum in Curator Lonnd's files. I remember all I see...' She took a deep, shuddering breath. 'It seemed a practical risk to take.'

'You seem to have a proclivity for risking your life,' he replied. 'You could have been killed.'

'That would have happened anyway.' As she said the words, Garro saw that she understood that truth as well, the reality of the danger she had just been in dawning on her. 'Other drones will be coming to take that one's place, and my trick won't work twice. Is there somewhere you can send me? Into custody of some kind?' Her tone became imploring. 'If you are Malcador's agent, then perhaps he can keep me safe until this is all out in the open.'

In spite of himself, Garro's scarred face twisted in a scowl. His presence on Riga was utterly unsanctioned, and he was reluctant to speculate on what might happen if he brought this before the Sigillite. Malcador was not a man to tolerate disobedience lightly, as others had learned to their cost.

He reluctantly shook his head. 'As much as I wish it, for now that option is not available. Circumstances mean we must remain together, scribe. I will have need of that perfect memory of yours, if I am to cut through the lies surrounding this conspiracy. *We* must find Othrys and learn its secrets.'

Garro thought she might oppose him, but then the scribe gave a hesitant nod. 'My life is in your hands, my lord. As it has been all along.'

THIRTEEN

Deadship
Long sleep
The hidden fortress

THEY FOUND THEIR way to the secondary docking ring beneath the lip of the orbital plate without further incident. Under Garro's unerring direction, the pair evaded fresh waves of the Thallaxii as they poured into the shipyards, and slipped the net.

Here, stalactite-like towers extended out from the underside of the floating metropolis, with nothing but open air beneath them and the surface of the Throne-world far below. Between each tower there were bays where war-wounded ships lay waiting for new orders. For many of these once-proud vessels, grievously mauled in battle against the traitors, the only fate before them was in the maw of a breaker's yard.

One such ship was the *Akulan*, a small, battered corvette that had served with the defence fleets outbound from Proxima Centauri. It lay at anchor nearby, a sad ruin of its former self, making ready to set sail for the last time.

In a cramped control compartment inside one of the towers, a lone control servitor worked the dock systems in an endless, monotonous cycle of arrivals and departures. 'Ready for decoupling,' it muttered, speaking into a vox-pickup. Its dull eyes blinked constantly as it processed complex shipping data. *'Stand by.'*

Behind it, a hatch opened out of turn and two humans entered. Without invitation. Correction: one human, one transhuman.

The servitor halted in its work cycle to address them. *'This area is restricted.'*

The transhuman (*gender: male, classification: Space Marine*) ignored the warning. 'Make sure this is the right one,' he growled, speaking to the other intruder.

The human (*gender: female, classification: Scribe-Adepta*) nodded and pushed past the servitor, moving to a console where she began to type out a string of commands on a keypad.

'Stop,' insisted the machine-slave. *'Identify yourself.'*

The transhuman strode forwards and towered over the dock controller. 'Look upon the brand on my armour, servitor,' it commanded. 'Recognise the authority.'

'And if it does not?' The human female's voice betrayed doubt. 'That didn't work the *last* time you tried it.'

'Then things will not end well for our half-brained friend here.' With the oiled clatter of metal on metal, the transhuman recovered a magazine of ammunition from a pouch on his belt and loaded it into a bolt pistol. The weapon was primed and aimed towards the servitor's chest.

The slave-worker hesitated, registering a faint fear-analogue as it realised its continued existence was being threatened. Its ruby-lensed optics clicked as they peered at the Sigil of Malcador, visible in the ultraviolet spectrum of its vision blocks. *'The mark of the Sigillite,'* it intoned, processing this radical new datum.

'Let me make this clear,' said the legionary. 'Obey me or I will end your wretched existence.'

The servitor executed a stiff bow. *'Understood, my lord. How may I assist you?'*

'It learns quickly,' said the female. The servitor watched her access the *Akulan's* resources packet and data queues, efficiently retrieving pages of information about the frigate. 'This is the right vessel, Garro. A "deadship" with the same registration I saw in the hidden files. Records indicate it is bound for the scrap-works of Jupiter's moons, but there's no terminus point logged.'

'Indeed?' The transhuman (*nomenclature: Garro*) shot the servitor a look. 'Where is this hulk really going?'

'Exact destination unknown.' The machine-slave had the same information in its head that the female had before her, and the troubling void in the *Akulan's* flight plan made it flinch with physical pain. *'Error condition,'* it amended.

'A different question, then.' The bolt pistol's black muzzle dropped away. 'Where is Othrys?'

The word lit a sudden, hateful fire inside the brain matter of the servitor, and it began to twitch like a victim of palsy. *'Unknown. Unknown.'* Pain analogues rippled through it, causing countless neural misfires in its cerebral matrix. *'Cannot answer. Data purged.'*

'Stop!' ordered the female, and the command brought a wash of relief through the servitor's hybrid body. It immediately purged the offending word from its short-term recall buffer, afraid to even consider it again. 'It must be a mnemonic block,' continued the human.

'It doesn't know that word because it *can't* know it. All references to "Othrys" have been burned from its mind.'

At the sound of the forbidden name repeated, the servitor jerked, running the purge program again and again before the word could take hold in its sluggish thoughts.

It became aware of the transhuman studying it coldly. 'Even a psyker would be unable to find anything in there,' the legionary told the female. 'Servitor. How long until this wreck is sent on its way?'

It bowed again. *'Egress will occur in ten minutes.'*

The transhuman paused, and the servitor knew he was considering the act of termination. It waited powerlessly for the killshot to come, but it never did. Instead, the legionary nodded to the female and they left as quickly as they had arrived.

After a moment, the dock servitor decided to purge its memory of everything that had happened in the last five minutes, just to be certain.

WHAT FEW GUARDS there were watching the docking bay had their attention elsewhere, allowing Garro and Tallery to steal aboard the derelict in short order. The scribe did her best to keep pace with him, but she was flagging. He frowned, holding open the *Akulan*'s wide airlock hatch so that she could enter. 'Hurry. The umbilicals are already detaching. The ship will be under power in a few seconds.'

'I hope you know what you are doing,' she panted, as all around the craft began to rumble and rattle into life.

'You have faith in the Emperor, Tallery. Grant me some fraction of the same. Actions of this kind are not new to me.' He let the hatch drop shut and led her down the corridor that ran the length of the corvette's spine.

She followed gingerly. 'I have never been to the Jovian yards…' Tallery swallowed a gasp. 'In all honesty, I have never left the orbit of Terra in my life.'

Garro glanced over his shoulder at her. 'I very much doubt that Jupiter or any of her moons are our final destination. Othrys, wherever it is, could lie anywhere within range of this ship's engines. A craft of this tonnage is fully capable of making a leap across the immaterium, clear across the Segmentum Solar at maximum potential.'

Tallery went pale. 'But, if we take to the warp, we could be in transit for days. *Months!*'

He nodded again. 'Or more.' Garro had already considered what duration of journey they could be letting themselves in for, and accepted it. 'But we are committed to this now.' He felt the vessel leave the dock, the iron walls about them creaking and grinding.

Garro went to a grimy portal in the hull and watched the departure, with Tallery silent at his side. Thrusters firing, the deadship disconnected from Riga and got under way; within minutes it had pulled away from the gravity of Terra, rising out of the atmosphere. It came about to put its broken bow towards the stars. The deck beneath their feet trembled as velocity increased, dim lights flickering over their heads as power ebbed away to maintain more vital systems.

A heavy chill began to descend. Rimes of frost formed on the metal walls, and their breath blossomed into streamers of white vapour. 'The cold,' said the scribe, releasing a cough. 'Where is it coming from?'

'I expected this,' he told her. 'We are aboard a derelict. The *Akulan* no longer has any human crew to speak of on board, only cogitators and servitors to run it, and they are confined to the command tiers. All the other decks will be empty. So there is no need for life support down here. Oxygen. Water. *Heat*. All unnecessary.'

Tallery's eyes widened. 'And how exactly am I supposed to survive a journey without those things? I have heard that Space Marines can endure even the vacuum of the deep void, but I am not so gifted!'

'Be calm,' he admonished. Garro gestured down the corridor, indicating a compartment off to one side, and beckoned Tallery to follow him. She drew her robes close and shivered, following him across the frost-rimed deck. 'I have not brought you this far only to let you suffocate or starve. You are correct that my genetically enhanced physiology allows me to live for extended periods in a state of suspension. For decades, if need be. I have something similar in mind for you.'

'Wh-what do you mean?'

Garro tapped a control stud and another hatch opened, vapour hissing out into the corridor from within.

Tallery stepped warily inside and the scribe baulked at the sight of dozens of glassy capsules, each the size of a coffin, wreathed in wisps of sub-zero gases. 'Stasis caskets. You're going to put me into deep-sleep?'

'I will stand guard while you slumber,' he promised.

'No! I can't!' Raw panic flared in her. 'What if I don't awaken?'

Garro reached for his helmet where it lay mag-locked to his thigh plate. 'Soon the atmosphere in this part of the ship will thin to the point where you will not be able to breathe. I have seen men lost to that manner of death and it is not a clean ending. You must survive. I need you so we can finish what we have started.'

She seemed to shrink before his eyes. 'This is all too much for me.'

He shook his head. 'I do not believe that. You are braver than you think. You faced that gunship without fear.'

Tallery gave a dry, humourless chuckle. 'Oh, there was quite a *lot* of fear, my lord.'

'You will be safe,' Garro insisted. 'You have my word as a legionary.' Before she could say more, he set to work activating one of the capsules. The operations of such stasis devices were known to Garro, recalled through old regimens of hypnogogic instruction given to him as a Legion recruit. The data implanted in him a lifetime ago as a Death Guard neophyte now returned, and he set to work bringing the system online. He knew that if he allowed Tallery to dwell upon her plight, the scribe's resolve would soon erode. He had to keep her focused on something else.

'I would know how it was you came to see the Emperor's divinity, scribe. Why do you think Him to be a god among men?'

She looked up at him with hooded eyes. 'I am not alone in such belief. Even if the Lords of Terra do not wish it, even if He Himself shies away from our Imperial Truth. Our numbers swell as time passes. Those who share true insight, who embrace the faith, we are many.'

'You did not answer my question.'

'I read a book.' Tallery sighed, as if a weight were lifting off her shoulders. 'It was called the *Lectitio Divinitatus*. A rough thing, printed on real paper, if you can believe that. Smuggled to me by a friend now dead and gone. What was written there...' She paused, then smiled slightly. 'All I can tell you is that it spoke to me. In a way I cannot articulate. But I felt as if I had been blind all my life, and only then learned how to see.' The smile deepened and became rueful. 'It sounds irrational when I say it aloud.'

'To some, perhaps,' Garro said earnestly. 'Not to me.'

'Do the Legions worship the Emperor?' Tallery shivered and hugged herself. 'You are the sons of His sons, the primarchs, after all.'

'We obey Him,' Garro allowed. 'But it is seen as *improper* to consider the Emperor as a divine being.'

She studied him closely. 'You think otherwise.'

He paused in his work. *She is perceptive, this one,* he thought. 'It is difficult for me to put into words also. I have seen horrors, Scribe Tallery. Worlds burning. Monsters. Brothers turning upon brothers. Death and war. All I rescued from that madness was my unbroken faith.'

'In what?'

'In Him.' Unbidden emotion, and reverence thickened his words. 'I believe He preserved me for something. He saw me to be of purpose.'

'Then I envy you,' she admitted. 'After what I have been through these past days, my conviction has been severely tested.'

Garro's gaze turned inwards. 'You are not alone in that. It is the nature of this conflict.' He met her gaze. 'I came to Riga because I was looking for answers. I have spoken of that to no other until now.'

'You are looking for the Saint Keeler, yes?'

Her answer shocked him with its truthfulness. 'You know of her?'

'How could I not?' Tallery shivered as she went on. 'They say she gives enlightenment with every word she utters. But I have never seen her. There are rumours that the Saint moves from station to station, never straying far from Terra. And so you came to Riga in the hope that she would be there.'

He looked away. 'I was mistaken. Euphrati Keeler once

helped me see clearly. I had hoped she might do the same again.' What seemed like an eternity ago, Garro had led a crew of fugitives on a desperate mission to escape Horus' treachery. The woman Keeler had been with them on that fateful journey, and along the way Garro learned that she had been changed by the Warmaster's actions just as he had. Keeler became, for want of a better word, a prophet... And he had become a *believer*.

'The air... is getting thinner.' The woman's words were laboured. 'Difficult... to breathe now.'

Garro cranked open the lid of the stasis casket and helped her climb stiffly inside. 'Here. It will preserve you for the duration of the journey.'

Cautiously, the woman settled herself into the padded interior. 'I am trusting you with my life once again. In the name of the Saint... and the Emperor.'

'Your faith is not misplaced,' he promised, and touched a control. The casket began to slide closed.

'Neither is yours,' she told him, her eyes fluttering closed as the stasis systems began to lull her towards deep-sleep. 'Like courage, that comes from within, not from... the words of others.' She gave a low chuckle. 'I read that in a book–'

The lid thudded shut and cut her off as it locked tight. Garro watched the stasis casket gather up Tallery's fragile life and hold it in check, the hiss of cryogenic gases and the crackle of ice sounding as she was rendered dormant. Frozen in an instant of time, she would survive for as long as it would take them to reach Othrys, wherever that might be.

'Sleep, Katanoh Tallery,' said Garro softly. 'I will keep watch.'

✠ ✠ ✠

TERRA FELL AWAY into the endless blackness, and the derelict ventured on alone. Its drives blazing against the void, the *Akulan* was only a guttering candle, a tiny shard of corroded steel in the unforgiving night.

As Tallery faded into the mindless slumber of stasis, Garro joined her in his own kind of suspended animation. The legionary allowed himself to drop into a fathomless trance-state. The catalepsean node implant deep in his cerebellum let him take rest without the need for true sleep as humans knew it. As one hemisphere of his brain went dormant, the other maintained a baseline level of alertness, shifting function back and forth so that he would never truly lose himself to unconsciousness.

The days stretched and thinned like heated glass, becoming unnumbered, their count forgotten. In the dark and dreamless abyss between worlds, the silence was all-encompassing. Out here, where stars turned upon pillars of gravity and the night went on forever, one might be able to briefly forget that this was a galaxy in flames.

But those who looked with sharper eyes, those who could perceive the foulness tainting those distant beacons of light, they saw the threads of corruption reaching from world to world. The suns burning out and the planets becoming ashen, barren and forgotten. In the silence, the galaxy screamed.

Nathaniel Garro did not hear it. He remained behind the walls of his own mind, in the company of thoughts that moved with a glacial slowness in the thrall of the half-sleep. For the former Death Guard there were only the questions that never left him. The doubts and the fears.

Keeler. Where are you?

His unquiet spirit pulled at the tethers of his soul,

resisting the truths he had set out for himself. If he did have faith, as he had told the scribe, then why was it so hard to accept the way of things? Was there still some small part of Garro that longed to see the rebellion end peacefully? Was there a vain hope that all the terrible acts he had seen committed might somehow be undone?

There were too many secrets, too many unknowns. Garro had come to Riga searching for meaning, driven by his doubts, by the words of Rogal Dorn and Meric Voyen, and more. And for his folly he had uncovered only more questions. And so a more pressing uncertainty was left at the fore.

What is Othrys?

The voyage seemed to go on forever, and he dreamed as only a legionary could dream, as the ship fell through space towards the answer.

BUT FINALLY, AT journey's end, after time unreckoned by the silent, unmoving warrior and his reluctant companion, the old and wounded corvette allowed itself to be captured by the gravity well of a cloudy, umber sphere.

Had there been an observer at the portals on the command deck, they would have noted that from a distance, the planetoid seemed to be without surface features of any kind. But upon closer approach, it became clear that this world was shrouded in a thick mantle of billowing haze, held aloft by constant, powerful winds.

The *Akulan* shifted course and dropped towards the ocean of shade, manoeuvring thrusters jetting out blasts of fire to set it on the correct path. Other craft that had come in from differing points of the aetheric compass were following the same mandated route. Some of them were near-wrecks like the corvette, others newer vessels fresh from forge world shipyards all across the Segmentum Solar and beyond. All of them had come here in secret purpose, their crews either lobotomised half-minds or a scant number of souls gifted with a most confidential trust.

Reaching the point of atmospheric interface, the craft cut into the dense, alien sky, briefly transforming into a lance of thunderous fire before tearing through. The *Akulan*'s last flight was almost over, and rather than be taken by the teeth of mindless breaker-rigs hungry for raw material, it would be reborn. The derelict's iron bones and steel skin would be repurposed here instead by other hands, for duties unguessed at by the Imperium at large.

Emerging from out of the thick, swirling cloud base, the ship began a wide turn over the coast of a rolling methane sea, tacking into the harsh wind and a driving wall of hydrocarbon rain. It passed through a howling primeval typhoon, crossing sculpted crags of black ice and cryovolcanic ridges, towards a forest of human-made structures jutting into the air. *Akulan*'s engines fired one final time to settle it into the grasp of the towering cranes that would disassemble it.

Swallowed by the unknown sky, the dying note of the main drives fell to stillness. Othrys had taken another claim and the count was far from ended.

THE CUTTERS SET to work before the old corvette had cooled from the heat of re-entry, paring it down as a servant might carve a roasted animal for the pleasure of their master's supper.

Garro shouldered open the hatch and stepped out into the harsh chemical rains, holding Tallery to him as he sprinted across the docking gantry. 'Quickly, scribe. We must get clear of the ship.'

She nodded weakly. 'All right. What is… ?' Tallery's hands rose as she became aware of her circumstances. 'What have you put on my face?'

'A breather mask,' he explained, letting her step down. 'The atmosphere on this planet is nitrogen-rich. My augmented lungs can process it, but you would choke to death.'

'Oh, of course.' She found her feet and staggered forwards a few steps. 'I feel weak.'

'A side effect of the stasis,' Garro explained. 'It will pass.'

Tallery clung to a support stanchion and peered out into the amber clouds. 'Have we found Othrys?'

Garro nodded. 'We have reached the end of our search.'

'Throne… Look at this place!' She pointed behind them, to where lines of decommissioning bays stretched away towards a broken ridgeline of dark peaks. They resembled the shipyards of Riga, but here it was clear that the reclaimed vessels were being remade into something quite different. A grand pattern of cannibalisation was in progress.

Monorails and grav-lifts carried repurposed metals towards a vast construction site in the shadow of a great black mountain, a gigantic circular pit that had been laser-cut into the stone-hard ice that lay underfoot. Garro glimpsed the work of countless construction teams in hazard gear and exoskeletons, some toiling as they laid rockcrete foundations, others assembling vast blocks of marble and granite into walls, battlements and donjons.

Scaffolding that reached from the lowest levels of the pit to beyond the height of the tallest crane swayed gently in the wind, warning lamps blinking through the constant, oily drizzle. He saw pieces of a large construction through the framework and, as his head tilted up to take it all in, he had a sudden jolt of insight.

Growing from the dead centre of the work pit was an artificial pinnacle that rose almost as high as the mountain that overlooked it. Although, like everything else before them, it remained unfinished, the legionary immediately understood that he was looking at a stronghold of some kind. The great citadel was the heart of the edifice, and at its feet the roots had been laid for many more buildings of similar scope and majesty.

'What are they building here?' whispered Tallery. 'I have never seen the like before.'

'I have,' said Garro, with grim certainty. 'On Barbarus, made after the coming of the Emperor. It is an echo of similar constructions on Baal, Macragge, Fenris and other worlds. This is a battle fortress. A place from which wars will be waged.'

Tallery shivered as a chill washed through her and she blinked, wiping rust-red rain from the lenses of her breather mask so that she might see more clearly. The closer she looked, the more it became clear that the fortress was nearing completion. Her gut twisted as she considered what kind of army such a bastion could house. The scribe was no tactician, but she understood numbers and logistics all too well. Even at a conservative estimate, she guessed that the great castle and its dominion would be able to support thousands of soldiers and war engines. Taking cover behind a rocky crag, they surveyed the site in greater detail. Garro was silent for a long time, but the grim cast of his expression spoke to his mood.

'I see no Legion sigil. No mark of garrison or company that I recognise anywhere in sight.'

'Just like your armour.' She glanced at him. 'So Othrys is a secret, hidden base, as we suspected. That makes sense. All the hardware, all the equipment being secretly diverted from Riga, it's been coming here. They're using it to build everything we can see.'

'Not just from Riga. I'll warrant that the data you uncovered on the orbital plate was just one stream of supplies.' Tallery could see Garro was deeply troubled by the portent of their discovery. 'To keep such a thing secret is no small feat. One would need to draw off just enough not to raise the alarm, and do it a hundredfold across the Imperium. In time of conflict, it would be a simple matter to misplace a ship here, a freight convoy there...' He trailed off.

Tallery felt sick inside. 'This is so much worse than I thought it could be. We have uncovered more than just some corrupt governor lining his pockets. This is a nest of the Warmaster's collaborators on *our* side of the battle lines! I can hardly believe it, that such a thing could go unseen.'

Garro's expression showed more a sense of grim resignation than concern. 'It has happened before, damnable though that truth is. Horus' cohorts built and then stole the warship *Furious Abyss*... This is an evolution of the same tactic, only played out on an even grander scale. Assemble a secret stronghold deep inside the territory of your enemy, use it to strike at their vulnerable underbelly. The genius of it is that the traitors have used our own infrastructure to build it.' He showed her a brittle smile. 'I almost admire the arrogance.' Garro raised a gauntleted hand and pointed towards a series of skeletal iron spires on the ridgeline surrounding the colossal construction site; purple-red energy crackled along their length, dissipating in clouds of sparks at their apex. 'Those are detector baffles,' he explained. 'There are dozens of them surrounding the whole site, projecting an energy grid that would confuse any scry-sensors looking this way. With that and the cloud cover, a ship passing within scanning range of this world would see nothing amiss here.'

'But who could orchestrate a scheme of this magnitude?' Tallery felt her indignation rise. 'No one could construct a fortress inside Imperial space and avoid detection forever.'

He eyed her. 'They did not avoid it, Scribe Tallery. *You found them.*' Garro was about to say more, but then he nodded over her shoulder and she turned to see a cadre of hooded figures.

They trudged in lockstep across the rain-slick ground, and each wore robes of muddy crimson lined with a cog-tooth trim. The brass shapes of their bionic limbs caught the weak light as they walked. 'The Mechanicum,' she said quietly, recognising the familiar cast of the figures.

'It would seem their treachery has grown beyond the insurrection on Mars,' said Garro. 'Come. We cannot tarry here.'

THE DIFFUSE GLOW of day through the orange sky waned, and night fell across the surface of the planetoid. It brought with it a chill that turned the oily rain into a greasy fall of chemical snow. Garro knew that remaining out on the perimeter of the construction site would eventually lead to their discovery. Keeping Tallery close to his side, he moved as fast as he dared, down into the work pit.

They stole aboard a pressurised monorail wagon and allowed it to take them the rest of the way to the citadel. Peering through a grate, he saw the skeletons of incomplete battle bunkers passing by, and gun towers armed with repurposed starship lascannon batteries. Nothing was going to waste in the forging of Othrys. It was a design that would rival the siege works of the Imperial Fists when complete.

But only if they allowed that to continue.

Garro considered the idea of making a stealthy approach into the heart of the citadel itself. If it followed the design protocols of a standard Imperial fortress template, there would be a mighty power reactor on the core levels. He knew how to weaponise such a device, but a catastrophic overload would obliterate everything for five kilometres in all directions. The secret of Othrys would be consumed in fire, but it would likely take him and Tallery with it in the blast.

Garro frowned. He had no way of knowing their exact location within the Imperium, and even if he managed to destroy this place, those responsible for creating it would not be brought to account unless word of their deed could be sent back to Terra. There would be nothing to stop them from beginning anew elsewhere. At best, he would only delay their plans. *And what if this was only one installation among many?*

To end this, the full truth behind the scribe's unwitting discovery had to be brought into the light.

'My lord.' Tallery called to him from further down the cargo wagon. 'Come look at these.'

'What have you found?' He approached, finding her standing over a pallet of pressed-metal cargo boxes.

'These all bear item codes I recall from Curator Lonnd's files.' Tallery had prised open the lids of several of the shipping containers. Inside, Garro recognised myriad offensive munitions and weapons elements. He saw racks of fusing cores for melta bombs, and boxes of heavy-gauge bolter ammunition. In another crate, there were complex frames for heavy weapons, directed energy cannons of a kind he had only a passing familiarity with.

'What kind of firearms are those?' asked the scribe.

Garro hefted one of the guns, turning it in his hands. 'These are conversion beamers. An uncommon firearm, not in wide use across the Legions or the auxilia. It is rare to see so many in one place.'

Tallery peered into the depths of the container. 'There are dozens here. No powercells in any of them, though.'

He returned the inert energy weapon to its rack and considered it. 'Whoever is gathering this army wants it to be very well-equipped. A single one of these beamers can obliterate heavy armour with one shot.'

In the distance, the mono-train sounded its horn and its motivators clattered over points in the overhead track.

'We're slowing down,' said Tallery.

'The loading bay is up ahead,' noted Garro. 'Reseal those cargo containers, quickly. Be ready to jump on my order. We can't be on this train when it reaches the dock.'

Tallery quickly closed the crates and pulled her breather mask back into place. He heard her whisper something under her breath, like a litany. '*Ave Imperator.*'

'Indeed,' he offered, and then pulled on the lever that opened the cargo wagon's hatch. The pressure change was instant and painful, but he shrugged it off, staring out at the deck flashing past outside.

He decided not to give Tallery the chance to question his choices and pulled her to him in a protective embrace. She cried out, but it was too late, and they had already leapt into the air.

FOURTEEN

Shield of lies
Titan
Obey or perish

DAMP DRIFTS OF methane slush cushioned their fall, allowing Garro and Tallery to make their way along the service course beneath the monorail platforms at the wide base of the fortress. Staring up through the gridded metal decking, they had a perfect view of the carriages as bipedal walker-mechs driven by gasmasked workers unloaded their cargo.

'You must take in all that you see here, scribe,' he told her. 'Study everything, omit nothing. That eidetic memory of yours will serve as witness.'

She nodded, but with little confidence. 'What good are my memories if I perish before I can recollect them?'

'You will survive, Tallery. You are the mission now. I will do everything in my power to see you to safety. The truth behind Othrys must be made known.'

Something slow and heavy darkened the low clouds as it descended from the sky, and presently a wallowing iron barge fell towards the citadel on spears of retro-thrust. At first, the legionary thought it was another cargo vessel, but Tallery corrected him. 'It's not a freighter. I recognise the configuration. That is a medicae transport. A mercy ship.'

The warrior frowned, watching as the great craft settled into a landing cradle extending out from the sheer walls of the citadel. As the sound of the thrusters faded, hatches clanged open all along its flanks. Instead of supplies, weapons or materiel, the new arrival deposited men. Garro's enhanced sight allowed him to pick out lines of injured soldiers, some being helped along by their comrades. The faces were recognisable to him – although he did not know these men, he knew their kind. *The war-wounded.*

Garro had seen such men alongside him in battle on many worlds during the Great Crusade, or in the halls of his Legion, amongst the neophytes. Warriors all, but young with it, and still untested even though the fires of their martial fury burned bright. It made no sense to see such men here. 'Each time I think I have some grasp upon this mystery, another twist reveals itself.'

The scribe agreed. 'This place is no hospice.'

But as she said the words, an answer began to form in Garro's mind, creeping into his thoughts like the cold wind over his flesh. Upon the hull of the mercy ship he saw the heraldry of a world that he knew. *Mertiol.*

Lost now, so the astropaths reported, lost to the warp storms and the iron grasp of the Warmaster, its cities burning and its people subjugated. Only a handful of ships had managed to flee the colony before Horus' war fleet blackened Mertiol's skies, and the question before Garro was now *why* this loyalist craft had fallen into the grip of Othrys, and not returned to safe harbour along with all the other refugees.

That cold understanding crystallised with a jolt. 'Those men are all *dead.'* Tallery gave him a curious look and he went on. 'Their names will have been struck from record, their ship listed as missing in the void. I think I understand. They will be healed, and then given purpose anew. Do you comprehend? The army of Othrys will be made of ghosts.'

The scribe rounded on him, her eyes wide behind the visor of her breather mask as terror took hold. 'How much more do we need to see? You have brought us to some misbegotten ball of black ice and poisoned skies, a place crawling with Mechanicum renegades. We have no means of escape, no way to call for help. You've doomed us both! And damn you if you tell me to have courage!' She tensed as if she wanted to run, but both of them knew there was nowhere to flee to.

Garro gave a solemn nod in return. 'We will both be damned if we do not finish what you began back on Riga. The Imperium must know of this place, this hidden outpost at the heart of a web of secrets. Othrys cannot be allowed to exist.'

'We'll need a ship,' panted Tallery. 'Something a lot faster than that barge.'

He drew his bolt pistol. 'Follow me.'

TALLERY MOVED AS quickly as she could in Garro's wake, but it was difficult to keep up with him. Even in the bulk of his unadorned, slate-grey battle armour, the legionary was more nimble than she could have hoped to be. He made it look effortless, and he moved without fear or doubt.

The scribe had worked hard to keep her panic sealed tight, drawing on her own inner strength, but it was challenging. She was so far outside her experience in this that it was beyond reason. Katanoh Tallery had been trained to be a calculator of numbers, a hand to compute figures and settle accounts. She was no spy, no agent of war, and yet Garro's single-minded determination had made her into that for the duration of this desperate mission. All at once she resented him for it, even as she knew that he was the only thing keeping her alive. So she did her best to keep pace.

Following the circumference of the citadel tower, they came to a huge elevator at the foot of the fortress. Cylindrical conveyor platforms as big as the monorail carriage they had ridden were moving up and down the length of the tower, carrying equipment and supplies to the upper levels. She watched them passing each other as they rose and fell in a complex ballet. Their motion reminded Tallery of the pneumatic vacuum tubes in the offices on Riga, where capsules containing sealed papers would jet away to the curator's chambers.

'Why are we here?' she asked.

'Look up,' said Garro. He indicated a circular landing stage halfway up the great length of the unfinished fortress. Growing out from the sheer rock of the tower like a disc of fungus from a tree trunk, the platform seemed small and insignificant. It was easily half a kilometre above ground level. 'That is our way out,' he explained.

Tallery's throat was dry. 'Shouldn't we be moving away from the centre of activity? I am not a tactician but what you suggest seems contrary to good sense.'

He smiled to himself. 'Don't make the mistake of thinking that you have a choice, scribe.'

Garro almost seemed to be enjoying their dire circumstances, but Tallery could only feel bitter about them. 'Yes. It seems my life is doomed to follow a path determined by everything but my will.' She pulled her robes close, shaking off the oily rainfall. 'Believing in the *Lectitio,* that is the only choice I have ever made for myself. And see where it has led me.'

A shadow passed over the warrior's face, and strangely, Tallery felt an unbidden pang of sorrow for him. 'That is the way of fate,' he told her. 'It takes us, makes us into what the universe needs us to be. Not what we want to be.' Then he shook off his own grim words with a turn of the head, returning to the matter at hand. 'We need to take control of a conveyor to reach the landing platform, without attracting attention. And for that, I require a distraction.'

He studied her intently, and fear crawled along the length of Tallery's spine as she realised what he was asking of her.

THE SCRIBE WALKED slowly towards one of the static conveyors, her hands raised, and her robe open to show that she concealed no weapons and posed no threat. She cleared her throat and managed a few words. 'Uh, hello?'

At the embarkation ramp, a number of skitarii, the heavily augmented foot soldiers of the Mechanicum, paused in their patrol pattern and turned their cold gaze upon her. With their bionic implants, cyber-weapons and dermal armour, the skitarii were formidable. Each had a steely limb with a built-in lasgun, and as she came closer they moved to put her in their sights.

'Halt,' came the demand. 'Identify yourself.'

Beneath their crimson hoods, what Tallery had first thought to be breather masks like her own were revealed, on closer inspection, to be surgically altered human flesh.

Eyes had been replaced with bulbous optical sensors and twitching antennae, mouths and noses permanently sealed behind featureless grilles fed by throbbing oxygen pipes. Unlike the servitors she knew from Riga, these man-machine hybrids moved with a quick economy of motion, exuding a sense of threat.

She began her performance. 'I… uh… require your assistance.'

'This site is restricted,' responded a second guardian. 'You are an intruder.'

'Quite so, yes.' Tallery made a point of being as affable in tone and as harmless in aspect as possible. 'That's why I'm surrendering, of course.'

'Restrain her,' said the other skitarii, and the two cyborgs closest to her approached. Steel talons extended to clamp around Tallery's arm and she was shoved towards the waiting conveyor car, the humming muzzle of a charged lasgun pressed into her back. She cast around desperately, her heart thudding in her chest. The scribe saw no sign of Garro in any direction, and for a terrible moment she was afraid that he had abandoned her.

The skitarii released its grip and pushed her over the lip of the ramp, into the cavernous space of the carriage. As the soldier kept a bead on her, the second skitarii yanked the heavy control lever. Rising on a thick chain-drive, each link as tall as a man, the conveyor slowly climbed away from the loading deck.

Peering out over the open edge of the platform, Tallery watched the ground fall away and she experienced a flash of sickly recollection, remembering the heart-stopping instant that she fell from the ledge on Riga. 'Not again…'

'Do not speak,' growled the cyborg.

Tallery looked away, and glimpsed movement from

the corner of her eye. A hunter. A *shadow*. 'I'm afraid I must,' she continued, digging deep to draw on her courage. 'How else would I be able to distract you?'

The skitarii began to demand that she explain herself. Light rippled behind the cyborg soldier, and with a flourish the Falsehood snapped off, revealing the towering form of the legionary beneath the metallic camo-cloak.

What came next happened almost too fast for Tallery to follow.

Garro surged forwards and grabbed the two skitarii about their throats. With a violent jerk, he slammed them together, cracking their augmented skulls against one another with enough force to break bone and splinter steel. They rebounded to the deck in broken heaps. One had perished instantly, but the other still possessed some animation and crawled away, jetting sparks and leaking vital fluids. She called out to Garro as the machine buzzed a warning to its comrades, but the warrior was already upon it for the killing blow, and he smashed it into the deck with the weight of his heavy boot. 'More resilient than they look,' he muttered.

The skitarii were dead, then, but already a distant bell sounded an alert. Tallery gasped. Their escape attempt had only just begun and it was in danger of ending prematurely. Garro accepted this new challenge with dour stoicism that was almost frustrating. 'So much for stealth,' he told her. 'It never was my strong suit.'

He reached down and snapped off one of the dead skitarii's cyber-limbs as easily as the scribe might have broken a twig, ripping the implanted lasgun free from its mounting. He offered it to Tallery.

'Take this.'

The weapon sat uneasily in her hands, wet with processor fluids. Her fingers found a trigger matrix and tentatively probed it. 'I have n-not been trained for use of firearms,' she stuttered.

'Then learn quickly,' said Garro. 'The Emperor protects those who protect themselves.'

Tallery dared to steal a glance over the edge and saw a dozen more skitarii soldiers staring back up at her. A second conveyor carriage was rising up from the lower levels, moving to match the climb of their own. Las-bolts cut at the air around her and she recoiled. 'They're coming after us... And a lot more of them than I would wish!'

'Good.' Garro's sword glittered as he drew it. 'I have had my fill of skulking in shadows.' Tallery did not share his hunger for battle, and told him so in no uncertain terms. He cocked his head. 'Fortunate for you, then, that one legionary is worth a thousand common soldiers.'

The second platform pulled level with their ascent and as one the skitarii troops leapt across the gap, hydraulic pistons in their legs propelling them up and over. Garro snarled and raised his bolt pistol, killing three of them with centre-mass shots before they passed the apex of their leaps.

The rest landed hard upon the deck and came up with claws and weapons deployed. Tallery found cover behind a control panel, las-beams slicing through the air around her. Hot droplets of superheated metal seared her robes as near hits gouged scars in the platform.

She fired back blindly, pointing her salvaged lasgun towards the sounds of battle, too afraid to raise her head above the console for fear of losing it.

GARRO WADED INTO the engagement with his weapons high. *Libertas* sang as it cut down any attacker who came within reach of the sword's edge, cold power flashing down the length of the blade. The legionary's bolt pistol barked, mass-reactive shells finding their targets and blasting them apart.

Slow to anger but strong in his fury, the warrior fell easily into the familiar mindset of battle. This was where he was at his best, engaged in death-dealing with a perfect, lethal precision. He fought without fanfare or great displays of martial flourish. It was his way, and the manner in which he had been trained. Once a Death Guard, always a Death Guard, Garro took to combat as the necessary means through which right was maintained. There was no glory in this, merely duty. Glory was something he had left behind, burned away in the ashes of his forgotten brotherhood. He was only a defender now, a crusader no more.

Shots deflecting off the ceramite of his battleplate, Garro spun away as a concentrated salvo of beam fire burned across the platform. Stray las-bolts ripped through the conveyor's drive mechanism and, with a sickening jolt, the carriage shuddered on its supports.

He felt more than heard the metallic shriek that ran through the deck. 'Tallery! The chain-drive has been hit.'

The scribe burst from cover as the platform canted sharply beneath their feet. 'We're going to fall!' she cried.

He shook his head. 'No. To me, *now!*' With a backhand blow, Garro knocked a skitarii gunman aside and bounded across the deck to Tallery, even as his boots began to lose their grip. Holstering his weapons, he swept the scribe off her feet, and before she could protest, he hurled her across the gap between the moving conveyors and to relative safety.

Her scream streaming through the air, Tallery landed

in a heap on the other platform. Then, Garro broke into a headlong sprint to follow her across, but the angle of the deck was already tilted too far, the gap widening with every second. A bulky, three-limbed skitarii tried and failed to grab at him as it slipped past and fell away into the smoky air.

The legionary sprinted and leapt, his arms extended towards the lip of the far platform. Encumbered by the weight of his armour and his weapons, it was almost too far for him to reach, but Garro's gauntlets barely caught the edge and he held fast. Behind him, the other carriage broke away and surrendered itself to gravity's embrace.

'Intruder!' grated a crackling vocoder. 'Intruder detected!' Garro was still in the process of dragging himself up when another skitarii came out of nowhere across the platform, training its implanted lasgun on Garro's head. One shot would blast him off the edge and send him spiralling down into the wreckage far below.

Crimson light flashed close and bright, air crackled along the path of a las-bolt, but the killing shot was not for Garro. With a grunt of effort, he hauled himself up, and found the scribe standing over the dead soldier, a smoking weapon in her trembling hands.

'D-did I kill it?' she breathed.

He turned her away from the dead cyborg. 'We live. That is all that matters.'

The chill breeze that pulled at Tallery's robes at ground level was a howling gale atop the landing stage, and the scribe gathered in her ragged hood to capture any warmth she could retain. Despite whatever attempts there had been to terraform the environment of this desolate planetoid, the noxious atmosphere, the deep cold and the poison snow were all hostile to anyone without a heavily augmented physiology. It was getting harder to breathe here, even with the mask clasped over her nose and mouth.

Following Garro off the elevator ramp, she could not stop herself from throwing a last look back at the corpse of the skitarii she had shot. An ugly burn-wound in the warrior's back showed where the bolt from the lasgun had hit, melting flesh and plasteel into a blackened slurry. What struck her was how swift the death had been. Alive one instant, ended the next.

Was that how Curator Lonnd had perished? she wondered. *Had there been time to see the end coming, time to understand and make peace with it?*

Tallery had dealt in life and death many times, through records of births in Riga's sprawling habitat blocks, to lists of casualties on battlefields across the Imperium. But those had always been abstract things. Numbers on a chart. Ones and zeroes. From this day on, she knew that she would never see them that way again.

'Scribe,' Garro called to her. She turned away and went to the warrior's side. A winged combat drop-ship stood before him, crouched on one of the landing pads like a sleeping hawk. 'This Stormbird is fully fuelled,' he explained. 'We will take it.'

'You do know how to fly this craft?'

He gave a worryingly vague shrug. 'I can get us into the void. From there, we will have to send a distress call on fleet channels and–'

Garro's words died in his throat and Tallery saw him tense. 'My lord, what's wrong?'

His eyes narrowed and his next words were so softly spoken she almost didn't hear. *'Damn them.'*

Unbidden, the Stormbird's drop ramp fell open, revealing a dozen shadowy forms within. Too late, Tallery realised what the legionary already had – that they had delivered themselves into the jaws of a trap.

A cohort of heavily armoured Mechanicum Praetorians advanced from the drop-ship's cargo bay. The machine-hybrids bristled with heavy weapons, each of them moving on a caterpillar-drive chassis that resembled the hull of a battle tank. They were more than a match for a lone Space Marine, and the maws of their plasma cannons and hellguns targeted the pair of them, never wavering.

Tallery sensed movement behind them and spun about. From out of the shadows came more soldiers, blocking off any escape route. But these new arrivals were not of the Mechanicum's red-cloaked tech-guard. Tallery felt a chilling sense of recognition run through her as she saw the colour of the carapace armour worn by the troopers. It was a stormy shade of grey, bereft of any symbols denoting unit, command or allegiance.

Garro saw it too, a question flickering behind those kind eyes of his before he locked it away. He raised his sword into a guard stance, his open hand dropping to the grip of his pistol. 'I am sorry, Katanoh. But it seems I will not be able to keep my vow… To you or to myself. I did not wish to bring you to such an end.'

A terrible inevitability settled upon her. 'We are going to die here.'

'That seems a likely outcome,' said Garro, and he stepped forwards and stared into the guns arrayed against him, glaring with defiance. 'Take your shot, if you will,' he bellowed. 'We shall see how many of you follow me into darkness!'

Tallery tensed, waiting for the first shriek of a las-blast, the first thunder of bolt-fire. She heard nothing but the howl of the wind.

Then the soldiers put up their guns and a grating voice issued out of the chest of the leading Praetorian. 'Battle-Captain Garro. Put up your weapons. You and the scribe will come with us.'

He faced the lethal machine-slave without fear. 'Why should we obey?'

'Our master would speak with you,' it told him.

FLANKED BY THE human troopers and the Praetorians, Garro and Tallery were escorted in silence to the uppermost level of the unfinished citadel. They emerged into a wide circular chamber that resembled the duelling arenas of a Legion training ground. Above them, the roof was a dome made from huge, triangular pieces of glass. The churning amber sky rolled over it, propelled by the constant winds.

Ahead of them, in the centre of the chamber, a raised dais of black marble glittered with reflected light. Garro spied an ill-defined shape beneath a dark cloak standing atop it, a hooded figure turned away from them. An aura of cold fury seemed to emanate from the figure, chilling the legionary even through his power armour. The air around him felt waxy and full of static, as though it were being held in check by some powerful force.

A creeping sense of foreboding gripped Garro's heart, and he chanced a look towards Tallery. The scribe had removed her breather mask and her eyes were wide with fear, but she held her terror under control. He gave her a nod that he hoped she would find reassuring, but in truth, the warrior's own mind was in turmoil as a sinister and potent possibility rose to the fore.

He knew then what he would see beneath that dark
mantle. The figure turned slowly, its face lost in shadow.
Gripped in one gnarled hand, a long staff of black iron
came out of the dimness and sent an echoing crack of
noise as it tapped the marble. Firelight from plasmatic
flames illuminated the space around the dais, spilling
from a narrow steel basket atop the staff. In those flames
sat a golden eagle, and inscribed links hung in chains
about its talons.

Garro knew the staff as he knew the man who wielded
it. The hood dropped back and the old-but-ageless face
of Malcador the Sigillite stared down at them, displeasure written clearly upon it.

Unable to resist the indoctrination that had been bred
into her since birth, the scribe dropped to her knees in
supplication. She bowed her head, and the skitarii did
the same, showing fealty to the man who stood second
only to the Emperor of Mankind. The First Lord of the
Council and Regent of Terra, and the master that Nathaniel Garro had sworn to obey.

But despite every impulse in his flesh to do so, the
legionary did not kneel. The question that burned in
his breast overshadowed all other compulsions. 'How
are you here?'

'I am everywhere and nowhere, Garro,' Malcador
intoned. 'This place belongs to me.' His words were
low and weighty with reproach. 'You should not have
come. You are not ready to see this. The preparations are
incomplete.'

'Are you a traitor?' Garro blurted out the demand,
desperately trying to square what he had learned from
Tallery with the reality now before him.

The hooded figure allowed a grim chuckle to escape

his thin lips. 'Open your eyes. You know what I am. The Sigillite is the Emperor's right hand. To betray Him would be impossible.'

'Horus Lupercal might once have said the same.'

Malcador's eyes flashed, and his face darkened. When he replied, it was with a chilling ferocity that cut Garro to his bones. 'Never compare me to the arch-traitor. I will burn your mind if you speak those words again.' He gestured with one hand. 'Kneel, Nathaniel. Obey me.'

The legionary shook his head wildly. 'Not until you explain all... *this!*' Garro cast around, gesturing at the walls, the Praetorians and the troopers in grey.

'I told you to *kneel*.' The Sigillite glared at him, and Garro lost control of his legs. In a heartbeat he was down on his knees, his great strength as nothing to the telepathic force pressing him to obey.

Locked in place inside his own armour, he could only turn his head to hold the other man's baleful gaze, even as he knew that it had taken a mere fraction of Malcador's monumental psionic power to humble him.

'I am the keeper of the secret of Othrys, the secret you were so eager to know,' said the Sigillite. 'So turn your sight to the skies, then. See where your blind path has brought you.'

Garro looked up, and saw Tallery daring to do the same. Out past the great dome, the sea of orange cloud thinned, as though some unnatural force were reaching out to part the veil. Black night sky beyond the planetoid's atmosphere was suddenly revealed, and there, hanging in the darkness like some shimmering jewel, lay a familiar gas giant world haloed by gossamer rings.

'Saturn...' whispered Tallery.

'Then we stand upon–'

'The Titan moon, *yes*,' Malcador answered for him. 'Did you think it to be some distant death world beyond the pale?'

Garro struggled to process what he was seeing. 'This makes no sense! If what you are building here is in service to the Emperor and the Imperium, why hide it behind this shield of lies? Why seek to silence anyone who learns of it?'

The Sigillite's dark eyes burned into him like star-fire. 'You question me?'

'I do!' It took all of Garro's effort to hold that gaze. 'This fortress citadel and the complex beneath it, it can be for only one intention. The creation and training of a new Space Marine Legion...'

'Only the Emperor Himself may grant life to the Legiones Astartes,' whispered Tallery, as if the thought itself was some kind of blasphemy.

'Does He know you are doing this, Malcador?' Garro pressed on, too far past the point of no return to turn back. 'Does the Emperor know what you do in His name?'

'My master...' The Sigillite's deathly stare lessened as he considered the question. 'He has His great tasks to occupy Him. And I have mine.'

PART OF KATANOH Tallery wanted to close herself off in the depths of her mind and wait for the inevitable end to come. But another, ever-inquisitive shard of her could not look away from the great psyker-lord. She could not meet her end without knowing the truth.

'Are these s-secrets worth my life?' Tallery forced out the words. 'And Curator Lonnd's?'

Malcador gave her a cold, indulgent look. 'My dear

scribe. The answer is *yes*. A hundred thousand times over, *yes*. For the greater good of our Imperium.'

At her side, Garro struggled to bring his fist to his chestplate. 'This is not enough, then? My strength? That of Rubio, Ison, Loken, Varren, Gallor and all the others? It is not enough for you to have your agents at large in the galaxy, now you must have an army?'

The litany of names meant nothing to Tallery, but they deepened the dark shadows over Malcador's face. 'You are my Agentia Primus, Nathaniel,' he told the legionary. 'But what I forge here will not be for me. A handful of Knights Errant are not enough. Not for the coming war.'

And now the scribe grasped a new measure of understanding, one so great that it made her feel hollow inside. 'You're not just talking about the Warmaster's rebellion, are you, Lord Regent? You mean something else. *Something worse.*'

The Sigillite raised an eyebrow. 'She has insight, this one. I see now why she has caused such problems.' With his iron staff tapping out each pace, Malcador stepped down from the dais and advanced towards them. 'Nathaniel has seen the dangers that lie beyond the edge of reason. He has fought them face-to-face. I have looked into that darkness, divining the myriad skeins of futures-yet-to-be. The things that Horus has allied himself to, these otherworldly and daemonic things, they will threaten humankind for millennia to come.' He eyed her. 'I know this in my blood. So we must be prepared for the war that will come after this one. A war that will be for our very souls.'

'And this is to be where those defenders are forged,' she said. 'Othrys.'

Malcador nodded once. 'In the old tongues the name

means "the home of the titans". The symbolism of it seemed fitting.' The Sigillite turned his back on Tallery and moved to Garro's side, removing the warrior's sword from its scabbard. 'Do you see now?' He asked the question as he examined the giant's blade, and Tallery knew no common man would have been able to lift it. 'These preparations must be made in secret, not only to conceal them from the eyes of Horus and his allies, but from our own people. From an Imperium that is not yet ready to accept the truth of what horrors lurk in the warp. Am I wrong, Nathaniel?'

After a long moment, Garro gave a reluctant nod. 'No, Lord Regent, you are not wrong.'

With a tilt of his head, the psyker relaxed the telepathic grip he held on Garro, and the warrior was released. Malcador turned *Libertas* in his hand and offered him the weapon's hilt. 'These secrets can only be kept by those of unflinching courage, through sacrifice and the shedding of blood. Because of an insignificant error, because of pure happenstance, Scribe-Adepta Tallery learned something she should never have known.'

Desperation fluttered against the inside of Tallery's chest. 'I am loyal,' she said, beseechingly. 'I will never speak of this. I swear it on the Throne of Terra, and in the Emperor's name!'

The Sigillite went on as if she had never spoken. 'She cannot live with this knowledge. Even the most loyal can be suborned, even those who never speak can have their secrets torn from them by arcane means. Only the dead cannot vouchsafe the truth.' He held up the hilt before Garro. 'Take the sword, Nathaniel. I am not cruel. Make it swift and without pain.'

The warrior hesitated, eyeing the weapon, and the

scribe felt the blood drain from her face. 'He tests me, Tallery,' said Garro. 'I defied him by taking my leave to Riga without his permission. I have stepped outside the bounds of his orders in days past. So now he tests me with this, to see if I will still obey.'

'It must be done. Even the scribe herself knows that.' Malcador glanced at her and in an instant her thoughts became his, stripped bare so that the Sigillite could be sure of her. 'She is truly loyal. She will not resist.'

The bleak truth was that Malcador did not lie. Tallery *was* willing to die in the Emperor's name, in the service of something greater than herself.

Garro's response took another path, however. 'I regret that I must refuse your command, Lord Regent.'

Malcador's eyes locked with Garro's, and his baleful stare was terrible to behold. 'I have only to think it and her heart will stop.'

The legionary nodded. 'Then it will be *you* who murders an innocent. *You* that takes the life of a faithful subject of the Emperor, who has done no wrong, who has committed no crime but to serve the Imperium.' He drew himself up. 'And if that is your choice, then end me into the bargain. For I do not wish to be party to such choices as an arch-traitor would make.'

'What other choice is there?' hissed the Sigillite.

Garro glanced at Tallery, and she drew strength from him. He looked away, once more matching the Sigillite's gaze without flinching. 'You said it yourself, my lord. The scribe has insight. I can attest to that, and to her courage and fidelity. So why not *use* those talents? Make her part of what is done here. Bring her into the circle.' The scribe dared to hope as Garro's impassioned plea for her life went on. 'Tallery was clever enough to find a flaw in the security of Othrys, from the other side of the Solar System. She could solve that for you, and seek out any other weaknesses that might yet be unknown.'

Tallery held her breath, knowing that her life hung in the balance. Closing her eyes, she knew also what she needed to do. Her fingers found the golden aquila about her wrist and gripped it tightly.

'The Emperor protects,' she whispered. 'The Emperor protects.'

GARRO HELD THE sword at eye-level and sighted down the length of the blade. There were no nicks in its edge, no discolorations in the metal. It seemed perfect, as if it had been newly forged that day. And yet, the weapon had lived for centuries in various forms, and been soaked in the blood of many souls long dead. He comforted himself in knowing that no innocents had fallen to the blade while he had been its master.

Returning the weapon to its scabbard, he turned to watch a Stormbird on a nearby landing pad as the flight crew prepared it for departure. It would take him away from Titan, not back to Terra, but towards his next mission under the Sigillite's command. The thought of that brought a frown to him, and he felt a bleak mood gathering on the horizon.

He heard footsteps approaching across the platform, and turned about to see a pale face peering up at him. 'Legionary!' Tallery looked very different in her new robes and finery, a million miles away from the fatigued, terrified woman he had first laid eyes on in Riga. 'Captain Garro, I should say. Did you intend to leave without saying farewell?'

He gave a shallow bow, making the sign of the aquila

across his chest. 'I did not wish to interrupt your new duties, scribe.' He paused, recalling her new rank and status. 'Forgive me. *Curator-Adepta Primus* Tallery.'

She showed a brief smile. 'The title seems a strange fit to me. And so does my life, if that makes any sense. Everything is different now.'

'It will never be the same,' he agreed. 'I know whereof I speak. After Isstvan, after the flight of the *Eisenstein*, I felt the same way.'

'Changed.'

'Yes. And for the worse as well as the better.' She seemed uncertain of his meaning and he went on. 'You will learn more in the days to come, Tallery. Terrible things. And there may come a time when you resent me for not doing as Malcador ordered.'

The woman hesitated, but then pushed her reluctance away. 'I will face those challenges with faith and courage. You reminded me where to find them. In this new role I will be able to serve my Imperium and my Emperor – my *God-Emperor* – to the very fullest in the days to come.'

Her use of the forbidden honorific dismayed him and he lowered his voice in a warning tone. 'You must never speak that name before Lord Malcador, or the others. They would not be receptive to it.'

'In time, perhaps,' she countered. 'But not now.'

He sighed. 'You will never be able to go home again.'

'A small price to pay,' said Tallery, and he knew she meant every word. 'I never had the chance to thank you for defending me. The Sigillite was correct. I would not have resisted, if my death served a greater good.'

Garro had known that about her from their earliest meeting, but he chose to say nothing of it. 'Fate had another path for you. For both of us. You will make a difference here, in the war against the insurrectionists.'

She reached up and laid a hand upon his armoured gauntlet. 'I hope you find the answers you are looking for. In the words of the Saint, or elsewhere.'

He wanted to share that hope, but despite the warmth in the woman's tone, Garro felt a darkness creeping across his spirit. The ghosts of emotions he could not fully articulate clouded his mind. This bleak sense of his future had been the spur that sent him looking for Keeler, searching her out on Riga and finding nothing. It was as though a hollow bell were ringing in the far distance, and with each peal Nathaniel Garro was slipping further and further away from it.

Tallery saw the haunted look in his eyes. 'What's wrong?'

'There is a shadow out there, Tallery,' he told her. 'A shadow of my future. I can only grasp the edges of it, but I fear that my path is not what I first thought it to be.' The Stormbird's engines rumbled to life and Garro stepped away, throwing her one last glance. 'I do not know where my destiny lies. I only know that it is not *here.*'

He turned his back on Tallery and strode up the drop ramp. 'You must have faith, Nathaniel!' she cried out. 'Remember that.' Her last words were almost lost to him as the thrusters fired and the hatch mechanism wound closed, but his genhanced hearing caught the final, faint entreaty on the Titan winds.

'The Emperor protects.'

PART THREE
THE VOW

'Belief is blindness of a kind so powerful that certain men willingly seek it out.'

– Shollegar Meketrix Yonparabas,
from *Words Matter Not* [M24]

'When all the Knights are gone, only their enemies will truly care. Those they saved and served will flock to the aegis of new protectors, never recalling their names.'

– attributed to the Imperial
remembrancer Ignace Karkasy

FIFTEEN

Crimson on white
Old ground
Leave-taking

As HE WAITED for the dawn glow to rise higher, the man turned in a slow circle and passed the time reading the history in the landscape around him. Some of it he gathered from his own instincts, more he took from flashes of mnemon-implants fed into his brain by the hypnogoges, long before he had come to Terra.

The forest of tall, mutated fir trees filled a valley that had once been a bay bordered by city sprawls now long-dead and lost. The iron-hard trunks, grey-green like ancient jade, ranged away in all directions beyond the clearing where he had landed the cargo lighter. He could see former islands that were now stubby mesas protruding from the valley floor, even pick out the distant shapes of old buildings swallowed by the tree line. But to the east, the clearest of the decrepit monuments to the dead city were the towers of a long-vanished highway bridge. Only the twisted remains of two narrow gates remained, rust-chewed and thousands of years old. Beyond them, in the time before the Fall of Night, there had been a great ocean; now, the strange forest petered out and became the endless desert of the Mendocine Plains.

The bleakness of that thought was somehow comforting. *Entropy is eternal*, it said. *Whatever we do today, it will matter not in centuries to come. Forests anew will rise and engulf all deeds.*

He turned and walked back to the lighter. The snow on the ground hissed beneath his footfalls as he came around to the drop ramp at the rear, open like a fallen drawbridge. Inside the flyer's otherwise empty hold, a man in a maintenance worker's oversuit looked up at his approach and pulled listlessly at the magnetic cuff tethering him to a support frame. The two of them were similarly dressed, alike in average height and nondescript aspect, but the chained man's face was swollen and florid.

'Haln,' he began, his words emerging in puffs of vapour, 'Look, comrade, this has gone far enough! I'm freezing my balls off–'

His real name was not Haln, but it was who he was today. He stepped in and punched the worker in the face three times to stop him talking. Then, while the man was dazed and reeling, Haln released the mag-cuff and used it to lead his captive out of the lighter. He chanced a look up into the cloudy sky. *Not long now.*

The worker tried to speak, but all that came out was a wet, breathy noise.

Perhaps he had thought they were friends. Perhaps the fiction that was Haln had been so good that the worker bought its reality without question. People usually did. Haln was a well-trained, highly accomplished liar.

He wanted to strike the worker again, but it was important that the man not bleed, not yet. With his free hand,

Haln pulled a metallic spider from one of the deep pockets of his overcoat and clamped it around the worker's throat. His captive whimpered and then cried out in pain as the neurodendrite probes that were the spider's legs entered his flesh, and found their way through meat and bone to nerve clusters and brain tissue.

Haln released him, but not before giving the worker another item – an Imperial soldier's battle knife. It was old, blackened by disuse and corrosion. There were stories in it, but they would not be heard today.

The worker accepted the blade, wide-eyed and confused. Wondering why he had been handed a weapon.

Haln didn't give him time to think too long about it. He pulled back the sleeve of his coat to reveal a control panel with hologlyph keys, secured around his wrist. Haln placed the fingers of his other hand on the panel and slid them around, feeling for the right position. In synchrony, the worker cried out and began a sudden, spastic series of motions. The spider device accepted the signals from the control and made him a puppet. He staggered back and forth as Haln got a sense of the range of motion. He began to weep, and through coughing sobs, the worker begged for his life.

Haln ignored his slurred entreaties, walking him away into the middle of the large clearing where the chemstained snow was still virgin. When he was satisfied, Haln looked again at the oncoming dawn and nodded once.

Highlighting two glyphs made the worker bring the old knife to his throat and draw it across. Manipulating other symbols forced his legs to work, walking him around in a perfect circle as blood jetted from the widening wound. Haln watched the spurts of crimson form jagged, steaming lines in the snowfall. Each wet red axis pointed away to the horizon.

Eventually, the cut killed the worker and he dropped, sprawled across the mark of his own making. Haln felt a change in the air, a grotesquely familiar acidity that was alien and uncanny. It was good, he decided.

He saw the object before he heard it. A hole melted through the low clouds and a flickering meteoric form fell from the sky. A heartbeat later, a supersonic scream came with it – although he knew no-one else beyond the valley would hear it, walled in and smothered as it was by the magicks the spilled blood provided.

The object slammed into the earth with enough shock force to toss Haln back ten yards, and rock the cargo lighter on its landing skids. When he rose to his feet, Haln saw that a shallow pit had been dug by the impact, revealing black dirt beneath the bloodstained snow. The worker's corpse had been directly beneath the fall, the very point upon which it was targeted – and if any of the man now remained, it was only shreds and rags.

In the pit was a capsule not unlike those used to eject the bodies of the dead into stars for solar cremation. Hot and sizzling, it creaked and shuddered as something moved inside. Haln looked up again and saw the hole in the cloud sealing up once more. He allowed himself a moment to wonder where the pod had come from – dropped by a ship from orbit, dragged from the immaterium itself, conjured out of a dream? – and then forgot his own question. It wasn't important. Only the mission mattered.

Heat seared him, even through his heavy gloves, but Haln found the seam of the capsule and pulled on it. A wash of thick air dense with human smells assaulted him, and fingers of fire-burned flesh emerged through the widening gap. Then presently a hand, an arm, a torso. A figure stepped onto Terran soil – a tall man with unkempt hair, a hawkish face and haunted, wild eyes – and glared at him.

'It worked,' he growled. 'Each time, I think it will not. I shouldn't. Should not doubt.' The words he spoke were rough and scratchy. The new arrival's tone made Haln imagine a feral animal taught to walk upright and speak like a person.

Haln gestured at the pod interior. 'You need to kill your pathfinder, before it–'

The other man's dark eyes flashed. 'I know. I've done this before.' He hesitated. 'Haven't I?' He shook off his own question and reached into the capsule. With a wet tearing noise, he ripped a bulb of gelatinous, oily flesh from where it had been nestled in among the pod's inner workings. It writhed and squealed, trying to squirm out of his grip.

Haln was going to offer the man another of his many knives with which to finish the task, but when he looked back the new arrival had a pistol in his fist. Haln had not seen him draw it, had not even seen a holster for the gun. Even the weapon itself seemed strange – he didn't really see it, it was more like he saw the impression of it. Something murderous and accursed made of chromed parts moving with no mechanical logic; or was it assembled out of glassy crystal and ruby-red liquid? He had no time to really understand, because it fired and his vision went purple with the afterimage.

Even the proscribed mech-enhancements of Haln's vision didn't stop the retina burn, and he blinked furiously. After a moment, his sight returned and there was only grey ash where the pathfinder-thing had been. The pistol had vanished.

He said nothing of it. These things, these moments of not-understanding, they were not new to Haln. He kept himself above them by remembering – once again – the mission, the mission, always the mission.

'Were you briefed?' said the man. His manner shifted like the winds. Now he was cold and professional.

'A basic summary. I am to provide operational support for the duration of your assignment,' he replied. 'My name is Haln, for the interim.'

'How long have you served Horus?'

Haln hesitated, glancing around. Even here in the deep wilds, far from the nearest settlement, he was reluctant to speak the Warmaster's name aloud. 'Longer than I have been aware,' he said, at length. A more honest answer to that question would be lengthy and complex.

That seemed to amuse the other man. 'Truth in that,' he allowed, and started for the cargo lighter. 'There are several avenues to follow but only one target. You'll help me locate it.'

Haln nodded and reached inside his coat for a melta grenade, priming the timer and radius so it would obliterate all trace of the pod and the sacrifice. 'As you wish,' he told the assassin.

HALF A WORLD away, a sky of artificial night made the wastes of Albia seem like a sketch in charcoal and slate. Miles above the ground, the aerotropolis of Kolob cast a massive shadow as it floated on a ring of colossal antigravs, causing microclimate veils of hard, cold rain to race across the stony hillsides.

The warrior had been walking for the better part of a

day. His Stormbird had climbed away and left him on a twisted crag somewhere in the northern sinks, just as ordered. He climbed down and started on a southerly path, his pace careful and the solid clanks and hisses of his power armour a steady metronome. He walked, waiting for the great emptiness of the landscape to clear his thoughts. It had not happened yet.

This place was home to him, or it would have been if that word held any true meaning for the legionary. His past was a gossamer thing, faint and ephemeral, so delicate that he wondered if looking too closely upon it would make it fade forever. The memories of the time before he took on oath and armour in service to the Imperium of Man were strange to him. In many ways, they were a fiction he had been told more than a chain of events he had actually experienced.

Had he ever really been the ragged youth that lurked in his deep recollection? The one that was sallow of face and always cold? If he reached for it, if he dug in and tried hard, he could pull some fragments back to the surface. Sensations, mostly. Pieces so small and dislocated that they hardly deserved to be thought of as memories. *Warmth in the embrace of a parent. The sight of shooting stars crossing the sky. A lake of captured sunlight, as gold as coin.*

Those events were centuries old. The outlines of the faces he saw there belonged to people long since dead and turned to dust, their voices lost to him. Wiped away by the bio-programming and hardwiring of his brain that made him a superlative warrior. Like all of his kind, the forgetting was required to reforge him into what he had become.

These grains of his old self were all that remained, trapped in the cracks of his newer nature, the one carved

out of the body he was born in and built anew with
implants, techno-organs and powerful genetic modifica-
tions. He carried a special, quiet apprehension that one
day he would look for these grains and they would be
gone. The legionary knew brothers like that, who had
lost whatever had made them human.

He looked up into the sky, watching the orbital plate's
slow progress, thinking of those men. Some of them were
like him, holding on to the threads of their better selves
in silent desperation, but more – far too many more –
had willingly opened their hands and let go of any ties
to Terra, to the past, to who they had once been.

Once, he would not have had the words to describe
these events, but ever since the insurrection, he did. He
thought of his battle-brothers as having given up their
souls, if there were such a thing.

The warrior halted at the edge of a crumbling ridge,
surrounding a vast pit that resembled a volcanic caldera.
There had been a city here long ago, assembled atop a
network of tunnels and caverns, but wars had washed
over it and torn it away. Remnants of the ancient caves
were visible down there, laid bare by forces that had
shredded mountains. He knew this place, the spectre of
it trapped in one of the memory-pieces. Perhaps he had
lived in the shanty-towns that clustered down along the
walls of the pit, or ventured from one of the hive towers in the far distance. He did not know. The content of
the memory was gone, only its empty vessel capable of
bringing him to this place.

Another hard pulse of rain lashed over him, and he
glimpsed his own flickering reflection in an elongated
puddle. A hulking shape in ghost-grey wargear, face hidden behind a beaked, cold-eyed battle helm. A cuirass

about his shoulders with golden detail, rendered dull and lifeless by the bleak sky. A great sword in the scabbard on his back, a master-crafted bolter clamped to his hip.

He reached up and removed the helmet, mag-locking it to a thigh plate, taking a breath of damp air laced with heavy pollutants. He met his own gaze on the water's surface.

The Knight Errant Nathaniel Garro looked back at himself, measuring the scars that were the map of his war record. He felt old and empty, a sensation that had been banished from him for a long while but now returned in full effect. The last time he had experienced such a thing, it had been as the madness unfolded over Isstvan III. As he stood aboard the frigate *Eisenstein* and slowly came to the shattering conclusion that his Legion had betrayed him. As the Warmaster Horus' rebellion had been birthed before him, the very personal treachery of his brethren and his primarch Mortarion hollowed him out.

Perhaps, if he had been without courage and honour, Garro might have faltered in that moment, might never have recovered from what he witnessed. But instead, he found a new kind of strength. Emboldened by the singular truth laid bare before him – that of his unswerving loyalty to Terra and the Emperor of Mankind – Garro defied the traitors and set upon a flight into danger, racing back to the Solar System with word of warning.

Had he been without focus, Garro's future and that of the refugees he brought with him might have ended with that deed. But his loyalty found reward, of a sort. The Emperor's right hand, the great psyker and Regent of Terra Malcador the Sigillite, took the reins of Garro's purpose. The former Battle-Captain of the Death Guard became Agentia Primus of the Sigillite's clandestine task

force. He became a Knight Errant, legionless but charged
with great deeds.

Or so he had believed. After years of working to Malcador's byzantine orders, recruiting others like himself,
chasing down Horus' spies, secretly crisscrossing the stars
beneath the shroud of a tormented galaxy, Garro's certainty of purpose became clouded. More and more, he
was coming to believe that fate had spared him at Isstvan for something larger than just the Sigillite's enigmatic
designs. Already he had openly challenged Malcador's
commands, in the Somnus Citadel on Luna and in the
halls of an unfinished fortress on distant Titan. How
long would it be before he spoke his doubts aloud and
in the fullest? Garro could not hold to silence forever. It
simply was not in his character.

His craggy face twisted in a scowl, annoyance flaring.
He had been foolish to come here. Some sentimental
part of his spirit hoped that walking these lands would
take him to a calmer place, where he could quiet his
uncertainties and find a measure of peace. But that
was not happening, and he knew it would never come.
He resented the lack of answers, the directionless una-
wareness that pushed and pulled at him whenever his
thoughts should have been at rest. More than anything,
he wanted to come to a place of tranquillity and in it,
find understanding. Garro was a legionary, a soldier born
to duty, but the one before him was not *right*. It was not
enough.

Everyone in the galaxy had been changed by Horus'
sedition, if they knew it or not. Garro knew with great
clarity how *he* had been altered. Something had broken
free inside him as his Legion's sworn oaths had blackened and disintegrated. He was more than just a weapon

of war, to be directed at a target and told to fight or perish. A heavier mantle had fallen upon him, a champion's duty.

Have faith, Nathaniel. You are of purpose.

The words echoed in his thoughts. The woman Keeler, she had opened his mind to that truth. She understood. Perhaps for Garro to understand too, he would need to find her again and–

On the wet breeze he sensed the stale odour of animals, and froze. Garro listened and picked out the footfalls of two quadrupeds, stalking him across the shale and mud. He turned his head and picked them out against the dark stone.

Lupenate forms, the pair of them. Predators evolved from the wolves that had once stalked the woodlands of this region, in the times before the trees had died off, never to return. Their large bodies were long and sinuous, their fur slick with secreted oils that sloughed off the toxic rains and made their thermal aspects harder to see. Arrow-shaped ears twitched and stiffened as they tracked Garro's smallest movement, while narrow eyes fixed him with a gelid, hungry gaze.

Normally, lupenates stayed away from the edges of human-habited zones, preferring to prey on the odd unwary traveller caught out alone. That a hunting pair had come so close to the shanty towns in the pit could only mean their life cycle was being disrupted as well as everyone else's on Terra. The global day-and-night preparations for Horus' inevitable invasion trickled down to even the most insignificant of the planet's creatures.

Garro had drawn his sword without being aware of it. The power blade *Libertas*, his stalwart war companion for a hundred years and a thousand conflicts, could slice through tank armour when fully charged. His lip curled. These animals were not worth that expenditure of energy.

'Go!' he barked at them, planting the sword in the ground with its hilt facing the sky. Garro took a menacing step towards the predators. 'Be gone!'

But the lupenates were starving and agitated beyond rationality. They attacked, flashing forward in a glistening arc of motion. Both leapt at him, smelling his breath, claws and teeth aiming to gain purchase on the bare flesh of his face.

The legionary's arm blurred and he snatched the closest of the creatures from the air at the top of its arc, grabbing it by the throat. The second he batted away with the back of his gauntlet – he saw it crash into the rocks with a furious yelp.

The lupenate in his grip spat venom at him, missing his face but spattering on his chest plate. The droplets sizzled where they landed, scorching the slate-coloured armour. Garro's lips thinned and he threw the creature in the direction of the standing sword. His aim was true enough, and the blade so sharp even in its inactive state, that the force of the throw bifurcated the creature and sent its parts tumbling over the edge of the pit. He stalked across to the second, wounded animal and stamped down on its head, crushing its skull beneath his heavy ceramite boot before it could rise.

Grim-faced, Garro returned to recover *Libertas*. If he had believed in omens, the appearance of the lupenates would mean ill portent.

'A wolf,' said a careful voice, 'attacking out of blind hate and savagery. That reminds me of someone.'

Garro withdrew his sword and replaced it in the scabbard, noting that the rain had suddenly stopped. 'Horus is not a savage. Unless he needs to be.'

ABOUT THE AUTHOR

James Swallow is best known for being the
author of the *Horus Heresy* novels *Fear to
Tread* and *Nemesis*, which both reached the
New York Times bestseller lists, *The Flight of
the Eisenstein* and a series of audio dramas
featuring the character Nathaniel Garro.
For Warhammer 40,000, he has written
four Blood Angels novels, the audio dramas
Corsair: The Face of the Void, Heart of Rage, and
two Sisters of Battle novels. His short fiction
has appeared in *Legends of the Space Marines*
and *Tales of Heresy.*

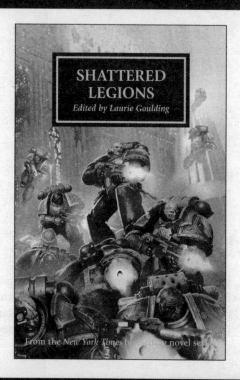

He turned and found Malcador studying the dead animal with mild disdain. Quite how the Sigillite was able to approach him without sound or signal, the legionary did not know. Garro had learned not to ask such questions, as there were never any answers that satisfied him.

'Was it necessary to kill them?' said the other man, rolling back the cloak that concealed his gaunt features. Pale, silver hair fell to his shoulders. 'The beasts have as much right to be here as you.'

'I gave them the chance to withdraw,' said the warrior. 'I would grant the same to any foe.'

'Honourable in all things.' Malcador gave a small shrug and looked away, dismissing the moment.

Is he actually here? Garro wondered. I could be perceiving some fragment of him projected by a psyker's might... It was very possible that in all the times Garro had stood before the Sigillite, he had in fact *never* stood before him, at least not in the most literal sense. The Regent of Terra's psionic power was said to be second only to that of the Emperor himself, and the Emperor...

Divine was not a word that Garro would have used, but there were few others that could encompass the power of the Master of Mankind. If the Emperor were not a god, then he was as near to it as had ever existed. The image of a golden icon, of a two-headed aquila dancing on the end of a chain, flitted through his thoughts and he pushed it away.

The Sigillite looked towards him, as if he could smell the memory just as the wolf-things had caught Garro's scent. 'You have not found what you are looking for, Nathaniel,' he said. 'This has become troubling to me.'

'I perform my duties to your order,' said the legionary.

Malcador smiled. 'There's more to it than that. Don't

deflect. I chose you to serve because of your honesty, your… simplicity. But as time passes, the clear view I have becomes more clouded.' The smile faded. 'Duty turns to burden. Obedience chafes and eventually becomes defiance. It was this way with the Luna Wolf.' He nodded toward the dead lupenate. 'I did not see it until it was too late. And so I am watchful for the same patterns now, closer to home.'

Garro stiffened. 'After I tallied all the things I lost in order to prove my allegiance,' he began, 'my legion, my brotherhood… I told myself that the next man who dared to suggest I was disloyal would bleed for it.'

'Ah, but your promise contains a fatal flaw,' Malcador replied, ignoring the threat. 'You begin from the assumption that loyalty is a fixed point, immutable once established…' The Sigillite broke off, and turned to look eastward, his eyes narrowing as if attracted by something only he could perceive. After a moment he turned away and continued, speaking as if nothing had happened. 'But it is a flag planted in sand, Nathaniel. It can and will drift under the action of outside forces you may never see, until you are challenged. You were loyal to Mortarion, until the moment you were not. You were loyal to the Warmaster, until you were not. You are loyal to me–'

'I am loyal to the Emperor,' Garro corrected him, 'and on my life, that flag will never fall.'

'I believe you,' said the Sigillite. 'But my point still stands. Your missions, the whole reason why I gave you the grey and my mark to carry…' He gestured to Garro's armour, where the small icon of a stylised eye was barely visible. 'They have been obscured of late by other issues.'

Garro looked away. 'You speak of what I glimpsed on Saturn's moon.'

Malcador shook his head. 'It began long before you ventured to places that are outside your purview.' The Sigillite wandered to the edge of the pit and looked down, taking in the gloomy settlement far below. 'You went to the Riga orbital plate at your own bidding. You have been casting out feelers in the time between your missions, looking for something. Someone.'

Garro became very still. *Of course Malcador knows*, he told himself. *How could I have believed he would not see the pattern?*

'Yes,' continued the Sigillite. 'I am aware of the Lectitio Divinitatus and the believers who have read Lorgar's book.'

'Lord Aurelian? The Word Bearer... ?' Garro's brow furrowed, unsure if he had heard Malcador correctly.

The Sigillite went on. 'I know they think of our Emperor as a living deity, despite all his words to the contrary.' He took a step back. 'And I know of the woman, Euphrati Keeler. The mere remembrancer who is now revered as a living saint.'

The question slipped out of Garro's mouth before he could stop himself from uttering it. 'Where is she?'

Malcador gave a rueful smile. 'Not *everything* is clear to me, Nathaniel. Even if that is the image I like to project. Some things...' The smile became brittle. 'Some places, even I cannot reach. As curious as that is.'

'But if you know of them, why do you allow the gatherings to go on unchecked?'

'There are so many, and more with each passing month.' The Sigillite opened his arms to the sky. 'But perhaps you have forgotten that we are embroiled in a war that threatens to consume the galaxy? There are many things of far greater import before me. They are not like the lodges that Horus used to suborn the legions. These believers are little more than groups of worried people drawing solace from the pages of a fanatic's scribblings.' He paused, thinking. 'That book proves my earlier point, when I spoke of malleable loyalty. Lorgar Aurelian was so very faithful when he wrote it. And look at him now.'

Garro nodded. 'I saw the Seventeenth Legion before Ullanor, and then after Isstvan. Like day and night, they were – but still a commonality of mad zeal in each incarnation.' He paused, marshalling his words. 'But I am not a Word Bearer. I am not even a Death Guard any more. I am only the Emperor's sword, and that I will remain until the day I die.'

'I believe you,' Malcador repeated. 'But even the best of blades can become blunted and careworn if left untended. It is clear that you cannot function fully as my Agentia Primus while you remain distracted by other concerns.' The Sigillite's tone hardened, and Garro found himself unconsciously taking up a combat stance.

His war-implants flexed and came alive, as they would if he were about to engage a foe. The very real possibility that Malcador was going to end him sang through Garro's nerves.

'You are of no use to me if you are preoccupied. I need agents who are here, in the moment. I need weapons and tools, if I am to end the war before it blackens Terra's skies.'

'Speak plainly, then,' Garro demanded. If the worst were to come, he would meet it head on; this was not the first time he had been ready for such an outcome.

Malcador sighed. 'After much consideration, I have decided to grant you a leave of absence, of a sort.' He gestured at the sky, the floating city still blotting out the weak sun above them. 'Go and find your answers, Nathaniel. Wherever they may lie.'

It was the last thing Garro had expected from the Sigillite. Censure and reprimand, indeed… But not *permission*. 'You would allow that?'

'I spoke the words. I have granted it.' Malcador eyed him. 'But there are certain conditions. You will leave behind your wargear, your power armour, your weapons. And more importantly, you will go without the authority I have conferred upon you. In this, you will be only Nathaniel Garro, late of the Death Guard Legiones Astartes. Whatever you want, you will find it on your own.'

In the distance, Garro heard the sound of powerful engines on a fast approach. A drop-ship was coming in. The warrior reached for his sword and removed it, scabbard and all, from his armour. 'I will not leave *Libertas* in the hands of another,' he intoned. 'All else, I agree to.'

'And still you challenge me, even in this…' Malcador folded his arms. 'Very well. Keep the sword. Perhaps you will need it.'

A Thunderhawk in unadorned grey livery crested the far ridgeline and tore over the pit, slowing to a hover on jets of flame. It pivoted in place as the pilot looked for somewhere to set down. Garro had done nothing to summon the drop-ship, nor seen Malcador do likewise, and yet here it was.

'They will take you where you want to go,' said the Sigillite, his words carrying over the howl of the engines. Garro raised a hand to shield his face as the Thunderhawk settled on the wide crag, the down-draft blasting a spray of rainwater up and about him. 'But do not tarry. Horus is coming and we must be ready. I will array every servant of the Emperor in preparation to resist him, and you are counted in that number. Am I clear?'

Garro nodded as the Thunderhawk's thrusters fell to an idling growl. 'Aye,' he replied, turning back to look at the Sigillite. 'It is–'

He stood alone on the ridge, as the rain began to fall once again.

SIXTEEN

Sanctuary
Last words
Confrontation

NDOLE CAST A nervous glance over his shoulder, towards the back of the ground-effect truck where the big man sat cloaked in shadows. He was large enough to fill the cargo bed of the hovercraft, even bent forward with his head turned down. The big man's eyes were closed, but Ndole knew he wasn't sleeping. His kind weren't capable of that, so someone had once told him.

The driver's lips thinned and he forced himself to concentrate on the path ahead. A haze of displaced sand moved in a constant wave front before the vehicle. Kicked up by its screaming blowers, the microscopic particles of rusty metal and mineral glass forever scoured at the truck's exterior. Ndole leaned in and out of shallow, drifting turns as he guided them over the desert landscape. He kept them on rivers of sand that snaked through the larger pieces of debris that studded the terrain; here the remains of a massive bat-winged strato-carrier from the Unification Wars, there a beached ocean

liner half-buried under the skeleton of a derelict arcology
dome. Smaller clumps of metallic waste formed hillocks
of corroded iron, all of it the collapsed remains of civi-
lisations that had died before the Age of the Imperium.

He knew he had to keep his attention on the journey,
because at the speed they were travelling across an area
this cluttered, even a glancing collision could tear the
truck in two and leave them stranded out here. Ndole
had no doubt the big man would survive something like
that, but he rated his own chances far lower.

It was hard not to keep stealing a peek, though. He had
never seen a legionary close at hand before, and to think
one of them was here, in his vehicle... Was it a dream
or a nightmare? He hoped neither, and reflected on how
he had come to give the warrior passage.

It wasn't as if the big man had threatened Ndole to
make him obey. It wasn't as if he had to. Back at the
border settlement, where the Wasted Ranges ended and
the Nordafrik Territories really began, everyone in the
tap house had heard the screech of the drop-ship passing overhead. It worried them all. Ndole listened to the
server fret about how it could mean the bastard archtraitor was finally here, but he knew that it would not be a
ship that came to warn them of that. Ndole fully expected
his first sign of Horus' invasion to be the sky catching fire.

The drop-ship must have let the big man out at the
edge of the settlement, because a few seconds later, two
panicked youths in rad-capes came hurtling through, falling over themselves to warn of the new arrival.

He came in only a moment after them. Curious, it was,
the sight of a legionary without his power armour, but no
less intimidating. At first, he had thought the man might
have been a genhanced worker from the breaker's station,

but something in his bearing – and myriad scars – spoke otherwise. Even in the hooded grey cloak, the warrior blocked the doorway with his bulk, and had to lower his head in order to enter. As he did that, the gigantic sword on his back briefly became visible and panic exploded. Everyone ran, fleeing for the rear exit. They did not do it because of anything the big man said or did, but because the sheer fact of his presence broke their nerve. And when one fled, all fled.

Except Ndole. He was too slow, too surprised by the new arrival to make his feet work.

His lip curling in irritation, the legionary surveyed the now-empty tap house and settled on the shabby, rail-thin driver. He evaluated him with a cursory glance, spying the tarnished neural jacks on his bare arms.

'You have a vehicle capable of ground transit.' The voice that emerged from the giant sounded almost high-born to Ndole's ears, and the words were less a question, more a statement. He was nodding before he realised it. 'You will take me into the scraplands.'

Ndole had to work hard to find his voice. 'W-will you kill me if I don't? Kill me if I do?'

'Why would I do that?' The warrior gave a curt shake of the head. 'But understand, I have no currency to pay you for the work.'

Despite the utter terror rooting Ndole to the spot, it was a credit to his avaricious nature that he actually frowned at that, and the question *what's in it for me?* danced on his lips, though he never dared give it voice.

The warrior answered him anyway. 'I will owe you a favour. I think a man in a town like this one, known to be in the debt of a Space Marine, would grow considerably in stature. Yes?'

Ndole nodded again, and smiled a little. Money was good, but reputation – that was better.

'Where do you want to go? There's nothing out there but rusted hulks and mutants.' That wasn't altogether true, though.

'I am looking for a place that has many names,' replied the big man. 'Asiel. Salvaguardia. Heilgtum. Muqaddas Jagah. Sanctuary.' He came closer, looming over Ndole. 'You know it, don't you?'

The driver considered continuing the casual lie, and then discarded the thought as idiotic. 'Some pass across the border looking for it. Those names are not often spoken.'

'You will take me,' the warrior repeated.

And of course, he had.

Everyone gathered across the street from the tap house when Ndole and the giant walked out the front door, and he heard them all whispering. Most of them were taking bets on how he would be killed. He kept a brave face, trying to project an aura of calm, as if he did this every day.

Only when the hover-truck was long past the settlement's outskirts did he entertain the thought that the warrior could be insincere. He'd heard the reports on the watch-wire of the Warmaster's perfidy and the warnings from the Lords of Terra to be wary of spies in their midst. He screwed up his courage and spoke for the first time in hours, shouting to be heard over the engine noise. 'What do you hope to find out here, with the… With those people?'

The warrior leaned forward, his massive head uncomfortably close to Ndole's in the close confines of the truck's cab. 'Answers. You know why they hide out here, I think. I am not the first you have brought to them.'

'Not the first pilgrim,' admitted the driver. 'But the first of *you*.'

'Pilgrim...' The giant weighed the meaning of the word. 'Do you know what they believe?'

'Aye, lord.' Ndole was suddenly sweating, despite the actions of the coolsuit he habitually wore beneath his crew gear. 'They say the Emperor is a god. The only real one, not like those out of the dead churches.'

'Is a being a god if it is more than a man?' The warrior's question seemed directed at nothing. 'How much more than human must one be, to be thought of as such?'

'I don't know.' Ndole felt compelled to answer, and nervously ran a hand over his shorn scalp. He dared another look at the warrior, seeing again the web-work of old scars that marred his pale face.

'What do you believe?' said the giant.

Terror bloomed inside Ndole and he cursed himself for a fool. If he gave the wrong reply now, this war-angel would kill him with a flick of its wrist and it would all be because of his weakness, his greed, his curiosity.

The legionary reached past him and pointed at something on the control panel on the roof of the hover-truck's cab. A tarnished brass charm on a length of grimy string, dangling from an inert flip-switch. The little aquila seemed to float in the air as the vehicle bounced over the rises in the dunes. 'Where did you get that?'

Ndole found his voice again. 'A pilgrim gave it to me. A-and some papers.'

'A book in crimson ink?'

He nodded. 'I didn't read it!'

'You should.'

'What?' Ndole blinked, and for the second time that day he felt as if he had barely escaped execution. 'But they say the book is dangerous. And the speaker, the one who goes from place to place and reads it... The Emperor is displeased with her.'

'Is he?' The warrior seemed troubled. 'How would we know?' His every word was filled with conflict, and if anything that frightened Ndole most of all. If this being, one of the Emperor's Angels of Death, could not navigate such questions, then what chance did a commoner have? 'I must find her,' the giant continued. 'I must know the truth.'

'We all want that.' The words escaped Ndole, coming from nowhere. 'But it is different for you, yes?'

He tried to find a way to express his thoughts, but the driver was a simple man and not given to great articulation. A Space Marine is born of the Emperor's sons, he told himself, so he's blood-kin to the Master of Terra, one step removed. Surely one so close to such magnificence could know the world better than a truck-hand raised in poverty?

The warrior's scarred face told a different story. He nodded towards a shape looming out of the sands. 'Is that it?'

Ndole blinked and refocused, his jacks clattering against the steering yoke. He saw a cracked minaret pointing skyward at a crooked angle – a thin tower that had once been covered in mirrors, now only a hollow skeleton that sang as the winds whistled through it. The 'sanctuary' hid at its base, clustered in a crater of fused glass beneath a skein of mimetic camouflage. Unless one knew where to look, it would have been nigh-invisible.

Or so it was on most days. Issuing out of the skein, pennants of black fire smoke were being pulled away on the stiff breeze, monstrous dark arrows frozen in flight above the settlement.

Ndole flinched and reflexively eased back on the throttle, but in the next second, the warrior's hand had enveloped his shoulder with firm, unyielding pressure.

'Get me there,' he commanded. *'Now'.*

GARRO KICKED OPEN the gate at the back of the truck and leapt down into the settling dust cloud, the keening whine of the hovercraft's engines falling away to nothing.

His battle-honed senses built an image of the site in less than a second. The crackle of fires and the acrid stink of burning plastic; spilled blood, still soaking into the sands where it fell; the snap and rustle of torn pergolas catching the mournful wind. He drew his sword and rested his thumb on the activator stud, stalking forward.

The driver clambered out of the cab, almost falling over himself as he squeezed out from beneath an arching gull wing door. His dark face was stiff with fear. 'This is not right,' he muttered. 'What happened... ?'

The legionary scanned the encampment. The great sail of energy-deadening cloth that concealed the sanctuary hid dozens of smaller tents, yurts and prefabricated dwelling cubes. Cables webbed the open spaces between them, some festooned with bio-lume clusters for lighting, others leading to dewcatchers for water reclamation. Most of the tents were blackened rags, a few patches of fire still burning here or there among them.

The first citizen of this refuge Garro encountered was a female, or rather what was left of her. He could only tell this by the dimensions of the skeleton that remained, crouched in a dark halo of thermal damage. As he approached, he could hear the hissing, ticking sound of something cooling, like metal taken too soon from a forge.

It was the bones. Fused solid into a sculpture that captured the dead woman's perfect agony, they had been transformed into dirty black glass.

He examined the seared skeleton, wondering. Garro had witnessed the effects of many kinds of weapons, from volkite ray guns to microwave throwers, and this was dissimilar to any of them. The threads of heat that radiated off the body were intense, enough that in any normal circumstance there should have been naught but a pile of grey ashes.

Behind him, the driver's boots crunched on the silicate floor of the crater. Garro shot him a look. 'Keep your distance,' he ordered, getting a wooden nod in return.

By the pattern of the thermal shock, Garro guessed the woman had been killed as she fell while trying to flee. He mentally tracked back to the place where her killer would have been standing and found a group of several more bodies. These ones were also burned, but in a different way. A group of irregular militiamen, he guessed, by the piecemeal soldier's attire they wore and the weapons still clutched in their rigor-stiffened hands.

It was impossible to tell what gender or ethnicity the five of them had been while they were alive. Their bodies were all uniform in the same terrible fashion – bloated and flayed by incredible heat, reeking meat in the form of human beings. Garro knelt by the closest one, the gears of his bionic leg clicking as it worked, and broke off its fingers so he could take the heavy stubber rifle the militiaman had been carrying. The charred sticks of flesh snapped easily, and where there should have been white bone, only grains of black powder spilled out.

'Their bone. It burned,' he said aloud. 'Burned them from within.'

The driver turned his head and retched into the dust. He made an attempt to recover and Garro heard him call out, doubtless trying to find someone still alive.

The legionary left him to it, instead raising the stubber to his nose, snapping open the weapon's breech. There was no smell of cordite. It had not been fired. He pulled the gun's drum magazine and confirmed it was still fully loaded. Garro repeated his actions with two more of the dead, and saw there were no signs of spent shell casings anywhere nearby. Five armed guards, and whomever had killed them burned them alive before anyone could let off a single round.

'Do you see that?' said the trembling driver. He was pointing with both hands, down at more heat-swollen corpses clustered in the lee of a tent pole. 'The... the path between the bodies?'

Garro nodded. A dry, inky pattern of burned ground seemed to join all the dead, as if the fire that killed them was a snake moving from one to another, scorching the earth in its wake.

'Oh, fate,' whimpered the other man. 'Dead. Dead. They're all burned and murdered.'

'Not all,' Garro began, his acute hearing picking up something deeper into the stale gloom of the camp. But the driver wasn't listening to him, and he staggered back towards the mouth of the camp, rubbing frantically at his face.

'In the air, that's all of them,' he gasped, his chest heaving. 'I can taste them in my mouth, it's in my lungs... The *smoke*. That's all that is left.' The driver's eyes were wide with panic. He threw Garro a look and made a split-second decision, choosing the terror that had wrought this destruction as the greater of the things he feared.

The legionary made no move to stop him as he ran away, and presently the thrusters of the hover-truck spun up to full power. Garro watched the vehicle bolt back in the direction they had come. He waited for the sound of the engines to grow fainter, and listened carefully.

Yes. There. Something shifted position, moving against loose rocks. Garro tightened his grip on *Libertas* and moved deeper into the foetid haze.

THERE WAS NO end to the horror that confronted the legionary in the charnel house that the sanctuary had become. Cruel flames had killed and destroyed here, yet the patterns of the fire were strange and irregular. The burning was *unnatural*. There was no other word for it.

Garro scowled. With each passing year in Horus' declared war, the legionary saw more that could fall into that category. The alien, that was something that the former Death Guard had faced on countless occasions, and no matter how grotesque and inhuman it was, there was some rationality to such a foe. But he swiftly came to the understanding that whatever powers the Warmaster had allied himself to, they were beyond reason. He took each step with care, ready to face anything.

Horus. For who else could have ordered this massacre? Who else would profit from sowing chaos on Terra?

Garro's question briefly illuminated another, more sinister answer, and the Sigillite's face rose in his thoughts. He pushed it away, silencing the treasonous impulse before it could fully form. That Malcador was not to be trusted, that was true. That Malcador had an agenda only he could see, and that it might not be in full synchrony with the Emperor's Will, that also was very possible. But Garro did not wish to believe that the Regent of Terra would permit the kind of unbounded malice that had been wrought on these civilians.

Malcador would do what he believed was for the good of the Imperium. Garro could not square that with this horror. No, another hand was at work here, and it sickened the legionary to know he had come too late to stop it.

He approached the centre of the settlement, finding an open space between the support poles and generator pods. A ring of salvaged chairs, cushions and pews in dozens of different designs clustered to form a kind of amphitheatre. There were hundreds of bodies here, fallen atop one another where they had gathered to face their attacker and died for it.

The wind caught a drift of scattered leaflets and whipped them up and past Garro's face, tugging on the folds of his robe. He snatched one out of the air with his free hand and the burned plaspaper crumbled into flakes – but not before he glimpsed a dense block of words written in common Low Gothic, the ink as red as blood.

He recognised phrases from the documents he had found in the personal affects of Kaleb Arin, the man who had once been Garro's housecarl. Poor Kaleb, dead and cast away to the screaming void of the warp. He had been a steadfast one, a weakling in the eyes of some because of his failure to pass the aspirant trials of the Death Guard legion, but strong by Garro's lights in how he endured and continued to serve.

The captain had not thought of the man for some time, and now he did, Garro felt a knife of sorrow turn in his gut. Kaleb's death had been a lesson for the warrior, and the price the housecarl paid to show it could never be

forgotten. Like those who lay dead and scattered around
Garro's feet, Kaleb had believed in the words of the Lectitio Divinitatus, believed it with all his heart. His soul
too, reflected the warrior. *But what do I believe?*

The empty question echoed in his thoughts, and Garro's frown deepened as he surveyed the bodies, hoping
that the one face he sought would not be among them. If
Euphrati Keeler were here, if the Saint had perished among
her faithful… Even the mere contemplation of that dark
possibility made the legionary's breath catch in his throat.

He shook his head. He had not come all this way only
to find a corpse.

The Saint was out there, he knew it in his marrow. In
recent months, Garro had stolen time to take his leave
unbidden and search for the woman, knowing that she
too was somewhere on or near Terra. His quest to find
her had taken him to secret places hidden in the cracks
of the Imperial Throneworld – the derelict Vostok Hives,
the Mothyards, the Nihon Peaks and Riga Suborbital –
and each time he had been a day late, finding only traces,
happening upon unexpected challenges.

And now here, in this sanctuary, where those who
believed as Kaleb did had gathered. The Saint had been
in this place, just as she had been at all the others. She
had stood on these sands and read from that book. If
Keeler was dead, Garro would know it. *Feel it*, even if he
could not explain how.

He heard the sound of movement once again, and this
time he knew for certain where it had come from. Stepping over the smashed remains of broken benches, he
came upon a survivor.

The man was young and fit, and that had been some
of what saved him. The other factor was the poor fools

who lay dead about him, each of them burned and flayed like the militiamen out by the entrance. They had taken the brunt of the inferno meant to end them all, and the survivor's loss had been one half of his body. On one side, his right arm and leg were withered things, black and red with new agony. In his gaze, there was such pain as could drive a man mad. Yet he still held on, quivering as his undamaged hand grasped a torn Divinitatus tract like it was his salvation.

The young man was beyond help, and Garro turned his sword in his hand, considering where best to place the edge that he might end the lad's agony with some measure of mercy.

'Who did this?' he asked.

The man's single unblinded eye refocused and found him. He took a shuddering breath. 'Serpents.' His voice was thick with fluid, and beads of dark arterial blood gathered at the corner of his lips as he spoke. 'Burning. Turned them loose among us.' He shook and began to sob.

'Who?' Garro repeated. 'Describe them.'

The survivor's head rocked back and forth in jerking motions. 'No. No. Not enough time.' His crippled gaze bored into Garro's. 'She told me we would meet. She did not know how or when.'

'Keeler...'

He managed a nod. 'We matter not. Only the truth. They seek her now... Serpents...' His voice was faltering, drowning in itself. 'Find her. Do not let her perish. Else we are lost.'

'Where is the Saint, lad?' Garro asked him, leaning close to catch what he knew would be the young man's final breath. 'Say it!'

'I know–'

The light and the sound came from nowhere. Above the sheath protecting the sanctuary, powerful daggers of radiance blazed down, drenching everything in stark white illumination. Screaming engines added their own cries to the winds, buffeting the cloth with a hurricane of jet wash, and Garro heard the familiar weighty thuds of heavy bolter cannons being primed for firing.

He looked up, the nictating membranes in his ocular implants flicking into place to stop the legionary from being blinded. Blocky avian shadows moved up there, searching for targets.

When Garro looked back, the survivor was dead.

The legionary pivoted on his heel and brought up his power sword, as six cloaked figures came falling through the canopy, tearing it apart with their violent descent.

THAT THEY WERE Space Marines was not in doubt. Even in the smoke-wreathed dimness of the encampment, Garro could not mistake the familiar tread of ceramite boots and the whine of servos. But as to their allegiance and the identity of their legion, he could only guess. They did not give him time to speak. It was an assault without question.

Bolters crashed and chewed up the gritty earth beneath Garro's feet. He leapt forward into a tumbling roll that took him over a broken pew and out of the line of fire. They came after him in a charge, breaking to the left and the right in an attempt to herd him and block off any routes of escape.

Flight, however, was the farthest thing from Nathaniel Garro's mind. Was he facing the same killers who had murdered all the devoted in the sanctuary? Had the arrival of the hover-truck somehow drawn their attention? Perhaps they had come back to make certain of their work, or to ensure that the legionary did not live to tell of it.

His jaw set as he spun about to face the intruders. No-one was left to speak for these poor souls, and so Garro would speak for them. He would let *Libertas* be their voice.

The mighty blade flashed blue-white as power pulsed through it, and Garro threw a hooked kick at a discarded water barrel lying near his feet. The empty container clanged as his foot connected with it, and flew up and at the nearest of the hooded warriors. By reflex, the cloaked figure opened fire and shredded the barrel with a burst of full-auto fire.

Garro used the split-second distraction to launch himself at one of the long tent poles that supported the fabric roof above their heads, and with a two-handed swing, he cut it clean through. The pole quivered and fell, dragging a swathe of camo-cloth, cables and other detritus on to the heads of the new arrivals.

As he planned, they broke apart from their careful formation, allowing him to pick single targets of opportunity rather than face a united force. But still, his improvised strategy did not go exactly as he wished. Even as they reacted on instinct, the attackers were still precisely ordered, moving with great economy of motion. There was no wasted effort here, no hesitation. A sudden sense of the familiar prickled Garro's thoughts, but he was not given time to consider it. Bolters barked and he moved again, falling on the nearest of his enemies.

From beneath the hood, he caught the briefest glimpse

of a blunt-faced helmet, a war-mask that resembled a
fortress wall lit by glowing eye slits. Then Garro was
swinging the pommel of his sword in a hard cross that
raked across at head height.

The tungsten hemisphere at the base of the blade struck
the helm with a sound like the peal of a dull bell, and
the impact shock travelled up Garro's arm. Out of his
wargear, he had sparred with other legionaries in the
training cages, and in full armour it had been his grim
duty to battle turncoats in theirs – but Garro had never
had cause to fight like this, bare genhanced flesh against
power-assisted ceramite and plasteel. He had agility and
speed on his foes, but they had the advantage of numbers and endurance. One well-aimed bolt shell could
end him instantly from range, whereas Garro needed to
be close to use his sword at full lethality.

The warrior he targeted stumbled and went down,
caught by the uneven ground underfoot. Garro wanted
to grab for his bolter, but he couldn't pause, not even for
a second. Instead, the legionary burst into a sprint, spinning *Libertas* around in a web of crackling power. Bolt
rounds deflected off the flashing edge of the weapon as
Garro scrambled up a half-collapsed habitat cube and
made a diving attack at the next closest target. This one
carried a smaller bolt pistol, and he panned it up to meet
Garro with a shot in the chest.

At the last second, the legionary jack-knifed and fell
on the attacker with his sword aimed down. The tip of
the blade *almost* hit the mark, a fraction of a centime-
tre from the point where the neck-ring of the attacker's
armour joined the helmet seal. Had it fallen true, *Libertas*
would have sliced down inside his collarbone, bursting
through lung and primary heart. Instead, the sword tip

slashed away hood and cloak, screeching down the chest plate to leave a sparking gouge in the ceramite.

In the bright aura of the power sword, Garro saw the colour of his adversary's wargear for the first time. A matt yellow-gold that could only belong to one legion.

He disengaged, reeling back. 'The Fists?'

In answer, a mailed gauntlet rocketed out of nowhere and stuck Garro in the side of the head, the shock and the force of it so great that he almost lost his balance. The few moments the surprise cost him were more than enough for the other warriors to close on him, and a savage kick to the back of Garro's knees planted him in the soot-caked dirt. A heavy boot clanged down on the blade of his sword, and Garro shook off the pain. When he looked up, he was ringed with the yawning mouths of bolters at point-blank range.

'Traitor swine,' came a snarl, as the warrior with the torn cloak angrily shook it off. His free hand traced the scratch *Libertas* had made down his chest. 'You'll pay for daring to come here.' Now revealed, Garro saw that the Imperial Fist was of sergeant's rank, and marked with many honours from countless campaigns.

'I am no traitor,' Garro retorted, turning his head to spit out a glob of blood, fighting off the ringing in his ears.

'He is of a Legion,' said one of the others. 'That much is plain. What is he doing here?'

'He fought us,' said the sergeant.

'You attacked me,' Garro corrected. 'Have you been waiting on the walls of the Imperial Palace so long that your trigger slips at the first hint of an adversary?' For a moment he was a battle-captain again, a command officer berating a lower rank for an error of judgement. 'Your primarch Lord Dorn would be displeased.'

The Imperial Fists stiffened, and Garro knew he had touched a raw nerve.

'This place is outside the law,' said the sergeant, his voice low and cold. 'Those settling here have no protection under Imperial edict, yet still we came. And we find you, without apparent purpose or sigil, armed and dangerous among hundreds of the dead. Give me a reason why I should not execute you and learn your name from your corpse.'

Garro hesitated. He had become used to the weight of the Sigillite's mark, of the doors that it could open for him as Agentia Primus, and it felt odd to suddenly be without it. He took a deep breath and stood up, the guns still tracking him. 'I am Nathaniel Garro. I was once a captain of the Fourteenth Legion–'

'*Death Guard*?' The other Imperial Fist who had spoken flinched at the name and aimed his bolter right at Garro's temple. 'Mortarion's accursed sons! How did–?'

The sergeant reached out a hand and pushed the muzzle of the weapon away. 'I have heard that name before, from my captain. You are Garro of the *Eisenstein*.'

He nodded. 'Aye, the very same.'

'I have also heard that he and his kinsmen, the ones who came to Terra after the archtraitor's defiance, are prisoners upon Luna. Held there until trust can be verified, or blame laid.' There was no ease in the words, not the smallest ember of credence. 'How have you come to be here?'

Garro frowned. 'There is more to the matter than what you have heard, sergeant,' he said carefully. 'I came to find this outpost... these people. But their deaths were not by my hand.'

'We are to take the word of a turncoat Legion's son?'

said another of the Imperial Fists. 'I say we finish what we started.'

But before the sergeant could decide on a course of action, heavy footfalls signified the approach of more armoured figures. The drop-ships that had circled overhead had since drifted away to make landings, and now more of Dorn's warriors were entering the desolated settlement.

A legionary with captain's laurels came into view. Garro saw he wore a heavy tabard of white ballistic cloth covered in jet-black detail, and chains about his wrist-guards. The device of a black cross, repeated on the armour of all the Imperial Fists, featured prominently upon him. This new arrival reached up to remove his helm and in a gesture of obedience, the sergeant did the same.

The captain's blond hair framed a face that Garro had seen before, what seemed like an age ago, in a meeting aboard the star-fortress *Phalanx*.

'He is who he says,' said the warrior, his eyes narrowing. 'Let him be.'

Garro gave a nod. 'First Captain Sigismund. Well met.'

Sigismund's cold gaze raked over him. 'That remains to be seen.'

SEVENTEEN

The Templar
Hesperides
Tracking

THEY SAT ACROSS from one another in the troop bay of one of the grounded Thunderhawks, alone after the First Captain had barked an order to clear the ship so that they might have some privacy.

The act seemed unusual to Garro. Knowing the character of Dorn's stone men as he did, the legionary expected to be clapped in irons and subjected to arrest. Instead, Sigismund reached forward with Garro's sword and scabbard, briefly confiscated by his subordinates, and laid the weapon on the deck between them.

Garro made no move to pick it up. His steady gaze held. 'Did your gene-father order that?' He tilted his head in the direction of the ruined settlement.

Sigismund's jaw clenched. 'You know better than to say such a thing, Death Guard.'

'I have not been a Death Guard for quite some time,' he replied. 'The insurrection has changed many things. Perhaps your master's countenance is among them.'

'I will choose to believe you are testing me,' growled the Imperial Fist. 'And poorly at that. The alternative is that you impugn the honour of the Seventh Legion, and were that to be so, it would go badly for you.' He pulled a device from a pouch at his waist and Garro saw it was a handheld auspex unit. Sigismund tossed it to him, and he caught it easily. 'Listen,' he told him.

Garro turned the device over in his hands and found that the display screen showed a blinking rune to indicate it carried an audio recording in its memory. He pressed the button to replay the data file, and for a few brief moments the interior of the troop bay echoed with sounds of screaming and the voices of the dead.

He listened to a man whose words were distorted with terror and feedback as he shouted into a vox-pickup, desperate for someone to hear him, pleading for rescuers to come and save them. The accent was thick and several of the words were from Afrik dialects Garro did not know, but the intent of the message was clear. It had been sent as the killing was in progress, as whatever force had come to murder the sanctuary had done its swift and merciless work. The recording cut off suddenly in the middle of a panicked shout.

'That was picked up on one of the common distress wavelengths,' Sigismund explained. 'We came to investigate.'

'And your men thought I was the cause?'

The First Captain looked away. 'They reacted with poor judgement. Inaction has made them lax. They'll be chastised for acting without thinking.'

Garro realised that was the closest he would get to any kind of an apology. Sigismund went on.

'What are you doing, battle-captain? I have heard tell that you were at large. But why here, and why today?'

'Both our missions have altered,' Garro offered, at length. 'Since the *Eisenstein*.'

Sigismund nodded. 'You are Malcador's attack dog now. With armour that bears no sigil or livery. What is it that you are called? A Knight Errant?'

Garro bristled at the off-hand description of his status. 'There is more to it than that.'

'Where the Sigillite is concerned, I have no doubt,' Sigismund shot back. 'He would build a scheme with a thousand players just to fetch him a cup of amasec.' He leaned back and cocked his head. 'But I wager he did not send you to this place. Have you escaped his employ, Garro?' He nodded at the sword. 'You've left your name-less armour behind. If not for that weapon, I might ask if you had decided to give up the warrior's calling in hopes of a monastic life.'

'I am here on a duty of my own, not by Malcador's orders,' Garro allowed. 'I came to the sanctuary looking for information.'

'About this?' Sigismund reached for something and threw a wad of burned devotional papers on the deck, across the sheathed sword.

Garro ignored the question and kept his eyes fixed on the Imperial Fist. 'If I am Malcador's attack dog,' he began, 'one might say that you are Lord Dorn's. What was the name they gave you? The Templar, I recall.' He gestured at the black cross on Sigismund's tabard. 'We both serve masters who seek to safeguard Terra and the Imperium.'

For the first time, Sigismund's expression shifted, and Garro saw a cold twist of humourless amusement on his lips. 'We are alike, is that what you wish me to believe? You, a man who moves in shadows under the aspect of a ghost, are the same as I? Who stands for all to see, his duty clear as daybreak?'

The First Captain's blunt truth cut Garro more deeply than he expected. 'I did not choose the path I am on,' he said tersely. 'But we each fight the battle we have, not the battle we want...' His words faded as a suspicion crystallised, one that had been gnawing at him since the moment the Imperial Fists had arrived. 'You answered that distress call.'

'Aye.'

Garro leaned forward. '*You* did. Captain Sigismund, commander of the First Company of the Imperial Fists, defender of this planet... You brought two drop-ships and a detachment of Space Marines into the desert for... what? The sake of a garbled message from some luckless civilian? There was nothing in that signal to warrant the deployment of such a force. Why not leave it to the local garrison instead?'

'We were passing through the area. It seemed expedient.'

Garro snorted. 'You do not lie well, cousin.' He pieced the facts together. 'The Imperial Fists were already monitoring this place. It is the only explanation that fits. My question is, for what reason?' He saw a flicker of doubt in Sigismund's eyes and chased it down. 'Or am I mistaken? These warriors are not here at Lord Dorn's behest... they are here at *yours*.'

Sigismund's face turned to stone, and it was then Garro knew he was right.

'When I first met you,' said the other captain, after a long moment, 'I thought you a deluded fool. We pulled you and your fellow refugees from that frozen hulk, dead in space, and you stood before my gene-father with stories about treachery and betrayal. I knew they were lies.

Knew it... until the very moment that remembrancer Oliton showed us her memories.' Sigismund shook his head. 'Emperor's Blood, Garro... Do you realise what damage you wrought with your flight?'

'More than you can know. I took no pleasure in it,' Garro said quietly, and he felt the shadow of that moment pass over him once again. It was not untrue to say that Nathaniel carried resentment for the burden that had been forced on him at Isstvan. 'I curse Horus Lupercal every day for forcing me to make the choices I did.'

The Templar looked away. 'The woman, Keeler. You know what she is.' It wasn't a question.

Garro frowned. 'I...' He halted, unable to frame his thoughts. 'We have spoken. I was... illuminated by her insights.' He nodded in the direction of the burned-out settlement. 'I hoped to find her here so we might talk again.'

'She spoke to me,' said Sigismund, and Garro could tell that the admission was a hard one for the Imperial Fist to voice. 'Told me things. *Showed* me things.'

He nodded. 'Yes. She has a way about her.' Garro thought back on the counsel Keeler had given him when he felt lost and rudderless. That she had become connected to some greater actuality, perhaps some fragment of the Emperor's manifested will, had never been in doubt. It came as no surprise to him that the so-called Saint shared that counsel with others. He looked at Sigismund with fresh eyes, assimilating this new truth.

It was as if he had given the First Captain permission to unburden himself. As he went on, hesitantly at first, Sigismund leaned close in the manner of a brother sharing a confidence. He described how he had crossed paths with Keeler aboard the *Phalanx*, and spoke of the futures she had laid out before him – one, to perish forgotten and alone under an alien sun; the other, to stand at Dorn's side when the inevitable invasion of Terra took place. Sigismund told him of his own grave choice, to go back on his primarch's command to lead a chastisement force against Horus, and beg a different posting closer to home.

Suddenly, Garro understood why the Imperial Fist had ordered his men to leave them aboard the Thunderhawk. He did not want anyone else to hear this, to glimpse what some might see as a fissure of weakness in the man's otherwise granite-hard exterior. If the Knight Errant ever spoke of what was said here, he knew he would be ignored and derided by Sigismund's brethren.

As Garro had become Malcador's agent in acts of preparation and retribution, so Sigismund had been tasked by Dorn along the same lines. The First Captain purged the Solar System of Horus' spies wherever he could find them – and Garro had frequently seen the results of his work from the sidelines as their missions crossed one another, always in parallel but never in unity.

But there had come a moment when Sigismund could no longer keep his secrets from his gene-father. That bleak mien Garro had seen pass over the Imperial Fist's face before returned, and he saw it for what it was – great sorrow and regret. Sigismund confessed to Dorn, and in turn his primarch tore him down for it. The master of the VII Legion decried Keeler as a charlatan trading in worthless religionist dogma, and reprimanded his son for allowing himself to be swayed by her.

Garro said nothing. Inwardly, he thought that it was Dorn who did not see clearly. It had been clear to him at their first meeting when he revealed Horus' perfidy, and then again when he stole aboard the *Phalanx* on a mission to recruit one of the Fists' psykers. The latter sortie had ultimately failed, but on both occasions Garro had known that for all his greatness, Rogal Dorn's rigidity of mind was a flaw. *As much as stone may endure*, he thought, *it cannot bend and so it may shatter*. He only had to look Sigismund in the eye to see that truth reflected in the Templar's troubled thoughts.

'Keeler showed me a vision of arcane horrors,' Sigismund concluded. 'And I have since seen them with my own eyes. You have too.'

'Aye.' Garro nodded grimly. 'That I have.'

'Then you know her gift is not worthless.' It was a hard admission for the Imperial Fist to make, to suggest that his liege-lord could be so mistaken. He took a long breath. 'I do not profess to know how all… this… is supposed to work. But I know the woman is important. With that in mind, I have watched over her from a distance, as best I could. I have used the assets of my Legion and the Imperial Court to track her movements.' He shook his head. 'She and her devotees have not made it simple. There are many gaps, many unknowns. It speaks to a great network of believers in existence, far larger than any of us suspected.'

Garro pressed him for more. 'But you knew she would be here, or was here, at the sanctuary?'

'Yes. As you surmised, I had the location monitored. One of many, in fact. When the call for help came, so did I.' Sigismund paused. 'Garro, you know how Horus' turncoats operate. Like the hydra of myth, we sever one head and two more rise to take its place. For all that we root out, others still lurk unseen. I believe that Keeler may perish at their hands if we do not prevent it.'

'The killings here, they show that the archtraitor is getting close to her...'

He nodded. 'She must be protected.' The Templar rose to his feet. 'But I have reached the limits of my agency. Tonight, I exceeded authority to come out here and Dorn will learn of it. He will be displeased once again. You see that the Imperial Fists do not have the freedoms of Malcador's Knights Errant. I can go no further with this.' He fixed Garro with a hard look. 'But you can. It is clear to me now that you are the only option.'

Sigismund reached down and took the auspex unit from Garro's hand and raised it to his face, allowing a retinal aura-reader to scan his eye. 'Identify me. Ex-load storage stack. Codeword *Iconoclast*. Unlock,' he told it. The device chimed and he passed it back.

Where before the unit's memory had been almost empty, there were now dozens of other files revealed – surveillance intercepts, intelligence files and more.

'What am I looking at?' said Garro.

'All that I have gleaned about Euphrati Keeler's movements over the past months. You may be able to fill in the gaps. I believe it will help you to predict where she will go next.'

'You are trusting me with this,' said Garro warily.

'We have to keep her safe, Nathaniel,' Sigismund replied. 'As much as I wish to, I can go no further. So the duty falls to you.' Some of the chilly fire of his earlier manner returned to his voice, and his next words were very much a warning. 'Do not fail.'

THE IMPERIAL FISTS called in a cohort of servitors to catalogue and then bury the dead, but Garro was gone before the first of them arrived. It took him the better part of a day to walk back across the scraplands, and the passage gave him the time he needed to digest the import of his conversation with the Templar.

As he walked, he pored over the content of the auspex, using hypnogogics to flash-read the vital data as a starving man might gorge himself on a banquet. As he expected from an Imperial Fist, Sigismund's record-keeping was precise and bereft of anything but cold fact.

The files tracked dozens of reports of illegal Lectitio Divinitatus gatherings, partial scans from sightings of women who matched Keeler's description, and dozens of other vectors, collating them into something that resembled a pattern. He found strings of intelligence that connected with his own research, including the same blind lead that months before had sent him to the Riga platform on what turned out to be a fool's errand. Although the journey to Riga led Garro to other things – and eventually to the uncovering of a secret the Sigillite had wanted to keep from him – the legionary found no traces of Keeler's passage.

She moved from place to place, slipping in and out of hive cities and metroplexes, space stations and orbital plates, never once being captured despite the iron grip the Imperium kept on the Throneworld and its satellites. What did that suggest, Garro wondered? Did Keeler's preternatural abilities enable her to weave through the security net that grew ever tighter as the Warmaster's threat encroached? Or was the truth more prosaic than that, was it that her association of followers was so large that those devoted to her simply looked away as she passed?

How far does the word of the Lectitio Divinitatus reach? Garro had no answer for that question, and it troubled him. The Imperium of Man was just that, and it had gone so far to stamp out the falsehood of religion, imposing secularity wherever its shadow fell – but what if that was impossible? What if there was something in the nature of humankind that meant they always needed something greater than themselves to believe in?

He scowled and displaced the nagging thought. For the moment, he cared not for what other men might think, feel or believe. He only knew what Nathaniel Garro felt... and that was loss.

'Where is this leading me?' he asked the air. The winds gave him no answer.

Garro returned to the data, moving from past records to present ones. According to Sigismund's sources, there were rumours that Keeler had visited the sanctuary less than four days ago – the closest Garro had been to her in a long time. There were a dozen other possible locations that the Saint could have journeyed to on the next step of her endless pilgrimage, but he quickly considered and discarded all but one. The guess was part instinct, part calculation.

Hesperides.

Garro halted and looked up into the night sky, craning his neck until he found a particular shadow off towards the south-eastern horizon. From here, it was little more than a blue-black smudge against a rare starry evening, low against the sallow glow of Luna. The orbital plate was one of the older aertropolis platforms, and he recalled it was an *insula minoris* that served Terra as a dioxide refinery and tertiary shipping hub. It was an ideal place upon which to deliver a sermon; much of the population were transients, system crews and unskilled labourers who moved as needed on contract indentures to Venus,

Mercury and the teeming null-grav work yards of the Belt. The kind of men and women, Garro reasoned, who would have empty lives overshadowed by the insurrection. The kind of people who, if so enticed by the Lectitio Divinitatus, could carry word of it to all corners of the Solar System.

A DAY LATER, Garro dropped from the wheel well of an automated cargo barge and fell a hundred feet to a landing deck on the western arc of the floating city. At a distance, Hesperides Plate recalled the shape and form of a great pipe organ, buoyant on a cushion of dirty clouds and wreathed in grey haze. Up close, the imagined form gave way to a less attractive reality, a great convoluted knot of tarnished tubes and gargantuan bell-mouths that resembled the fatal collision of a thousand giant brass instruments, crushed into a clump by the hand of a mad god.

Nowhere on Hesperides could one find silence. Every passage and walkway was walled in by lines of rattling, echoing pipes that hummed and gurgled with chemical reaction. Deep in the bowels of the platform, engines that had operated for centuries sucked in polluted air and fractioned it into its component elements, desperately trying to salvage some breath of purity from the wounded atmosphere of the planet.

The constant noise made it difficult for Garro to extend his battle-senses to the full, and he mentally recalibrated the parameters of his actions. A place like this would make it harder to see an enemy coming, and the confined byways were perfect territory for ambushes, choke-points and murder boxes.

Pulling his hood down and his robes close, Garro

made sure his sword was hidden where none could see it, and ventured deeper into the endless range of narrow alleyways.

Hesperides had never been designed to be a city – it was a glorified atmosphere processor with a few support modules bolted on – but someone had neglected to reveal that to the people who lived there. Humanity crammed itself into every nook and cranny of the structure, with ramshackle hovels built around spaces between the great brass tubes that snaked this way and that. Parts of the makeshift city were permanently cold, platforms rimed with hoarfrost from the chilly aura of vast coolant towers. Others were always tropical-hot and damp from the steaming output of chemical fractionators. Frequently, both extremes could be found within a few hundred yards of one another.

Poverty was rife here. The legionary saw no souls who were not clothed in shabby, grimy cuts of worker garb, and their hollow faces and averted gazes spoke to him of people who were beaten down, who hung on by their fingertips. Unseen, he grimaced in the shadows of his hood. It seemed wrong that here, above the planet that was the bright heart of the Imperium, citizens had no taste of the glorious future the Emperor wanted for them all.

Garro pushed the thought away as he came upon what he was looking for – a 'village square' for want of a better term, a larger open space between two towering smokestacks that the locals had repurposed into a marketplace and meeting point. The legionary found a shaded perch above from which he could observe the area and scanned the milling crowd for his targets.

The group were dressed no differently than those around them, but to a warrior's trained eye they stood out like magnesium flares on a dark night. A trio of earnest-looking men, two keeping watch while the third carefully offered slips of paper to anyone who would take one. Garro saw red ink on the paper, text he could not read from this distance and the shapes of icon-symbols to aid any illiterates to understand the leaflet's intent.

He smiled thinly. The followers of the Lectitio Divinitatus were becoming bolder, and that would give him what he needed. Garro planned to wait for them to finish their proselytising and then track the men back to their point of origin. Somewhere amid this hissing, clanking mess of conduits there was a clandestine church, and if he found it…

A low cry came to him, arresting his train of thought. Four more figures had emerged from the passers-by – rough types with the build of Imperial Army troopers about them, although none of the quartet wore anything approaching a uniform. The new arrivals were haranguing the believers, and Garro speculated on what was happening below him from body language and the snatches of snarled words captured by his augmented hearing.

The four were members of the group in charge of this part of Hesperides. Garro had not seen a single Arbites officer since he arrived on the orbital plate, not even a monitor drone. He guessed that whichever member of the Tech-Barony was charged with rule of Hesperides had little interest in the people who lived in between the air machines, as long as the processors kept working. In this kind of environment, thugs of a certain stripe flourished where law enforcement was absent and weakness was rife.

Demands were being made. From his vantage point, Garro glimpsed the flash of silver from Throne coins as the larger of the thugs – a broad barrel of a man with a wild beard – pulled tribute from the hands of one of the believers. It clearly wasn't enough, because the thug produced a push-sword from under his coat and ran through the man who had been holding the leaflets. It was a basic but efficient kill, up under the ribcage. The victim went down, dead before he hit the platform, the papers he had been clutching scattering like windblown leaves.

There were shouts and screams, and the two remaining believers exploded into panicked motion, bolting through the crowd, heading towards rat-runs on the western side of the marketplace. One of the thugs stayed behind to pick over the dead man's corpse, but the bearded killer led the other two on a chase.

Garro cursed silently. If these fools killed his only leads, he would be stymied. All the members of Keeler's church would draw back and hide themselves, and the Saint – if she was here – would be spirited away by nightfall.

Moving as quickly as he could without drawing attention, Garro went after them, leaping from one cluster of conduits to another. The terrain became increasingly difficult, as his elevated path was blocked at random intervals by outcrops of machinery or shrieking steam grilles. Twice he lost sight of the fleeing believers and the men in pursuit, but their shouts allowed him to zero in and keep them from vanishing into the complex root system of brassy tubes.

The legionary heard the bass cough of a heavy-calibre gunshot and a wail of pain. Away from the crowds, the thugs were happy to start shooting where collateral damage would be minimal. Garro's enhanced senses smelled fresh blood, and plenty of it. The injured believer was bleeding badly.

He managed to get ahead of the thugs, closing the

distance to the running men below along a high maintenance walkway. Amid the constant background chorus
of rattling apparatus and clanking vents, Garro's heavy
footfalls went unnoticed. Forced to a halt as the walkway came to a sudden dead end, he paused to take in
the scene.

Fifty feet beneath him, the uninjured man was struggling to help his wounded comrade stagger forward, but
the slick of blood that trailed behind them was enough
for Garro to know that one of them would be dead in
minutes.

That estimate fell to zero when the thugs emerged from
a side-passage, and the one with the gun put a second
round into the bleeding man. The hydrostatic shock of
the impact parted the two believers, sending the injured
one over a safety rail and into oblivion. Garro glimpsed
the body spinning away towards the filthy clouds.

The one with the beard shouted something about
being owed more money, about promises made, and
the dimensions of this sordid drama became full and
clear to the legionary. The thugs ran this part of Hesperides Plate, and they were letting Keeler's followers
have a safe haven here in return for hard currency. But
belief alone was not enough to mint coin, and the greed
of men like these had few limits. He imagined that no
matter what they had been given, it would not have been
enough. They were going to kill all three of the believers to send a message.

*What other reason was there to have committed brutal
murder before so many eyes, if not to sow fear?* For a brief
moment, the Warmaster's snarling aspect rose and fell in
Garro's thoughts. He shook off the memory.

Out came the push-sword again, still red with the gore

of the man it had killed. The last of the believers was
looking back and forth between the killers and a narrow
passage ten yards away. Asking himself if he could make
it there before a bullet buried itself in his back.

Garro had seen enough. He stepped up and over the
edge of the suspended walkway and dropped the distance
to the deck below, hitting with the impact of a demoli-
tion hammer. The metal flooring flexed under the force
of his arrival, putting the thugs and their would-be victim
off their feet. The panicked believer was quick to recover,
however, and scrambled away towards the gaping alley.

Furious at the interruption, the three thugs turned
on Garro and fear was not what they showed him. He
was so used to seeing that barely-controlled terror on
the faces of common humans that it struck him as odd
to find it absent. Without his power armour, they must
have thought Garro was some kind of mutant affected
by gigantism. It never occurred to them that he was a
Space Marine; after all, why would one of the Emperor's
Angels of Death ever come to this light-forsaken place,
much less so without armour or fanfare?

'What are you?' spat the one with the pistol, taking
aim. 'Go away, freak.'

The bearded man hesitated – perhaps he had some clue
about Garro's actual origin – but his rat-faced cohorts
were too snappish and blood-hungry to think twice
about what they were facing.

'Y'heard him,' bellowed the third member of the group,
whose mouth was full of teeth filed to points and whose
flesh was a canvas for dozens of obscene electoos. 'Piss
off!'

Garro took a step forward and met four bullets fired
in quick succession by the gunman. The shots hit him

in the chest and belly, breaking the outer layer of his epidermis but penetrating no deeper. He grunted with irritation and reached into each of the wounds with thumb and forefinger, pulling out the flattened heads of the kinetic rounds and flicking them away. Blood, thick with gene-engineered Larraman cells, was already clotting the trivial wounds.

The one with the gun was clearly an imbecile. Instead of putting distance between himself and Garro, he came closer, aiming the heavy pistol up to target the legionary's head.

Garro stepped in to meet him. With a lazy backhand, he smacked away the weapon, shattering the bones in the gunman's forearm. He could have left it there, but there was a lesson to be taught, and so he put what he considered to be a light punch into the squealing gunman's chest. The blow caved in the thug's ribcage, collapsed his lungs and stopped his heart.

The man covered in phosphor-glowing tattoos cried out the dead man's name, and turned tail and fled back in the direction of the marketplace.

The thug with the beard and the push-sword yelled and slashed at the air before Garro, attempting to force the legionary back with a wild, uncontrolled feint. He was trying to put Garro on the back foot, perhaps so he could extend away and flee as well.

The warrior watched the criminal's pattern, saw it, and in the next breath he grabbed the razor-sharp blade and yanked it forward. A seasoned swordsman would have let go of the handle, but the thug's best challengers had only been untrained civilians with no grasp of bladecraft, and he had no more moves to make. Ignoring the distant sting of pain as the push-sword cut into his palm,

Garro twisted his wrist and disarmed the bearded thug, the motion breaking fingers in his opponent's hand.

The blade fell to the deck and he stamped on it, the steel heel of his bionic leg snapping it in two. Garro reached out and grabbed the thug by the shoulder and squeezed, feeling bone grind on bone.

'You have made several mistakes,' he told the man, as he listened to him panting. 'And your path brings you to me.'

'Please… ! Don't… !'

Garro shook his head. 'That time has passed.' He shook back the cuff of his robes and showed the man one of the sigils branded into his flesh, the device of a skull against a six-pointed star. 'You attacked a legionary. Do you understand that?'

The bearded man's eyes were wet and streaming. A patch of dark colour spread on his breeches as he soiled himself in fear.

'I want to know where they are.' Garro nodded in the direction that the surviving believer had gone. 'You know. Tell me.'

'Don't… don't know!' gasped the thug. 'Don't remember… .'

'You do,' Garro corrected gently. He tapped the thug's forehead. 'Memory chains in your brain tissue. Either you access them… or I will.'

'What… ?'

Garro put his other hand around the man's skull and slowly began to apply pressure. He would need to be careful, to crack the bone without destroying the soft organ inside. The warrior took on a gentle, lecturing tone. 'When the genesmiths made me what I am, they placed an implant in my belly called a preomnor. A stomach within a stomach, if you will. It allows me to ingest poison and toxics, subsist on edible materials that would kill any other living thing...'

A wet crackle sounded from beneath Garro's fingers, and the thug cried out in terrible pain, fruitlessly trying to peel the legionary's grip apart.

'Moreover,' he went on, as if this were instruction for some neophyte battle-brother, 'there is a second implant, the omophagea. Capable of separating genetic memory from ingested matter, if you can conceive of that.' He leaned close and looked the thug in the eyes. 'What I *eat*,' he said, with cold clarity, 'I take the memories from. Do you understand?'

The thug's cries became whimpers, and Garro knew that he did.

'One way or another,' said the legionary as he increased the pressure, 'you will tell me where to find the hidden church.'

EIGHTEEN

The mark, and the marked
Sermon
A burned figure

HALN SPENT AN hour or two getting used to the steady rocking motion of the Walking City, but eventually he had taken to it like a local, and now he could move through the mile-long corridors without scuffing his elbows on the iron walls with each gyration. It made spotting other new arrivals very easy. Even the most experienced counterspy would take a time to get in synch with the *lurch-drop, lurch-rise* rhythm of the great mobile platform.

That was part of the reason Haln had picked the city as their means of transit down the continental spine, an extra way to help him flush out any potential followers on their trail.

His caution was yet to be tested, however. Haln always kept to the tenets of his tradecraft, following rules of espionage that had been set down centuries before humans had even left this blighted planet. He took circuitous routes, never used the same vox module twice, varied his pattern, his gait, his appearance. He assumed nothing, distrusted everything, just as he had been trained.

And yet, in all the time he had been active on Terra, there had never been a moment where he was truly afraid. Never a point where he had glimpsed a flash of an enemy's blade and known he was close to being discovered. Was it that his opposite numbers in service to the Sigillite were so good that he never saw them? Were they watching and waiting to see where he would lead them? Or was the opposite true, that Malcador's agents were as ignorant to his like as the people about this platform were to Haln's real intention?

He suspected the latter, but he would not allow the opposition's laxity to infect him. It was acceptable – desirable, even – for one's enemy to be lazy, but that didn't mean Haln could slacken off. He had to behave as if those out to stop him were as competent as he was, even if that had never been true.

Haln halted at the iron door to his rented cabin, and rearranged the cups and plaspaper bags he carried so he could recover the beam-key that opened it. Checking the alcove to make sure he was alone and unseen – he had already disabled the primitive security monitor at the far corner – Haln unlocked the hatch and kicked it open with his boot.

The room was small and gloomy. It smelled of old metal and sweat. Haln deposited his load on the collapsible table in the middle of the compartment and went to the circular window, pivoting it to open outward. Immediately, the steady crunch and grind of massive gears entered the space, and he stole a glance out. The cabin was above and to the aft of the eighth leg mechanism on the port side of Walking City, a massive iron limb as tall as a hab-tower that ended in a splay-toed foot large enough to crush a city block. Twenty legs on both sides of the gargantuan moving platform provided motive action for the slab-like mobile settlement as it laboured southwards towards the equator, endlessly marching through a dustbowl that stretched from horizon to horizon.

Rising from a corner, the assassin helped himself to a cup of lukewarm tisane and scowled at the taste. Then, he found a bag with skewers of cooked arthropod meat and set to work devouring them. Haln sat on a stool, took his own meagre portions and ate in silence, observing the killer without directly watching him.

Haln was only ever honest with himself, and he was so now as he considered how much he disliked the mission he had been given by his handler, his Aleph. What he knew for sure was that the directive had come from outside the legion to which he was oath-sworn. Haln was one of many non-Lords, part of a vast army of commons who toiled for his masters the First and the Last, and he gleaned that his assignment had been handed down from the Sons of Horus… Perhaps even from the Lupercal's Court itself.

He had been diverted from the midst of other duties and forced to leave work undone for this, to be the chaperone for a man who woke screaming in the middle of the night, who constantly shifted back and forth between icy lucidity and morose disengagement. At first, Haln wondered what was so special about this particular killer – there were many capable of that act, he reasoned, Haln among them – until the moment he saw the assassin at his work.

The killings at the sanctuary were unlike anything he had witnessed before. That horrific weapon that seemed to hide away until the assassin called it forth, and the things it did to living flesh… If Haln had still been capable of sleeping, he imagined it would have given him nightmares. As it was, he used chem-shunts to edit his own memories of those scenes, softening his recall of the worst moments. What he could not remember fully, he could not dwell on – that was the idea. In reality, it didn't work. He had to hold much of it untouched in his mind, for the sake of the operation. And so Haln still recalled enough to be fearful of the assassin and that cursed gun of his.

He wanted this to be over and done. The work he had come to Terra for, that the Aleph had tasked him to prepare, that would now go on without him. Dozens of operatives, primed to spring a great feint against Rogal Dorn's defences, an invasion *before* the invasion that would entice the primarch of the Imperial Fists into tipping his hand. It was an elegant endeavour that Haln had been enthused by. He liked the clockwork of the notion, the sheer *game* of it.

By contrast, conveying a murderer – no matter how monstrous his ways might be – seemed like a lesser work. *Any bloody fool can pull a trigger*, the spy told himself.

As the thought crossed his mind, the assassin stopped chewing and stared directly at him. 'How do I know I can trust you?'

Haln arranged his features into a neutral aspect. 'We've already had this conversation. Don't you recall? Before you… sterilised the settlement.'

The assassin nodded slowly. 'What did we learn from them? The killed?'

'There are several possible vectors for the target.' Haln took another sip of tisane and with patience, gave the same report he had twice already. He reminded the assassin about the half-dead, burned souls who had begged for quick ends while Haln flensed them for intelligence on the target. There were many probable locations, and it was taking time to narrow them down. Haln had contacts he was using to follow up leads, and that data was yet to mature.

'You have told me this,' snapped the assassin, his hard eyes glittering, his manner becoming stony once again. 'Is there no more you have? What use are you to me?' He held out his hand. 'Show me your mark.'

'I don't have a–'

'Show me your gods-damned mark, you stinking whoreson!' The words exploded from the assassin with such venom that Haln actually jerked back, the stool scraping across the metal deck. Before he could get out of reach, the assassin grabbed his arm by the wrist and pulled him over the tiny table. Haln toppled off the stool and his cup emptied its contents over the floor.

Still, he was quick enough to will his own tattoo into quiescence before the killer could wrench back his sleeve and glare owlishly at his hand, his forearm. Had he been unready, the thin greenish tracery of a many-headed form would have been visible there. Instead, there was only umber-coloured flesh with the texture of worked leather.

'You don't have it,' said the assassin, his towering fury smothered in a moment. He released his rigid grip, disgusted. 'You don't,' he repeated. Then the killer pulled off one of the black ballistic-fabric gloves he habitually wore and offered Haln his bare palm.

The mutant shape on his pale skin could not be called a scar. That word simply wasn't grotesque enough to encompass the abhorrent nature of the brand on the assassin's flesh. It was, in some fashion, an eight-armed star. An octed, Haln had heard it called. But it was also a festering stigmata, ever-bleeding and raw, a cut that smoked rather than oozed, a monstrous and abnormal wound not just in the meat of the man, but greater than that. Haln instinctively sensed that the mark went soul-deep.

He shrank back, recoiling as carefully as he could so as not to show how squeamish it made him feel. Haln had opened the flesh of hundreds and never felt anything as base as the repulsion he experienced at that sight.

Mercifully, the assassin hid his horrible grace back inside the glove, eyeing him. 'You have been here a while. How was that possible? They couldn't send too many with the pathfinders, the scry-seers in the towers would read it…'

'I came here through more conventional methods,' Haln said, gripped by a sudden need to fill the air in the cramped cabin with anything other than the thought of that cursed mark. 'My insertion was with a group of refugees… Previously I served my masters with disinformational sorties and proxy attrition. Then I was tasked with a direct intervention.' Normally, Haln would never have voiced even a fraction of this detail to someone from outside the legion hierarchy, but he suspected that the assassin would never live beyond the completion of this mission to tell of it. He had swept the cabin and pronounced it clean of listening devices that very afternoon. *The only person who can hear my words is a dead man walking*, he thought.

'On Terra?' prompted the assassin.

'Not at first.' Haln shook his head as the room tilted, the Walking City clanking and heaving over some ravine far below. 'I was put aboard a flotilla of ships running to Sol after escaping the rebellion…' He had to remember to call Horus' act a rebellion, not an insurrection or a revolt, as he did when speaking in the character of his cover. 'It went… poorly. The Custodian Guard intervened and there were many deaths. But I was able to escape in a small craft and reconnect with our assets already in-situ.'

The assassin grimaced at the mention of the Legio Custodes and looked away. 'Those arrogant, gold-plated wretches! I should like to kill one of them, under the gaze of all their cohorts. Just once. To remind them they are not perfect. Let them know there are better weapons.' He glared up at Haln and the barely restrained violence the man had shown earlier was back again. 'I want a target, do you hear me? I *need* it. There's no purpose for me otherwise!'

Haln's eyes narrowed. 'I can't just find you someone to murder, even in a place like this. Not in the way that you do it.' He nodded toward the marked hand, the killer's gun hand, and remembered the dead at the sanctuary once again. 'It would be too risky. Traces would be left behind, too difficult to explain away.'

'Then find me what I came here for,' spat the killer. 'Quickly.'

WHAT THE FOLLOWERS had made their church had once been a vast section of a sluice mechanism, a crevice between two large coolant channels that could direct waste water away from the atmosphere processors and into the air below Hesperides as dirty rainfall. Accumulated layers of rust and grime told Garro that the system had not worked for years, perhaps decades. This was borne out by the silence coming from the coolant pipes;

nothing flowed in there. The whole area of the orbital plate was inert and largely abandoned, buried as it was deep on the floating city's keel where sunlight never fell.

The church was suspended on one of dozens of grid-work deck frames, each of them layered atop one another in complex profusion. He made his way down to one of the lower levels and found a point to watch what took place overhead, and wait.

Above the legionary, the believers moved back and forth, none of them pausing to consider that an intruder had already found his way into their house. Once, he saw the believer who had escaped the thugs in the marketplace, heard him talking to his comrades about the dangers out there in the alleyways. While the specific threat of the bearded man and his friends had been removed by Garro, there were others that these poor fools were only vaguely aware of.

The best part of a day passed. Garro willed his body into a state of solidity, becoming static and unmoving as he lingered. He did not require water or food. His bio-implants were more than capable of sustaining him for months on the stored nourishment distributed throughout his artificial organs. He let his mind drift, absorbing the sounds of the believers at their worship. He listened to them as they quietly sang old forbidden hymnals, or recited pieces of the Lectitio's texts. For the most part, though, they kept together in small groups and their conversations, no matter what aspect they wore, orbited around the same unpromising subject. *When will the Warmaster come to Terra?*

Then a voice Garro had not heard for years reached into his quiet mind and brought him back to the surface of full awareness.

'Hello, my friends.' The legionary raised his head to get a better view of the church's dais, just visible through the holes in the floor plates, and there he saw an old man. 'I'm pleased to find so many of you here.'

Once upon a time, that old man had worn the robes of a high Imperial iterator and he had spoken only of the Emperor's crusade against idolatry, religionism and the plague of superstition. But since the evolution of one young woman into Sainthood, the man had become the greatest convert to a new understanding – the veneration of the Emperor of Mankind as a living god.

Kyril Sindermann clasped his hands together and bowed to the assembled group. Garro could tell by the creaking of the deck above his head that the makeshift church was filled to capacity, even though none of the attendees spoke louder than a murmur.

Despite his advanced years, Sindermann's voice carried over them with the clarity born of zeal. 'I know you are afraid,' he began. 'Of course you are. It is true, what many of you fear. We are on the edge of an abyss, and a step too far will send us to our end. Not just death, mind. Not the material ending of our flesh and bone, but of our souls. Our faith.' He broke off, chuckling to himself. 'There were days when I did not believe in such ephemeral notions,' admitted the iterator. 'No longer. My eyes were opened by the Saint, who in her glory, showed me a brief glimpse of the God-Emperor's will… and the darkness He is ranged against.'

A ripple of apprehension echoed through the space, and Garro held his own counsel on the exemplars of that darkness that he too had seen.

'The archenemy has a force of such great fatality at his fingertips,' Sindermann continued. 'And as we stand here and draw breath, it closes the distance to Terra. Inevitable. Inexorable. When Horus… arrives…' The iterator stumbled over the Warmaster's name, as if it were ashes in his mouth. '…there will be such horror. This *will* come to pass. The God-Emperor knows it, and by His wish so does the Saint and so do we. Know that I speak truth to you when I say we have gruelling days to come. The sky will burn and blacken. Death in manners undreamt of shall stalk the world.'

The crowd were utterly silent now, and even Garro felt his breath stilled in his chest by the old man's steady, purposeful sermon.

'Some of you question,' said Sindermann, the deck rasping as he walked off the dais and out among the gathered followers. 'You ask why we must face this terror. Why does He not leave the Imperial Palace and show His face, why does He not cast down the Ruinstorm from the sky and take the war to His errant sons? I tell you it is because even now, in the bowels of this planet, the God-Emperor fights on another front, in another war. A war that only He can wage.'

The legionary's eyes narrowed. How was it possible that Sindermann could know such a thing? Garro had heard many rumours about the Emperor's absence on the stage of conflict, but never anything stated with such certitude.

'We are being tested, my friends,' Sindermann was saying, his words echoing off the iron walls. 'Tempered in these moments to become something greater for the coming battle. To be made ready for the advance of such chaos, we must be primed for it. We must grow to be unafraid.' He took a long breath, and his tone became almost fatherly. 'Doubts are not forbidden. Questions are not silenced in this chapel. Ours is not a faith that is so delicate that it cannot stand up to hard questions. That is why we swept away the old churches and the false gods during the Great Crusade! We erased every ancient, crumbling belief because they were weak. Their credo could not resist the test of a keen mind, or questions not easily answered. They asked for blind faith in something that could not be perceived, touched or experienced. We do nothing of the kind. Our deity lives among us. He can be seen, and in some small manner, He can be known to us!'

A few of the believers picked up on Sindermann's words and called out in affirmation, and he continued. 'We question, and we have answers. We emerge the stronger for it, and so we shed our fears.' He paused again, and the room quieted. 'I am unafraid because I have walked the path to reach this place and on that journey I have *learned*. Now I look to the road ahead, the road that leads to the edge of the abyss and see it for what it is. Not fate. Not some pre-destiny scripted by a phantom deity that puppets me like a toy. No. *No!*'

Sindermann's voice shifted again, taking on a hard, defiant edge that seemed strange coming from the elderly iterator. 'This is the duty we have! This is the path we are on! *Resist*! Resist and survive and resist again! For the God-Emperor of Mankind is not the engine of our future, no, my friends. *We* are the engine of *His.*' The old man's words rose to fill the chamber. 'He empowers us and we empower Him! And through that unity, we will know glory!'

The church erupted in a cacophony of cries and applause, and for a moment even the legionary felt his spirit lifted by the power of Sindermann's oratory. The decking above his head shuddered, resonating with the righteous power of

the followers. That was why Garro did not become aware
of the child until it was too late.

Beneath the shouting, he heard the clank of movement
somewhere nearby, on the same underlevel. Moving as
quickly as he could in the cramped space, Garro came
about and found himself face to face with a small girl.
The child had the delicate features and red hair charac-
teristic of some Jovian commoner bloodlines, and her
dirty clothes suggested she might be a refugee from one
of the outer moons.

Her eyes were very wide and her face was pale with
shock. 'Wait,' he rumbled, keeping his words soft.

Her scream was high and piercing, and it seemed to go
on and on. How a little frame with such tiny lungs was
capable of emitting so sharp a sound was beyond the
legionary, and the girl scrambled away before he could
reach her. Cursing himself for his momentary lack of
focus, Garro pushed out of his hiding place and took two
quick steps across the lower deck. The child vanished up
towards the church proper, scrambling along pipes and
through gaps that would barely have accommodated the
warrior's hand, let alone his body. Cries of alarm were
spreading through the gathered followers, and he caught
the sound of lasguns powering up. Clearly, the beliefs of
the Saint's followers did not stretch to pacifism.

There was no point trying to hold on to his meagre cover now it had been well and truly blown. Better
instead, he decided, to use what Space Marines were best
at. *Shock and awe.*

With a growl of effort, Garro launched himself upwards
and bulled his way through layers of the metal deck,
forcing rusted metal outward until he crashed out on to
the floor before the dais. He rose to his full height, his

face set in an imperious glare, casting a cold gaze over
the followers as they stood terror-struck before him. In
the front rank there were eight people with short-frame
Naval-issue beam rifles, and as one they trained their
weapons on the giant that had risen into their midst.

Of the child who had raised the alarm there was no
sign, nor could Garro see Kyril Sindermann. He guessed
that the iterator had been rushed out of the chamber the
moment the screaming started.

'Is that it?' said a frightened voice, from somewhere
among the faces hiding behind the ranks of pews.

'First Salvaguardia and now here!' said another. 'He's
come to kill us all!'

Garro raised his hand, but panic detonated like a
bomb, and suddenly the crowd behind the followers
with guns was fragmenting, some groups rooted to the
spot, others flooding towards the hanging blackout cloths
that were the entrance to the church.

The legionary read the faces of the believers before him
and he saw the glitter of determination in the eyes of the
one that would shoot first – a wind-burned woman with
hair in tight black rows. Garro's right hand was already
snapping back to the hilt of *Libertas* with transhuman
speed, running to a clock that was far faster than any
unaugmented response. His tactical mind told him that
he could put down these eight with only two cuts of the
blade, killing outright at least half of them and leaving
the rest to bleed out in minutes. Without his armour, the
concentrated las-fire of multiple rifles at close range could
gravely wound him. A lucky shot might even end his life.

But he was not here for battle. These people had been
waiting for an enemy, and in his haste, Garro had presented that to them. *No killing today*, he told himself.

Not here, at least. Even though this chapel was nothing more than a repurposed drain-way, it felt disrespectful to shed blood here.

In a lightning-fast flash, Garro drew the sword in a downward flourish that took off the front quarter of the woman's rifle as easily as trimming a plant stem. She recoiled, staring at the sparks bleeding from the end of the ruined gun.

The sharp crack of superheated air sounded, and Garro hissed – more in annoyance than genuine pain – as a single laser bolt grazed his shoulder. He turned a hard glare on one of the other armed followers, a gangly dark-skinned youth who looked at his rifle as if it had betrayed him by going off on its own.

Garro's unflinching gaze was enough that the youth dropped the weapon and backed away. 'I am not here to kill anyone,' intoned the legionary. 'I was at… Salvaguardia, or whatever you wish to call it. The Afrik sanctuary. But I was too late to halt what happened there.'

The woman with the broken gun tossed it away, trying to recover some of her earlier courage. 'Or maybe you did it. Maybe the Regent sends you and his phantoms to cross us off, eh? One at a time.' She shook her head, her wary gaze never leaving his. 'Men of the Legion, they don't come to read the book. We don't trust.'

'You're wrong,' Garro told her. 'The book… Its reach is further and higher than you can know.'

'You need to go,' she shot back, unwilling to listen to him. She knew – they all knew – he could end them, and yet they still stood against Garro. They were as brave as they were devoted.

He opened his mouth to reply, but a commotion at the back of the chamber stilled his words. He heard an argument taking place, and Sindermann's voice raised in great annoyance. Suddenly, the iterator burst through the blackout cloths, shrugging off the grip of those around him as he went.

The old man took a few steps and stopped, his hand rising to his mouth as he caught sight of the standoff. 'Oh, infinite. Yes.' He came forward, an honest smile breaking out across his lined face. 'Captain Garro... ? It is you, isn't it? Alive and well.'

What happened next was quite alien to the legionary. The iterator pushed his way through the armed followers and embraced Garro like a long-lost sibling – or at least, as much as he could given the discrepancy in their heights.

'Do you know who this is?' Sindermann demanded of the believers, some of whom were now warily filing back into the chamber. He threw a derisive wave at the woman and her armed cohort, speaking to them like they were disobedient children. 'Do not court further insult. Put those guns away. This person is a friend to the Imperial Truth. He is always welcome among us.' Sindermann's manner shifted and briefly he was the great orator again, his words filling the air. 'You look upon the face of Battle-Captain Nathaniel Garro, and you should be honoured! He is a true hero, a rescuer! He saved my life, and that of the Saint... We would be long dead at the hands of the archtraitor if not for his fortitude and daring.'

Garro heard his name rush back and forth across the church in a wave of whispers, and the strange moment made his skin prickle. 'Well met, Kyril Sindermann,' he offered, then faltered over his next words. Now he was here, he was not sure how to ask the question that had been gnawing at him for months.

'The last time you came to my chancel, you made a forthright entrance.' Sindermann nodded towards the buckled floor plates. 'And so again. You could have used the door, Captain.' He smiled up at the legionary.

'I… erred on the side of caution. Perhaps too much so.'

The iterator nodded gravely. 'Zeun was right when she said that the Legiones Astartes are uncommon in these halls… but all are welcome. After a fashion.'

'There are many among my kindred who would hear you,' Garro told him. 'If they could.'

Sindermann touched Garro's hand and his smile returned. 'They will. In time.' He gestured towards the dais and an area beyond it hidden behind more of the heavy black drapes. 'Come, my throat is parched and I need a drink. We'll talk.'

Garro nodded, and carefully returned his sword to its sheath. As he turned away, he met the gaze of the dark-haired woman Sindermann had called Zeun.

'You owe me a weapon, phantom,' she told him. 'You good for it?'

'We'll see,' he replied.

ABOVE THE ENDLESS clanking tread of the Walking City, there came a sharp rapping on the metal hatch of the cabin. The assassin burst from the place where he had been crouched for the past few hours with such velocity that Haln almost drew his shimmerknife in shock. The killer had been so silent, so still, that Haln had begun to wonder if he had fallen into a slumber of some kind. Now he realised that the man had only been at rest, waiting for a target of opportunity.

Inky black smoke gathered in the assassin's hand and began to take on a familiar shape, but Haln was quickly on his feet, stepping between the hatch and his twitching charge. 'No,' he said firmly. 'Put that away. This isn't the time.'

'You don't tell me what to do,' hissed the killer. 'I tell *you*.'

Haln let the exasperation show on his face. 'My orders don't come from you,' he hissed. 'They don't even come from *him*. So back off, and let me do my job.'

The assassin muttered something foul and venomous under his breath, slinking away to the open window. His scarred hand was empty again, and his fingers toyed with the growth of unkempt stubble on his chin.

The scent of brimstone lingered in the air as Haln peered through a spy hole in the hatch and then cracked it open to allow a wiry deckhand to slip inside. She had a pict-slate in her hand. 'Got you something,' she explained, her accent thick with the heavy vowels that betrayed a tech-nomad upbringing. 'Did just like you asked.'

When they had boarded the Walking City, Haln had paid this woman to slip a code-spike into a port on the maintenance level of the central interlingua, the Walking City's core vox nexus, through which ran a steady stream of pirated data.

The woman's employers, the mistresses of the city, were information brokers with great access to the decrepit digital networks in this part of the world. Haln could have paid them for the data he wanted, but that would have drawn too much attention. It was easier to steal it using a greedy cat's-paw like the deckhand.

'Give,' demanded Haln, and he snatched the slate away. He leaned forward, allowing his right eye to open like a quartered fruit. Long ago, Haln had killed a Mechanicum adept for the optic implant and added it to his own repertoire of tools – it extruded a fine mechadendrite that wormed across the surface of the slate and into a connector slot.

Immediately, his forebrain was assailed by a storm of images and sounds, pieces of data captured in the net of scrapcode that had been lurking inside the spike. The demi-intelligent software device had sifted the torrent of raw data passing through the Walking City's servers – much of it so grossly illegal that the mistresses would have been executed if they were known to possess it – and plucked out what Haln needed to complete his mission.

He drifted into a mechanically-induced fugue state, the data temporarily becoming his whole world. Much of it was useless, redundant or vague, but the valuable gems among the silt shone through. The trawl of data slowly confirmed what he had suspected from the start. The woman called Keeler, the target that they had missed at the sanctuary, was on the Hesperides orbital plate. Snatches of vox chatter, pieces of raw machine-code, probability percentiles, all of it accreted into a solid, high-order chance that Keeler was there. *Confidence is strong*, Haln told himself. *This time we will have her.*

But there was something else that rose out of the stolen data. An outlier.

For a moment Haln thought some programming anomaly had crept into his feed, but as the information presented itself he realised that it was what it appeared to be. Someone else was in the mix, following the same path, looking for the same thing.

He found a partial pict-capture from a monitor bird of a huge, muscular figure in robes, caught in the act of killing a man. Legiones Astartes. There was no doubt in

Haln's mind. Bereft of armour and guns, it appeared, but still very much a grave danger.

And the face… Haln knew that face. He had seen it before, back when he himself had worn a different aspect. The legionary had been clad in storm-shade wargear then, the decks of the starship *Daggerline* reverberating beneath his boots as he strode past the alcove where Haln stood. Not seeing him. Not knowing what he really was.

Haln got off the ship as soon as he could after that, learning that the legionary had another of his kind with him, a psyker whose gaze might pierce Haln's otherwise flawless disguise. He kept out of sight, with no other choice but to let things take their course… That he had escaped the confrontation out beyond Eris had been a miracle.

But at least the legionary was alone this time. That shifted the odds against them from insurmountable to merely incredible.

'There's a problem,' Haln began, his voice sounding slow and drawn out to his own ears as he disengaged from the data mass and returned himself to a more human thought-mode. 'There may be a…'

He halted as he became aware of what was going on around him. Being inside the information cluster caused Haln to lose focus on the real world. Time could pass, events could occur right in front of him and he would remain only vaguely aware.

Haln's face was wet. He reached up and wiped away hot specks of blood.

In the middle of the cabin, a slagged thing that was some repugnant fusion of a melted metal stool and a burned human body lay on its side, emitting high-pitched squeals as it cooled in the breeze from the window. What was left of a face there sat locked in freakish horror.

The assassin stood over his work, black smoke coiling back into his hand as a gun-shaped object deliquesced and vanished.

Haln blew out a breath, secretly pleased that the killer had sated his needs but also irritated at his lack of restraint. 'You couldn't wait? Now I'll be forced to find a way to dispose of her that doesn't draw notice.'

'That's one of the things you're good at,' whispered the assassin. 'What is the problem?'

'You have very poor impulse control.'

The killer shook his head, gesturing at the data-slate. 'With that.'

'I believe we have the target's location. But there's an added complication. A Space Marine is also on site. He may be there to protect the target.'

'Oh.' The assassin leaned in towards the burned corpse, until his face was almost touching the blackened bone of its skull. 'I've killed that kind before.' He looked away, glaring at Haln with glittering eyes. 'More than once.'

NINETEEN

Ask the question
Lucidity
The Gallery

GARRO SAT AWKWARDLY on a chair that, while large, was still too small for a transhuman. He accepted a flask of water from Sindermann more out of ritual than actual thirst, and presently the iterator found a seat for himself, where he could look the legionary in the eye and consider him.

'It makes me glad to see you alive,' said the old man. 'There were times when I wondered if you might have fallen victim to this damnable conflict.'

'The war has tried to kill me. Many times,' Garro allowed, one hand falling to rest atop his augmetic leg. 'It's taken pieces but not the whole.'

'It *is* a war,' Sindermann said, nodding gravely. 'There are people out there who still think it is just a minor revolt. A thing that can be put down with the correct application of reasoning, gunfire and belligerence.' *We know otherwise.* The unspoken coda hung in the air between them, and the moment stretched.

'I am here to see Euphrati,' Garro said, pushing out the words with some effort.

'I know.' The iterator nodded again. 'But why do you *need* to, Captain?'

'You of all men ask me that?' Garro looked away, his gaze ranging around the room. The chamber they sat in was another part of the drain-way, walled off with pieces of repurposed decking and old girders. It was an anteroom of sorts, with an entrance at either end. One passage led back to the makeshift chapel, and the other vanished into an unlit tunnel. Sailcloth shrouds hung from the ceiling to pool on the floor, deadening the sound of distant atmosphere processors.

'I can only imagine the things you have seen,' Sindermann prompted. 'I witnessed horror enough at Horus' hands, and I would live a happy life if I never saw the like again. But you? You brought us back to Terra and then threw yourself into the fight anew.'

Garro eyed him. 'I never did learn how you were able to leave the Somnus Citadel on Luna. I recall that the Sisters of Silence were determined to hold you in custody for as long as they desired.'

The iterator smiled slightly. 'Some of the Null Maidens have read the book. They understood. And dear Iacton played a role for us. We found our way out.'

The mention of the Luna Wolf veteran's name cast a shadow over Garro's thoughts for a brief moment. 'Qruze was a great warrior, a better man. His loss is keenly felt.'

Sindermann pointed back towards the chapel. 'I keep a sacrament lit in his name. He won't be forgotten.' He took a breath. 'You still haven't answered the question.'

Garro took a sip of the water, tasting the impurities in it, delaying the moment of his reply. Now he was here, he was reluctant to go forward. But eventually the words came, as he knew they would.

'After the *Eisenstein*, after we made it to Sol... I thought I understood what my duty was. Before, it had been simple. Serve my Legion, my primarch, my Emperor, fight the crusade, bring about the golden age... But Mortarion and the Death Guard broke that covenant. The moment he allied with the Warmaster, my purpose was sundered. I lost my identity, do you see? Great pieces of who I was, stripped away or corrupted. And for a time, I clung to what was in front of me. I reached for the last thing I had left... My only compass was my honour, Sindermann. My only path was to do what was right.'

'And so you have,' said the iterator. 'You took a warning to Lord Dorn and then to Terra. You saved many lives.'

A bleak mood settled on the legionary. 'I believe now that the Emperor and the Sigillite already knew about the rebellion, even before we reached Terra. I carried that warning for nothing. Men were lost – good men like Kaleb Arin and Solun Decius – and for what? Because I did not stand and fight.'

'And die?' Sindermann snapped. 'We all would have been destroyed, had you not taken us to the warp. Or worse!'

Garro shook off the moment of self-pity. 'Aye, perhaps so. But it stings no less. And I wonder if it was my arrogance at play to believe that I would find new purpose when I shed the Fourteenth Legion's colours. Was I a fool to take up Malcador's offer of patronage? He promised me I would serve the Imperium, and I thought that would be enough.'

'But what have you really done?' The iterator's question was plucked from Garro's own thoughts.

'I have passed back and forth across the stars through secretive byways, and by means that only the Sigillite understands,' he said quietly. 'I have dug up a dead man who lost his mind, stolen a loyal son from his brothers... These and many others, all to press-gang them into the same ghost army I now march with. For what? For a purpose whose design is beyond my ken? So that Malcador can have his grey legion for tomorrow's wars? That is not what I hoped for. It is not who I wish to be.'

'You are of purpose,' intoned Sindermann, and the familiar words sent a chill down Garro's spine. For a moment, it was as if he heard other voices speaking the words in synchrony with the old man. 'The Saint told you that. And you believed that purpose was the one Malcador presented to you.'

'It is not.' It was the first time Garro had given voice to the nagging notion that had grown, slowly and surely, in the depths of his thoughts over the passing months. 'Whatever great schema the Sigillite plans to assemble, I am not a part of his endgame. He confronted me on Titan, in the hall of the hidden fortress that even now he builds for his knights. I knew then. I am his tool. It is true that his purpose aligned with mine, for a while... but I look over my shoulder now and see that they diverged a long time ago.'

'And you fear you will never find your way back.'

He nodded, his gaze dropping. 'Euphrati... the Saint... gave me clarity once before. I need that again. If not... I will slip back to what I was that one day over Isstvan. A man who does not know himself.'

'That will never...' Garro's head snapped up as he heard the strange echo-voice beneath Sindermann's words, clear and distinct now. A woman's voice.

'Never be so,' said Euphrati Keeler. She stood at the iterator's shoulder, as if she had been there all along. Garro half-expected her to be bathed in some kind of ethereal radiance, but there was nothing of that – only a warm serenity that flowed from her peaceful smile. Sindermann mimicked her words, and the legionary realised that in some manner, she had been speaking *through* him.

Keeler saw the question in Garro's eyes and shook her head. 'No, no, Nathaniel. Nothing like that. But dear Kyril is elderly and he has not endured our fugitive life well. Sometimes I can help him. Strengthen him.'

Sindermann rose, colouring slightly. 'I should let you two talk alone.' He bowed to the woman. 'Blessed,' he said, and then walked away, pausing only a moment to pat Garro on the shoulder. 'Captain. I am so glad you found your way back to us. This is meant to be.'

Garro accepted that without a word, and watched the iterator disappear through the blackout cloths, back into the church proper. 'I've been looking for you for some time,' he said, without turning back. 'Often, I was so close I could swear I sensed your presence in the room as it faded.'

'Yes,' she agreed. 'I'm sorry that was necessary.'

He shot her a look. 'You knew, then?'

'That you sought me? I did. The time wasn't right before.' She took a step away, walking towards the dark tunnel. 'No longer. We shall talk, Nathaniel. I will help you.'

Then he was alone, as the sound of a banned hymnal began in the nearby chamber.

SOMEONE HAD TAKEN the ruined shell of a passenger shuttle, ripped away the pilot space and the aft drive modules, and then by enthusiasm and a lot of molecular welding, bonded it to the edge of a yawning gap between two huge thermal runoffs. Dangling out into naked air over a sheer drop, the ramshackle cantina was a nexus for every lowlife chancer, petty criminal and thug who wanted to numb themselves against the unpleasant reality of life on Hesperides.

Haln nursed two fingers' worth of something brackish and electric blue in a tumbler cut from the bottom of a water bottle. It tasted like spindle oil and ingesting too much of it in one go would have blinded a normal human, but he was only simulating the act of drinking. Occupying the sparse end of the cantina's grubby steel bar, he kept watch on the place through a wireless link to the spare eye he cupped in his free hand. Now and then he would roll it back and forth across the countertop with the idle motion of someone who wasn't looking for companionship or conversation.

His charge, the assassin, had changed his manner once again on the voyage up from the surface to the orbital plate. He was actually in a frame of behaviour that Haln would have been willing to call 'lucid', and the spy wondered if the horrific murder aboard the Walking City had aided with that. He dismissed the thought. The assassin was a short distance away, near a hololith tank showing a playlist of tawdry burlesques and sanctioned watchwire broadcasts. Mostly, though, he was pretending to be interested in the ranting of a stocky, rat-like man covered in shimmering electoos. The obvious social dynamics of the room revealed that the tattooed thug was in some position of authority here, and after slipping unnoticed into the cantina a few hours earlier, Haln and the assassin had swiftly built up a model of the power structure in this sordid little corner of the Emperor's mighty Imperium.

The thug had recently ascended to the top of his gang through attrition, and not by his own guile. The termination of two of his closest allies had forced the tattooed man to become the leader, and it was abundantly clear to Haln he did not have the acumen for it. The thug talked again and again about the circumstances in which his comrades had perished, embellishing it a little more each time to make the story play like he had been its focus. Haln read through all that, of course, nodding along with the rest of the audience and laughing in the right places. The assassin was particularly good at this sort of subterfuge, even volunteering the occasional comment in an accent that passed muster. He was like a different person now, and Haln hoped this version of him would stick around for a while.

The thug's story wound round again and the broad strokes remained the same. A killer Space Marine, undoubtedly dispatched by personal order of Horus the Whoreson himself, had come to Hesperides to join up with the chanting religionist freaks living in the underlevels, clearly on a mission to kill, defile or eat those hardy souls who called the platform home, in the name of something or other unhallowed. The thug and his comrades had bravely set out to stand in their way, and despite a spirited fight that claimed the lives of all his friends, he alone had survived. His pyrrhic victory had been to chase the slavering monster into the underlevels, where it had either perished of its wounds or found safety with the god-lovers. If the Space Marine or the believers knew what was good for them, they'd stay there.

Haln ignored the gaping lapses in the story's logic

and sifted for facts. So the legionary was alive, and most likely with the target. But the location of the followers and their 'church' would be difficult to find. By the thug's own admission, the body of the last man to know where it was had been thrown off the gantry and buried in the sky.

Then someone else mentioned that there were other followers who had come to this quadrant, and how it amused the gang greatly to kidnap and keep them chained up for beatings. There were suggestions that the captives be sold to harvesters in the nearby Mindano Plex, who reportedly paid good coin for fresh organs.

This was the information they needed. The assassin gave a pre-arranged signal, and at the next thing the tattooed thug said, Haln burst out laughing. He pocketed the spare eye, turned on the thug and told him how all the effluent he had been spouting for the last two hours made his brain ache. Missing nothing, Haln called out each and every point where the thug's tissue of lies made no sense, giving special focus to the places where he had obviously covered up his own cowardice.

The fight blew up in an instant. Haln fought off the gang's lesser members, giving the assassin the chance to step in and 'assist' the thug in disposing of this mouthy interloper. He made it look convincing – too convincing, in fact – and ended up pitching Haln out of a window towards what would seem to be his grisly death.

In fact, Haln scrambled out across the underside of the ramshackle construction and waited there, clinging on with a web of cables while the assassin ingratiated himself with his new best friend. He observed through the remote eye, which he had deftly dropped into the killer's jacket pocket while they struggled.

The plan had made Haln nervous when the assassin described it, but now it was in play, it proceeded exactly as expected. Another surprise, he considered.

Hanging there, with the wind pulling at him and the thud of worker books drumming through the deck over his head, Haln eavesdropped on the lie the assassin unfolded for the thug.

He hadn't been totally honest. He wasn't just someone passing through. The truth was, he was here as a servant of the Emperor himself, oh yes. As an agent of the Legio Custodes, the Emperor's personal guard, no less. Hard to believe? But true, a truth that could only be told to a patriot. Someone like you. And that Space Marine, that enormous freak that had dared to kill your friends and sully your city with his presence? He was here to hunt it down.

Haln could not deny that the assassin knew how to play his part. The thug's reaction was lamentably predictable. His initial wariness was soon overridden by greed, vanity, and no small amount of self-preservation. He had to know his newfound status was shaky, but what better way to cement his role than by ending the threat that had already claimed the lives of his betters? Someone more intelligent, less desperate, might have questioned it a little more. But the thug wanted it to be true, and Haln knew that the fictions most easily imposed were the ones that were willingly swallowed.

Of course, the only way to locate this monstrous traitor-kin will be to find the place where these fanatics are hiding their filthy place of worship... But who could know where that might be?

The thug was not intelligent enough to realise that he had been guided to his answer before he gave it.

The pilgrims, of course! They had to have some idea, didn't they? All it would take was someone to cut on them for a time, and the location would be freely given...

He was telling the assassin where to find them as Haln began to navigate a slow and careful path across the underside of the platform and back to the decks of the lower levels. By the time he had made it to safety, Haln witnessed the two men speaking in coarse good humour like they were old friends.

The spy found a good place to wait, a short way from the cantina, and settled in to prepare for the next phase of the deception. He didn't have to linger too long; the tattooed thug, a couple of his cohorts and the assassin emerged on one of the swaying gangways and set off towards a satellite platform, connected to the main bulk of Hesperides Plate by a series of interwoven conduits.

Haln followed at a distance, still listening to the feed being transmitted to the short-range receiver implanted in his skull. The mutter of their conversation echoed through his mastoid bone, and he listened for the trigger word.

Lupercal. The assassin said it twice so that Haln didn't miss the moment. The spy burst into a run, drawing his shimmerknife as he came out of the shadows.

He put the blade across the backs of the thug's men in two short sweeping motions, the weapon's aura-generating edge slashing through bone and nerve and flesh to sever their spinal columns. They fell screaming and he sneered. Their tradecraft was appalling, barely the smallest inkling of situational awareness that dull, almost bovine reactions did nothing to improve. He declined to give them mercy-kills to end their lives swiftly, and let them bleed out as they lay paralysed and screaming.

Haln saw the assassin raise his hand as the tattooed

man's face twisted in shock and surprise, and for a moment he was afraid the killer would conjure his daemon weapon there in broad daylight. But something odd flashed over the assassin's face instead. The open hand became a heavy fist, and he sent it crashing into the thug's jaw. The man went down, and more blows rained upon him. Each time the assassin struck, a spasmodic feedback pulse went through the thug's electoos and they gave off a desultory flicker of light.

The assassin lost himself in beating the thug to a pulp, and Haln hesitated, unsure if he should intervene. Raw emotion twisted the killer's expression into something filled with rage and pain. Haln heard him cursing the thug – who by now was quite dead, his nasal bone having been smashed into the front of his brain – and saying a woman's name, over and over.

'Who is Jenniker?' He asked the question without thinking.

The assassin let the thug drop to the deck amid a pool of his own blood. 'What are you talking about?' His expression was stony once more, and he fished in a pocket to find the spare bionic eye. 'You don't know that name.' He tossed the eye at Haln, who snatched it out of the air. 'Why are you asking me pointless questions?'

Haln's lips thinned. Was his charge losing clarity of mind again, so soon? Perhaps that was the price of having such a horror of a weapon bound to him by that gruesome scar. 'It doesn't matter. You know where the pilgrims are being held?'

'We'll need another story to tell, if we are to find the target. Torture will take too long, and we've wasted too much time already on this effluent.' He gave the dead thug a kick, gaining a dull blink of light in return.

'I have a suggestion,' Haln ventured. 'The same game we played in the cantina, but for a different audience.'

'As long as there will be kills for me,' muttered the assassin.

'Soon enough,' promised Haln. 'Soon enough.'

THE WOMAN CALLED Zeun grudgingly found Garro some privacy in a meditation cell of sorts, cut out of the side of a feeder pipe. Her distrust of him hung in the air like acrid smoke, but he made no effort to assuage it. The legionary was tired of having to answer every single challenge made to his character, no matter how large or how small. If this woman thought ill of him, then so be it. All that mattered was the Saint, and what she would tell him.

Garro had a very real sense that he was reaching the end of a chapter of his life, turning a page from what he was now to what he would be next. It had happened before, this profound state of transition – when he was a youth, recruited to become a neophyte of the Dusk Raiders, again when his Legion had bent the knee to Mortarion and become the Death Guard, then on Luna when Malcador had spoken to him... But this time there was something more. A feeling, not of dread or anxiety, but of grim understanding. A sense, perhaps, that the next chapter of his life might be the last.

'So serious,' said a light, warm voice, and Garro turned to see that Zeun was long gone and Euphrati Keeler stood in her stead. 'And so troubled. Sometimes I wonder what your face would look like if your heart was lighter.' She cocked her head, studying him. 'You'd make a good subject.'

He frowned. 'For what?'

Keeler smiled, holding up her hands, thumbs and

forefingers making a rectangular frame that she held in front of her. 'A pict-image or three. That used to be my canvas, Nathaniel. I miss those days, sometimes. When all I had to do was capture a moment of time.' She let her hands fall. 'The language of an image can be understood by anyone, anywhere. It's timeless. It can communicate so much... I wish it were so easy for me to pass on the message I carry now.'

'I'm not sure I understand...' he began.

'I can show you.' Keeler moved towards him, and unaccountably, Garro retreated a step, motivated by something that he could not quantify. 'What's wrong? You've come so far, but now you have doubts?'

'I have come this far precisely *because* I have doubts!' he retorted. 'It is a state that is anathema to me. I am a legionary and I was made to be *certain*. It eats at me that I am not.'

'The curse of the intelligent man,' she offered. 'To question all things, while those less gifted act without hesitation.'

On an impulse he couldn't explain, Garro surged forward and grabbed her wrist. 'Then answer the question,' he demanded. Keeler's forearm seemed a tiny, fragile thing like spun glass, and he knew that with the slightest pressure he could crush her bones to powder.

The Saint showed no reaction to what he had done. Instead, her other hand snaked down and found his, gripping it gently but firmly. Garro felt a strange, electric thrill run though his nerves. 'Let me show you the gallery,' she told him. 'The place where I hang all the images that come to me.'

Keeler's voice was melodic and strangely distant. Garro felt a chill crawl over his bare arms beneath his travelling robes. He tried to speak, but the action was difficult to complete.

He blinked, and a shade had been drawn across the world. The room looked different, the light of it falling in odd ways, as if through a prism.

'See here, Nathaniel. In this one, I am killed.' Keeler was showing him a still image, sharper than any hololith or high-definition pict, brighter and more detailed than reality itself. It engulfed him. He could not look away from the hyper-saturated, overwhelming composition of it. 'I don't care for it myself,' she said.

Somehow, in this non-moment, he was *inside* the image with her, both of them observers who had stepped into this trick of the mind. The transition had been so subtle, so easy, that Garro had barely felt it happen.

He beheld a tragic scene. Keeler, draped across ouslite steps that were pock-marked with bolter hits, surrounded by common soldiery and weeping helots. She was quite dead, but angelic in her repose. 'Where... is this?' he asked.

'The Annapurna Gate of the Imperial Palace. This is one of my fates.' She paused. 'Here, another.'

Darkness eclipsed the moment and it became another time and place. A near-lightless dungeon, all sallow illumination coming from the glow-flash of a meltagun about to discharge. It was impossible to see the hand on the weapon, but the shadow behind it was a hulking one, unquestionably a Space Marine. Keeler knelt on the stony floor before the muzzle of the weapon, still meditating in the split second before the beam destroyed her.

'Another,' Keeler went on. This time, in the hold of a shuttlecraft that was on fire around her. 'Another.' At the foot of the Byzant Minaret beyond the Petitioner's City,

a sword at her neck. 'Another.' Desperate hands dragging away mounds of rubble, finding beneath them the
hem of her tattered robes. 'Another.' Garro saw himself
cradling her limp body in his arms, his face and his
shattered grey armour a monument to the hardest-fought
battle of his life.

On and on it went, visions of futures that might come
to pass, a cascade of unhappened days where the only
constant was Euphrati Keeler's death. He thought he
glimpsed other places he knew – the Somnus Citadel
on Luna, the tacticarium of the *Phalanx*, even the nave
of the makeshift chapel.

'Stop!' he demanded. 'Why are you showing me this?'

The Saint looked up into his eyes and the sorrow he
saw there was pure and endless. 'These are the lives that
extend out before me, dear Nathaniel. I capture glimpses
of them, and fate ends my life again and again.'

'I reject that,' Garro snarled. 'There is no fate but what
we make for ourselves. Nothing is pre-ordained. If destiny exists, it is to guide us, not yoke us!'

'And yet, I perish,' said Keeler. 'Here, and here and here
and here…' She paused. 'In all skeins of time I am dead…
save one.' She shook her head as all around them became
darkness. 'And that place, I have not seen.'

Garro blinked as she released her grip on his hand, and
he let go of her arm. All was as it had been, and they
stood unmoved from the anteroom beyond the makeshift church. Keeler's 'gallery' faded from his memory
like a sunset. 'You must not die like that.'

She smiled gently. 'I won't live forever, Nathaniel. None
of us will. Only the God-Emperor has that gift… That
curse.'

We have to keep her safe, Nathaniel. Sigismund's solemn

words tolled through his thoughts, and suddenly Garro's own troubles seemed small and inconsequential. 'You bring hope to millions in these darkest of days. I can't let you be killed.' He shook his head. 'The Templar was right. I let my own uncertainties cloud the duty before me. You must be protected.' He nodded to himself as the doubt that had plagued him suddenly melted away. 'I wasn't certain what that purpose was… I think I am now.' The clarity was stark and dazzling.

But then the Saint shook her head. 'You see and you still do not see.'

Garro stiffened. 'You must leave Hesperides immediately.'

'No, battle-captain. I will not.'

'You *shall* leave!' Garro barked, and his shout drew Sindermann's attention, the iterator dashing back through the blackout cloths with a look of fear on his lined face.

'What is going on–?' he began, but Garro spoke over him.

'You are exposed, Euphrati,' the legionary insisted, forcing himself to meter his tone. 'This place is not safe. Horus sent killers for you at the sanctuary, and they hunt you still. I know a place where we can protect you, a remote outpost in the Ishtar Range…'

'On Venus?' interrupted Sindermann.

Garro went on, formulating the plan as he spoke. 'There are automated cargo ships that ply the run to the Venusian protectorate. It's isolated, lightly populated, and you will be out of harm's way. From there, we will be able to gain passage from the Solar System and out across the segmentum.'

A flash of disappointment crossed Keeler's face. 'Why would I ever want to flee, Nathaniel?'

How could she not comprehend this? 'Because if you

stay on Terra, you will die here! Your own insight showed
you that!'

'I have you to protect me.' Keeler turned away from
him. 'And you should know by now – nothing is that
simple.'

A CLOUD OF conflicted emotions swirling about him,
Garro strode out to the gantry beyond the chapel of the
followers and scowled at the night sky. He struggled to
process the churn of his thoughts.

'I am of purpose,' he muttered.

For too long, he had vexed himself over what the
meaning of those words might be. For a time, he had
thought that purpose was the same as the Sigillite's plan,
but events had shown him otherwise. Garro wondered
if there really was a kind of fate, and if it were playing
him for a fool.

Keeler was the hub around which his future was turning. He saw that now, looking back at the path his life
had taken. The escape of the starship *Eisenstein* had not
just been about his passage from last loyal son to Knight
Errant, or the warning brought to Terra – it had been the
Saint's journey as well. It fell to him to keep her safe, and
he had done so. Now that duty was coming full circle
and the undeniable realities of those grim futures Keeler
showed him could not be ignored.

'Sigismund…' For a moment, Garro wished the Imperial Fist could hear his words. 'You were more correct
than you realised…'

'Do you know yourself now, Captain?' Garro turned
as he heard Sindermann approaching him. 'Those cross
words in the chapel, I admit I did not expect–'

'I don't remember her being that wilful,' he snapped.

The iterator chuckled. 'Then you have not spent enough
time in the Saint's presence.' He folded his arms. 'She's
much more than she was last time you saw her. The
changes the Saint has been through… Can you imagine
what it must be like for her? To awaken one day and
know that you have been chosen as a vessel for the will
of a higher being?'

'I am a legionary,' Garro said simply. 'That is every day
for me. Or it was once.'

Sindermann came to the guide rail where Garro stood
and looked out at the same sky. 'She's more than just a
symbol of hope for those who believe. She is the embod-
iment of that potential. The Imperial Truth… the *real*
Imperial Truth.'

'That makes her dangerous,' Garro insisted. 'It puts her
at risk.' He shook his head. 'Ever since Isstvan I have
been searching for a true reason to keep on going, to
keep fighting and striving. She may be it, Sindermann.
I should have seen it all along. I can protect her. If she
will only let me.'

'But are you certain you know what you are protecting her from?'

Garro shot him an acid glare. 'This is not a moment to
give me riddles, iterator. My patience wears thin! Speak
plainly or not at all.'

He sighed. 'The Saint is a flashpoint, Captain. Her life
or death will affect the course of this war, even if it seems
like great hubris to say so. If the Warmaster's agents reach
her now, while the word of the Lectitio Divinitatus is
still finding its level, it could trigger a religious uprising
here on Terra. That is what Horus wants. The common-
ers touched by the words of the book finding cause for
fury… It could destabilise the planet, perhaps the whole

star system, ahead of any invasion. Think of it… While
Lord Dorn toils building a fortress and hemming in
Mars, while Malcador schemes and the God-Emperor
faces what we cannot in the secret realms of His palace,
as each of them is distracted the book could sour the
common people without the Saint's guidance. Chaos,
Captain Garro. The seeds of chaos would bloom.'

'I can prevent that,' said the legionary. 'I've seen the
weapons the Warmaster uses, with blood in their teeth
and murder in their eyes. I know how to kill them.'

'But Horus Lupercal is not the only one with designs
upon the Saint,' Sindermann replied, watching him
intently. 'The Sigillite is not ignorant of her potential.
A man like him… How could he not be concerned by
what she might become?'

'I am not here as Malcador's instrument,' said Garro
firmly.

Sindermann waved away that notion. 'Of course not.
No one thinks that.'

'Zeun does.'

The iterator chuckled again. 'She'll learn. But her suspicion is a valid one. If the Sigillite were to find some
way to fetter the spread of the book, he would usurp it.
Turn it into something that serves his interests.'

'Malcador told me all he does is in service to the
Imperium.'

'But not to the God-Emperor?' Sindermann leaned
closer. 'They are not the same thing, Captain. Think on
this, sir – Euphrati is what the people need… a con-
duit to His glory, uncluttered by other intentions. She is
the hope they so desperately want in this time of great
uncertainty.'

Garro was silent for a long moment, before he stepped

away from the guard rail. 'She will not leave for Venus and beyond.'

Sindermann shook his head. 'She will not.'

'Then it falls to me to ensure that the Saint survives to fulfil her potential.' The legionary drew himself up, reaching inside for the familiar sense of his warrior soul that had been muted these past few months. 'To do that, I must shift the balance of the battleground. Anticipate the enemy... and destroy him.'

TWENTY

Interception
Revelations
Infernal

THEY LOOKED, BUT they did not find the shimmerknife on Haln when they searched him. The spy had hidden it inside a flesh-pocket on his inner arm that only a close inspection with a medicae auspex would have revealed. The other pilgrims surrounding him submitted to the same checks without question, some of them quietly accepting, others giddy with anticipation. When the believers in the makeshift chapel were satisfied, the pilgrims were allowed into the wide, curved space of the chancel proper.

Haln melted into the group, drifting forward to the front without obvious effort on his part. It had been little challenge to set these people free from the thugs who captured them on the upper tiers of Hesperides. He watched the assassin murder the hapless guards left behind with casual brutality, making use of his bare hands to do the deed. Under cover of darkness, Haln inserted himself into the group of captives, many of

whom had seen no light for days. In the dank, dripping
gloom of their haphazard prison, one more frightened
face was easy to overlook.

He was ready to push them on to the right course with
some choice words, but the moment never came. Someone eventually figured out that the silence outside meant
the guards were gone, and gingerly pushed open one of
the hatches. There they found dead bodies, and in one
of the rooms off the main corridor, somebody else discovered another prisoner chained to a chair – a prisoner
with a hawkish face and a scarred palm. The hostage pilgrims were so deliriously relieved to be free, not one of
them stopped to think that their escape was part of a
larger gambit. As the spy hoped, several of them knew
where to locate the hidden chapel in the lower levels,
and all he needed to do was follow them.

Haln heard one man saying that this was the God-
Emperor's will, and the ease with which the others
accepted that meant Haln's armoury of prepared lies
went unused. He allowed himself a smile, and enter-
tained the thought that this might actually be easy. He
liked that idea. The sooner they could bring this mission
to a close, the sooner Haln could jettison the mercurial
assassin with his monstrous gun and his see-saw moods.
The sooner, he reasoned, he could return to the work
assigned by his lords. That was where the real war lay,
not in these foolish games–

He snapped back to the moment. The pilgrims were
forming into a queue that wound back through the
chapel, and Haln was close to the head of it. He shot a
look over his shoulder, seeing fifty or more of the faithful
who had journeyed to this rusting hulk of a city on little
more than a word and a hope. The believers who had

met them with open arms stood in clusters all around, some of them linking hands and speaking litanies to one another.

He was very careful not to look upwards, into the dark shadows among the gantries overhead. The assassin had vanished from the group as soon as they arrived in the chapel, and he had to be up there somewhere, waiting for the right moment.

Step by step, the pilgrims advanced towards the stage at the far end of the chapel, and Haln felt the ebb and flow of emotion from everyone around him. He put away his smile and kept a fixed expression of humility on his face, not wishing to betray even the smallest iota of his true feeling to the others.

In point of fact, Haln despised these religionists. The spy considered their dogged acceptance of a mythical deity to be backward and childish. He would admit that, indeed, the Emperor was an incredibly powerful being, but then so were his sons, and so were their scions, the legionaries. Power of that kind could command fear and loyalty, that was a given – but to suddenly attest numinous nature to a real and quantifiable thing? Such thoughts came from limited minds unable to appreciate the true nature of existence... There were no gods in the universe, only unknowns. Life existed in a cruel space that neither rewarded nor punished. If Haln believed in anything, he believed in that.

The followers in front of him moved forward in a jerky surge and Haln suddenly found himself at the foot of the stage, near a jury-rigged wooden stair that would allow the pilgrims to climb up and walk across the dais. He looked ahead and saw an old man in what looked like the robes of an Imperial iterator, standing close to a dark-skinned woman who scowled at every one of the new arrivals, as if searching for a face that disagreed with her. Haln glanced away without making it obvious as the group shifted forward again, and he heard a female voice cut through the air.

'Blessings of the God-Emperor be with you,' she said, the words soft and perfect. 'Go forward in His light. The Emperor protects.'

Haln found the speaker and something strange happened. He was at a loss for words.

Revealed as another of the pilgrims moved away, there stood *the target*. Haln had seen a hololithic image of the woman taken years earlier, something dredged up from the public data nets, unflattering and basic. It hardly seemed possible that it was the same woman whom he looked upon now. She was changed in a way he could not put into words. She seemed more alive, and there was an energy to her that he could sense even yards away. Charisma, for want of a better term.

As he watched, she said the holy litany again for the man who stood in front of him, giving him the blessing of her god. Haln felt a peculiar energy around him and his heart pounded against the inside of his ribs. Against all willingness, the spy felt a pulse of elation run through him. It was like moving closer to a naked flame, bright and warm and enticing. The target – the Saint – looked to him and met his gaze for the first time.

Her radiance washed over him, and Haln was torn in two. One voice inside his thoughts rejected whatever gentle witchery she was casting over him, another throwing itself into the glow of it with abandon. The pressure built inside him.

It would be easy to take her hand, and admit it all.

Give up the darkness he had shackled himself to. Surrender. Redeem whatever remnants of a faded spirit still remained in him.

But the other voice won out. He shook it off and ran a hand down his arm. Flesh parted, blood oozed, and the shimmerknife slid into his grip. *This is who I am*, Haln told himself, his smile growing wide and cold. He wished he could see the face of the assassin as the blade came alive. The killer had sent him into the crowd to sow distraction, but now chance had put Haln directly at the point of the execution.

He laughed aloud at the thought that it would be he and not Horus' broken vassal who would end her. The sound was swallowed up in a crash from the other side of the chamber.

'*No–!*' The dark-skinned woman saw the vibrating glow of the shimmerknife and shouted, throwing herself into Haln's path.

THE KILLS AT the sanctuary had not been the random murder of an untrained mind. From the first sight of the fallen, fire-twisted corpses, Garro had instinctively known that he was dealing with an expert in the art of death. The way the infernal flames had been laid down defied analysis in some places, and there the legionary suspected sorcery was at work. But elsewhere, the pattern of shots and kills fell into a state that approached regularity. The hand that wielded the weapon at the gutted stronghold was methodical and callous, leaving nothing to chance, chasing down every last wounded believer and burning them alive.

He wondered if the killer took some form of pleasure from the slow, agonising deaths – or was it more arcane than that? Did the killer literally consume that pain? With all the horrors Garro had faced since the eclipse of the insurrection, he doubted nothing any more.

He believed in what he could see, even if that was something preternatural and horrific – and what he had seen at the sanctuary gave him insight into the mentality of the killer. Knowing that gunsight mind, grasping and understanding it, Garro knew where such an assassin would strike, and fathomed how it might be done.

The legionary stood up for the first time in hours, allowing his body to snap back from a low-heartbeat, slow-slumber state to full combat readiness. Concealing himself in a cluster of coolant pipes, he had blended in and become a piece of the darkness. Now that shadow came apart and he strode forward, each step ringing on the plates of the suspended gantry.

The man stood before him, balanced on the edge of the raised catwalk with a hand that grasped a bell made of black smoke. He turned to see the new foe that had presented itself, and Garro glimpsed a masked face. Tarnished steel and shredded synskin surrounded a baleful viridian mono-eye strip. The mask was damaged, but it was unmistakably that of a Clade Assassinorum.

Garro drew his sword. 'I should have known. The kill profile was familiar to me. You are Vindicare. The outcome that justifies the deed.'

The assassin cocked his head. 'I haven't been that for a long time.'

Garro heard the echo of his own words in the reply and grimaced. 'What you are now is a traitor.'

The barb had no effect on the killer. The coil of inky haze in his hand shifted and changed, becoming a solid, glassy form. 'Can one betrayed become the betrayer?' He pointed with his other hand. 'You are deceived, legionary, as much as I was. We're all just weapons in the end. But they lie to us, they make us think we are more.'

There was uncomfortable truth in those words, but now was not the moment to dwell on them. Garro raised his sword, thumbing the stud that brought the blade's power field to life. 'There will be mercy, if you surrender. I can promise no more than that.'

The smoke gathered into a great pistol of blocky crystal shapes, lit from within by a liquid, hellish luminosity. The form of it was sickly and unreal, and just the act of looking at it made Garro's jaw clench. The killer balanced the daemonic gun easily, making lazy aim towards the chapel below. Garro saw the recently-arrived pilgrims and the rest of Keeler's followers mingled down there, all unaware of what was happening just above them.

The former Vindicare shook his head. 'I cannot accept your offer. That choice can only be made by a man. And I told you... I am the weapon.'

With a sudden jerk of motion, before Garro could strike, the assassin tipped backwards over the edge of the gantry and fell to the floor below with a clattering din.

HALN PLANTED THE shimmerknife in the dark-skinned woman's chest, a quick in-and-out blow that punctured her aorta. She went down on the dais in a jumble of arms and legs, blood jetting from the wound in her torso.

'Zeun!' The old man in the robes stumbled after her, too slow and too feeble to catch her before she collapsed. Impotent rage flared on the elderly iterator's face and he foolishly turned his ire on the spy. He tried to shove Haln back, but he had little strength behind him.

Haln batted the old fool away with a hard backhand

blow, and it was no different from punching a wrap of dry twigs. The iterator tumbled headfirst off the stage and into the screaming crowd of believers.

The fixed, rigid grin on Haln's face faltered a moment as he caught the sound of a fire catching. He paused in his grisly duty and saw the assassin rising from among a pile of crushed chairs. The unhallowed pistol was massive in his pale fist, and Haln knew what would come next.

Just as before in the extermination of the Afrik settlement, the daemon gun discharged with a firedrake's roar and vomited up a stream of plasma flame. The murderous lance of burning warp-energy was itself alive, and it wound through the stale air of the chapel as a sea-serpent would move through open water. Blindingly fast, the blazing streamer described twists and turns that no conventional munition would ever have been able to achieve – and everything it touched came alight, consumed from within by a shrieking internal fire. The assassin kept firing, and more snakes of hellish plasma were unleashed into the chamber, dancing and killing as they went.

None would survive this, just as none had lived to tell the tale of the deaths at the sanctuary, and this time the tally of kills would include the greatest prize of this idiotic little cult. Haln turned back with the bloody shimmerknife still humming in his grip and saw the target down on her knees, draped over the body of the woman he had stabbed through the heart.

The target had her pale, long-fingered hands over the gushing knife wound, and Haln saw strange glittering motes of gold misting the air around the injury. She was singing a hymnal to the dying woman, and by no means Haln could grasp, that act was pulling energy from nowhere, keeping her from perishing.

With all her attention on her charge, the target seemed barely aware of Haln coming towards her. He decided that he would make his fatal cut across the back of her neck, severing the spinal cord.

GARRO SPRINTED TO the edge of the gantry as the odour of burned flesh and scorched metal filled his nostrils. He heard screams and saw bodies falling, their skin seared away in the same grisly fashion as the dead at the sanctuary. Below, the turncoat killer was firing into the crowd with cold abandon. The discharges moved as only living things did, whips of fire coiling around their victims, burning them, moving on to the next.

Perhaps they were some minor phylum of warp-creature, squeezed into this plane of reality though the annulus of the daemon-gun. Garro understood why the burn patterns in the sanctuary had been so haphazard and unreal – the fire from the weapon was *toying* with its victims.

I must end this–

The thought perished half-formed as his genhanced hearing pulled a cry from Sindermann out of the melee. Finding the old man through the chorus of shouting and screaming, he glimpsed the iterator fall at the hands of some nondescript man in shabby work clothes. From up here, Garro could clearly see that the other man had a powered blade of some kind in his grip. He was advancing on Keeler, who had ignored all sense to flee and instead knelt over the bleeding body of Zeun. The Saint was a heartbeat away from joining the injured woman on the road to a painful death.

The assassin with the sorcerous pistol was immediately, undoubtedly, the greater threat – Garro's tactical mind pushed options into his thoughts, weighing how he could end the gunman's existence as quickly as possible and save the bulk of the followers. But Keeler would die if he chose that target over her preservation. Was she worth it? Did this woman have the right to be saved over all the others in the chapel?

She would say not, Garro told himself. That it why she must not perish.

Blotting out the screams, the legionary gave himself over to the detached, clinical battle-skill that ran through his flesh like a second spirit. He ceded control to muscle-memory and the precise, unflinching proficiency that was forged into him. With a snarl, Garro spun *Libertas* up and around his head, putting might and momentum into the hilt of the crackling power sword. At exactly the right instant, the weapon slipped from his grip as if it were escaping of its own accord, and it looped away over the heads of the panicked believers.

HALN RAISED HIS arm at the beginning of the downward arc that would slash through the Saint's unprotected back, and saw a blink of motion from the corner of his eye. He had no time to register it, not even enough for his adapted nervous system to react and push him away.

Like a sight from the holy tales of gods and monsters he so reviled, a titan's sword fell from the shadows and cut though him. The blade severed his forearm just above the elbow and then went across his neck and shoulder. Haln was still trying to understand as his head fell away from his body and tumbled to the stage. He glimpsed the mighty weapon embedded in the curved steel wall, his own blood vaporising into pink smoke off the energised flat of the blade. Beneath it, flung there by force of impact, his bifurcated arm with the hand still clutching the shimmerknife. Without a consciousness to control the skin reactives, his concealed mark of fealty darkened and reappeared. The blue-black ink of the hydra tattoo, the many heads curving in on themselves. His true fealty as covert auxilia of the XX Legion, there for all to witness.

Haln's severed head rolled, the cut that removed it so fine that nerve impulses were only now starting to misfire, fluids spilling from the clean-cut meat of his neck. Consciousness stayed with him, brain-death still long seconds away.

He saw his own body, the headless mass sinking to its knees and jetting blood from its stumps. There was enough energy in him to blink once and move his eyes.

In the spy's last moments, his gaze was filled by a woman's face. The target.

Haln felt the terrible, final panic of this instant, and all he wanted was to get out one last thought, one last regret. *I wanted to see victory.*

The woman's sorrow washed over him, and then darkness.

NOW WITHOUT A weapon, Garro was not unarmed. More than his sword, more than a bolter or a suit of powered armour, a legionary alone was the greatest weapon in the arsenal of righteousness – that was an axiom that had been drilled into the warrior as a neophyte, back when he trained hard under Terra's storm-blackened skies, and the gloom of Barbarus and all it augured were still a lifetime away.

He followed the gunman down to the lower level in the same fashion, leaping the gantry and allowing himself to drop twenty feet to the steel deck. For Garro, it was barely a step, and he struck the metal in a perfect three-point landing, his robes snapping out around him.

Fires burned everywhere, and each one of the shrieking torches was a human being engulfed by cruel witchflame. They were not allowed to die quickly. Whatever brutal animal instinct drove the fire-serpents unleashed by the gun, they clearly liked the taste of pain.

Garro ignored the agony around him and broke towards the assassin as he reeled around to bring his accursed weapon to bear. The legionary had no time to make a definitive killing blow; the angle was wrong and the moment off-kilter. All he could manage was a sweeping backhand that clipped the killer and sent him spinning up and away. The assassin landed hard atop a line of cracked wooden pews and tumbled across them.

The strike dislodged the killer's battle-damaged mask and Garro came storming towards him, sweeping low to scoop it up as he approached. The corroded, stained metal of the faceplate made it resemble an object centuries old. Garro sneered and crushed the mask in his hand, shattering delicate crystal circuits and visi-lenses. 'Let me see your true face,' he spat, as the assassin rose shakily to his feet.

The legionary's sword was rooted in the wall, across the chaotic, smoke-wreathed chamber and well beyond his reach. But no matter; Garro would end this wretch without it if he had to.

The assassin glared at him, and Garro saw an angular, unkempt face that was a mess of hatred and grim determination. If not for the hell-gun in his hand and the wraiths of morbid light it cast across his features, the killer could have been mistaken for a vagrant pulled from the foetid alleys of some overcrowded hive city.

Garro closed the distance. 'I gave you a chance. You should have taken it.'

The assassin did not grace him with a reply. He *fired*.

A gush of volcanic flame erupted from the yawning maw of the glassy pistol, opening into a multitude of blazing streamers that flicked towards the legionary. Garro thought he saw dark spots at the tips of the fire-streaks, reminiscent of arachnid eyes. Then the weapon's war shot was striking him and he staggered into the infernal deluge. A conflagration hotter than any natural flame he had ever encountered bent and moved around him, holding close to Garro in a tormented embrace. He felt the material of his robes crisp and catch alight, polymerised synthetic plasti-threads flexible enough to turn a knife blow now burning like a common weave. The hood rolled at his back spat and burned, searing the fuzz of shorn hair on his scarred scalp.

Garro forced himself to advance, step upon step towards the gunman, hands raised to protect his face. The halo of flames sang as they consumed the air around him, filling his lungs with choking smoke. He uttered the Warmaster's name as the curse it had become, and snatched handfuls of his burning robes. With a grunt of effort, Garro ripped the flaming material from his back and flung it away. Beneath, he had only the form-fitting body-sheath that he would have worn under his Mark VI Corvus-pattern battleplate, the connector ports to his implanted black carapace glittering in the muddy firelight.

He shrugged off his own tide of fire, a terrible phoenix intent only on stopping cold this killer's mission. Leaping at him, Garro grabbed the assassin's gun hand and forced it up and away, his other hand snatching at the greasy tunic his target wore.

The legionary lifted his foe easily off the deck and shook him hard, but the obscene pistol would not be dislodged from the assassin's grip. From the corner of his eye, Garro saw that the daemon weapon appeared to be a seamless part of the man's hand, the glassy matter of the breech, grip and barrel morphing out of flesh, bone and blood. Aimed uselessly at the ceiling, the muzzle grunted and flexed like a gasping mouth.

'Why did you turn?' Garro bit out the words as he increased pressure with his other hand, feeling ribs crack and grind on one another beneath his implacable grip. 'What did they offer you?'

The uncertainty curdled in his throat. It was a question he could never answer for himself, one that troubled him deeply. So many of his battle-brothers in the Death Guard – led, to his eternal shame, by their gene-sire Mortarion himself – had made the same pact as this man, surrendering their honour to Horus Lupercal's new vision.

'What could be enough?' he roared, anger fuelling him as much as the pain from his burned flesh.

'...*Truth*,' said the assassin, forcing out the reply.

'What?' The word hit Garro like a slap in the face, and there was an instant when he lost focus. 'What truth? Speak it!'

'My name... is Eristede Kell.' The assassin choked in the legionary's death-grasp. 'Your God-Emperor took... everything from me. Your Sigillite sent... sent me to die.' He showed a mouth of blood-flecked teeth and shouted back at Garro. '*Horus set me free!*'

The daemon-gun was an impossible weapon, and so its next transformation, the act sudden and ugly, was no shock to Garro. He saw it happening and realised that this man Kell had drawn him in, used a moment of hesitation against him.

The weapon and the hand that gripped its blocky, crystalline form both dissembled into a pulse of seething black smoke that remade the component parts. Bone and glass, blood and mist, fed by hatred. In the blink of an eye, the gun was Kell's hand and Kell's hand was the gun, shifting and moving, a writhing eel-thing that bent itself out of Garro's grip. It turned back along an axis that no bones could have accepted without shattering, to aim point blank at his face.

Garro had no choice but to let go, arms coming up once more to shield himself. A breath of white-hot plasma ignited before him and shrieking overpressure blasted the legionary back into a mass of blackened corpses and smouldering matter.

He lost precious seconds reeling from the fiery shock front. Garro's skin sizzled and cracked where the bite of the flames marked him, and had it not been for the autonomic nerve-shunts and the agony inhibitors generated by his bio-implants, every breath would have been misery for the legionary.

He was back on his feet, flexing his hands into fists, when a voice cried out his name. 'Nathaniel! Here! Look to me!'

Garro turned and saw old Sindermann staggering towards him. The elderly iterator was dragging something behind him, all his strength put into hauling his burden across the chamber.

Libertas. Somehow the old man had managed to dislodge it from the wall where the thrown sword had embedded itself, and was attempting to bring it to him. Conflicted thoughts crossed Garro's mind – respect for the aging preacher that he could do such a thing, even though he was bruised and bleeding; annoyance that the old fool was putting himself in harm's way. He let the latter take the lead.

Garro dived towards the iterator and shoved him to the floor, pulling the blow as best he could. Even as he moved, he felt new surges of witchfire at his back. The assassin Kell would not stop until he had reduced the legionary to ashes. Sindermann went down in a heap as Garro snatched back the hilt of his power sword. A surge of confidence bloomed as the familiar weight of the weapon settled into his hand. He had always felt a special bond with the blade, something above and beyond the simple equation of warrior and weapon. A bright object clattered about *Libertas'* cross guard and Garro saw a golden chain wrapped around it, the links ending in an icon of a two-headed eagle. *The Emperor protects, aye*, he thought. *But today, that responsibility falls to me.*

Kell shouted a foul curse and Garro reacted without hesitation. He dragged Sindermann close and shielded the iterator's body as a new wave of murderous flame bathed them both. A hiss of pain escaped the warrior's lips as the outer layer of skin across his back was burned away, exposing the plasti-form sheath of his black carapace implant. The torrent of heat seemed to go on forever, and not even the legionary's pain blocks were enough to dam the flow of raw, searing torture.

Then at last it ceased, but Garro knew it would only be a few moments before Kell fired again, unleashing another blazing serpent-thing from the immaterium even as the echo of the last shots faded.

Drawing a breath laced with the sweet stink of burned human meat, Garro forced himself to his feet.

Sindermann lay on the deck before him, white as milk and trembling in terror. 'Get her out of here,' Garro growled, forcing the words out of his damaged throat. 'There's a dock platform at the edge of the district. Go now, and stop for nothing.'

As Sindermann nodded, a question fell from him. 'Can that witch-gun kill you?'

'I will find out,' Garro managed. He came about, each step jamming razors into the dozens of open wounds across his torso and his limbs, and advanced on the assassin through the wreaths of dirty smoke.

Sickly vapour streamed from the mouth of the glittering glass pistol as Kell brandished it towards him. 'I think I understand how the Clade Eversor find such joy in their kills,' he said, as if speaking to some unseen audience. 'Every murder I made before, it was distant and cold. I saw their faces but I never really knew the moment of death.' He showed Garro the daemonic gun. 'This makes it different. When you are close, you can taste it. It allows you to love the act.'

'You are quite mad,' spat Garro. 'Horus did that? Or did he just make use of it?'

Kell's face twisted. 'He let me *see*. And I've seen you dead, Death Guard. Your heart broken and bleeding black.'

'Perhaps,' he allowed, fighting back a weariness that reached up from the darkness. 'But it will not be your hand behind it, murderer.'

The assassin bared yellowed teeth in a feral snarl and took the daemon weapon in a two-handed grip, bracing to aim towards him. The square-cut shape of the muzzle undulated and snapped open into a glass flower, its maw widening in a funnel of crystal petals. Garro saw baleful fire shimmer within the impossible spaces of the gun's interior a split-second before it vomited forth a great comet of flames. The air screamed as it was torn open by the power of such elemental horror forcing its way into reality.

A mass of living fire, dancing and swooping above him, came at Garro in a blinding rush. It had no shape that could be held in the mind for more than a few moments, shifting between forms that could have been avian, arachnid or humanoid.

There might have been a time – before becoming a Knight Errant, before the Warmaster's betrayal – when Nathaniel Garro would have beheld this horror and wondered how he would fight something so utterly unreal. He was no longer that man.

This war – Horus' war – had changed him in ways he had never expected, and in this second Garro realised that whatever doubts he had were now ashes. They had burned away, just like the skin across his body. He was free of them.

He did not question how he would fight the daemon. He would destroy it as he had every other enemy put before him. *With the weapon in my hand and the strength of my soul.*

Garro triggered the power field surrounding *Libertas'* blade at its maximum potentiality. Lethal jags of captured lightning scintillated along the length of the sword, generated and collimated by ancient, time-lost technology. This weapon had brought down tyrants, it had slaughtered rampaging beasts, ended the lives of traitors and, when called upon, given the Emperor's Peace. One more monster would not be its match.

Ignoring all sense of caution, Garro threw himself at

the fire-form as it swept down on him. Raising his power
sword high into a jousting thrust, he pushed himself
past the pain from the lashes of flame bombarding his
tormented body and let the point of the blade find the
pulsing heart of the daemon. The creature, a primitive
predator-form from the abyssal deeps of the immaterium,
did not possess the wit to realise that the legionary had
used its own momentum against it.

Libertas plunged into the core of the abhorrent form
and the energy resonating through its blade flashed free
in a catastrophic shock of unleashed power. Unknowable
science from the age of Old Night met unreal anti-life
from another dimension and cancelled out its existence.
Blue aurorae rippled through the fire-daemon, and with
a cry that chilled the blood it combusted into a haze of
orange-black embers. Whatever malevolent quintessence
had motivated the creature was sent screaming back to
the warp, and Garro's sword became dead metal once
again, its power drained for now.

'No!' Kell shook his head wildly, whatever brief clarity
his tortured mind had known now dispersed like the daemon. He raised the gun again, aiming at Garro's chest.
'You should die! You are supposed to die, that is how it
will be, I have done it before, I will do it again–'

'Enough,' snarled the legionary, and *Libertas* sang
through the choking air on a downward arc. Powered
or not, the age-old sword was still a formidable tool of
battle. The cut cleanly severed Kell's hand at the wrist,
the shock knocking him back as the lump of flesh and
glass spun to the deck.

The assassin's howls echoed off the curved walls, but
Garro ignored him. He watched as the severed hand
flopped back and forth of its own accord like a landed

fish, dragging the profane crystal mass of the gun with it. Meat and bone became molten, changing shape once more. The weapon took control of the flesh and remade itself into a form that resembled a scarab beetle, grimy fingers for legs and a vitreous block for a shell.

Garro stepped to the thing and impaled it on the tip of his sword before it could completely reconfigure itself. It burst in a welter of blood, oil and silvery pus. For good measure, the legionary stamped what remained into the deck plates, grinding it to nothing beneath his heel.

A trail of dark fluid led him to the assassin, as the man stumbled across the makeshift chapel towards the altar. 'She is gone,' Garro called after him. 'You failed in your mission.'

'Not the first time,' gasped Kell, refusing to accept defeat. 'No.'

Fatigue pulled at Garro, and he knew it was his body's energy racing to repair the grievous damage wrought by the witchfire. He shook it off and aimed a finger at the other man. 'Eristede Kell. I name you traitor. Stand and answer for your crime.'

'Traitor?' echoed the assassin. 'We are all traitors in the end, legionary! We are all betrayed and then the betrayer... You are no different than I!'

Garro's lip curled. 'I did not swear fealty to the first primarch to turn against his father!'

'*But you did turn against your father!*' Kell shot back, cradling the bloody stump of his wrist close to his chest. 'Your kinsmen too! Traitor... What does the word mean? It changes colour depending on where you stand... All that anyone can know is that we will eventually be betrayed...' His words trailed off into a painful wheeze. 'Are you prepared to save her?'

The question came from nowhere. 'Save who?'

'You know! Are you ready to surrender everything for her?' Kell looked away, his watery gaze suddenly lost and distant. 'I was. All for nothing.'

Garro's sword turned in his hand, shifting to a back-hand grip as he closed the distance between them. 'This ends now.' He raised the weapon, point downward.

'It won't,' said Kell, but then the blade dropped through his clavicle and down inside his ribcage, cutting his heart in two and freeing the assassin from whatever bargain he had made with the Warmaster.

Alone now, with only the murdered and the ashen fires surrounding him, Garro withdrew the sword from the corpse and watched it fall.

TWENTY-ONE

Betrayal
Of purpose
Never seen

THE BURN-PAIN LINGERED along with the stench of the dead, pressing into Garro with a throbbing ache. A cursory search of the makeshift chapel found not a single follower there still alive, and with a grim cast to his face, the legionary left it behind.

He crossed through the blackout sails and followed a route through the derelict overflow conduits, the path that he had ordered Sindermann to take towards the upper tiers of Hesperides. With each step, he wondered if he would come across more flame-crisped bodies like those killed by the daemon-serpents. His thoughts tormented him as he walked, suggesting ways of death for the Saint and the others that were manifold and horrible.

He recalled Sigismund, and the Imperial Fist's entreaty to protect Keeler at all costs. If she perished under his watch, Garro knew that the Templar would hunt him down and see her pay for her loss.

These were the thoughts that plagued him as he

ascended a vent shaft by means of an iron ladder. Wan light streamed down on him from an open grille at the shaft's exit, and presently Garro emerged on to a shadowed landing platform that extended out from the western side of the orbital plate.

He took a deep breath of damp air, and there was faint, brackish moisture on his face. A fine rain was falling. The industrial aertropolis' weather screen was poorly maintained, and as Hesperides skirted a dense cloud formation, some of it wandered in past the city limits. Garro nodded to himself. That would be useful; it could cover an escape.

'Sindermann.' He spoke the iterator's name aloud, and the word was a husky growl from his smoke-scarred throat. 'Show yourself.'

He glanced around, finding a pair of stubby oxy-tankers parked line abreast in the middle of the platform, little more than clusters of spherical pressure tanks in winged frames with gravitic motors to get them in the air. They would do as a way off this wretched place.

Garro sensed the survivors before he saw them, hearing the rattle and creak of their footsteps over the rusting deck. Limping badly, Kyril Sindermann emerged from the shadows. He was leaning heavily on a young man, one of the armed posse of believers that had surrounded Garro when he first arrived. With them were a handful of others who crowded an unseen figure in the middle of their group. Zeun was leading these followers, and she was almost corpse-pale, her tunic covered with drying blood. Still, she walked towards him with brittle strength, those hard eyes once more daring him to cross her.

'You live, then,' he said, with a nod. 'I thought I saw Kell's accomplice take you down.'

'Kell?' she echoed, making it a challenge. She waved a hand in front of her face, mimicking a mask. 'That one?'

He nodded again. 'That one. I killed him.'

'Good…' Zeun was going to say more, but she trailed off as she got a better look at him. He had to appear as something barely alive to them, the burns on his body so fierce that they had only ever seen the like upon the dead. She struggled with her reaction – was that disgust or pity? Amazement or revulsion?

Garro peeled open part of his body-glove, where it had become stuck to his bloody torso, to remove an object he had placed there. With care, he cleaned it off. 'Here. You should have this.' He handed it to her, and Zeun looked down at the shimmerknife dagger lying across her palm.

She held it like it was a poisonous snake, fascinated as much as she was repelled by it. After a moment, Zeun took the weight of the energised blade in her hand and rolled it in her fingers. Garro could see that she had the skills of a street fighter, and the pragmatism too. Some might have baulked at taking the very weapon that had almost ended them, but not this one.

From where he stood, he could see the cut in Zeun's tunic where the blade had gone in. If there had been a wound behind it, that injury was gone now. 'You said I owed you a weapon.' He gestured at the blade. 'My debt is paid.'

He didn't linger to see if she had more to add, and turned towards Sindermann – but not before casting a glance at the knot of hooded believers. One among them seemed to move differently to the others. Keeler. Hiding in plain sight.

'Captain,' began the iterator, labouring a breath with the words he uttered. 'What of our people… ?'

'None remain.' He saw no merit in softening the blow. 'Your secret church of Hesperides, such as it was, has suffered the same fate as the sanctuary in Afrik.'

'And others too, that you know not.' Saying the words aged Sindermann terribly, and his young companion had to hold him steady. 'But the killers are dead. I heard you say that.'

'*These* killers are dead,' Garro corrected. 'But there will be others. The archtraitor has many more broken souls to call upon.' Frustration rose in him, his growl becoming harder and colder. 'You should have listened to me.' He turned and glared at the hooded figures. 'Euphrati!' barked Garro. 'You should have listened!'

The group parted and there she was in the middle of them. He wondered if they really thought the act of surrounding her with their frail human bodies would be armour enough to keep her safe.

The Saint rolled back her hood and showed him a weeping face. 'I did not want this,' she breathed, coming to him. 'I don't want it to happen any more.' She halted and looked up at the sky, as if seeing something Garro could not.

He glanced at the iterator. 'You must go into hiding, that is clear. I will stand with you. I have contacts. I will find us a safe haven.'

'You would reject the Sigillite's dominion over you?' said Sindermann. 'You would become a renegade?'

'I will never reject Terra and the throne,' Garro snapped back. 'Lord Malcador, however...'

But before his thought could fully form, the legionary felt the wet air around him take on a taut quality. He tasted ozone on his crackled lips and knew the familiar sensation for what it was – the precursor effect to a battlefield shock transit.

He had *Libertas* clear of its sheath as the first emerald flash emerged out of nothing, across the platform past the prow of the second tanker. In the span of milliseconds, other motes of green lightning blinked into existence all around them, and then came a low crack of displaced air molecules as multiple teleport fields deposited a dozen faceless figures at all points of the compass.

Garro wheeled, seeing human soldiers in blank-eyed carapace armour bearing high-power laser carbines. His gaze settled on their leader – a Space Marine in full Corvus-pattern war-plate, a heavy bolt pistol already drawn and ready in his grip.

Like the soldiers', the other legionary's armour was the shade of storm clouds and bereft of all sigils, honours or iconography – or at least, no marks that were immediately apparent to the eye. But if Garro had looked closely, he would have found the ghostly imprint of a stylised eye upon their shoulder pauldrons.

The bolt pistol – the sole object that carried a splash of colour upon it – was a clue to the face behind the beaked helmet. Then, as the legionary advanced towards Garro, the way he moved confirmed his identity. 'Ison? Malcador sent you, then?'

Ison reached up and twisted off his helm as he walked closer, snapping it to a magnetic pad at his waist. The other legionary's face was olive-hued and his eyes were dark and almond-shaped. A duelling scar ran the length of his jaw and it had not healed well, giving him a permanent half-scowl. The bolt pistol floated in his mailed fist, lazy and deceptive. Garro could almost believe it wasn't aimed at him, but he had seen the warrior in action and knew how he fought.

'Captain Garro,' Ison said formally, giving him a slow

look up and down, his gaze lingering on the worst of the burns. 'Do you require an Apothecary?' His voice was a steady murmur.

'I'm well enough to fight.' He tightened his grip on his sword.

Ison cocked his head, and as one the soldiers raised their rifles to firing stance. 'Will it come to that?'

'The choice is yours.'

The other legionary released a weary sigh. 'The order falls, Garro. Stand down. You are recalled to duty.'

'Malcador tracked me...' Garro's lips thinned as he considered this turn of events. 'He used me to find Keeler?' He nodded towards the Saint, who had gathered Sindermann and Zeun to her.

'He is the Sigillite,' Ison replied, and tapped a long finger against his temple. 'Did you ever think he would *not* know where you were?'

'He sees so much, aye... But not enough to intervene below?' Garro pointed at the deck, in the direction of the underlevels. 'Or is it that he cares little for civilians who lose their lives daring to seek a different truth?'

'I know nothing of what you speak.' Ison's expression remained neutral, and Garro realised he was telling the truth. The Knight Errant went on. 'By the command of the Regent of Terra, you must stand down and allow the woman Keeler to be taken into Imperial custody. She won't be harmed. No blood will be shed... if there is co-operation.'

Garro's damaged features turned stony, and he let his weight shift away from his bionic leg. If it came to combat, he did not trust the replacement limb to work flawlessly after all the heat damage it had suffered. *Libertas* was at the ready. He could strike at any instant. 'I do not wish to comply.'

'Out of respect for what you have done for me, I suggest you reconsider that statement.' Ison stiffened, tightening his grip on the pistol. 'I say this for the final time, Captain. Stand down.'

The sword began to move, but then Garro felt a delicate touch on the blackened flesh of his arm and he looked down to see Keeler's hand resting there.

'*Wait*,' she said, and all at once the air became slow and heavy. The gauzy haze of raindrops around them gained sudden definition as they were suspended, and every motion was arrested.

He looked back to Ison and saw that the other legionary was as motionless as a statue. The soldiers and the believers, Sindermann and Zeun alike, all were frozen in a timeless instant.

'How... are you... doing this?'

There was a peculiar echo to his voice, the sound flat and contained.

The Saint was pale, the effort taxing her greatly. 'It doesn't matter.' She took a shaky breath. 'Don't fight him, Nathaniel. That act cannot be called back.'

'I have taken the lives of brother legionaries before,' he said, regret weighing down the words.

'Not like this. Ison is not your enemy.' She gestured at the soldiers, whom Garro knew he would have to butcher to a man if it came to blades and guns. 'They are only doing what they believe to be right, as you are.'

He turned on her, *Libertas* dragging in the air as if moving through thick oil. 'I did not protect you from Horus' agents only to turn you over to the Sigillite! Malcador's schemes are known only to him, and I will no longer place my trust nor yours in his hands! Not while he has so many secrets.'

She shook her head. 'I told you before. You see and you do not see.'

'So tell me,' he demanded.

The Saint's head bobbed. 'Have you not considered that I am *meant* to go with Ison? That this confrontation was always going to happen?'

'Malcador fears your influence,' Garro retorted. 'He hides it, but there can be no doubt! If the Knights Errant take you this day, you will vanish... There are myriad dungeons buried deep in the rock of the Imperial Palace. You will disappear into one of them and never see light again!'

'I don't believe that,' she said firmly, with enough conviction to give the legionary pause. 'Not as long as you still draw breath.' Keeler leaned closer to him, and he felt an ethereal warmth radiating from her face. 'You told me before I am in danger. What better fortress walls for me to shelter behind than those of the greatest bastion in the Imperium?'

'As a prisoner?'

She smiled. 'If the esteemed Regent wishes to consider me that, I won't correct him until I have to. And the word will out, Nathaniel, even if I am not there to speak it. I am the Truth, but the Truth is not me. The book continues to spread across all human worlds. The work will go on. We approach our darkest hour, and the people need that light to guide them, now more than ever.'

His heart felt leaden. 'Then this is to be my doing? I do not protect you. I step aside, stand down... What am I then? What value do I have any more, if not this?' The sword in his hand had never weighed as much as it did now.

'Nathaniel Garro, you are as you have always been.' The

smile on her face became radiant, and her eyes shimmered. 'You are of purpose. When the moment comes, and mark me when I tell you, you *will* know it… It will be your hand that sees me set to freedom, your sword that holds fast my safety. Do you believe me?'

How could he not? The force of veracity behind every word she said resonated with him in a way few things ever had. Garro knew now that he was sworn to her, that he had been from the very moment they first met on board the *Eisenstein*. If there was a fate, then this woman was its hand upon his. He nodded. 'Aye.'

'When the time is right,' she told him, 'you will release me.'

'From what?'

'You'll know,' said the Saint. 'Until then… you must have faith, Nathaniel.'

There were so many other questions he had, but then Keeler withdrew her hand from his arm. The gossamer rain resumed its fall and the moment was in motion once again.

'Put up your sword,' Ison was saying.

Without breaking the Saint's gaze, Garro tapped the stud that deactivated the power field around *Libertas'* blade, and then carefully returned the sword to its scabbard. He took a step back from the woman's side, and at a nod from the other Knight Errant, a trio of soldiers detached from the group and came in to escort her towards the edge of the platform. His hearing picked out the muted thunder of a stealth-rigged Stormbird approaching from the north.

Garro eyed the troopers with cold malice. 'She is to be respected, understand?'

'Of course,' Ison replied. There was a faint note of

reproach in his words, as if he was insulted by the suggestion of any other behaviour. He nodded again, and
the remainder of the grey-armoured soldiers stepped forward, moving towards Sindermann, Zeun and the other
followers.

'*No.*' Garro's hand had not left the hilt of his sword,
even though it remained sheathed. 'You won't take them.
She is all you'll have today.'

Ison hesitated. 'It is true that Lord Malcador did not
make specific reference to any others beyond Keeler…
As you wish, Captain.' He gestured to the soldiers, who
stood back.

The weak scattering of rainfall was briefly whipped
into a fury as the Stormbird rose into view, hovering at
the edge of the landing platform. Its thrusters turned
the air to a turbulent squall as it moved to present a
drop ramp for boarding. The Saint gave a bow to Sindermann and the others, and then walked directly into
the ship without waiting for her escorts. Garro watched
the iterator take two shaky steps after her and then falter, his face falling. Zeun shot the legionary a poisonous
glare, blaming him for all of this. *She has good cause*,
Garro told himself.

Ison crossed to his side, his voice rising to be heard
over the engine noise. 'You'll accompany us, then? I have
been told your wargear has been repaired and renewed
during your leave. Your mantle as Agentia Primus awaits
your return.'

Garro let go of the sword's hilt and watched as Sindermann and the other followers came to the realization
that they were free to leave. Slowly, they turned to face
the Stormbird, and without any bidding from the iterator they all bowed in the direction of the Saint. Against

their breasts, they crossed the flats of their hands over one another, forming the shape of the aquila.

As elderly as he was, Sindermann's old mind still held a fire of oratory that would continue to carry the truth of the Lectitio Divinitatus, even without Keeler's ephemeral support. And perhaps a quiet word to Brother-Captain Sigismund would help that on its way – if the Templar ever forgave Garro for letting Keeler fall beneath Malcador's shadow.

'Is there anything more to hold you here?' said Ison.

'My questions have been answered,' Garro told him, walking towards the drop ramp.

WEEKS PASSED, AND Garro left Hesperides behind in thought and memory – first in the non-sleep of a curative trance to heal his wounds, and then with new duties. There were many tasks to be addressed, fresh missions to be attended to. It seemed that with every passing day, the clandestine work of the Knights Errant grew in scope and complexity.

In a lull before his next deployment, Garro travelled back to the surface of Terra, back to the forbidding hills of Albia. Now he walked there once again, alone with his thoughts, refreshed by the silence.

It felt right to be back in his war-plate once again. Without it, he was less than the sum of his parts, incomplete – and Ison had been right when he said the armour had been well cared for in his absence. While outwardly it still bore many of the scars earned in decades of long battle, beneath the skin the mechanisms that drove it had been invigorated with new components and the loving care of the armourium's tech-wardens.

With flesh regrown across his burns, his bionics newly

attuned, he was whole again, not just in physicality but in spirit – something that had eluded him for too long.

Garro walked on, wondering how many others there were like him, at large in the galaxy at this moment. How many men in grey, featureless armour at the Sigillite's beck and call? He considered what he had seen on a mist-wreathed moon of Saturn and the moment of insight that had come to him there. *My fate does not lie on Titan*, he had told himself. He would have to trust that it would reveal itself in due time, rather than allow itself to be sought out.

His gauntlet closed into a fist. Garro had been a Death Guard legionary, and a Dusk Raider before that. He understood the acts of patience, dedication and unyielding perseverance better than any scion of the Legiones Astartes. *So be it*, he thought. *I will be ready. Until then…*

He sensed movement on one of the nearby crags and halted, his hand dropping to his mag-locked bolter. Presently, a trio of oily black shapes detached themselves from the dark granite outcroppings and gingerly skirted around him. Garro halted and let the lupenates come a little closer.

The wolf-things sniffed at the air, tasting his scent on the stiff breeze, and lowed mournfully to one another. A simple communication passed between the animals and they slowly backed away, giving him a wide berth. An intelligent predator learned from its errors, and the lupenates had learned not to challenge the warrior in grey, instead to respect him. But as they moved to a distance, the creatures became twitchy and skittish, finally breaking into a loping run and vanishing over the ridge line.

Garro knew without needing to turn around what

apparition had frightened them into headlong flight. 'Am I never again to have my own counsel, my lord?'

Malcador walked past him, marking out each step he took with the black iron staff in his hand. 'Is that why you come here? To be alone?' The Sigillite looked at everything except the legionary, a pool of light cast around him from the slow-burning fires in the basket atop the rod.

'I find something in this place that exists nowhere else.'

'Indeed?' Malcador's eyebrow arched.

'Clarity,' explained Garro. 'I have learned that as time passes, it becomes a more valuable commodity.'

'And what does your clear vision grant you?' Malcador turned to face Garro, that ice-cold gaze washing over him. 'A greater understanding of the threats we face, I hope.'

'I know those things well enough.'

The Sigillite gave a nod. 'Yes, I think that may be so. Your conduct proves it.' Garro wondered what that might mean, and Malcador told him. 'When we stood here before, and I granted you leave to follow your own path for a time... I confess, there were many ways in which that might have unfolded. But in the end, you did what I would have ordered you to do regardless, even without my command. You did what best served the Throne and Terra. What does that say about you, Captain?'

Garro held the Sigillite's burning gaze. 'That I am as I have always been. Loyal to the vow I swore.'

'No doubt...' Malcador seemed about to break off, but then the smallest of expressions pulled at his lined features.

Garro saw it clearly for what it was – puzzlement. For a brief moment, the air stiffened around him and the legionary sensed the Sigillite turning a greater force of his

powerful psionic ability to bear on him. Then the strange
pressure fell away, like a wave retreating from shore.

'Something has changed,' said Malcador. 'I did not see
it before, but now I perceive it clearly.' He tilted the head
of the iron staff towards Garro, the flames atop it quietly
crackling. 'There is a part of your spirit that is opaque,
Nathaniel. Obscured, even to my insight.' A faint, brittle
smile played upon the Sigillite's lips. He seemed at once
amused and dismayed by the possibility.

'Aye, lord.' Garro remembered a touch of gentle radiance against his seared skin, of how it passed through
him and what that might portend for the unwritten
future. 'That place you cannot see into? That part of me
that remains forever closed to you?'

He broke Malcador's gaze and turned away from him.
'That is my faith.'

When his name is spoken, it is often in the context of what he meant to those telling the tale. I have been guilty of this. I often speak of what Nathaniel Garro meant to me.

But what did we mean to him?

The legionaries were the creation of the God-Emperor, and they were a part of the Master of Mankind's great plan. But they were also part of us, of we common humans. Perhaps that was why some of them succumbed so forcefully to the worst of our natures. They magnified all elements of our spirit, the noble and the horrific.

Garro was the former.

But there was more to him. What he allowed few to see was the most human part of himself – his doubt. He questioned his place in the universe, as all of us are wont to do at some time in our lives.

For him, that question came wrapped in the tragedy of Horus Lupercal's heresy. And when everything he loved was stripped away from him, when Garro's oath, his brotherhood, his very sense of belonging was made ashes, there was some of him that became lost.

He came to us to find it again. He sought us out, the Saint and I, to find a path that had meaning.

It was the question we were asked over and over again in those days. We struggled to understand what had brought his great tragedy to pass, and what our place was in it. And in many ways, he was the first of the legionaries with the courage to admit he did not know the answer.

For there were many of his kind who simply did not question, who took up arms against their kinsmen because they had been ordered to do so, not through any great enmity or corruption. That came later, at the hands of those among them who were already tainted, who had been so since long before the murder of Isstvan III.

But Garro was the first to make the leap of faith. He was the first who truly dared to believe.

I am proud to say I saw him at the moments when his spirit was at its most wounded and when he was at the purest height of his selflessness.

And as to those who have asked me, in the years since then, of the price he paid – what can I say that will carry the full measure of that? I will say with no false modesty that my name is known for my oratory on the matters of the Imperial Truth, but even I find it hard to conjure the right words.

His path was the path of this conflict.

A journey from a place of bright and shining unity, a place where all things were possible, into a shadowed valley of darkness and betrayal. Onwards to a future forged by a god.

Euphrati was the first Saint of our new Church, but Nathaniel…

Nathaniel was its first true martyr.

Sorrow clutches at my heart now as I commit these words to the page. Yet it is strangely tinged with a hope, a thin golden thread of it that cannot be broken. It exists now and will exist into eternity, I am certain of this. It may never pull us entirely from the dark, but it was never meant to. Light cannot flourish anywhere else.

There are other stories I might recount, of course. Of hells and heroism. Swords and shields, truth and lies, oaths and Legions. Fate. Faith.

Let me tell you about Nathaniel Garro.